The
Shock

Marc Raabe

MANILLA

First published in Germany in 2013 by Ullstein Buchverlage GmbH, Berlin

First published in Great Britain in 2017 by Manilla Publishing,
80–81 Wimpole St, London, W1G 9RE
www.manillabooks.com

FIFE COUNCIL LIBRARIES

FIFE COUNCIL LIBRARIES	
HJ491817	
Askews & Holts	24-Aug-2017
AF	£7.99
THR	AN

A CIP catalogue record for this book is available from the British Library.

Paperback ISBN: 978-1-7865-8025-2
E-book ISBN: 978-1-7865-8021-4

2

Printed and bound in Great Britain by Clays Ltd, St Ives plc

MIX
Paper from
responsible sources
FSC® C018072

Manilla Publishing is an imprint of Bonnier Zaffre,
a Bonnier Publishing company
www.bonnierzaffre.co.uk
www.bonnierpublishing.co.uk

For Meike and my boys

The road to Hell is paved with good intentions.

Prologue

Berlin, 26 December 1969

Froggy was ten years old. Three thousand seven hundred and nine days old, to be precise. And every one of those days he wished desperately that something would change.

Froggy wasn't daft. He knew there were certain cast-iron rules in life, and one of those rules was that wishes don't come true. But, still, he hoped.

It was the second day of the Christmas holidays, late evening. It had snowed, suffocating the whole world beneath a skin of white. Ice crystals glowed under street lamps like phosphorous, and the plain detached house sat awkwardly amongst the bulky blocks of flats.

Froggy, having slunk a little way up the dark staircase, was lying stomach-down on the uncomfortable steps, staring between them down into the living room. Through the window in the door he had a good view of the television.

His parents sat on the sofa further to the right, hidden in the alcove, where they would remain glued for the rest of the evening. Every now and again bluish tendrils of cigarette smoke came floating into view.

After the film came the news. Froggy hated the news. Always the same stilted people talking like machines, interspersed with nothing but boring pictures. Maybe a few dead bodies, if you were lucky.

Tonight there were no dead bodies.

Tiredness crept into his eyes. He wished he had a button that would fast-forward to the late-night film.

As his eyes closed, he dreamt of Jenny.

She was the same age as him and he dreamt of her often, nearly always the same dream. He went over to her, stretching out his hand, close enough to smell her, wanting to touch her shoulder, wanting her to turn and look at him. But then someone thumped him painfully in the ribs and laughed a mocking laugh.

He opened his eyes with a jolt.

He was still lying on the staircase, the edges of the steps pressing into his ribs. The pyjama sleeve where his head had rested was damp, and out of the corner of his mouth ran a thread of drool.

Had he been . . . asleep?

Cringing, he looked at the television. The news was over. The late-night film was playing.

Oh no! How could he have been so careless? His panicked gaze flew to the alcove, where a slender plume of smoke was drifting out of the corner. He exhaled. They were still sitting there, still rooted to the spot.

Time to get going. Without a sound he tensed his weak muscles and straightened up, but as he did so his eyes happened to fall back on the television, and he froze mid-movement. There was a man on the screen, his entire body wrapped in wide bandages; Froggy couldn't see so much as a centimetre of skin. Very slowly, with hands that were also tightly wrapped, the man undid the bandages from his head.

Mesmerised, Froggy gawped.

Behind the bandages was – nothing.

Nothing at all.

The man was invisible!

Froggy's skin broke into gooseflesh. Suddenly nothing else mattered. The damp pyjama sleeve, the fact that he'd fallen asleep, that he could have been discovered. He had to watch this film.

At the end of the film, he crawled stiffly upstairs, slipping into the cramped confines of his bedroom. The street lamps cast a poisonous light through the window. Exhausted, he went over to his bed – and his blood ran cold.

Someone was sitting there.

A massive figure that reeked of smoke and alcohol. The figure got up from the mattress, a black ghost against the wallpaper, illuminated in yellowish-grey. From its hand dangled a leather belt.

'Your ma saw you on the stairs,' said his father. His voice was heavy and tired, yet clear, even though the stench on his breath suggested he wasn't sober.

Froggy began to shiver.

'Do you have any idea how much worry you cause her by being like this?'

Froggy kept silent. It worried him too. He'd rather not be there at all.

'*I* could forgive you,' said his father. 'I know where you get it from, after all. But she knows too, you see, and she hates me for it. *Me!* Do you know how much that hurts?'

Froggy bit his lip. Yes! He knew! He hated himself for it too. He'd been trying his whole life to be someone else.

As he took his punishment, he bit down on his tongue. The metallic taste helped him not to scream. He wanted to vanish, to step outside himself, to no be longer there.

His father was puffing with exertion by the time he left. His sweat still hung in the air. Froggy lay face-down on his bed, his back stinging. He felt pathetic, weak. He wanted to crawl into the furthest recess of his soul, to a place where nobody would see him, a place where he could sob his heart out quietly to himself.

He thought longingly of the film he'd just watched. If only he could be invisible, like that man.

Invisible people couldn't make fools of themselves. They couldn't be laughed at. Invisible people couldn't be punished.

The urge overwhelmed him like a swarm of locusts, dark and deafening. If he were invisible, he could do *anything* he liked!

And nobody could stop him.

His religious education teacher popped into his head. She'd told them once about a doctor for madmen. This doctor had found out that people have different creatures inside them. There was the *id*, something a bit like a ravenous animal, then the *superego*, controlling like his mother, and somewhere in between them was you yourself, at least if you were normal.

But if you were like the man in the film, there'd be no more superego. There'd be nobody to tell you what to do.

That must be awesome.

He imagined creeping into Jenny's parents' house and into Jenny's room without her being able to see him. Observing her, watching her get undressed until she was completely naked like the women in Pa's magazines. Or he could trip up Herr Broich, his German teacher. Ideally right next to the kerb. If he knocked out his front teeth, Broich would finally know what it felt like to have everyone gawping at you all the time.

Slowly he got out of bed, his back one long agonising burn. Going over to the window, he opened it wide. The icy winter air covered his skin like white frost. His breath was foggy.

If I were invisible, he thought, that's all you'd be able to see of me right now.

If I were invisible, I could creep into Ma and Pa's room. I could cut off Pa's balls and stuff them in his yellow gob. Until he choked on them.

And Ma would have to watch. That'd teach her.

Chapter One

The moment his mobile rang was the moment that all hell broke loose for Jan Floss.

Seventeen minutes earlier he'd been standing absent-mindedly in front of the panoramic window, staring through his own reflection out into the darkness. Four hundred metres beneath him, the sea was churning. The bright blue of the Côte d'Azur had morphed into black lead, and the sky seemed to be flowing directly into the sea.

It had been bucketing down for three days already, and a dank chill atypical of this part of the coast was creeping into his limbs. Bloody heating. Bloody house. How many years had it been since his father was last here? Not since his mother had moved out, and that was when Jan had just turned ten. Twenty-four years, then. No wonder nothing worked in this house any more. What a crazy idea to come here, of all places. Too little heating, too many memories.

For three days the four of them had been living on top of each other in a 120-square-metre holiday home barely a quarter of which was halfway habitable: his parents' bedroom and the large, open-plan living-and-dining space with the panoramic window. Theo's old childhood bedroom was still locked, as if his ghost had taken up residence behind the door. Jan didn't know where the key was. And even if he did, he couldn't have brought himself to use it.

Greg, Katy and Laura had been unable to stand it any more; they had taken Greg's Jeep and gone shopping in town – to Beaulieu-sur-Mer, not far from Nice.

Jan had decided to stay behind. Swapping thirty square metres of house for four square metres of car? No thanks! Certainly not in this rain. In any case, he couldn't take much more of watching his thirty-seven-year-old sister Katy gaze adoringly at Greg, as if she didn't have a husband or twins back home. Jan didn't care for supermarket shopping anyway. Endless shelving, gaudy products and ceaseless, babbling ads. For years he'd researched that kind of bollocks and its effect on customers. The psychology of instant soup had been his life for far too long.

When Greg and Katy had announced they wanted to go to Beaulieu-sur-Mer, Jan had hoped that Laura would stay. The memory of last night was still quickening his heartbeat. But Laura was evidently suffering from cabin fever too, because she'd stepped into her wellies and left the house with Greg and Katy.

Jan stared through the windowpane. His reflection stood out clearly on the glass, the exhausted face of a thirty-four-year-old loner. His brown eyes were black dots; his dark hair stuck out wildly from his head like the thoughts whirling around in his brain. And then there was the port-wine stain, which spread like a reddish island from his left temple down his cheek to the corner of his mouth. After what happened to Theo it had always seemed to him as though somebody up there had decided to mark him from birth. Look, this boy brings misfortune. Be careful. Avoid him.

When the phone rang, Jan simply reached out, blindly pressed the green button and lifted the device to his ear. Her voice was already fizzing.

'Hi. It's Katy. Is Laura with you?'

'What?' asked Jan.

'Am I speaking Spanish? Is Laura with you?'

Jan frowned. 'Well, she was just sitting next to you in the car, but hang on a minute, I'll just see if she's behind the curtains.' He rustled the fabric loudly. 'Oops. Nope. Not there.'

'Ha ha. Very funny, brother dearest.'

'Garbage in, garbage out,' said Jan laconically.

'Eh?'

He sighed. 'I mean if your question's rubbish the answer's going to be rubbish too.'

'Could you please try to stop being obstructive and answer my question?'

'I'm not obstructive,' said Jan, 'I'm just not at my best right now.'

'Can you just tell me whether Laura's with you? Or if she's called you?'

'Is she gone, then?'

'As if off the face of the earth. Otherwise I wouldn't be asking, would I?'

'Where are you right now?'

'At the supermarket.'

'At *which* supermarket?'

Katy snorted. 'The *hypermarché*. On the edge of Beaulieu. Where else? Now could you please just answer my question?'

'You've just answered it yourself.'

Katy groaned into the receiver.

'Katy, please! You set off half an hour ago. It takes ten minutes to get down there. Climbing back up the mountain on foot takes considerably longer. Assuming Laura didn't leap out of the car mid-journey because she couldn't bear another second of Greg's crap, she can't possibly be here.'

'Thank you for the brief course in logic, professor! I'm just worried, all right? Laura's gone and we have no idea why. Look, if she calls you or shows up there, then at least let me know,' said Katy caustically, before abruptly hanging up.

Jan sighed as the pipes clanked. He was immediately sorry that yet again he hadn't just let it go. It was always the same. He could never talk to Katy without a thousand tiny devils leaping on his shoulder, making him act like a stubborn teenager instead of a grown man.

He stared out into the rain. The cliff edge, beyond which was a steep drop into the sea, was visible only as a vague, jagged shadow in the dark. He thought of Laura. Her face looked so different from the way it had at school. Fuller. More adult. Not only because she was older – there was something else, too. Something closed that fascinated him. No – that drew him magically in.

Even in school, aged fourteen, Laura's presence had always got him into trouble. His head grew hot, and he knew only too well that the port-wine stain would be practically glowing. Nonetheless he still sought her out, and at night he had such intense dreams that the next day he averted his gaze in shame whenever their eyes met. He didn't know how to cope with all those emotions; he felt stupid and somehow guilty, as if what came over him wasn't normal.

Then, suddenly, Laura hadn't been there any more, whisked away from one day to the next. Later he found out that she'd switched schools; to this day he didn't know why. That was the last time he'd seen her – until Katy had suggested this trip to France.

He glanced left towards the narrow road that wound up the slope towards Èze. The water was flowing in broad streams to the car turning bay in front of the house, gathering in large puddles. Disappearing acts seemed to be one of Laura's specialties. But why had she chosen this dump in France, in this weather, in front of a supermarket that was closing in a few minutes' time? He was growing uneasy.

Instinctively he reached for his mobile. He didn't have Laura's number, so he phoned Katy.

The number you are trying to reach is not available, it droned.

Well, that wasn't helpful. What now?

For a moment he felt silly. A grown woman had gone off for a few minutes and already he was in a tailspin. Must be the rain, he thought. Rain like this always makes you crazy.

He closed his eyes and leant his forehead against the glass. It pressed coldly against his skin.

Most likely the three of them were in their Jeep somewhere along the coastal road, on their way back. There were definitely a few places around there with bad phone coverage.

Another ten minutes. Maybe a bit more. That's how long it took to get from the *hypermarché* to the house by car.

That's how long he'd wait.

Chapter Two

The taut skin had briefly resisted, then the cannula's sharp, V-shaped point had gone through. Beneath the skin shimmered bluish veins. The thin tube had filled with red. A second artery, one with a small white plastic tap.

Beyond that the tube was still virginal. Transparent.

For as long as he wanted.

He began to shave her. Wet. Some of the white foam dripped onto the steel table. Freshly fallen snow with dark pubic hairs. A moment earlier she'd been resisting. Begging. Shaking. As he'd brought the three-bladed razor near her clitoris, she'd frozen. Now she was only weeping. The salt in her stupid tears was spoiling her complexion. He had to dab them away, as if he didn't already have enough to be getting on with.

The electric fork-lift was ready. For fifty minutes now the first twenty centimetres had been hardening on the bottom of Tub One. It smelled appropriately caustic. The ventilation was working full blast. So was his penis. Every stroke of the razor made it pulse.

She stared at the ceiling and continued to sob.

Princesses don't sob.

Not his ones.

He felt annoyed with her.

Although his penis seemed to like it. He wiped away the mess with the much-too-dark hairs. Climbed onto the steel plate. Stood above her, his member like a revolver. She looked at him, and knew what was about to happen. It had taken a bloody long time. But he was finally there.

He pushed into her and thrust, putting his left hand around her neck and squeezing. No strangulation marks: with his right hand he loosened the small white plastic tap. Blood flowed into both tubes, splashing onto the floor where they ended. She grew paler, and his penis stiffened still further. The stink of chemicals, the metallic scent of blood, his overheated memories – it was all one giant whirl.

Then something burst and began spraying.

He looked up. Fixer was leaking out of the pipes above Tub One, directly into the basin. He leapt to his feet, nearly slipping in the sticky red puddle, and ran over.

But it was already too late.

Fucking hell.

The timing was totally screwed up.

He stared at the defective connector, remembering the salesman who'd palmed the bloody thing off on him. 'Of course it's durable. It's plastic. It lasts for ever.' Fucking moron.

That had been three days ago, in Berlin.

Today he had to admit that without the burst pipe he wouldn't have gone outside. He wouldn't have seen *her*. And then he wouldn't be here: in the rain, in an isolated car park outside a French supermarket.

He could almost smell it. And see it. They were afraid, the tall blond man and the dark-haired woman. The way they edged around the car. Like two stupid flamingos.

Fear enshrouded them like a sweet, heavy miasma of perfume, which he greedily inhaled. For twenty minutes they'd been in this cloud, searching, phoning and getting soaking wet in the rain. Now the pretty, dark-haired one was stuffing her mobile furiously back in her pocket. Her boyfriend, the all-American kid with the ugly tan, didn't look particularly happy either. More like he'd rather be on his surfboard at Venice Beach.

Then he saw *her*.

She came out of the supermarket like it was the most natural thing in the world, as if only a few seconds had gone by. Such grace in her step. The way her long hair swung overwhelmed him, even though she wasn't blonde. Everything about her overwhelmed him. The narrow face with prominent cheekbones, and then those eyes, their high brows giving her a perpetual expression of surprise – eyes that were strangely guarded, as if she were hiding a silent sorrow. Sorrow. Hiding. How well he knew those things! By now they were a part of him. And as for the hair – well, hair could be dyed. Or bleached.

Even in Berlin, catching sight of her by chance on the street as she joined the others with her suitcase, had taken his breath away. He had been on his way to find replacement parts. Instinctively he'd slammed on the brakes and peered through the tinted rear window. If he hadn't known better he'd have sworn there was such a thing as reincarnation, she reminded him of Jenny so much.

As the Jeep Cherokee carrying her and the others set off, he'd had to make a lightning-fast decision – to fly blind. Without a plan, without preparation. He couldn't even clean up first. He had to drop everything or lose her. And losing her wasn't an option. She was too special for that.

So he'd followed her: 1,324 kilometres thus far. He'd used a rest stop on the motorway to switch his plates. He always had one in reserve; he had a back-up for everything.

Once they'd arrived in Èze, the waiting had begun. It had been punishingly hard. Yesterday evening was the first time an opportunity had presented itself: his heart had begun to beat faster as she stepped outside the door and lit a cigarette. He'd raised the weapon, taken aim, strained the sinews in his index finger to the limit – and then, at the last moment, *he* had shown up.

Fucking arsehole!

And that birthmark. Dark, violet and ugly.

He'd been hoping the guy would go back inside the house at some point. Instead he'd come on to her. Groped her. Grabbed hold of her.

Forced to watch the two of them, he'd been tormented by the same piercing feeling he'd been tormented by before, back when he was still Froggy – *just Froggy* – and had to put up with the others undressing Jenny with their eyes as she danced.

The telescopic view had brought everything unbearably close. Only when she suddenly froze and gave Herr Birthmark a furious glare in response to something did his spirits briefly lift. Maybe she was telling him to go to hell. Just so long as he pissed off! But instead she left him standing there and disappeared into the house.

Shit.

More waiting, then. More self-restraint.

As far as restraint was concerned, his schooling had been harsh. But here and now, in this car park in front of this supermarket, he could hardly contain himself. He was seized by arousal, his cock swelling, and a feeling of limitless power and strength flooded through him like hot magma. He stared at her from within his cave under the black hood. The rain-soaked material was cold against his bare scalp.

Keep calm, he admonished himself. Concentrate!

He saw the dark-haired flamingo storm towards the woman, gesticulating wildly. What did flamingo taste like? He wondered whether he'd ever tried it, and what colour it had been. Was it pink?

Now they were getting into the car.

The Cherokee's headlights flared, and as the Jeep turned rapidly they swept over him, like a spotlight grazing a dancer who's still standing in the wings, waiting for his music to begin.

Chapter Three

Beaulieu-sur-Mer, Côte d'Azur, 17 October, 10.07 p.m.

Laura had hardly sat down on the back seat of the Cherokee before Greg trod on the accelerator and turned sharply. She only just managed to pull the door closed with an effort.

'Could you do me a favour and not drive like a teenager on speed?' snapped Laura.

'Sure,' growled Greg, 'if you let us know next time you decide to disappear into the supermarket bathroom for twenty minutes. Just before closing time, as well! We were worried.'

'You think that was fun for me? I didn't have any choice.'

'You didn't have any choice?'

'I'm a woman, for fuck's sake!'

'Oh yeah?' growled Greg. 'And women can't let people know what they're doing?'

Laura rolled her eyes. 'Katy, can you explain it to him please?'

Silently, Katy turned her head aside and looked out of the window.

'Ah, fuck it,' murmured Laura.

She leant forward; rain had run down the collar of her jacket, and now her wet clothing was clinging to her back. Her belly was still acting up, and between her hips and vertebrae shot a cramping pain. Then there were the headaches and the nausea. She'd had an inkling yesterday that it was that time of the month again, but as always she'd ignored it until it had burst out of her.

To describe her period as a necessary evil would be an understatement. Evil, certainly. But necessary? *Why?* In her first life she'd been too young for children. In her second, too lost and broken.

And now, in her third life?

She didn't even have a partner, let alone somebody she wanted to have a child with. The mere thought of having to take responsibility for a child made her throat tighten; it always reminded her of her childhood, of the oppressive loneliness of that villa in Finkenstrasse, of her father, who was perpetually absent, either on business trips to Vienna or in one of his rooms, always unapproachable. As for her mother . . . well . . .

Better to be properly alone, then. Like now. She had her apartment, her job at Ultimate Action, a sporting events agency, and the rest of the time she kept busy not falling back into old habits. Whichever way you looked at it, she was constantly fleeing from Life Number Two.

She was lucky that Gerald, her boss, still liked her as much as ever, even though she'd persistently ignored his advances.

Laura sighed and looked out of the side window of the Cherokee. Beyond the rivulets of rain, distorted by the headwind, the last houses of Beaulieu whipped by. Her damp back reminded her of last night, of Jan and what had happened outside the house.

She'd had enough and was desperate for some fresh air. She never could stand enclosed spaces. In her jacket pocket she found an open packet of Lucky Strikes put there by a colleague. She was an occasional smoker, at most, but every once in a while it was the perfect excuse to slip outside for a few moments – especially if the others didn't smoke. Fifteen minutes alone with nothing but a cigarette. That seemed like paradise.

This paradise lasted all of three minutes. She'd been standing outside, her back to the door. Above her loomed the overhanging living room of the house, which was crammed into the upper part of the steep incline like an enormous packet of cigarettes. Water poured from the roof before her gaze, and the end of her cigarette glowed as she drew on it.

In the darkness, to her right, between the trees on the slope, something suddenly caught her eye. Was that a shadow? She squinted, peering into the night. An animal, maybe?

At that moment Jan stepped out behind her, moving silently nearby and gazing at the dark sea and low-hanging clouds. They said nothing, by tacit agreement. The rain pelted down, and the waves broke against the rocks far beneath them.

Flicking her cigarette into the rain, Laura lit a second.

'You don't really smoke, do you?' asked Jan, without taking his eyes off the sea.

'Don't I?'

'No,' said Jan.

Laura blew smoke into the rain and laughed. It sounded surprisingly rough and rather mocking. 'What gave me away, Inspector Floss?'

Jan smiled and shrugged. 'Your posture. The hands . . .'

'I see,' said Laura, 'I'm dealing with an expert. Want one?' She held out the packet.

'Thanks. I don't smoke.'

She looked at him sceptically. 'Like I don't, you mean?'

Shivering, Jan hunched his head between his shoulders. 'I feel more like a coffee right now.'

'Coffee? At *this* hour? I'd be wide awake all night.'

Jan gave a crooked grin. 'It's all a question of practice.'

'Oh yeah? And where do you practise drinking coffee at night?'

'Market research. Or advertising. You start in the morning and keep your caffeine level constant while you work.'

Laura dimly remembered that Jan's and Katy's father had owned an advertising agency. Hence the holiday home on the Côte d'Azur. It was getting a bit run-down now, but at one time it must have cost a small fortune. 'Long days on the job, then?'

Jan nodded. 'Twenty-four/seven. Felt like that, anyway.'

'Nice. Great way to set yourself up for a burn-out.'

'Yep,' said Jan.

'So why do you do it?'

Another crooked smile. 'I don't any more. I'm out. It's over.'

'Aha. Did you jump, or were you . . .?'

'More "or",' said Jan, and fell silent a moment. 'It's a complicated story.'

'I see.' Laura drew on her cigarette. If he didn't want to talk about it, that was fine. After all, she didn't like being interrogated either. Turning the cigarette in her hand, she examined the glowing tip eating through the tobacco.

'My father had a stroke,' said Jan unexpectedly.

'Oh.' The words slipped out. 'I'm so sorry, I—'

'No, no,' Jan hurried to say. 'It's all right, he survived. He's at a really good care home now, the Blankenburg Residence. But I was stupid enough to think he needed my help. So I resigned. I was doing market research, and for eight years I'd had a pretty decent job as a psychologist at an institute. They were a bit annoyed when I just up and quit.'

'And then?'

'I looked after my father's ad agency.'

'Was it that easy? I thought you were a psychologist.'

'You'll laugh,' said Jan without a trace of humour, 'but I actually studied psychology because I wanted to end up doing something different from my father.'

'Sounds like you didn't always see eye to eye.'

Jan was quiet for a long moment. 'Always demand two hundred per cent, but never be there when you need him. That's my dad.'

Laura said nothing. She knew only too well what Jan meant – and how it felt. Except her father had never demanded anything. He couldn't have cared less about her.

'After university,' continued Jan, 'I started training to be a psychotherapist, and I interned at a day clinic for a year. On only my third day I was supposed to lead a group. Eighteen alcoholics – and I was a trainee without any practical experience. You might as well put a medical student in an operating theatre and ask him to perform open-heart surgery all by himself. Some of my patients were highly aggressive, and they weren't remotely keen to be treated. One of them went nuts and broke my nose. After that I had a bit of a rethink and went into market research. Which is pretty closely connected to advertising, when it comes down to it.'

'Precisely what you didn't want to do.'

'Yeah, well.' Jan shrugged. 'I didn't have anything against advertising in principle. It was more about my father . . .'

'And how did he feel? He must have been pleased when the lost sheep finally returned home.'

'Nothing pleases my father. Nothing I do, at least.'

'Maybe he is pleased but he just can't say it,' suggested Laura. Jan laughed bitterly.

'Got it.'

'Even if that were true, it wouldn't make me feel better,' said Jan. 'Anyway, as he lay in hospital the agency was spinning out of control. I felt like such an arse just watching as everything went down the drain. So I quit and started running it.'

'So what's the problem?' asked Laura. 'Did the agency go broke?'

'Not at all. It's still going strong.'

'Sounds like a happy ending.'

'An ending, yes. Not sure I'd call it happy. He sold the agency as soon as he could. Just like that. Without a word to me. One of the clauses in the contract was that I'd have to leave with immediate effect.'

Laura gazed at him speechlessly.

'That was six weeks ago. Since then I've been a bit of a mess.'

'Wow,' said Laura.

Jan took a deep breath and shrugged. 'Anyway, I badly needed a change of scene. That's why I'm here.'

Laura nodded, blew a cloud of smoke and wondered why Jan had come to his father's house, of all places, for his change of scene.

'What about you?' asked Jan. 'How did Katy get you to agree to this trip?'

'What do you mean?'

Jan threw her a long look. 'Well, you don't exactly look overjoyed to be here.'

'Is that so?' Laura laughed. A little too shrilly, he thought. 'What makes you say that?'

Calmly and wordlessly, Jan fixed her with his brown eyes, and suddenly she felt as though he could see straight through her. To a place nobody was allowed to look.

She blew another plume of smoke into the night, watching the raindrops plunge noiselessly through it. The cigarette was burning dark red. She felt on her guard, and cast him a swift and chilly sidelong glance. 'You don't want to know.'

'That bad?'

Worse, she thought. High time for a change of subject. 'Maybe not as bad as your sister's attempts to pair us off.'

Jan laughed. An awkward, embarrassed laugh, thought Laura.

'That's how she is, my big sister. It was like that even before my mother ran off. Do this, Jan, stop that . . . it's not the first time she's tried her hand at matchmaking for me. It's always a bit . . . awkward.'

'Does it work?'

'Does what work?'

'The matchmaking,' asked Laura. 'I mean, um, in general.' She felt like biting her tongue.

Jan considered for a moment. 'I don't do what my sister says. Just on principle.'

'Good,' said Laura. 'So that's sorted.' She flicked the burned-down cigarette butt into the rain, where it traced a red arc and was extinguished in the wet gravel outside the house.

She stared at Jan. The mark on his cheek looked like a dark and ragged lake on some map. Even at school, it had never bothered her. It had attracted her, in fact.

I shouldn't have thrown away the cigarette, she thought. And I'm standing much too close to him.

She felt his gaze. Saw the way it flickered, as if he were as uncertain as she. He should turn around now, she thought, go up the stairs and disappear into the house.

But he stayed. Standing much too close to her. Glancing down between her breasts, where her black gothic cross hung on a thin silver chain she'd stolen from her mother.

When she parted her lips, an electric current crackled between them even before she'd touched his mouth. She knew she tasted of smoke, but it didn't seem to bother him. He was careful, as if unsure, and it made her keener still. She staggered, catching herself on him and feeling rainwater run down her collar. She wanted to laugh but stopped herself – she couldn't help gazing at his lips and kissing him again, much more passionately than she wanted. She remembered how they were, like a flashback: her in the schoolyard aged fourteen, peeping furtively at Jan, her hands sweaty and her heart pounding unbearably quickly. Jan had been so different. Quiet and sensitive. Not constantly beating his chest like the other boys. He was like 'It Could Be Sweet' by Portishead sounded, just as lost, just as melancholy, just as sweet.

The kisses set off a firework in her head, and she grew dizzy. Was that it?

No, it was impossible. Not like this. They were only kisses!

She felt the tips of her breasts, the gooseflesh everywhere. In her back was the familiar nagging pain. Internally she cursed her cycle, but at the same time she was deeply grateful. If it hadn't been her time of the month she would have slept with him then and there, because being with Jan suddenly felt like coming home, although home was not something she'd ever really had. As if it hadn't been just a teenage crush at school. As if, even then, he'd been the only person who could have understood her. A soulmate.

'I always wanted this, back then,' Jan whispered into her ear.

She pressed herself against him. 'Why didn't you say anything?'

'*You* didn't say anything. And suddenly you were gone. Just like that.'

She stiffened in his arms. As if it had been her fault that she'd had to leave. How could he think such a thing?

A bump brought her back to the present. Katy gave an astonished yelp, and Greg braked the Cherokee with a jerk. Behind them a bigger SUV lurched left, moved up beside them and kept pace with them for a moment. At the wheel sat a dark figure which seemed to be glaring accusingly at them through the wet glass – a dangerous move on the increasingly steep coastal road.

'Yeah, yeah, all right,' Greg growled in the driver's direction. 'Chill out.'

The vehicle shifted even closer. 'Get lost,' growled Greg, giving the middle finger with his left hand.

The man – if it was a man – didn't react. For a moment it seemed to Laura that his gaze was fixed exclusively on *her*.

Seconds later the SUV slowed down and fell back.

'Dickhead,' murmured Katy, laying a soothing hand on Greg's arm.

Laura rolled her eyes. Even on the journey over, Katy had taken every opportunity to touch Greg. Her wide, dark eyes were practically burning into him, and she was gradually starting to wonder whether Katy only wanted to pair her off with Jan so that she could get Greg alone.

There was a dull splash as the Cherokee drove through a large puddle and turned onto the D6007, Avenue Bella Vista, towards

Èze. After a few hundred metres the road split and became two lanes. Curving street lamps cast islands of light onto the wet asphalt at regular intervals. To the right, beneath them, the lights of Beaulieu were growing ever smaller. To the left towered walls of rock or wooded slopes that were lost in darkness.

Laura thought of Jan again, and how she'd secretly hoped he would come with them to Beaulieu. Reaching into her jacket pocket, she pulled out her mobile and considered calling him. But the display read *No signal*. Out of the corner of her eye she suddenly registered a beam reflected in the window, then a bulky shadow next to her. The SUV was back, and it evidently wanted to overtake.

'What the hell does *he* want now?' muttered Greg. He must have stepped on the gas, because the Cherokee sped up.

For a long moment it seemed as though the driver of the SUV couldn't decide whether to overtake or go more slowly. Instead, he kept pace with the Cherokee as it accelerated, drawing up beside it. The two vehicles' garish halogen headlamps cut through the rain. The speedometer climbed to eighty, then ninety kilometres per hour.

'Greg . . .' said Katy softly.

Greg just glowered obstinately ahead, his jawbone clearly visible.

For a second Laura was afraid the SUV might force them off the road, over the crash barrier and into the abyss. She craned her neck, trying to make out the driver, who was openly staring straight at her.

That again.

Pressing a few buttons, she activated the video app on her phone and did what usually frightened off most of these dodgy guys: she raised her camera and filmed the man as ostentatiously as possible. Could he see her, in the dark back seat of the car? Perhaps: the street lamps were casting a pool of light over the two cars every fifty metres.

Then, out of nowhere, there was a sudden flash of light at the edge of the road.

Laura sucked in a sharp breath of air. 'Oh my God,' she murmured faintly. For an instant she thought she'd seen the face of the driver, but it had looked so unreal, so grotesque, that she didn't trust her eyes. She lowered the phone. A chill crept up her spine.

'Well, that's just great,' growled Greg. 'Speed limit's seventy here.'

'So? How quickly were you going?' asked Katy.

'Faster than that, at any rate.'

Laura saw the SUV fall back again. She wanted to turn and reassure herself that it had actually disappeared, but something told her not to, that the strange figure at the wheel might take it as a challenge.

'Did you see that?' she asked.

'Oh yeah, I looked straight into the light and put on a nice smile,' said Greg sarcastically, 'so I can at least get a decent photo.'

'All right,' said Katy. 'We'll share the fine.'

The Cherokee drove through a deep puddle, tossing noisy splashes of water left and right.

Katy squealed and clutched Greg's arm.

Laura groaned with irritation.

Ahead of them the tunnel appeared, and the D6007 was getting increasingly narrow, with only one lane in each direction. All Laura wanted to do was get out of this bloody tin can. If it hadn't been bucketing down, and if that weird guy hadn't been hanging around, she would have got out and walked.

Next time, she told herself, I'm staying with Jan.

She was annoyed to realise how much she was looking forward to seeing him. Another five minutes, she thought. A few kilometres along the Moyenne coastal road to Èze, and from there a few twists and turns up the steep incline to the house . . .

Then came the tunnel. It opened like a mouth, swallowing the Cherokee into a black, two-hundred-metre long tube of rock.

Chapter Four

Jan had tried everything to stop himself going crazy, to resist the nagging thought that Laura might have vanished from a supermarket in a foreign city.

But nothing helped.

Since last night his mind had kept returning incessantly to Laura. It was like there'd been no break between then and now. He felt fourteen again, gnawed by those same abruptly flaring emotions, that same swiftly beating heart, except that his reflection in the pane of glass was that of a thirty-four-year old. A grown man.

Does it work, the matchmaking? Laura had asked him last night.

He could have replied with something charming, could have dodged the question or played for time. He could simply have smiled. Instead he'd blurted out something brusque: *I don't do what my sister says. Just on principle.*

Even as he spoke, he wished he'd held his tongue. Why did the wrong thing always come to him at the right moment? He had no idea why she'd kissed him anyway. When it happened it had felt like a release, like a white cloud forming out of black smoke. Time had stood still, as if there were no past, as if Theo hadn't gone flying through the windshield and his mother had never run away.

Here and now, with Laura, everything felt fine. He felt fine. Not like an abandoned child, not like a *guilty* child.

And then the thread had been cut again.

'Why didn't you say anything?' she'd asked him.

'*You* didn't say anything. And suddenly you were gone.'

It had only struck him later that she might have taken it as an accusation. Whatever the reason for her disappearance, he was sure it couldn't have been easy for her.

She'd gone stiff as a board, pulling away from his embrace and stepping back. 'What do you mean *you*?'

'No, don't get me wrong, I could have said something, but ...' He hesitated briefly, looking at her. 'You were so ... unapproachable ...'

'Unapproachable?' Her eyes narrowed, her cheeks flushing. 'Like the patients at your day clinic, you mean? The ones who didn't want therapy from you? The ones you ran away from?'

Bang. He felt himself redden too. With anger. With embarrassment. 'What's that supposed to mean? That's got nothing to do with it. They were alcoholics. Lots of them had been admitted for the umpteenth time blowing 0.2, and ... they wanted lots of things, but certainly not help from a clueless newbie. Unless I was bringing them schnapps.'

She'd stared at him with a strange expression. Furious, and somehow just as hurt as he was, as if he'd hit a nerve. 'You think the only people who need help are the ones who ask for it?'

'Do you seriously want to debate the psychology of alcoholics with me?' he asked.

Her gaze flickered briefly. She stared mutely past him into the darkness, her eyes empty, past him towards the sea.

'No, I don't,' she said roughly, then turned on her heel and opened the door. Her silhouette stood out sharply against the light indoors.

Why was she being so sensitive? Could it be that . . . He hesitated. It suddenly occurred to him that Laura was the only person who'd drunk no wine at all that evening.

'Laura, I—'

She raised her hand to cut him off without even turning around. The sound as she pulled the door shut gave him déjà vu. Only one other sound had burned itself as deeply into his memory as that door: the skidding of tyres on wet asphalt, seamlessly followed by shattering glass and tearing metal.

The door had come after the accident. He'd just turned ten. His mother had probably thought he was asleep. But he wasn't. And he heard the door. Quickly getting to his feet, he went over to the window of his bedroom on the first floor and stared outside as she dragged her pale leather suitcase behind her on little wheels. His heart nearly stopped. Hurriedly he opened the window. Cold air struck him in the face, fear nearly robbing him of breath. 'Mum?'

She jumped.

Somehow he'd expected her – no, wanted her – to turn around. But she simply ducked her head, hunching it between her shoulders, and her steps grew quicker.

'*Mum!* Where are you going?'

No answer. No glance. Only ice-cold air.

In those first weeks he'd been paralysed. Then came the rage and emptiness. She hadn't left so much as a letter. Later he'd come to realise that it wouldn't have made any difference if she had. He knew the reason. It was because of Theo. Because Theo was no longer alive. Because *he* hadn't taken better care of him.

Jan stared through the pattern of raindrops on the huge panoramic window and brushed the memories aside. More than twenty minutes had passed since Katy's call, and he'd been unable to reach either her or Laura.

Something was wrong, that much he knew.

So he went downstairs into the hallway, stepped into his father's old wellington boots, shrugged on his much-too-thin rain jacket and picked up the only umbrella left on the coat hooks, a shabby black fold-up thing, before grabbing an LED torch.

The umbrella was a joke, better suited to a woman's handbag than rough coastal weather. Yet as the water beat down onto the taut fabric, he was glad of it. Switching on the torch, he braced the umbrella against the wind and strode off. The rain flashed in the white beam of light, and a skin of water covered the asphalt.

He followed the narrow mountain track that led from the house up to Èze, a town of two and a half thousand inhabitants that sat lonely and enthroned on a mountaintop 403 metres above the sea. From there the road led down towards the coast.

Approaching the outskirts of Èze, he stepped onto the viaduct.

He kept a safe distance from the railing as he walked. Gusts of wind tugged at him as he went, and the gorge seemed eager to suck him into its depths.

The tunnel at the end of the viaduct was a relief, dry and protected from the wind, although at thirty paces it was significantly shorter than the second tunnel that lay below, just outside Beaulieu-sur-Mer.

Jan's steps echoed off the fissured rock walls. Water flowed downhill over the asphalt; it sounded like the whispering of mountain spirits.

Hardly had he stepped out of the tunnel's protection than a gust caught him and ripped the umbrella out of his hand. Jan stumbled after it, but the spindly wire frame went somersaulting away.

Cursing, Jan pulled his hood tighter. After barely two minutes his face was wet, and he felt the dampness creeping into his jacket. Shivering with cold, he continued walking down the coastal road, which by now had widened to two lanes on both sides. At any moment he expected a car to swing towards him round the next bend. But the road was empty.

Until, suddenly, he saw it.

Headlights beyond a turn in the road.

Only the lights weren't moving. The vehicle seemed to be standing still.

All at once he felt queasy.

No. This can't be happening, he thought. Please don't let it be happening.

He swallowed, trying to ignore the old images rearing up inside his head.

Walking quickly he headed for the beams. The road veered gently to the right. The Cherokee was angled as if it had pulled up too abruptly. The rain was refracted in the light of the headlamps, which were shining into the bushes. Droplets of water danced on the still-warm bonnet like tiny devils. The passenger door was open, all others closed.

The car was empty.

No sign of Laura, Katy or Greg.

Although the Cherokee was completely undamaged, he suddenly thought he saw bent metal, shattered glass, a smashed windshield.

The silence after the crash, that had been the worst thing. It had been pouring with rain, the droplets hammering on the car roof, but it was as though he were deaf. He'd been sitting in the middle at the back, between Katy and Theo. His mother was in the passenger seat. She'd turned around and seen him first, but then her gaze had fallen on the child seat next to him and her eyes had widened. The whole world seemed to stand still: no sound, no movement, no intake of breath. Only his mother's eyes on the empty child seat.

When someone dies, they say the light in their eyes goes out. At that moment the light went out in his mother's eyes. But she didn't die.

Jan gritted his teeth, trying to shake away the memories. You're an adult! There's no empty child seat here!

Slowly, very slowly, he approached the wide-open passenger door of the Cherokee. His fingers touched the cold metal. It helped a little to bring him into the here and now. His gaze fell on the light beige leather seat, which was soaking wet, as was the footwell. The ignition key was missing.

Shutting the passenger door, Jan climbed onto the dry back seat. Once he'd pulled the door closed behind him, he felt as if he were sitting in a pocket of air at the bottom of some dark lake. Feeling something hard beneath the sole of his right boot, he bent down and picked up a flat, rectangular object. Laura's mobile phone, a shiny silver Nokia with a small crack near the edge of the case.

What the hell had happened here?

For a long while, paralysed, he stared at the mobile. Water dripped from his hood onto the display. He blinked, trying to shake off the feeling of apprehension. Perhaps calling the police would be best. But what number did you dial for the police in France?

Then he noticed there wasn't any signal anyway.

He pocketed Laura's mobile, climbed out and shouted into the darkness: 'Laura?'

No answer.

'LAUUURA!'

Nothing. Only the pelting rain and the distant roar of the sea. Beyond the next bend a set of headlights appeared. Standing in the pool of light cast by the Cherokee, Jan raised his hand and waved. The vehicle, a small van, moved into the inside lane without altering its speed.

Jan stepped into its path and flailed both arms wildly. The headlights shone straight at him, and he squinted. A Citroën logo flashed on the grille.

For a moment it looked as if the vehicle were slowing down, but then the Citroën accelerated sharply. Jan leapt aside. A torrent of water soaked his trousers. Through the side window he saw the silhouette of a woman at the wheel.

Then the tail lights disappeared in the direction of Èze. He swore. Still, he could understand the woman's reluctance to stop. Bucketing rain, a strange man in the middle of a lonely road – in her shoes he wouldn't have stopped either.

Onward, then, to Beaulieu. There must be a police station there.

He set off, walking quickly, keeping to the left-hand side. The next bend but one was a hairpin; the crash barrier there was broken, the chasm beyond it an open grave. Pushed into the earth nearby was a covered wooden cross and a statue of the Virgin Mary, the colour peeling off it. The hood was clinging to his hair, water running over his face like sweat. As he walked his torch caught a signpost: *Beaulieu 2 km.*

He stopped. Two kilometres. That meant at least twenty minutes to the edge of town. Èze was ten at the most.

Turning on his heel, he hurried back up the road towards Èze. The statue of Mary gazed at him impassively. Going uphill took significantly more effort, and he broke into a sweat beneath his rain jacket. He thought of Laura, Katy and Greg. What on God's green earth had *happened* to the three of them? He took his mobile out to see if he had a signal. Nothing doing. He looked up again, and couldn't believe his eyes.

Slowing his steps, he came to a halt and stared uncomprehendingly at the wet, empty road.

Greg's black Cherokee had disappeared.

Chapter Five

Èze, Côte d'Azur, 17 October, 11.01 p.m.

Jan hurried down the final stretch of road. Below him, his parents' house jutted out of the rock like a stunted diving board. Behind the panoramic window there was a faint light. The rain had eased off over the last few metres, but Jan cast an angry glance at his dripping trousers. The water was already inside his wellington boots. Raising his head, he stopped as abruptly as if he'd run into a wall.

In the middle of the turning bay outside the house was the Cherokee.

He trudged furiously past the Jeep, up the stone steps and inside, stomping into the living room.

In the middle of the room stood Katy, wearing nothing but a slip, her hair damp and tousled. Greg, also half naked, was rubbing her upper body warm with a towel.

They both froze as Jan burst in.

Greg dropped his hands, and the towel fell to the floor. 'Bloody hell, mate. You gave me a fright,' he growled.

'A fright, eh?' said Jan viciously. 'Would you mind telling me what's going on?'

Katy's eyes narrowed. 'Leave it, will you? This is my business, not yours.' She picked up the towel and covered herself. 'I was soaked to the skin, and I'm freezing cold. That's all.'

Jan looked from Katy to Greg and back again. His mind went to her husband Sören and their twins, Anna and Nele. Jan liked his nieces, especially Nele, the quieter of the two. Whenever they went out she demanded the spot on his narrow shoulders – not by saying anything, but simply by looking at him, her blue eyes surrounded by freckles. The Sweden Look, Katy called it, in deference to Sören. 'Yeah, that's all,' muttered Jan.

Katy raised her eyebrows warningly. Her slip was damp, sitting crooked on her hips and revealing a dark triangle beneath.

'As far as I'm concerned,' said Jan irritably, 'you can be dried off by whoever you like. I'm only asking where you were, for Christ's sake. I was worried after your call. I went looking for you.'

'You did *what*?' asked Katy in consternation. 'In this weather?'

'Clearly.' He gestured to his soaking-wet things. 'Where's Laura?'

Katy threw an uncertain look at Greg. 'Isn't she with you?'

'Would I be asking if she were?'

Katy fell into embarrassed silence, and cast another glance at Greg. Suddenly Jan was gripped with a feeling of unease. Something wasn't right.

'We . . . we argued,' said Katy.

'Who?'

'Well, Laura and—'

'We were pissed off,' Greg interrupted her. 'She just buggered off at the supermarket without saying a word. We searched high and low, but then she just showed up like nothing had happened. Had to go to the toilet, apparently. For half an hour!'

'Twenty minutes, Greg. It was twenty minutes,' interjected Katy.

Greg threw out his upturned palms in mock helplessness.

'Yeah, and?' asked Jan.

Greg shrugged. 'Women's problems.'

'Excuse me?'

'She had her period,' murmured Katy.

'Just get to the point,' said Jan, reaching the end of his tether. 'I want to know where she is. Or am I the only one here who cares?'

Katy opened her mouth, but Greg cut her off. 'Frankly, I've got no idea. She ran off.'

Katy shut her mouth and averted her eyes.

'You mean you left her down in Beaulieu?'

'She's a grown-up,' replied Greg. 'Am I supposed to tell a thirty-four-year-old what she can and can't do?'

'Then why,' asked Jan softly, 'was her mobile in your car?' He pulled the phone from his rain jacket with the tips of his fingers.

Greg's grin faded. 'Where did you get that?'

'As I said, from your car.'

'You don't have a key to my car.'

'I didn't need one. The door was wide open when I found it, slap-bang in the middle of the road. It was bucketing down and your stupid hunk of crap was just left there. Lights on, abandoned, in the middle of the mountains.'

Greg blinked.

'Do you still want me to believe that Laura ran off after your little fight at the supermarket?'

'I didn't say she ran off at the supermarket. You said that.'

'*What?*'

'Greg threw her out,' said Katy softly. 'Near where you saw the car.'

'Threw her out?' Jan stared at Greg in bewilderment. '*Why*?'

Greg shrugged. 'Argument. Like I said.'

'About what, for Christ's sake?'

'What does that matter? She got out.'

Katy was gazing at him in thin-lipped silence.

'Look, all I said was that if she couldn't pull herself together she should get out of my car,' Greg said defensively.

'And you let her get out and just drove on?' asked Jan in disbelief.

Greg shook his head.

'At first, yes,' murmured Katy. 'At Èze we turned around and drove all the way back, nearly as far as Beaulieu. But she was gone. Then we went to the spot where she got out. There's a way back to Beaulieu from there, a sort of footpath down the mountain. Greg left the headlights on so we could see where we were going, then we walked a little way down the path. But eventually we gave up.'

Jan felt dizzy. His cold, damp clothes were clinging to his body. A small puddle had formed around him. He groaned, grabbed a chair and sat down. He didn't know whether to be furious or despondent. His gaze went first to his sister, then to Greg. 'I don't get it,' he murmured. 'You threw a woman out of the car in the middle of the night, on a lonely mountain road in the pouring rain.'

'It was a few minutes past ten. And I didn't throw her out. She got out under her own steam.'

'Why didn't you just tell me what happened straight away, for fuck's sake?'

'OK, that's enough,' said Katy, getting agitated. 'It's not as if we're making up a pack of lies here.'

'Surely I don't have to explain to a woman at the tender age of thirty-seven how thin the line between lying and keeping quiet is, do I?'

'Don't you start acting the psychologist with me! I've got two kids, I know the difference between keeping silent and lying.'

'Exactly,' said Jan drily. And what would you tell the two of them if they could see you now? He looked his sister up and down.

She felt his gaze, blushed and tried to rewrap herself in the towel so that it covered her better.

A leaden silence fell.

The rain had stopped. Outside, water splashed from the guttering.

'Look, don't worry,' said Katy finally. 'I know Laura. She's always pulling stunts like this, especially when she's in a mood. She's probably in some hotel in Beaulieu right now, and tomorrow morning she'll go back to Berlin.'

'Without her phone? Without any money or her clothes?'

'She's got her wallet. At least, she did when we were in the supermarket. Or did you find that in the car too?'

Jan shook his head.

'Fine. Like I said, I know her. She'll turn up.'

'Funny,' replied Jan caustically, 'that doesn't sound remotely like the Laura *I've* got to know.'

'Believe me, Jan,' said Katy, 'you only know a tiny part of her. Don't worry.'

'Look who's talking! Weren't you the one who called up in a panic because Laura spent a little too long on the loo?'

Katy swallowed. 'That was different.'

'My thoughts exactly,' retorted Jan. He looked at Greg, who was leaning against the edge of the dining table and glowering sullenly at the floor. Jan's instincts were rebelling. Something about this story didn't add up; he just wasn't sure what it was. Nor was he sure how to proceed.

Should he call the police? But what would he tell them? That a couple of grown-ups had been bickering like children? That a woman had got out of a car in the rain and walked away on foot? They'd hardly start a major search on that account.

A swelling patter broke the oppressive silence. The rain was back, stronger than before.

He wished he could be standing on the porch outside with Laura, tasting the smoke on her lips.

Chapter Six

Berlin, 18 October, 10.21 a.m.

Laura felt the pain first. A stinging like a thousand needles at the top of her skull. She opened her eyes, but the darkness remained. Dazed, she closed them again. Where was the rain? The road?

A few minutes ago she'd been stomping up the road, alone and utterly enraged. She'd glared at the tips of her wellies, counting the steps so as not to think about how far it was to the house.

The dull gurgle of a diesel engine had crept up behind her. She heard the water spraying from beneath the tyres, but kept her eyes stubbornly focused ahead as she strode up the mountain. No way in hell was she getting back into that car. She was used to going it alone. *Totally alone.*

Even in the glare of the headlamps, she didn't turn around. Spray drenched her trousers, and she saw heavy silver wheel rims digging into the road, a German number plate, a black rear bumper.

She stopped short, staring at the back of the car, the grooved tyre tracks in the wet asphalt and the glowing red brake lights. About ten metres ahead of her, the SUV had come to a halt. The tracks in the water broke off; the vehicle stood there like a phantom.

Then the driver-side door opened. A figure got out, moving at a leisurely pace. The lights inside the car cast a yellowish glow. In the figure's right hand something flashed – a long, narrow object.

Laura stared at the object as though paralysed. Suddenly she was aware of every hair and every pore in her body. Gooseflesh set her skin alight. The object was a narrow tube about a metre long with a grip at the middle and the end, and above the middle grip was a second, shorter tube.

A scope, thought Laura. *That's a rifle*!

The fraction of a second between realisation and running seemed incalculably long; time slowed, the rain a glistening curtain of knife-sharp strips through which the car's tail lights burned.

She turned and took to her heels. Out of the corner of her eye she could see the man raise the weapon. Her imagination filled in the rest: the way he took aim, rested the hind grip on his shoulder and his right cheek on the stock, put his eye to the scope. Her wellington boots splashed clumsily over the road, her brain whipping her muscles onwards. She smelled earth, salt and rotting vegetation. I'm athletic, she thought, I'm fit. I only have to get far enough away for him to miss.

She saw his index finger curl around the trigger. The wind tore back her hood. She felt naked, and the rain whipped into her face without her even feeling it. Behind her was only the man and his rifle, and before her the black coastal road, wide and long, refuge-less.

I should zigzag, she thought, so he doesn't . . .

Then came the noise. A *thwack*. Dry, brief, sharp.

At the same instant something struck her neck. A stinging pain tore through her body. She stumbled but didn't fall, kept running.

She registered her slowing legs.

Don't flag! she thought. Or he'll catch you with the next shot.

But her muscles seemed to freeze up mid-stride, as if she were running through icy waist-deep water, and her strength dwindled second by second.

He hit my carotid, she thought in a panic, that's why I'm running out of strength! But then wouldn't blood be spurting out of my neck?

She fell to her knees, sinking onto the wet road. She turned, forcing herself to keep the man in her field of vision – maybe she could dodge the next shot . . .

She lay with her cheek turned to the asphalt. Her neck was throbbing; she felt something flowing, though whether it was blood or water or both she couldn't tell.

And now she had this headache, and it made no difference whether her eyes were open or closed. Everything was black.

Then: a blaze of light.

Someone was approaching.

A breath of exhaled air wafted into her face. It stank of rot, and mouthwash used in vain.

She opened her eyes.

Bright spots of light burned into her retinas. She squeezed her eyelids shut, blinked and looked through her lashes as though through a protective filter. Everything was blurry. Directly in front of her hovered something oval, black and white like zebra hide, and it was coming closer – much too close. Another exhalation hit her face, the revolting smell penetrating deep into her nostrils. Her eyelids fluttered; her vision grew sharper.

Right in front of her, at eye level, was a mouth: masculine, pinkish, slightly open, with chapped lips. Chin and cheeks were shaved smooth, and covered in a symmetrical pattern of wide black tattooed stripes, as if someone had cut the stripes off a zebra, painstakingly rearranged them, bent them into shape and applied them to their own face. The blank strips of skin between the tattoos looked as if they'd been painted white.

Laura frowned woozily.

She wanted to raise her head and look the man in the eye, but some sort of padding prevented her bending her neck. The man's nostrils were flared like an animal's, and he seemed to be inhaling her scent through his nose. A smile played around the corners of his mouth: concentrated, ecstatic and bewitched.

He breathed in – and back out again. Laura panted, trying to move. But she couldn't. She was sitting naked on a wooden chair with armrests. Plastic wrap was wound tightly around her limbs, giving her not so much as a millimetre's leeway.

Laura wanted to get out of this dream. To wake up on the dusty mattress in France, in the house that belonged to Jan's father. And where was Jan? Suddenly she remembered that evening, the trip to the supermarket, the journey back, and . . .

All at once she was ice cold.

The SUV.

The man at the wheel, the grotesque face.

With a jerk her brain shifted into gear. *This was no dream.* Fear struck her like a fist, echoing in the pit of her stomach.

The man must have noticed. His smile grew wider, and he was breathing more quickly. 'Welcome,' he whispered. 'Welcome to my gallery.' He stepped aside, offering Laura a clear view of the large windowless room. It was sunk in gloom, despite the white walls. From the ceiling hung countless spotlights, throwing bright patches onto the surrounding walls and the whitish, shimmering objects mounted to her left and right.

The man stepped back into her field of vision, his pose like that of a gallery owner at an opening, awaiting a response from his audience.

He was tall, clad entirely in white and had a shaved head. The black stripes ran not only over his face but his scalp as well, like a whole-body tattoo.

Throwing out his arms, he gestured to the walls. 'Look around you. Aren't they breathtaking?'

Only now had Laura's pupils adjusted to the light enough to make out the details. At intervals of about one-and-a-half metres, massive transparent blocks were embedded into the wall, more than a dozen in total. Each was the size of a narrow door, and the edges were covered with plaster so that it looked as though someone had scratched windows into blocks of frosted ice, allowing you to see inside. Every single one held a floating woman.

The women were naked, and the effect was like some ethereal vision. A light source somewhere behind the blocks lent the bodies a special aura, shimmering magically past them into the room, and Laura felt as though she were at the bottom of an illuminated swimming pool, surrounded by the drifting dead.

They were near-identical. Each woman had unnaturally pale skin, and all were young, with similar figures, shaved pubic areas and long white-blond hair that floated around their heads.

A chill ran through Laura as she realised that the women had one other thing in common: they all looked like *her*.

She didn't have blond hair, of course, her skin wasn't nearly as white, and she was older than the women around her. But the resemblance was unmistakable.

'Ah,' whispered the man. 'You're thinking about the hair. And the skin. Are you afraid? It's hard to bear the presence of so much beauty, isn't it? You feel you don't belong. But don't worry. We'll manage. I can manage nearly anything.' His voice was rough, and in any other room would have been drowned out. But here, in this dead silence, Laura could hear every smack of his tongue against his gums.

'It doesn't matter that you're older, either.' His tongue licked his dry lips. 'You're perfect, you know. You've no idea *how* perfect. Or I wouldn't have gone all that way for you.'

What did he mean, *perfect*? thought Laura. Despair over-whelmed her, and she fought not to cry. 'What . . . what do you want from me? Who are you?'

The man jumped. For a moment his eyes widened, his gaze flickering. The smile died on his lips. 'What . . . who the hell . . .' he whispered, staring at her.

Laura bit her lip. Had she said the wrong thing? Maybe she wasn't supposed to say anything at all?

'Say that again,' he whispered hoarsely.

Laura pressed her lips together. It's a trap, she thought. *He's crazy*. Anything I say now will make him—

'SPEAK,' roared the man.

Laura flinched. Tears welled up in her eyes. 'I . . . I wanted to know who you are. And what you want from me.'

'*More.*' He waved his hand. 'Speak *more!*'

'Please . . . I don't know what you . . . I don't even know what's going on,' stammered Laura. 'What is this place?'

The tattooed man gazed at her open-mouthed. His already white skin was now practically translucent. He groaned, threw back his head and ran his hand over his scalp. One of the ceiling lamps shone into his face. For a brief moment his pupils glowed red, and he screwed up his eyes as if it scorched him.

Laura's breath faltered. It's not possible, she thought. Nobody has red eyes, nobody.

The man lowered his head. He looked like a wild animal that couldn't decide whether to kill its prey or run for its life. 'What are you doing here?' he asked in disbelief. 'What the *hell* are you doing here?'

What am *I* doing here? Laura didn't understand the question. *He* was the one who'd brought her.

'Tell me!' he shrieked.

His voice triggered something in her more disturbing than his appearance. It was something diffuse; a memory crept like a snake out of its hole in the earth, but she couldn't catch it, and it escaped her.

The man was staring at her as if *she* were the monster instead of him. Then he groaned loudly, clenched his right hand into a fist and struck his bald skull several times in quick succession.

Breathing heavily, he stopped at last. He staggered briefly, and for a moment Laura thought he was going to collapse.

Then he turned with a jerk, walked stiffly to the door, flung it open, switched off the lights in the gallery and slammed the door behind him.

Laura was left in total darkness, trembling.

This isn't real, this isn't happening! she told herself.

But the image in her mind's eye wouldn't leave. She could still see his face and those red eyes, glowing in the darkness like cigarettes. The pale bodies of the young women surrounded her like ghosts.

Chapter Seven

The door banged shut behind him like a shot. His head felt about to burst. It can't be true, he thought. It – can't – be – true!

Yet there sat Laura, on the other side of the door.

He slammed his fist repeatedly into his skull. It resonated dully, the bones vibrating. He hoped the pain would distract him, but it only reminded him that all of this was real.

He was *so* blind.

He thought of Jenny, what she'd been like – back then. He was always thinking of her, really. Always, and with every woman. The memory was so lifelike he could grasp it.

Thirty-first of October 1977 had been the day to end all days. The day his most fervent wish had been fulfilled. Even though wishes were *never* fulfilled. You didn't just get what you wanted. It was a cast-iron rule.

That day, he'd broken the rule.

He'd always hated dressing up, even as a little boy, and he'd hated just as much the occasions when you had to do it, like carnival, for instance, when every arsehole and his mother went wandering around in a costume and make-up.

Thirty-first of October 1977 had been just such a day: Halloween.

That Halloween came from America and that according to 'Buck', alias Bernhard Stelzer, running around like a zombie was the latest craze hadn't made it any better. Frankly, staying at home seemed by far the best course of action. Only one argument spoke against it, and that argument was named Jenny. Jenny, the unattainable. She was seventeen and had firm round breasts, a pink tongue so sharp he couldn't bring himself to think about it and hips that mesmerised him. It was no exaggeration to say that he literally lost his mind when he stole furtive glances at the middle of her body, no matter the angle, from the side, from behind or from the front. He could do it for hours, just watching her and pining.

And naturally Jenny was attending Buck Stelzer's Halloween party too – Buck, the son of a surgeon, Dr Stelzer, who made such a packet out of his patients that it made you dizzy to think of it. A surgeon. That was a good job. Slicing people up and getting paid for it. Apparently Dr Stelzer had perfected his slicing in the USA, which meant he could charge more than his colleagues. And since his son had nothing better to do than throw his father's cash around, he soon had his nickname: Buck, like the American one-dollar bill.

So now Buck had invited people to a Halloween party – in costume. And Jenny would be there. Not that Buck had invited him; he never got invitations like that. But if he showed up in costume, nobody would recognise him. He'd be a ghost among ghosts. And if nobody recognised him, then nobody would throw him out.

That left only one question: what costume?

He didn't have one.

He ransacked the house, nervous, and sick with jealousy at the thought that he might get there too late, all because of a stupid costume – that the others would already be there, ogling Jenny on the dance floor.

He started turning every room in the house upside down. His father's study, the kitchen, the wardrobe in the bedroom, the tool room in the basement, the hobby room, which was being renovated. His gaze fell on the freshly glued strips of wallpaper in the hobby room, with the striking pattern. On the pasting table lay a cut-off piece. The idea came to him at that very moment, and suddenly it all seemed like a string of pearls on a necklace: shimmering and brilliant.

He took the knife and followed the pattern of the wallpaper until he had templates for the various symmetrical curves and jagged lines. Then he hurried into the bathroom and tied back his black, straw-like strands of hair which he hated, smoothing them down with gel. Taking all his mother's black make-up sticks, he tried them out on his hand.

The eyeliner was the best.

With a steady hand he copied the wallpaper pattern onto his face. He'd always been able to paint, but doing a mirror-image was harder and one of the lines slipped. Still, that was the only mistake. After twenty minutes he lowered the eyeliner, which he'd had to sharpen several times, and gazed into the mirror.

In front of him stood an unfamiliar man with the face of a – well, of what? A demon? A voodoo priest? He hardly recognised himself, yet suddenly he liked it. It wasn't just a disguise; it was better than that. *He* was better. He was someone else.

He was gripped by a strange arousal. At first he wasn't sure what it was, and he didn't waste any further thought on it. The party took priority. Jenny took priority. He was about to leave when it occurred to him that the make-up might run. Grabbing a can of hairspray, he closed his eyes, held his breath and sprayed a fine mist over his face to fix the colour, just as he'd always done with his pencil sketches. Finally he took a pair of white trousers out of his wardrobe. No white shirt, though; only his father had those. In normal circumstances he'd never have dared open his father's wardrobe. But today everything was different.

He pulled on the white shirt, tucked it tightly around him, and set off.

People on the train kept eyeing him nervously, as if he were mad and might bite. It felt nice.

Buck Stelzer's parents' villa was a Grecian palace, with columns like a temple. Buck's parents were out of town, so Stelzer junior had taken the opportunity to throw exactly the kind of party that would have sent them round the bend.

Everywhere in the pitch-black garden torches were burning, small islands of fire. The tall columns flickered in the glow of orange globes. As always, he found it difficult to see clearly when things were far away. As he approached he realised that the globes were pumpkins, heads lit from within, their skulls broken open, their toothless mouths frozen into joyless grins. Gooseflesh prickled on his skin, and he wondered whether Jenny, too, had been overcome by a strange arousal when she saw the heads. What he wouldn't have given to see her nipples then.

The party was in full swing. Hundreds of ghosts, and he one of them. Nobody recognised him, nobody laughed. It smelled like sweat and cheap costumes, like cigarettes and alcohol. Shards of glass crunched on the parquet. Buck was an idiot. What did he think his parents were going to say? What was going through his head?

Suddenly he saw Jenny. In the middle of the dance floor, exactly where he'd have wanted her to be if she hadn't already been there. No – he'd have wanted her somewhere else entirely, really, but there was no hope of that.

So he stood still, losing track of time.

Five minutes, fifteen minutes, thirty-five minutes.

He could have stood there for ever, watching her dance. She'd done something to her skin. She was shimmering, white as alabaster, pale and seductive. Her blond hair was pinned up into a tower, and looked as though it had been powdered. From her red lips a trickle of blood ran down her chin and over her neck, as if she'd just bitten somebody. Never had he seen so much beauty brought to such bewitching perfection. Then, like a bolt from the blue, she looked at him and reached out her arm, beckoning, reaching for his hand. Yes, *his* hand! She was beckoning to *him*! He tried not to make his feelings obvious. More certain, more self-assured. Instinctively he puffed out his chest and gave a firm smile.

He was somebody now. Somebody else.

Jenny beckoned again. 'Come here,' she twittered in her bright, clear voice above the blaring music. Her pink tongue flicked between her lips, and he was on fire. Slowly he moved onto the dance floor.

He smiled.

He was strong and assured.

The make-up made anything possible!

He outdid himself and took her hand. Her fingertips were cool and slightly damp. More deftly than he'd thought he could, he raised her hand with his. He'd seen it once in a dance film. She understood the invitation and danced beneath the crook of his arm, turning into him so that her back nestled against his body. 'Who are you?' she whispered over her shoulder into his ear.

An overpowering jolt ran from his ear down into the tips of his toes. He'd never thought such a feeling was possible. As if in a fever, he said hoarsely: 'Does it matter?'

She laughed. For a moment he thought it was an alcohol-fuelled laugh. But she was too steady on her legs for that, wasn't she? 'Maybe I can figure it out,' she said provocatively.

I bloody hope not, he thought.

'Maybe you can figure it out when we go upstairs,' he heard himself say.

A slap or a mocking laugh wouldn't have surprised him. He was certain she'd collapse to the floor, rolling around laughing and bawling, 'Froggy, don't be such a stupid sod!' and the whole room would agree. Everybody would laugh at Froggy, and he'd probably be called that all life long, because no princess ever wanted to kiss him and because he always wore those glasses with the dark-green lenses.

Instead she pressed her arse against him. 'Come on. I know where we can go.'

As the door of Dr Stelzer's bedroom fell shut behind them, he still wasn't sure whether she might not take his cock out of his trousers then run off snorting with laughter. I'm not me, he told himself. I'm somebody else. Froggy's the one people despise. Not me!

Jenny stared at him, her gaze practically licking his face. 'I love that tattoo thing,' she whispered. 'Is it voodoo, or what?'

'It makes me stronger,' he said.

'How strong?' she asked, half drunk and half clear.

'A thousand times stronger,' he said, intoxicated. And it wasn't even a lie.

A second later she did the unthinkable. What he'd pictured in his head a thousand times, but which had always been reserved for others. She kissed him. Him! Her tongue went into his mouth, and a firework went off inside his mind. As if of its own accord, his hand reached for her, and he wondered again who *he* was now, who the hell this *other* person was.

He tugged her clothes off, feeling like there was an animal inside him, and pushed her to the bed. She pulled his trousers down eagerly, and his penis almost leapt out. He poked awkwardly between her legs until suddenly he felt himself slip inside and fill with heat. He bit her neck, digging his right hand into her buttocks until his fingertips burned. She screamed, but it wasn't just pain, it couldn't just be pain.

It was perfect. Equal to equal, pure magic.

And then in a torrent it was over. The arousal was simply too much. Abruptly his make-up seemed to shrink, and so did his penis.

God, he was so ashamed. Jenny looked at him in surprise. 'Wow, that was fast,' she muttered. 'Are you always so speedy?'

Yes, would have been the honest answer. It was his first time, after all, so 'always' was accurate. But he said nothing.

He stood up, his heart pounding, and grinned. A crappy smile, he thought. But better than forcing some stupid sentence.

'Who are you?' asked Jenny. She narrowed her eyes interroga-
tively and stood up. Her skin was glowing white. Around her
neck his make-up had left black marks. Licking the tip of her
finger with her tongue, she reached out her hand to his face.
'Your eyes,' she slurred. 'For a moment I thought they were red.'

He blinked and tried to keep grinning, but it was a struggle.

Using her saliva, she began to rub the make-up from his face.
Jenny could have done anything with her saliva. Anything and
anywhere. But not the make-up! Not that! Froggy wasn't there,
and it had to stay that way.

In a panic he raised his arm and slapped her hands aside.
She gave a shriek of astonishment and jabbed him in the chest.
'What the hell was that, you arsehole? Who are you?'

Enraged, he grabbed her by the throat, flung her to the floor
and sprang on top of her. He had no idea who he was. Arousal
engulfed him like a nuclear meltdown. He took her a second
time, his hands around her throat. Finally he was the one with
the power. The power to control Jenny. The power to control
himself – and yet to step totally outside himself at the same time.

It only took a little longer than the first time, or so it seemed
to him. When it was over, he straightened up – and froze.

Jenny wasn't moving.

Why the fuck wasn't she moving?

He stood up and looked at her.

Was she unconscious?

Had she been unconscious the whole time?

The unconsciousness lent her an entrancing beauty. On the
dark wooden floor her body looked like freshly fallen snow, like
you could sink into her up to your neck.

Was she . . .?

No. Not possible. He'd have noticed. You had to notice something when . . .

He gazed down at her, and the idea took on a monstrous quality, something so huge and powerful that he felt sick, as if from a drug his body craved but had to get accustomed to.

Slowly he edged backwards towards the door. Zipped up his trousers. *Get out of here. That wasn't you. That wasn't Froggy. That was somebody else.*

But who the fuck was it?

He fled the room in a frenzy. Walking down the stairs to the ground floor, he was afraid. But nobody recognised him. Froggy wasn't there. He was invisible.

He left the house and the street where the Stelzers' folly stood, swearing to himself in the darkness that he'd never wash again. He'd carry her taste on himself for the rest of time. And he'd stay invisible.

For the first time in his life, his dream had come true.

Free at last, he'd thought.

And now?

Now, suddenly, Laura was sitting on the other side of the door.

He remembered how he'd watched her two days earlier, outside the house near Èze. The way she'd kissed that guy.

Kissed?

No. It had been more than a kiss. Jenny had kissed other men too, and it had made him furious. But this thing with Laura was something else entirely. It virtually ate him up, knowing that that man had touched her.

He had to know how Laura felt.

He turned on his heel, his white shoes squeaking on the stone floor. Handle, light switch, steady pulse.

There she sat, her eyelids fluttering, bound to the chair.

Slowly he approached her.

He knew now what he had to do. A clear goal, at last. Clearer than he'd had in many years.

No, it was more than a goal.

It was a *mission*.

He leant down to her.

He smiled. Opened his mouth.

Chapter Eight

Berlin, 18 October, 10.39 a.m.

Laura shut her eyes as he approached. There was nothing else she could do to rebuff him. His hot breath caressed her face. Her eyelids fluttered, and everything inside her flinched.

'What's his name?' he whispered.

'W . . . what?' She opened her eyes, not understanding the question.

'There's nothing I can do for you if you don't tell me his name.' He edged closer still, strangely over-enunciating every sound. 'Tell me his name, and I can protect you.'

Laura stared at him. This was madness. Utter raving madness.

'I saw you outside the house, the night before last.'

Jan! He meant the evening with Jan. How long had he been watching her? What else did he know about her?

'The name.' He lifted his right hand, stroking a finger down her cheek.

'You can trust me. Just tell me his name.'

'Why?' whispered Laura.

'I have to make things right. And I need your help to do it.'

Make things right? She felt tears spring to her eyes.

Fiercely she pressed her lips shut.

'Betray him,' his voice rolled on. 'Betray him, and I'll let you go.'

She felt faint with hope. But she'd rather bite off her tongue than let slip Jan's name. There had to be another way. 'What do you want with him?'

He said nothing. Merely smiled.

'Tell me his name and you can go.'

Go. The word was like a drug in her brain. Her gaze flitted across the women on the walls.

The man leant further forward.

Oh God, don't come closer, thought Laura. Don't come *even closer* to me.

The tattooed man leant back and peered alertly into her face. 'His name,' he insisted. At that moment he shot forward again, grabbing the chair where her arms were resting. His grip was so strong, so frenzied, that despite Laura's weight the chair should have moved. But it didn't even quiver; evidently it was bolted to the floor.

'Tell me, and I'll let you go!' His black nostrils were nearly touching hers.

Laura felt his physical nearness like a painful jolt of electricity. Her nerves jangled. She wanted to hit him, to push him away. What if I don't? she thought frantically. What if I don't tell you? Would that change anything?

'Why are you fighting?' he asked. 'For him, perhaps?'

She gritted her teeth. Get out of my face, goddammit . . .

'Are you going to tell me his name?'

Like hell I will, she thought, and spat in his face.

He jerked back, blinking. His eyes blazed coldly.

Laura tried to brace herself for what was coming next.

'Think you've won, do you?' He was audibly struggling to control himself. 'Then listen closely. His name – the name you're so bloody determined not to tell me – is Jan!'

Silence.

For a moment Laura thought she'd misheard. Had he actually said Jan?

A triumphant smile was on his face. 'And the name on the bell at that French dump, that's his, isn't it? *Floss!*' He paused, enjoying Laura's bewilderment. 'Does the house belong to him? Or his parents? Probably his parents, right?'

Laura didn't answer.

'You and me,' he said softly, 'we share a secret. Did you know that?'

If she could have shaken her head, she would have.

'Do you remember that night in Nordholm Woods? You were fifteen at the time.'

Laura froze.

'Do you remember?'

What a question. Of course she did. That night had been hideous. In her nightmares she was still running through Nordholm Woods. Only – how did *he* know about it? It was impossible. Totally impossible!

She stared at him.

He smiled back.

'It wasn't your fault,' he said.

She blinked and had to swallow. She refused to believe it.

As the tattooed man took a step back, one of the spotlights grazed his shiny scalp. A burning fleck slid across his brow and made his eyes glow red, before he squinted and retreated from the light.

Nobody has red eyes, thought Laura again. There's no such thing!

Suddenly she heard a faint, dull sound, as if metal were struck against stone. Then again. And again and again. Her gazed flitted to the right, where the sound was coming from. But there was nothing except the wall and the women floating in it.

The tattooed man stood stock-still, eyes resting on Laura; yet his gaze was empty, absent, as though something else were absorbing all his concentration.

Between the dull thuds Laura thought she could make out other noises, a kind of clattering and something high, complaining, like a voice. A woman's voice.

An icy chill ran down her spine. Somewhere behind that wall was a woman. A living woman.

The tattooed man reached into his trouser pocket and took out a packet of white tablets. Pressing three into his palm, he held one directly in front of Laura's lips.

'What's that?'

'A precaution.'

She compressed her lips and teeth so hard that it hurt. Again she heard the woman's voice.

'If you don't swallow the tablets, I'll give you an injection.'

Laura capitulated. Reluctantly she opened her mouth, and he put the tablet in.

'Swallow,' he ordered, eyes on her larynx.

She choked the tablet down dry.

The tattooed man nodded in satisfaction, gave her the two remaining tablets and watched her larynx bob as she swallowed. Then he stood up with a jerk, hurried to the door, switched off the light and locked up behind him.

The woman's voice penetrated through the wall for another minute. Then it fell quiet.

Chapter Nine

Germany, 18 October, 7.38 p.m.

Jan sat in the back seat of the Cherokee and peered at the speedometer. The needle was hovering around 170 kilometres per hour. The water on the motorway created an unbroken film, in which rain and clouds were mirrored like visions.

The lorry to his right suddenly began to swerve. Jan opened his mouth, but before he could scream there was a shockwave. The lorry side-swiped the Cherokee, the Jeep lost its traction and veered out of control. The tyres howled frantically, the car turned soundlessly on its axis, and Jan's gaze flew to the child seat beside him. It was enormous and empty, the two unfastened halves of the seatbelt twirling weightlessly. Only a few seconds earlier, Katy had been sitting in that seat. The car was still turning in the air. His father and mother had twisted around in the front seats, staring at him accusingly.

Centimetres before the car hit the ground, Jan woke from the dream with a start.

His heart was pounding wildly, and it took him a moment to orientate himself. Outside the window of the ICE, the country-side was slipping past; he felt the draught of the air conditioning on his skin, and the seat covering smelled of strangers.

He glanced at the display on his phone. Twenty to eight. Shortly before nine, the ICE 914 would reach Berlin's main railway station.

That morning he'd still been in Èze, he and Katy by themselves – Greg had driven to the baker's at Beaulieu. The heavens had opened, fading to a watery grey. The sea had glinted wanly outside the panoramic window. On the dining table Katy's mobile vibrated. She tapped the screen, read something briefly and raised her eyebrows. Without a word she passed Jan the phone.

At the top of the screen was an unknown number, and below it a text sent at 10.48 last night:

Hello Jan. Couldn't take it any more. Needed some space. Went back to Berlin. Please don't worry, and say hi to the others for me. Laura.

Jan felt a twinge in his stomach.

'Told you,' murmured Katy. 'Typical.'

'Hm?'

'She used to do that all the time at school. When it came to running off or skiving, she was always the expert.'

'Really? I never picked up on that.'

'You wouldn't have picked up on stuff like that.'

Jan's mouth twisted. There was plenty from his school years that he could only hazily remember. After Theo's death and the disappearance of his mother, he'd drifted through much of his life in a kind of waking coma.

'In the end that's why she left and had to go to boarding school.'

'Boarding school?' Jan hesitated. 'How do you know that?'

Katy was silent – for a fraction too long.

'Or did you know back then, too?' asked Jan suspiciously.

Katy shrugged. 'I didn't think it was that important.'

'Rubbish. You didn't want me to know, did you?'

Katy shrugged once more, her expression mulish, as ever when she'd been caught out. 'You were fourteen and totally unstable. And Laura was completely bonkers. I mean, I liked her, but Laura and you – it would have knocked you for six. Especially after . . . well, you know. What do you think I should have done, eh?'

'Not act like my mum, for a change.'

'You know, I'd rather Mum hadn't left us too. I had it up to here with playing that role.' Katy's hand cut through the air at eye level.

Jan thought of her husband Sören and the twins. Probably she still had it 'up to here' with playing that role. At the same moment, he realised something else. 'Oh, that's why,' he muttered.

'That's exactly why,' said Katy.

'It's because of your guilty conscience.'

'What?'

'You invited Laura on our trip to Beaulieu because you still feel bad about what happened.'

'OK, that's enough,' said Katy, her chin jutting out. 'I just happened to bump into her and thought it would do you good, after all that stuff with Dad.'

'You're doing it again,' warned Jan.

'Doing *what*?'

'Do I really have to explain?'

A brief, unpleasant pause followed. Katy inhaled noisily, struggling visibly to be patient. 'I meant well, all right?'

'I know. That's the problem. You've got to stop it.'

'What's wrong with you? Is this about Laura? Are you pissed off because she's done a bunk?'

'Certainly not. Unlike you, I'm not on the hunt for a partner.'

'Ugh, don't start *that* again!' Katy's cheeks had flushed, her voice suddenly shrill. Inside Jan was boiling, but he knew only too well how this would end: in tears or an outburst of rage from his sister, and he wanted neither of those things.

Then Greg's Cherokee had driven up, tearing Jan from his thoughts. The front door opened, Greg came up the stairs and burst in on the embarrassed silence. 'What's the matter?'

'You're the matter,' growled Jan. Then, turning to Katy: 'Do what you think is right. But at least don't leave Anna and Nele in the lurch.'

Greg's gaze darted back and forth between them. 'Fraternal love, eh?'

'Moron.' Jan pushed past Katy into the next room and started throwing his clothes into a suitcase.

'Where are you going?' called Greg.

'Home. Where else.' As he slammed the front door behind him, the panes of glass in the window rattled.

At least now he was on the train, sitting peacefully on his way home.

He drew Laura's mobile out of his jacket pocket and tried to switch it on. But nothing happened. Either the battery was dead or the phone had got wet.

Taking out his own phone, he dialled the number from which Laura had texted Katy. He'd noted it down just in case.

Nothing.

There it was again. The queasy feeling. He thought of what the text had said. *Needed some space. Went back to Berlin.* So far, so good. But why had she written, *Please don't worry, and say hi to the others for me*? Why would Laura want to say hello to Katy and Greg? The three of them had fought.

He gazed uneasily out of the window, while the trees and pylons shot past the ICE 914 on its way to Berlin.

Chapter Ten

Berlin, 18 October, 7.49 p.m.

The hot water burned his back. He'd act tonight. The sooner the better. Tilting his head, he let the searing torrent hit his face. The pain gave him a sense of purification. Around his closed eyes, black streaks ran down his face then down his body, blurring into a dark eddy around the drain.

Purification was control.

And control meant power.

He thought of Laura, of the moment he'd mentioned Nordholm. Of her widened eyes.

Steam rose as he stepped out of the shower. His skin was still red. Later it would shimmer like marble with a tangle of fine veins. He gazed at himself in the mirror.

Froggy was invisible. Just like Peter. That's what his parents had called him. Two shitty names. He'd shed them like an old skin.

Now there was only Fjodor.

Fjodor derived from Theodor, and meant something like *gift from God*. According to his birth certificate, it was his middle name. His parents had always avoided using it, and it had never appeared in his passport. At some point he'd found an old tin box in the basement, full of faded black-and-white photos. One showed his grandfather, a tall, white-haired man with an elegant pallor. On the back was scrawled his name, *Fjodor*.

Truly a gift from God.

The name Jan, however, meant *he has shown mercy*. That sounded like weakness. Fjodor spat into the washbasin. For Jan there would be no mercy.

Only just now had he been able to pick up where he'd left off. Repairing the pipes, getting new resin and fixer, cleaning the tub and finishing his work. But for now that would have to wait.

His priorities had shifted.

Jan was in the way, like a fat toad on a too-small street.

He would have liked to believe that Jan meant nothing to her. He'd even given her the chance to prove it. She only had to reveal Jan's name. Instead she'd spat in his face.

The fat, oozing toad had to be removed.

Two hours later he was turning into Stephanstraße in Moabit. He parked the car, having just switched its plates again with new, stolen ones, got out and walked purposefully away, clad in the overlong dark coat with the white hood that shadowed his face. His feet in their polished shoes stepped only between the cracks in the pavement, never on them.

Inside he was laughing. It was unbelievable how easy everything was today. A name, a telephone number, a computer. Assuming somebody wasn't actively hiding, you could find them in a heartbeat. Especially people like Jan Floss. Stuck-up, greedily materialistic, at the top of the social heap. That much was clear from his profile on LinkedIn, his connections, CV and photographs.

Fjodor turned down Stendaler Straße, striding past the house numbers until he was standing in front of a newly renovated period block. Red brick with grey-painted stone, no weeds between the gaps in the front path. He pressed the bell with the name 'Floss', and waited for a moment.

Nothing.

He read the other names, then rang at an apartment on the fourth floor. A woman's voice answered through the intercom.

''Scuse me,' he droned, 'GLS courier here. I've got a delivery for Patiz. Nobody's answering, but I don't want to disturb them again later . . .'

'At this time of night?' crackled the speaker.

'It's been busy today. Could you open up? I'll just leave it outside the door.' There came an indistinct muttering from the speaker, then the door buzzed and he stepped inside.

In the hall Fjodor stood for a moment outside the door marked *Patiz*, then he went back to the main door, opened it and let it fall shut. After waiting silently in the corridor for another five minutes, he quietly mounted the stairs, climbing all the way up to the fifth floor. Three doors. Two of them with names that meant nothing to him.

He took the lock-picking tool out of his coat pocket, an object roughly the size and shape of an electric toothbrush. House-breaking wasn't his greatest talent, but anybody capable of researching and ordering things online didn't need talent – only a bit of practice. Especially when you were dealing with an ordinary standard lock. Gingerly he slid the thin metal implement into the cylinder. Inside the lock there was a barely audible click. Then he added pressure and turned the mechanism.

It was done in under a minute. He smiled and stepped into the dark apartment, closed the door softly behind him and pushed back his hood. Closing his eyes and flaring his nostrils, he drank in the air. Earthy, woody, aromatic, with a hint of fruit, maybe lemon. Something else, too. The smell of coffee.

So that's your scent, Jan Floss.

Fjodor opened his eyes and felt along the wall for the light switch. A row of halogen bulbs lit up, reflected faintly in the parquet. The corridor was surprisingly small, leading to a parquet-covered staircase on the left, which led up to the top floor like a vertical shaft. There was a white built-in cupboard in the hallway, a storage area in the style of the parquet, and nothing else. No pictures, no ornaments. Not even a mirror.

You don't like yourself, Jan Floss. Is it because of your birthmark?

He thought back to the Côte d'Azur, to the house on the slope in the pouring rain. If he'd known then what he knew now, he wouldn't have hesitated. It would be over and done with by now.

Fjodor went upstairs, finding himself in a sizeable living room and kitchen. The open attic roof consisted of old square-cut beams, skylights and large dormer windows set into its sloping walls.

In one bay window stood an old, plain, cottage-style table, on it a silver wire basket of oranges and lemons. One of them was growing a tiny patch of mould.

The back wall of the open-plan kitchen was clad in brick. A shiny silver ECM espresso machine stood on the work surface, a colossal grinder next to it. The lid wasn't shut firmly on the container, and the scent of espresso beans suffused the room.

Fjodor wrinkled his nose contemptuously. Mould, and coffee beans left out. How could anyone who . . . he paused, and his eyes narrowed. Jan Floss, he thought, you love coffee. Anybody with an espresso machine like that loves coffee. You'd never leave the lid off that container. The beans would lose their aroma, and you know that.

But if it wasn't *you*, then who was it?

He glanced around.

Listened to the silence.

But nobody was there.

He went into the bedroom. The bed was a hundred and forty centimetres wide, he could tell at once. Wide enough for two, but narrow enough that you'd always be touching if you slept next to someone.

He thought of Laura.

Always touching.

Had Laura already been here?

The thought made him sick to his stomach.

At that moment he heard the soft metallic sound of a key being slid into a lock, then the click of the mechanism.

His eyes narrowed to slits, his nostrils dilating. He was ready.

Chapter Eleven

Berlin, 18 October, 9.57 p.m.

As the main door swung open, a skinny Pekinese with tattered ears yapped frenetically at Jan.

'Franzi, shhhh! Stop that.' The old woman tugged at the lead, and the dog hung with its front paws in the air, but kept yapping. She manoeuvred awkwardly past Jan onto the street, but not without stealing a glance at his birthmark. Her coat smelled of mothballs and old sweat. Jan hurried over the doorstep into the hall.

As he stood outside his apartment door, key in hand, he hesitated for a second. Glanced around. All was quiet in the corridor.

The sound of the opening door echoed faintly in the stairwell. Inside the flat, everything was dark. Softly he stepped inside, pressed the door closed behind him and held his breath. What was that?

His heart was thudding so loudly he wondered if it could be heard in the neighbour's flat.

He groped for the light switch next to the door. His fingers met plastic. A breath of air stroked his neck, as if someone had exhaled behind him.

Rapidly he flicked the switch.

A red paper lamp, with Japanese lettering and golden tassels, came on. The hall in Laura's apartment was tube-like and sparsely furnished, containing nothing but a narrow chest of draws with a telephone. The walls, on the other hand, were downright cluttered. To his left and right hung a hundred, perhaps even two hundred photographs, all without frames, one next to another, and among them postcards and notes covered in tiny scribbles.

Jan stared at the hotchpotch of images, and got the uneasy feeling that Laura really wouldn't like him standing here.

Half an hour earlier he had phoned Katy and asked her for Laura's address. 'Moabit, Bremer Straße 10,' was Katy's answer. When it came to addresses, Katy was meticulous. She never took down just a telephone number but always insisted on full contact details, as if she were worried people might vanish otherwise.

After slipping past the old lady in the lobby, he'd first rung Laura's doorbell. Getting no response, he'd checked under the mat and finally groped along the top of the door frame with his fingers. In a small hollow had been a single key.

He spun slowly around, examining the collection of photos. They were all pictures of homeless people in Berlin. Lots of them looked a bit blurred, as if they'd been taken from a great distance. Again and again there were large, indistinct patches in the foreground. Clumsy snapshots taken close-up were noticeably absent.

All the photos were of the same subject. A chubby girl with various dye jobs, from acid green to dark red. Her haircut was asymmetrical: on one side a short buzz cut, on the other long and matted, hanging over half her face. In her one exposed ear was a row of five piercings, and in her left nostril was a ring. In several photos she was holding a bottle. Her face looked puffy, and her eyes . . . what was it about her eyes?

Jan inhaled sharply. In disbelief, he stepped closer to the pictures. Only now did he realise whose eyes they were.

Two days ago he'd been lost in them.

The homeless girl in the pictures was Laura.

Jan could easily recall the way Laura had looked at school. She'd always been slender. Mostly she wore the same outfit, although her parents had money to burn. She always looked great in it. God knew he wasn't the only person who'd stolen glances at her.

What the hell had gone wrong?

It struck him that Katy had mentioned Laura running away and ending up at boarding school. But what had happened to her *after* that? And why were all these photos hanging in the hall?

He began to inspect all the pictures systematically. In some Laura looked to be just fifteen, in others maybe twenty. So the photos spanned a period of about five years, eight at the most, in which Laura had lived on the street.

After a while he came across a picture of Laura sleeping under a bridge, huddled against a wall. Directly beside it was one taken on the banks of the river Spree, showing Laura sitting and staring into the water. A star consisting of five crossed lines was scrawled onto the picture in black marker, and on the back 7/8.

Only rarely did the images feature another person, but now and again Jan saw a scruffy older man with a long, bushy grey beard.

Suddenly he heard footsteps on the landing outside. His pulse instantly quickened.

The footsteps grew louder.

Instinctively he drew back, quietly opening a door at the end of the hall without taking his eyes off the main entrance.

The footsteps were now immediately outside.

He darted soundlessly into the shadowy room and flattened himself against the wall.

The footsteps were fading now, climbing further up the staircase. He closed his eyes and sighed. His pulse grew calmer, disappointment mingling with relief. It struck him that he wouldn't mind her catching him. Just so long as she came back.

He switched on the light and blinked in astonishment. The bedroom was bright and friendly, with a window overlooking the courtyard that took up almost the whole wall. Unlike the morbid and cluttered hallway, in here there were only two Rothko prints on the wall. The bed was a simple futon, the wardrobe an old, richly ornamented rustic piece.

He sat down on the futon. Only now did he notice the bedside lamp, which was placed on the floor directly beside the bed. It was the same lamp Katy had bought for Nele, one that had stood for years in his niece's bedroom. Three small spherical feet and a red lampshade with delicate flowers in yellow, light blue and pink. One time, when he'd been putting Nele to bed, he'd asked her to blow out the lamp. Nele had giggled and looked at him as if he wasn't quite all there. 'Try it,' Jan had said. Nele blew – and the lamp went out.

Jan had been sure she'd eventually figure out that he'd stealthily pressed the button on the cable as she blew. Yet blowing out the lamp had been her favourite ritual for years.

He smiled, burying his hands in his jacket pockets. In the right one, he still had Laura's mobile. He pulled it out and attempted once more to switch it on.

Unexpectedly the display lit up, and the phone demanded a PIN. Jan frowned. Then, trying his luck, he tapped in 0708, the number scrawled on the photo. Maybe it was significant?

Incorrect PIN entered. Two more attempts, announced the phone. Would have been too easy, he thought disappointedly.

After a moment's thought, he switched the digits around. 8070.

Incorrect PIN entered. One more attempt.

Jan swore under his breath.

If he was wrong about this, how was he going to explain to Laura why he was giving her back a locked phone? I meant well? I was worried?

But he did, and he was. One more go, then. What other possibilities were there? A 78 and then the year she was born? Or were there other ways of writing dates? The American one, maybe. Hadn't Laura's grandfather spent years in the USA?

He swapped the day and month like they did in the States, and entered 0807. Then he pressed OK.

Success!

His guilty conscience instantly came flooding back. Still, he flicked through the most important things: the texts, the last calls, the photo folder, which contained no more than half a dozen innocuous images. Then he found a video clip dated the day before yesterday: 17.10.2011, 10.09 p.m.

Just minutes before Laura had gone missing! Electrified, he pressed play.

The image wobbled and hissed. He recognised Greg in the driver's seat and Katy next to him. Laura was evidently sitting behind, filming. The camera panned outside, where you could see the vague outline of a car in the darkness. Large and black.

For a fraction of a second the licence plate came into view. Jan glimpsed a B for Berlin, but nothing else.

Oddly, the car seemed to drive parallel to Greg's Cherokee for a while. Jan tried to make out the driver, but could see nothing but a dark figure and a pale blob, probably his face. He seemed to be looking directly at Laura's smartphone.

'Greg . . .' Katy's voice. Uncertain. Warning. Maybe it was the speed? The car seemed to be racing. A high whooshing sound came through the speaker. Then, very suddenly, Laura's voice: 'Oh my God.'

Jan rewound the clip a bit. There it was again. 'Oh my God.'

He played that bit again repeatedly, staring intently at the display. There was a flash of light immediately before Laura's 'Oh my God'. He scrolled back and forth, trying to capture the flash of light as a still image so that he could see the driver, but the controls were too imprecise. Then, abruptly, the screen went dark. Jan swore, pressing the on/off button several times, but the battery was evidently completely flat. And he didn't have a charger for the Nokia.

He got to his feet. Red light drifted in from the corridor. The fringe on the lampshade fluttered in the draught, casting trembling shadows on the walls. This whole situation was getting more and more bizarre. Laura going missing. The strange text. A video clip with an unfamiliar black car and Berlin number plates. Laura's 'Oh my God'. And then those photos.

He went back into the hallway and began systematically photographing the pictures. Reaching the one with Laura's birthday, he paused. Removed the drawing pin. Took the photo from the wall and tucked it into his jacket pocket.

This left a hole in the wall. An empty space, like when Laura had vanished from school one day as if she'd fallen off the map. He'd searched back then, too. He could still remember calling at the black iron gate in Finkenstrasse.

She's gone away, they told him, without even opening the door.

Tomorrow morning he'd ring that bell again, and this time she'd open the door. Surely she must. After all, it was about her own child.

Chapter Twelve

Berlin, 18 October, 11.58 p.m.

After swallowing the tablets, Laura had slumped into a daze. The world around her no longer existed; she was locked in her own head. Spectral, glowing female bodies emerged out of the darkness, trapped in a rubbery, transparent substance. 'Run,' they whispered. 'Run!'

Laura tried to answer, but her tongue was swollen. In the middle of her head grew trees, tall and black. Between their knotty branches the moon was shimmering, and somewhere beyond the trunks gleamed the waters of a lake. Somebody picked her up, although she didn't want them to. It disgusted her.

Picking up a stone from the ground she flailed wildly, but nothing happened. Strong arms lifted her over the edge of a tub and lowered her inside. Then – dead silence.

This isn't a tub, she thought, this is a grave. An upright grave, with her inside. She wanted to scream, to scramble up, to run away. Yet somehow she was paralysed, and the walls that towered above her were smooth as glass.

Her naked body shimmered bloodlessly in the moonlight. Again she heard the voices. *'Run. Run!'*

She gazed upward in despair. A drop of something fell towards her, landing on her cheek. She wiped it away with her index finger.

It was a rubbery, transparent substance.

Then the rain began. It was coming from a shower: thousands and thousands of droplets of the viscous fluid.

It ran stickily down her body, gathering around her feet and climbing ever higher. First her shinbones, then her knees, her thighs. It felt cold around her pubic area, then it climbed to her stomach, her arms and breasts.

She tried to move her legs, but realised that the substance around them had already solidified. She gasped for air, feeling her neck grow cold. Then her chin. Then her bottom lip.

She clamped her mouth shut. Closed her eyes.

Everything fell dark, silent and cold.

Trying to scream, she wrenched her mouth open, and the coldness slunk inside her, filling her from within.

'Lory,' she suddenly heard someone whisper. Voices, she thought, I'm always hearing voices.

'Lory, is that you?'

Yes, she wanted to scream, but her mouth was full of the liquid. The seductive scent of whisky crept into her nose – and of foul breath. Then she tasted whisky on her lips, Jack Daniels, unmistakable, she thought, and it ran down her throat. The sticky fluid tasted like Jack Daniels. She coughed and spat. Her insides were on fire, as if the fluid were caustic.

She heard the faint noise of running water and the soft tapping of pebbles, as if she were sitting under the bridge on Teltow canal, spitting cherry stones. But how could she be spitting cherry stones when she was dead, naked, preserved like an insect inside some transparent liquid that was hardening second by second?

Chapter Thirteen

Berlin, 19 October, 9.41 a.m.

Jan got out of the taxi. A brisk wind drove grey clouds over Grunewald. At least it wasn't raining. He stared down Finkenstrasse. On the next street down, Am Hirschsprung, lived Karl Eisner – the man who'd bought his father's agency – in a 450-square-metre period home with an English lawn, dense hedges and a covered pool.

Finkenstrasse had houses like that too. Number 71, however, was looking a little neglected. The wall that enclosed the plot was partly overgrown with ivy. The black gate in delicate wrought iron showed traces of rust, and the grass outside was covered in patches of brown.

He was about to press the bell when his mobile rang.

'Katy?'

'Hi. You called earlier?' She sounded irritable and half-hearted.

'Where are you?'

'On our way back. Has Laura turned up?'

'Not yet.'

Katy sighed. In the background he could hear an even hum. The motorway. 'What do you want?' she asked.

'On the night she went missing, when—'

'She hasn't gone missing, Jan. She's just taken off. You read the text yourself.'

'What if it wasn't from her?'

Katy was silent a moment. 'What makes you think that?'

'There was a car following you that night, wasn't there? A large black SUV. Laura filmed it. I think she recognised the driver and got scared.'

'That was some crazy guy. We were all scared, because he drove like a nutter. Until we got caught on a speed camera, and after that I guess he wasn't in the mood for games.'

'Does that seem strange to you?'

Instead of an answer, he heard the line rustle.

'Listen. I'm reaching the end of my tether here.' It was Greg's voice. 'Can you just leave us in peace? This topic is closed.'

'Give Katy back the phone,' said Jan, controlling himself.

'So you can spoil the rest of our holiday? Forget it.'

'*Our* holiday?'

'Yeah, I do happen to like your sister. And it's mutual. Which is more than I can say for you and Laura, otherwise she'd hardly have run off.'

'She didn't run off,' hissed Jan.

'Laura's been running all her life. When are you finally going to get that through your skull?' There was a crackle, and the line went dead.

'Arsehole,' growled Jan. He stuffed the phone angrily back in his pocket, although he felt more like hurling it against the wall. Who did that twat think he was? He took a deep breath and turned back to the house. Above the silver bell a camera was mounted in a dark recess. Next to the letterbox, out of which an envelope was peeping, was a small '71'. Nothing else. The envelope was addressed to *Frau Ava Bjely*.

Jan rang the bell.

'Hello?' A voice crackled out of the intercom.

'Good morning. Frau Bjely?'

'Who wants to know?'

'My name is Floss. I'm a friend of your daughter Laura, and—'

'My daughter doesn't live here any more.'

'Could you spare a minute? It's important. I think your daughter—'

A faint click interrupted him.

'Hello?' Jan tapped the speaker with his finger.

No answer.

He pulled the envelope out of the letterbox and rang a second time, waited a while then rang again.

Finally the intercom crackled. 'Get lost!' growled the voice.

'I've got a letter for you. From Laura.' Jan waved the envelope in front of the camera.

For a moment there was silence.

'Fine. Put it through the letterbox.'

'No,' replied Jan.

'Excuse me?'

'I said no!'

More silence.

'Are you alone?' asked the speaker eventually, warily.

'Yes. Why?'

'All right, then. Come on up.' The gate buzzed and opened.

The house was about thirty metres from the gate, a white, three-storey period building with a grey-tiled roof and four classical columns supporting the balcony over the entrance.

Jan shuddered. Laura's parental home was as colourless as the grey sky. Even the green areas of grass and the colourful autumn foliage appeared strangely wan; he found it hard to imagine Laura playing carefree games on this lawn.

Involuntarily, Jan's mind turned to his own parents. The house reminded him of his father. Large, proud and cold. Anyone living inside was inevitably too small, just as nothing was ever good enough. For a long time Jan had thought it didn't bother him any more. The agency's last set of half-yearly accounts had proved what he was capable of. Until his father had sold up and sent him packing. Suddenly everything was back the way it was before. He was the little one. The one who hadn't fastened Theo's seatbelt properly. The one to blame for the family's brokenness. And now his father was stuck in that old folks' home, and Jan had deleted all his phone numbers.

Jan's footsteps crunched over the gravel as he approached the house. Three steps led up to the entrance. Next to them was a gently sloping ramp, which stopped at the front door. The massive, grey-painted door swung wide open. A woman in a wheelchair rolled over the threshold and looked Jan up and down. He guessed her to be in her mid-fifties; she wore a black suit, her grey hair severely pulled back, her face narrow, with prominent cheekbones. The resemblance to Laura was impossible to overlook.

'Young man, has anyone ever told you that extortion is an extremely inauspicious way to begin a conversation?'

'You didn't want a conversation,' responded Jan. 'That's not a very good start either.'

Ava Bjely surveyed him, her gaze lingering briefly on his birthmark. 'You're rather articulate for a postman.' She stretched out her hand for the letter. Jan gave it to her.

'From the gas company?' She glanced up from the envelope.

He smiled apologetically.

'Everything all right, Frau Bjely?' Behind the lady in the wheelchair appeared a woman of about sixty, short, with cropped hair and astonishingly broad shoulders, wearing a coarse white blouse and grey cargo trousers that didn't seem to fit the overall image.

'It's all right, Fanny, thank you. I'll manage.'

The woman nodded and disappeared.

Ava Bjely's gaze was still resting on Jan. 'What do you want?'

'I'm looking for your daughter Laura. She's been missing since the night before last—'

'I'm not,' said Ava Bjely brusquely.

'I'm sorry?'

'*You* may be looking for my daughter. I'm not.'

Jan stared at her, perplexed.

Ava Bjely sighed, like someone being forced to explain the obvious. 'Young man, I'm unwell enough already. I see no reason to waste my strength on other sicknesses. And that's exactly what my daughter is – a sickness.'

Jan's jaw dropped. 'A sickness?' He felt rage well up inside him. At a single stroke he was back to being a small boy standing at an open window, watching his mother leave the house with her suitcase.

'You'd better go now.' Ava Bjely grabbed the wheels of her chair and swivelled round on the spot with a practised movement. Unless he could come up with something in short order, the conversation was over.

'You're not the only one who has a problem with Laura,' he said quietly.

Ava Bjely paused in the doorway, then turned around and looked at him out of narrow, watery blue eyes. 'What's this now? Soft soap? "We've got something in common?" Don't make me laugh! You should have stuck with your postman strategy. That was direct, at least.'

'What makes you call Laura a sickness?'

'Ha!' Ava Bjely laughed. It sounded like a dry cough, joyless and cynical. She studied Jan, pointing finally at his face. 'Had that long?'

'What? The birthmark?'

Ava Bjely nodded.

'From birth. That's why they're called birthmarks.'

She nodded again. Then, rolling back from the door, she beckoned Jan inside. On her scrawny arm clinked two plain silver bangles, a gold signet ring with a dark crest in a light-blue oval flashing on her ring finger.

'Coming in, then?' asked Ava Bjely. 'Or have you changed your mind?'

Jan stepped inside the house and closed the door behind him. The corridor was floored with white-and-grey marble. The wheelchair's rubber tyres squeaked softly on the smooth stone. Ava Bjely rolled past a staircase and through a wide double door, beyond which was the living area. A whiff of faeces and bodily fluids reached Jan's nose.

As he entered, he glanced around in confusion. Evidently the whole ground floor consisted of this one room, which enclosed the entrance hall like a horseshoe. The walls were as white as the opulent stucco on the high ceiling, while the floor was laid with limed grey parquet. One end of the horseshoe ended in an open kitchen, white and shiny with stainless-steel fittings, and the other end of the U was hidden from sight. The dining table by the kitchen area was the same grey as the floorboards, and the chairs were likewise fitted with grey covers. It was as though somebody had sucked all the colour out of the world. Silver picture frames, white curtains, grey mantelpiece and grey books, their spines lettered in black. Whichever way he turned, there was nothing but shades of white and grey.

'Your birthmark,' said Ava Bjely, rolling towards the dining table. 'Have you ever wished you could have it removed?'

Jan sat down on the chair she offered him. 'Often,' he admitted. 'But in the old days it wasn't possible. Now there's laser treatment, but it's slow and painful.'

'My birthmark is Laura. No matter what I do, I'll never be rid of her. Look around you. This house, this wheelchair' – her hand struck the armrest, then her legs – 'these useless things here, that smell – you've already noticed, haven't you? – that's all Laura. She'll never let me go. *You* could have laser treatment to get rid of your mark. I've got to die, or at least lose my memory.'

'You mean it's Laura's fault you're in a wheelchair?'

Ava Bjely grimaced. 'Do you have children?'

Jan shook his head.

'Then you have no idea.'

'I have two nieces.'

'You have no idea,' repeated Ava Bjely. She laid her hands demonstratively in her lap and interlaced her fingers. 'What's your problem with Laura? What has she done to you?'

Done to you. Her choice of words made Jan's hackles rise. 'She's gone missing, like I said.'

'Gone missing. Is that all?'

'The circumstances are peculiar. It . . . it almost looks as if somebody . . .' He fell silent.

Ava Bjely looked at him enquiringly.

'Well, as if somebody was stalking her. Or kidnapped her.'

'Kidnapped?' Ava Bjely raised her eyebrows.

'I'm not sure,' conceded Jan. 'She was being followed by a black SUV with Berlin number plates, and when she recognised the driver it gave her a fright. Sometime after that she disappeared.'

Ava Bjely turned away, gazing out of the window in silence. Her lips were pale and narrow. 'How do you know that?'

'I found Laura's mobile. She filmed it.'

'Can I see the film?'

'The battery's dead.'

Ava Bjely sneered. 'Dead. I see. And what am I supposed to do? Roll through the streets to look for her? Call the police? Or pay a ransom?'

'No, no,' Jan protested. 'It's not about—'

'I'll tell you what I'm going to do about all this: nothing. Absolutely nothing. If I went to the police I'd only make myself look ridiculous. They know about her already. And if she has been kidnapped, then I'm not paying a cent.'

Jan was speechless. He tried to read in her eyes whether she really meant what she'd said, but she wouldn't meet his gaze. 'I don't think it's about money,' he said. 'Rather . . . well, something personal. Something from her past. Like I said, she seemed to know the driver. She spent several years living on the street, didn't she?'

'If I know Laura, she's not been kidnapped so much as she's run off. Clearly you like my daughter, and you might even think she's a good person. You look like someone who sees the good in people. But there's a side of Laura you don't know. A side you've never even glimpsed. And if Laura's disappeared, it's because she *wanted* to. She always did know how to vanish into thin air when trouble came along.' Trailing off for a moment, she suddenly seemed far away.

'At school she used to skip class all the time, just skiving constantly. Later she repeatedly ran away from boarding school, and at one point the police had to pick her up from the red-light district with acute alcohol poisoning. I took her to more than one clinic, believe me. But she'd fallen in with a bad crowd. Eventually I put her in a special clinic for alcohol and drug addiction. Three weeks later she was gone again. The day she left, this place was burgled. She stole jewellery from me, cash – not for the first time, mind you. There's a lot you don't know about her. Trust me, if she's disappeared, it's for the best.'

Jan's eyes flashed with indignation. Whatever Laura may have done, it was nothing compared to the coldness of her unfeeling mother, and he wondered what was really behind it.

'Have I shocked you?' asked Ava Bjely.

Jan was silent.

'I think you'd better go now.'

'That's probably best,' replied Jan icily. He was already at the door when something else occurred to him. 'One more question. The photos in Laura's apartment – do you know who took them?'

'What photos?'

'From her time living on the street.'

'Do I look like someone who goes driving around Berlin photographing beggars?' hissed Ava Bjely.

'That wasn't my question,' said Jan. 'And no, you don't. But you could have asked someone and—'

'Rubbish! I've no use for photographs of my daughter. Would you have your birthmark photographed? Put it in a nice frame on the bedside table so you can be reminded every day when you wake up how much it disfigures you?'

Jan swallowed his fury with an effort. What a childhood Laura must have had with this mother. Was her father the same? 'You don't mince words,' he said bitterly.

'I prefer clarity.'

'Or poison.'

Outside on the gravel path, he felt Ava Bjely's gaze at his back like an icy wind. Like a black widow in her web, he thought, with her signet ring, her wheelchair and her ileostomy.

His own mother crossed his mind. He wondered where she was at that moment, whether she was even alive.

If somebody went to her and asked about me, what would she say?

Chapter Fourteen

Berlin, 19 October, 2.01 p.m.

Rain hammered furiously against the window. Jan was lying in Laura's bed, in her childhood room in her parents' house, and Laura was stretching out her hand to him. So much longing.

He was thirteen. But why did Laura look so much older? So much more grown-up?

As she unbuttoned his shirt, his breathing quickened. Hadn't she just been wearing something? Her ribcage pumped, quivered. Her breasts were fuller than he'd thought.

She took his hand and pressed his fingers between her legs, sliding his index and middle fingers inside her. Everything was wet. He pulled back his fingers, and she took them and sucked them, then immediately kissed him. The kiss tasted of nicotine and tobacco and his fingers and her.

The rain was coming through the cracks in the window, the room filling up like a sinking ship. The water was already lapping at the mattress.

By the time he finally noticed, it was too late. He wanted to jump up, but Laura was sitting on him. 'Are you afraid?' she whispered.

Afraid? He was panicking! He stared at her.

Suddenly she had grey hair, wrinkles and blotchy grey skin. On top of him sat not Laura but Ava Bjely.

Feeling cold water at his back, he made to rear up, but her weight pressed him down onto the mattress. Her deflated breasts dangled above him. Her hips gyrated. His penis disappeared between the lips of her labia and the straggling grey hairs that clung dark and damp to her sagging skin.

'No,' he gasped.

She laughed, bending over him, slipping her tongue into his ear with a smack of her lips. The water was rising unstoppably, running into his eyes and sloshing into his open mouth. He struggled for air, his lungs screaming for oxygen, but only water came. Ava Bjely opened her mouth wide, baring two rows of sharp, pointed teeth, then sank them into his neck and tore out a mass of flesh.

Jan's eyes flew open; he sat bolt upright and gulped down air.

He was alone.

In his bed.

The sheets were drenched with sweat.

The relief of being at home, in his own apartment, calmed his breathing somewhat.

He got up. The cotton shirt he'd slept in clung damply to his back, and he felt weakened and unsteady. He urgently needed something to eat. Maybe a pizza, he thought. Salami.

Without bothering to put on socks or trousers, which lay in a jumble next to the bed, he went into the kitchen.

Dogging every step was Ava Bjely. He shuddered, wondering how Laura's father had coped with the woman. Probably by retreating into his work. Perpetual absence. Jan knew a thing or two about that.

He tugged at the freezer door, which opened with a squelch and a puff of cold air. Automatically, without looking inside, he reached into the top drawer for the frozen pizzas. His gaze fell on the espresso-machine grinder. It looked remarkably empty of beans. His hand groped for the familiar pizza boxes, but instead it found a peculiar shape, hard as stone, and furry.

He looked into the freezer.

What he saw made his heart stop. He gasped and shrank back; his knees gave way and he crumpled to the floor.

Inside the freezer was a cowering woman. Delicate, naked, her arms and legs pressed unnaturally close to her body. Frozen, pale blue skin encrusted with frost. Her eyes were open, the pupils dull and empty as lumps of ice.

Jan recognised her instantly. It was Nikki Reichert from the fourth floor. He'd asked her to water the flowers while he was in France. Smeared on her forehead in dark red letters were the words *NOT LAURA*.

Jan vomited onto the floor. Then he sat down on the parquet, trembling, his legs drawn up to his chest. 'Calm down,' he whispered. 'Calm down and think.'

He stared at the dead girl. Noticed the kitchen knife – *his* kitchen knife – sticking out from beneath the corpse's left breast. Hardened blood had left a dark trail from her heart to the white plastic bottom of the freezer. Nikki Reichert had been forced violently into the space, her unnatural position testifying to numerous broken joints. He retched again. Swallowed. Breathed.

NOT LAURA.

Who in the world had . . .

A shrill buzz at the door made him jump.

Silence.

Only a dull throbbing in his head.

Then a second ring.

Jan didn't move. It'll stop any second, he tried to reassure himself.

The bell rang again, longer this time. More adamant.

Jan got to his feet and tiptoed down the stairs to the door, still wearing nothing but underwear and a shirt. In the corridor he could hear voices. 'He's *must* be in there. He got back some time after eleven and hasn't come out since.' There was no mistaking Norbert, Nikki's boyfriend.

'Are you sure she's here?' came a second, sterner voice. 'I mean, she could have gone out.'

'In her pyjamas? Where to? We were watching a DVD. *Lost*, Season 6, the finale. You don't just get up and leg it. She only wanted to pop upstairs and water the plants.'

Jan held his breath as he listened. There was another press of the bell, directly beside his ear. Piercing and strident.

'It's weird he's not answering, don't you think? Can't you open the door somehow?'

'Let's not get ahead of ourselves,' said the stern voice camingly.

'But I'm sure she's in there, hundred per cent.'

'She might be. But maybe she's in there voluntarily.'

'What are you trying to say?'

'There does seem something fishy about this, Phil,' said a third male voice. 'The two of them are sitting on the sofa at ten in the evening, watching TV, and she goes upstairs in her pyjamas and disappears. That's sixteen hours ago. And she's got no shoes, no jacket, no phone, no wallet . . .'

Silently Jan padded closer to the door and squinted through the peep-hole. Outside stood three men. One of them was Norbert: chubby, with a red squishy neck and close-set eyes. The other two were uniformed police. One banged against the door with the flat of his hand. 'Herr Floss? Police. We know you're in there. Please open the door.'

Chapter Fifteen

Berlin, 19 October, 2.22 p.m.

Fjodor pushed the question of whether he'd made a mistake with Laura to the back of his mind.

It was what it was.

He pointed the hose at the floor, driving the red puddles towards the drain with the steaming jet of water. The steel table was already gleaming again, the tubes had been disposed of, the electric fork-lift neatly parked and the tubs emptied, cleaned and sealed. Dust and dirt were a specimen's two worst enemies. Only pockets of air were uglier still.

He still had Laura's face before his eyes. Pale and peaceful. A face for all eternity. Not like the photo on Laura's ID card, which was tucked inside her wallet. In the biometric photograph she looked serious, hard, and her skin had a greenish quality.

Memories of his own first ID card photo crossed his mind. Mother had taken greater care than usual. Expensive make-up, better dye, a tighter grip. Her fingers around his neck had been iron, as if she were holding his head under water, under the hot jet. His eyes were barely five centimetres from the drain, where the water spiralled into the trap black as poison, smelling of mixed dye, cut hair and particles of skin.

Afterwards the person in the mirror had always seemed like an alien being, one who also had red marks on its neck. For the ID card photo he'd had to wear a scarf. The photographer had stared at him the whole time, but like all the others he'd shut his mouth and concentrated on the job.

Fjodor had tucked Laura's ID card carefully into her wallet – and something else, too, to make the signal clearer. To make sure she would understand. She had to know he was on her side. She had to feel safe.

He'd learned how important signals were. Like the woman in the freezer. And the writing on her forehead.

Chapter Sixteen

Berlin, 19 October, 2.24 p.m.

'What are you waiting for?' urged Norbert.

'Look here . . .' the policeman kept his voice calm with an effort. 'I can understand that you're upset, but if you don't let us do our job in peace I'll have to ask you to wait somewhere else.'

Norbert made an indeterminate noise.

The officer rang the bell again. 'Herr Floss? Police. Open up, please.'

Jan held his breath. Were they allowed to break down the door? Almost certainly not, unless there was immediate danger. But was he making himself look suspicious if he didn't open the door? They might take it into their heads to ask the building manager for the master key. What then?

Suddenly there was a piercing beep. Jan jumped. The sound was coming from upstairs, from the kitchen. If the door to the freezer was left open too long, it made a loud, high, warning noise.

'Do you hear that?' asked Norbert.

'An alarm clock, maybe.'

'I told you he was in there.'

The bell, again.

'Herr Floss?'

White as chalk, Jan shrank back from the door and tiptoed hurriedly up the stairs. In the kitchen he nearly stepped in his own vomit. The sour smell wrinkled his nose. He pushed the freezer door quickly shut and the beeping broke off with a sigh.

Downstairs the bell rang yet again.

Jan ran a hand through his hair to tousle it, then trudged loudly down the stairs. 'All right, all right. I'm coming.'

His pulse was racing as he opened the door. Norbert stared at him mistrustfully, thin yellow hair falling into his ruddy face.

'What's going on?' asked Jan, putting on the best *I'm-feeling-wretched* face he could muster.

The officer standing outside looked him up and down. He was a burly man in his mid-forties, his bright, alert eyes strangely shrunk by Coke-bottle lenses. 'Are you Herr Floss?'

Jan nodded and gave a cough.

The policeman grimaced as Jan's sour breath wafted into his face.

'Sorry,' muttered Jan. 'I'm not feeling well. I just threw up.'

'I see,' said the officer. 'Herr Floss, my name is Schüssler, and this is my colleague, Peters. We're looking for Miss Reichert, your neighbour. She's been missing since yesterday, and Herr Weinrich here' – he gestured to Norbert – 'believes she went into your apartment around ten last night to water the plants. She hasn't been seen since.'

Jan raised his eyebrows. 'I . . . don't quite understand.'

'For God's sake, stop beating about the bush,' Norbert blurted. 'She's got to be here.'

'Ten last night?' Jan scratched his head. 'Look, I only got back from France yesterday, around half eleven. And there was nobody here.' Only now did he realise how narrowly he must have missed the killer.

For a moment nobody said anything.

Jan looked at them in turn. 'Don't you believe me?'

Schüssler cleared his throat. 'So, just to be clear, Miss Reichert is *not* in your apartment, correct?' It was evident from his manner that he was becoming increasingly exasperated, and wanted nothing more than to wash his hands of the tedious business.

'No, she isn't. As I said.'

'Bullshit!' cried Norbert, getting agitated. 'Where else would she be?'

'Herr Weinrich, please!' Schüssler interrupted. 'Stay out of this.'

Good, thought Jan. Norbert was doing a first-class job of getting the officers riled. 'Were you arguing again?'

The officers exchanged a glance.

The corners of Norbert's mouth twitched. 'What would you know about that?'

Jan shrugged. 'Only what she's told me,' he lied. 'That you're always sneaking off somewhere. Down the betting shop, for instance. She was getting pretty sick of it.' Jan knew he was pushing his luck, but he was fairly sure that Norbert was a gambler. He pointed to Norbert's right wrist, where there was a patch of lighter skin. 'She thought you'd lose the Breitling on it sooner or later.'

Instinctively Norbert gripped his wrist, but let it go a split-second later. 'Bollocks. It's downstairs,' he shot back angrily. 'What is all this crap?'

'Now, now,' rumbled Peters, the second officer, a gangly man with a walrus moustache who seemed poised at any moment to teach his interlocutor some manners with a few practised moves. 'Calm down, both of you.'

'Calm down? You're telling me to calm down?' Norbert had turned beet-red. 'Does that mean you believe him?'

'I don't believe anything yet,' replied Peters.

An unpleasant silence settled.

Schüssler coughed. 'I'm sure this is all a misunderstanding, Herr Floss, but we've got to look into it. We can get it sorted for you in a jiffy, if you'll just let us have a quick peek around your apartment.'

Jan's heart skipped a beat. 'I assume,' he said calmly, 'that you need a search warrant for that. Don't you?'

Schüssler's eyes narrowed, and he stared at Jan. 'A search warrant?'

Jan bit his lip. He sensed what was coming.

'Herr Floss,' sighed Schüssler, 'you can refuse us entry, of course. But I was under the impression you wanted this cleared up as soon as possible, in which case you should be cooperating. After all, we're talking about a missing woman here. It's a serious matter, wouldn't you say?'

Peters, the officer with the walrus moustache, backed up him with a nod.

Jan said nothing. His pulse was hammering. The image of the frozen blue corpse had seized him, and wouldn't let him go.

Schüssler raised his eyebrows, waiting for an answer with visible impatience. 'Look, there are other ways we could resolve this. I could stay here outside your door while my colleague goes back to HQ and obtains a warrant. Then next time we ring your bell it'll be with a crowd of people and a far less generous frame of mind.'

'OK, fine,' muttered Jan. 'So long as you don't mind unmade beds and vomit in the kitchen.' He opened the door and moved aside.

'Vomit,' murmured Norbert, frowning. Schüssler and Peters, Norbert in their wake, stepped into the flat. Tramping up the staircase, their footfalls echoed in Jan's ears like an entire forensics squad. For a split second Jan saw people in white overalls, with taut latex gloves and piles of little plastic bags for evidence-collecting in his kitchen.

'I'll take a look around,' announced Schüssler, throwing a glance at the lumpy yellowish puke on the floor. His colleague remained in the kitchen with Jan. Norbert loitered nearby, fidgety and unsure of what to do with himself.

Jan leant his back against the freezer; at least that way his eyes wouldn't betray him. 'Be my guest,' he muttered. He considered offering Peters an espresso to distract him, but realised that his hands were shaking.

Hastily crossing his arms, he fixed his gaze on the floor as he heard Schüssler wheezing in his bedroom. It sounded like he was getting down on his hands and knees to peer under the bed. Then the wardrobe doors were opened. Hangers clacked.

'Bedroom's clean.'

Norbert grunted, shuffling from one foot to the other.

Jan was staring at the floor, wondering frantically how he could stop them searching the kitchen just as thoroughly, when his gaze suddenly fell on a spot in the middle of the parquet. It was dark red, about half a centimetre long, at the foot of the island: exactly where Norbert was standing.

Jan began to sweat.

'What's this here?' asked Schüssler, tapping at a narrow door in the corridor outside the bedroom.

'Storage closet,' said Jan, his voice raw.

'And why is water coming out of it?'

Water? In the storage closet? Jan hesitated.

Every alarm bell inside his head went off with a jolt, the hairs rose on the back of his neck, and he felt his legs turn to jelly.

The handle to the storage closet was turned. The hinges gave a short, high squeak.

'Come and take a look at *this* mess,' said Schüssler.

Peters and Norbert both went over at once.

'Frozen pizza,' came Schüssler's voice from the storage closet. 'And chicken and ice-cubes. Thawed, all of it!'

As quietly as possible Jan crept along the kitchen unit, past the pool of vomit and towards the staircase, hoping his legs wouldn't give way.

'Who *does* this?' snorted Peters, now evidently standing beside his colleague.

Jan put one foot on the stairs, then the second.

'I'm telling you, the guy's not right in the head,' declared Norbert.

'Oh, for Christ's sake, keep your mouth shut!'

The stairs seemed infinitely long. Arriving at the bottom, he took his leather jacket off the peg with trembling hands, picked up his wallet, his and Laura's mobile phones, and his keys.

Shit! he thought. My trousers! They were still in the bedroom.

'Doesn't this chap have a freezer?' He heard Peters's voice from upstairs.

'A freezer?' repeated Schüssler slowly. Jan could hear the wheels turning in his brain, and they were clearly turning swiftly. 'Herr Floss?'

Jan opened the door, kicked his Converse shoes onto the landing and slipped out.

'Herr Floss? *Hello?*'

The door fell shut behind Jan. His hand trembled as he made to slide the key into the lock. Why the hell were the bloody things so tiny?

Finally it slid into the hole. Jan turned the key twice and pulled it out. Inside, footsteps were clomping down the stairs. Jan reached for his shoes. Panic was welling up inside him, hot and paralysing. As if in slow motion, he shrank back from the door.

'HEY! HELLO!' That was Schüssler, directly behind the door. The handle was pressed rapidly up and down, the policeman tugging so hard the door shook in its frame.

Jan legged it, rushing barefoot down the stairs. On the fourth floor he stumbled and banged his head against Nikki Reichert's door.

He got back up and lurched away, a dull ache in his forehead. The sound of thumping fists echoed through the stairwell. Throwing on his jacket, he shoved the phones and wallet into the pockets.

Reaching the bottom of the stairs he threw open the front door, turned left and bolted down Stendaler Straße before turning right into Havelberger. His lungs were bursting, and the sunlight stung his eyes.

The entrance to Westhafen underground station was a yawning black hole, but he dashed down the steps. Anywhere, so long as he was off the street. Arriving on the platform, he saw the yellow U9 come thundering out of the tunnel. He climbed aboard and flung himself onto the wine-red seats.

An older woman with tousled hair gave him a disapproving look. He was still trouser-less, barefoot and holding his shoes with both hands. He attempted a smile, but got nothing more than a harsher glare in return. As if she knew there were a body in his freezer.

With a sharp jolt the train began to move; he still had no idea which direction it was going.

Nikki's dead, his head throbbed. *She's hidden in my freezer, stabbed with my kitchen knife. And the message on her forehead was doubtless left for him.*

NOT LAURA.

What on earth was that supposed to mean? A warning? Should he stop looking for Laura?

Inside the pocket of his brown, scuffed leather jacket, his hand gripped Laura's phone. *I've got to see that video again,* he thought. Another few stops, then he'd get out and find a Nokia charger. And a pair of trousers.

He held onto that thought, closing his eyes to shut out the world for a moment. He didn't care that he was still barefoot. The chilly carriage floor felt good beneath his feet. The vibration of the train, the rattle of the tracks.

Chapter Seventeen

Berlin, 19 October, 3.06 p.m.

Laura was already awake, but she kept her eyes shut. Like in the old days, when she'd woken under the bridge with a splitting headache and hadn't wanted to let the daylight in. When she'd been desperate for a drink or two to take the edge off.

Her limbs were stiff. Her head was pounding. Before her mind's eye she could see the tattooed man. Pale pink lips, cracked, surrounded by black stripes over white skin. And that toneless whisper: 'Do you remember that night in Nordholm Woods?'

A split-second flash. Water glittering between tree trunks, a three-quarter moon, branches casting shadows. Wind, heavy over the forest floor. The scent of moss, earth and leaves in her hair, there must be a fucking stone around here somewhere—

Her eyes sprang open.

Her heart was racing.

The memory had been so tangible she'd thought she was in the woods for real.

But this wasn't the woods.

Nor was it the gallery.

She was lying underneath a bridge. A smattering of cars came rushing overhead, and the familiar babble of the water picked up below the massive columns supporting the concrete flyover. This wasn't just any bridge – it was Gandalf's bridge!

I'm dreaming, she thought. Closed her eyes. Opened them again.

She was still lying under the bridge.

Her heart leapt, and she sat up with a lurch. For a second the sharp movement made her blood pressure drop: stars danced before her eyes.

She was naked and wrapped in a sleeping bag. Her clothes were hanging on the branches next to the bridge; beneath her lay a tatty camping mat. To her left was a pile of old plastic bags, the logos partially worn away, and among them an ancient transistor radio with its antenna snapped off.

Gandalf's radio. She really was with Gandalf!

But how? The last thing she could remember was swallowing the tablets. He must have let her go.

Except – she didn't understand why. Her head was whirling madly. And she was desperately thirsty.

Rifling through the first bag that came to hand, she found a battered plastic bottle of water as well as a virtually empty bottle of Johnnie Walker. Laura put the water bottle to her lips and drank so greedily the sides dented inward with a crack. The Johnnie Walker was next – drained to the last drop. No more than four centimetres left, unfortunately. The whisky burned pleasantly in her throat, before trickling into her stomach as though into a dried-up pond.

'Awake at last,' came a guttural voice behind her.

Laura spun around. The man had deep grooves in his face and a full grey beard; he could easily have been in his mid-sixties, but was actually a good ten years younger. He wore a green parka, baggy pleated trousers with a brownish herring-bone pattern and a stained beige pullover. Dirt had gathered in the furrows of his face and in his clothes, and his eyes were as dull as his long, sparse grey hair.

'Gandalf,' groaned Laura.

'Didn't recognise you at first,' mumbled Gandalf. 'The hair and that . . .'

'Was that you?' Laura nodded at her clothes.

'You were shivering,' he murmured. 'Pissing it down, it was.'

Laura nodded, although she couldn't remember a thing. 'Thanks.'

Gandalf twisted his beard, which had earned him his nick-name: Gandalf the Grey.

'How did I get here?'

'Found you. In the university gardens.'

'Oh.' *The university gardens*. Still nothing. Not a single shred of memory. 'Was anyone else there? Did you see anybody?'

'Nah.'

Laura furrowed her brow.

'Everything all right?'

She shook her head.

Gandalf scratched his neck and waited to see if she had more to say. If not, he'd leave it at that. Laura's eyes flitted nervously over the plastic bags. Her stomach was burning, her throat craving more. Maybe Gandalf . . .

She swallowed, forcing the thought aside. 'I was kidnapped.'

Gandalf's eyes widened. 'For cash?'

Laura couldn't help laughing. Her hoarse voice was much the worse for wear. 'Oh yeah, sure. I can just imagine the poor bastard phoning up my parents and asking for money, and my mother saying, "I'd rather you kept her," and hanging up.'

Gandalf giggled. He knew all Laura's stories. The boarding school, the thefts, the home, the clinic.

'Nah,' said Laura, becoming serious again. 'It was a psycho.'

'Psycho,' repeated Gandalf. The dull eyes in his tired face were suddenly alert. 'A *dangerous* psycho?'

Laura nodded. God knew it was a reasonable question. The streets were wall-to-wall with psychos, but most of them were relatively harmless. Gandalf, for instance. 'One who kills women. That kind of psycho.'

'And you got away.'

'That's the weird thing. I don't know why.'

Gandalf frowned.

'He gave me some stuff, tablets. Next thing I know, I'm here.'

Gandalf nodded and fell silent for a while. It didn't occur to him to question what she'd said. He'd seen too much for that. 'And now? What are you going to do?'

'Don't know. Go home, maybe, to my—' suddenly she paused. 'Gandalf?'

'Eh?'

'Did you find my wallet in my clothes?'

Gandalf considered briefly. Then he shook his head.

'Shit,' whispered Laura. 'Shit, shit, *shit*.'

'Was there much in there?'

Laura rolled her eyes. 'Not because of the money, Gandalf. My ID! The guy has my ID card. Now he knows where I live.'

'Oh,' said Gandalf, looking at the floor.

Laura drew her knees up to her chest and wrapped her arms around them. She should be happy to be free, breathing fresh air and sitting under the bridge with Gandalf instead of ending up as a naked corpse in some nutter's cabinet of horrors. But something was wrong; that much was crystal clear. The fact that he knew about Nordholm Woods made her deeply uneasy.

'Maybe it would be best,' said Gandalf slowly, 'to go to the cops?'

Laura stared at her knees. 'They know me, though,' she said. 'If I come to them with a story like this they'll think I was plastered or high or something.' She was petrified of everything boiling up again. The thefts, her mother's police reports – and Nordholm. 'In the end,' she said, 'they'll stick me back in some rehab clinic. And who says the psycho can't find me there.'

'It's your business, but that's what I would do. I can't stand the cops either, but with this kind of thing . . .'

'You don't understand.'

'No,' murmured Gandalf. 'I don't.'

Silence.

'Have you got anything to eat?'

Wordlessly Gandalf handed her half a loaf of cheap brown bread from the supermarket. Laura snatched it greedily and began to eat.

'Gandalf?' she asked after a while. 'Can I stay here for a while?'

He nodded. 'I share it with Benny sometimes, though.'

'That's OK, I'll ask her too.'

Gandalf hummed. 'What do you think the psycho's doing now?'

That's the big question, thought Laura.

She remembered the pale lips, the bald head and the self-administered beating, as if he'd had to punish himself. And then that moment when he'd thrown his head back and his eyes had glowed red. What had he said when he came back in?

She froze.

Jan! He'd asked about Jan. Because he thought – how had he put it? – that he had to protect her.

The idea that the tattooed psycho might be after Jan turned her stomach. She had to find him and warn him. The question was how: she had no clue where he lived, or even whether he was back in Berlin. Her mobile was gone, and with it all the numbers and addresses she'd saved, including Katy's. She didn't even have any money. What if the tattooed man turned up again, the way he had in Èze? She cringed. The memory was as lifelike as it was unreal. The pouring rain, the black car, the rifle in his hands, the shot to her neck. She knew it couldn't have been an ordinary rifle – maybe a tranquilliser dart of some kind. But a gun was a gun. She had no way to defend herself against it.

'Think he'll come back?' asked Gandalf.

Laura looked at him. In his eyes lay a touch of fear. God knows Gandalf was no hero, and the last thing she wanted was for him to send her packing. 'Don't worry about it,' she lied, wishing she had a weapon – ideally a pistol. Then, out of the blue, she remembered where she'd last seen one. 'Gandalf,' she said quietly, 'I've got to go.'

Gandalf watched silently as she climbed naked out of the sleeping bag, plucked her dirty, still-damp clothes off the branches and put them on.

'There's a couple of old boots over there. You can have 'em if you like.'

'Benny's?'

'Nah, mine.'

Laura smiled at him and stepped into a pair of battered Caterpillars. They were at least four sizes too large, but better than nothing. 'I drank the rest of the Johnnie Walker.'

Gandalf nodded serenely.

After hesitating a moment, Laura asked, 'Got any more?'

Gandalf's eyes grew narrow. His shake of the head came a fraction too late.

'Cheapskate,' said Laura, sending a curse and quick prayer up to heaven.

Gandalf merely shrugged his shoulders and grinned broadly. The gaps in his teeth were the size of sugar cubes.

'Still – thanks. I owe you. And now I'd better be off.'

Gandalf was still grinning.

'Oh, Gandalf, one more thing. Can I borrow your pocket knife?'

The grin vanished. Gandalf's pocket knife was his most prized possession.

'Please,' whispered Laura. 'You'll have it back tomorrow, I promise.'

With a sour expression, Gandalf reached into his parka. It was an old Swiss Army knife, with a screwdriver, tiny saw and various other tools. 'Until tomorrow,' he said curtly.

Laura nodded. 'And maybe a few euros?'

Gandalf gave a sigh, reached back into his parka and counted out three euros.

'You're the best.' She took the knife and the coins.

Raising her hand in farewell, she stepped out from the protection of the bridge and climbed up towards Königsberger Straße.

A lorry thundered past, the airstream tugging at her clothes. The sky stretched above her like a milky grey skin.

Walking down Drakestraße, she scanned the roadside for a payphone, but there was none to be seen. Obviously, she thought. Why would there be, when everyone in the world has a mobile by now?

Then she noticed a sign. *Hostage – Table Dance*. It was hanging above the door of a plain, boxy house that had once been painted a cheerful yellow. Laura made a beeline for the front door and rang the bell.

A woman of sixty-odd, clad in a white towelling dressing gown, opened the door. On her feet were shiny black boots, the laces trailing on the floor. The dressing gown offered a glimpse of deep, wrinkled cleavage between her two heavy breasts. Under sharply drawn black brows twinkled a pair of mocking eyes which inspected Laura, coming to rest on her shabby Caterpillar boots. 'Do you have an appointment, love?'

Laura shook her head. 'My phone's been nicked. I've got to make a call.'

'Does this look like a phone box?'

'There aren't any phone boxes around here.'

The woman raised her eyebrows. 'And you decided this would be the right bell to push?'

Laura shrugged.

'Got any money?'

'A few euros. But I might need longer than that.'

The woman gave a hoarse, barking laugh. 'And you thought, "If anybody's going to open the door to me in this get-up, it'll be *that* place."'

She'd hit the nail on the head, and knew it. Laura smiled apologetically. Her damp clothes were clinging to her body, and she was freezing.

'If you pinch anything,' said the woman, 'then I'll have your pretty little guts for garters. Trust me, I'm capable of it.' Then she stepped aside.

'Thanks.'

Laura's first call was to directory enquiries. As expected, Jan's mobile number wasn't available, and neither were Katy's or Greg's, but there was a landline in Stendaler Straße under the name Jan Floss.

Her heart was thudding as she dialled the number and pressed the receiver to her ear, hoping fervently that he would be there. Partly because she had to warn him, but also because—

'Floss residence.'

She paused. 'Hello? Who's that?'

'Who are *you*, if I may ask?' The voice sounded oddly stiff and wooden.

'A friend of Jan's. Can I talk to him? Or is he not back from France yet?'

'France?' Laura heard muttering in the background. Something wasn't right. 'No. He's back. Do you have any idea where he might be staying?'

'I . . . er . . . no.'

'Please tell me your name.'

My name? Laura's sixth sense was kicking into overdrive: there was only one kind of person who kept asking for your name. In a heartbeat she was ice-cold. 'Has . . . has something happened to him?'

Silence.

Then a sigh. 'This is Inspector Berendt, Berlin Office of Criminal Investigation. I'll ask you again: do you know where Herr Floss is?'

'No,' said Laura huskily. 'What's happened?'

'I'm not at liberty to tell you that. If you could just give me your name—'

Laura hung up without another word.

Police.

Paralysed, she stared at the wall in front of her. Evidently Jan had returned to Berlin – and something had happened to him.

'All right, love? What's the matter?'

She wheeled around. Before her stood the woman in the towelling dressing gown.

'You're white as a sheet.'

Laura swallowed. She wanted to run outside and find Jan, but her legs rebelled. In her heart there opened up an old, dark wound, and her brain was screaming for more Mr Walker. Screaming to feel nothing but the heft of a glass, like the old days. No fear, no loneliness, no Nordholm.

And a glass wasn't the bottom of a bottle, was it?

Control, she thought.

I just have to control how much.

She was an expert at self-control. After all, she hadn't touched a drop for years. 'Do you have any . . .' Laura paused and cleared her throat. 'Do you have anything to drink?'

Chapter Eighteen

Berlin, 19 October, 3.12 p.m.

Jan gazed through his reflection in the window at the walls of the tunnel flitting past. At each station, the juddering doors opened and closed. He stayed seated every time, even when they reached the end of the line at Rathaus Steglitz and the U9 set off back in the opposite direction. He wished he was back in his old wardrobe; its dark and stuffy confines had rescued him many times after Theo's death. No sight, no sound, no feeling. Although the no feeling part hadn't worked out so well.

By now Jan had put on his Converse shoes. Tying the bright white laces had done him good: a few seconds' normality amid all this madness.

He was still picturing Nikki Reichert's body, the bloody writing on her forehead. He'd never seen a corpse before, let alone touched one, and the brief moment when his finger had brushed her frozen hair and skin was etched horribly into his memory.

NOT LAURA.

What the hell was that supposed to mean? That he should keep away from Laura?

His eyes rested on the ceiling of the train, on a CCTV camera. He had no idea how quickly the police could initiate a manhunt, but he was an obligingly easy target: a man with no trousers and a prominent birthmark on his left cheek.

At the next stop he got off the train.

Immediately adjoining the station was a row of shops, and he entered the first one he came to. The sales assistant, twenty at the most and dressed like a clone of David Beckham, scanned him with hostile eyes while he picked out size 32 dark-blue jeans, a pair of warm socks and a baseball cap. He was still glancing warily at Jan as they stood at the till, and only when the card machine beeped its approval did he crack a brief smile. Jan hurried into the changing room and pulled on the socks, trousers and cap. A few shops further down he found a Nokia charger for Laura's phone.

Hardly had he left the shop before he froze, rooted to the pavement.

He'd paid with a debit card!

What a bloody idiot. The first thing the police would do was check to see where his card had been used.

Heading straight to the nearest bank, he took out as much money as he could from the ATM: eighteen hundred euros. From now on he'd pay for everything in cash.

But what now?

Where should he go? Hotels and hostels usually wanted to see ID, and that was out of the question. To Katy? The police would almost certainly turn up there, too, asking for him. Then he remembered Laura's apartment. For now, at least, it seemed like the best option.

As a precaution he avoided public transport and taxis, going on foot instead, and barely two hours later Jan was standing outside her apartment door. His fingers groped along the upper edge of the doorframe and found the key. Unlocking the door, he stepped inside.

It was dark, like last time, and he flicked the light switch. The red lamp with Japanese writing came on.

Dumbfounded, he stared at the hallway.

At first he thought he must be in the wrong apartment. But everything else was the same: the colour of the walls, the floor, the doors, the red lamp with the gold tassels, which were still swaying in the draught from the opening and shutting door.

Only the photographs were gone. All of them. Without exception.

Somebody had been here – or was here still. His heartbeat quickened. 'Laura?'

No answer.

'Is anybody there? Hello?'

The silence was oppressive, uncanny. From the kitchen came the faint whir of the fridge.

Calm down, he thought. There's no one here.

He traced his fingertips across the bare wall. Thin edges of dirt, bits of Sellotape and tiny holes marked the places where the pictures had been.

He went into the bedroom. Then the kitchen and the bathroom. In the silence, every step and every rustle of his clothes seemed much too loud. At first glance it all seemed unchanged. The sink was dry. There was no toothbrush. The bin was empty.

The telephone's ring cut like a knife through the silence. It was coming from the hallway, from the landline on the chest of drawers. A red button blinked, and the answering machine kicked in. From the speaker came the faint sound of breathing.

Ten seconds. Fifteen seconds. Then there was a crackle, and the red light disappeared.

Jan took a series of deep breaths, until his pulse had slowed. From somewhere far away he heard a siren howling, and instantly his heart was thudding again. All they had to do was find Katy, question her about her fugitive brother and ask whether the name Laura meant anything to her. Then they'd have him.

Swiftly he reached for his phone and dialled Katy's number. She didn't pick up until the sixth ring. 'Hello, Sherlock,' she joked instead of a greeting.

'Hi,' he replied tersely. He wasn't in the mood for banter.

'How's your current case going?'

If she's this relaxed, thought Jan, then at least it means the police aren't with her. 'You've got to do me a favour.'

Katy sighed. 'Let me guess, it has something to do with Laura.'

'Promise me you won't tell anybody about Laura, no matter who asks. OK?'

'What? What are you talking about?'

'If somebody comes to you and asks about me or her, just pretend you don't know any Laura and—'

'Jan, what's going on?' interrupted Katy. 'Who's going to come and ask me about you?'

Jan groaned, annoyed with himself. 'The police,' he said softly. Silence. Of course.

Outside on the street, someone honked their horn.

'Katy? Are you still there?'

'The police? What's happened?'

'Do you promise?'

'Jan, I'm not promising you anything. Not if I don't know what it's about.'

Jan's hand clenched the mobile. It was tearing him up; it would have been such a relief to tell Katy everything. But how would she respond when the police showed up and confronted her with the killing? He doubted she would manage to feign genuine surprise or horror. Very few people were capable of that. And the investigators were no fools, he was sure. Lying about Laura would be difficult enough. 'Please, Katy. Don't ask,' he said. 'Just pretend the name Laura means nothing to you, OK?'

'Why?'

Jan was silent.

'Have you fucked up?'

'No.'

'Honestly?'

'I swear. You know me. Just give me a day or two, then I'll get back in touch and explain everything.'

More silence.

'Fine,' said Katy at last.

Jan exhaled. 'Thanks.'

'The things I do for my little brother, eh?'

'How can I reach you over the next few days?'

'Only via mobile.'

'I'll call you.'

She hesitated. 'Jan?'

'What?'

'Look after yourself.'

'I will.' He hung up rapidly and sighed. At least he didn't have to worry about the police tracing him to Laura's apartment.

A few minutes later he was sitting in the kitchen, unplugging the toaster and charging the Nokia instead. Then he entered the PIN and played the video.

Again he watched the clip of the black SUV, heard Laura's horrified 'Oh my God', stopped and scrolled back. It tested his patience, but eventually he captured the video still with the flash of light. Involuntarily holding his breath, he bent over the little display.

The flash had illuminated the driver and a few details of the interior. Everything else was lost in blackness. A chill ran down Jan's spine.

A man was looking at him – a man with a grotesque mask. The skin of his face and his whole skull was covered in black stripes, and his eyes glowed red.

The telephone rang again in the hallway, making Jan jump. The answering machine picked up once more. Nobody spoke. Only quiet breathing could be heard. Then a click.

Jan leant back. He felt as though he were in a film. The wooden chair protested with a squeak. His eyes rested on the fridge, a bulbous Smeg in classic Fifties style.

Something told him that Laura hadn't ended up in this guy's clutches accidentally. Why else would the man leave him such a vivid warning. *NOT LAURA*.

And then, suddenly, he was struck by a thought, and wondered why it hadn't come to him before. His heart clenched as if gripped by an icy fist.

The man wouldn't have been after Nikki Reichert. He had broken into his apartment because he wanted to kill *Jan*.

The phone rang a third time. He leant forward, looking through the open door into the hallway, where the answering machine picked up. He waited for the sound of breathing.

From the speaker came an uncertain voice. 'Laura? It's Katy. Are you there? – If you are, then please pick up – we . . . we're getting a bit worried, and wondering where you've got to – if you hear this, please give me a call . . .'

Click.

A faint smile darted across Jan's face. His stomach rumbled loudly, reminding him that it had been a long while since he ate.

His eyes turned to the fridge.

Chapter Nineteen

Berlin, 20 October, 12.52 a.m.

Laura gazed through the black wrought-iron bars at her former home. How long had it been since she was last here? An eternity. Yet it didn't appear to have altered much. The lawn spread like a dark carpet before the house, the outline of which loomed through the darkness. The trees were dark grey blots. Not a single window was lit.

Finding a spot where the wall was covered with ivy, she scrambled over, her clothes getting wet as she swung over the top of the foliage. Dizziness welled up in her brain. Too much Mr Walker. Or too little.

Ronda – the woman in the dressing gown – had wordlessly taken the bottle away after her fourth glass of Bowmore Single Malt. Doing her a favour, perhaps; or maybe she just wanted to stop Laura drinking her dry of expensive liquor.

Laura had been staggering a little as Ronda showed her the tumble drier for her wet clothes. Laundry was spinning in the window of the washing machine next to it. The sight of the rotating drum made her queasy. Everything in her head was muddled up, nothing in its rightful place.

Why were the police looking for Jan? Her thoughts tripped over themselves. Like a demon, the tattooed man kept taking shape, his twisted red-eyed louring face. Had he already done something to Jan? She kept wanting to run and warn him, but the dizziness was too strong.

The pizza Ronda had put into the oven for her wasn't much help. Laura choked down about a quarter of it and nearly threw up. Somehow she was bundled off to bed. She fell asleep.

When she woke, she could hear the faint sound of music.

Beside the bed was a cheap white digital alarm clock. Noticing the time, she jerked upright: almost midnight.

She pulled on her dry things and slipped her feet into Gandalf's boots. Opening the door, she listened; the sound of muffled club music echoed down the hall. Gingerly she stepped out onto the landing, but stumbled at the top of the stairs and nearly toppled down them: a parting gift from Mr Walker.

And now?

Now she was standing in front of her parents' place, yearning for a sip or two to drown the memories that surfaced at the sight of the house.

She thought about the sound of the light grey tyres on her mother's wheelchair as they squeaked over the marble. About Fanny with her bucket and the constant hissing of the vacuum cleaner. How old would Fanny be now? Early fifties? Did she still come every day? Or could she no longer cope with heaving her mother out of the bath?

Avoiding the front entrance with its tall, showy columns, Laura went left around the house, careful not to crunch on the gravel along the wall. She kept to the grass – the grass she'd never been allowed to set foot on as a child for fear it would get patchy.

She peered up at the dark wall, knowing that the windows on the ground and first floors weren't an option; her mother had installed an alarm system. On the second floor the windows weren't secured, but most burglars would be scared off by the nine-metre drop.

To the far right, on the second floor, one window was ajar. Her father's bathroom – or it had been, anyway. And from there she was only two doors from her goal!

She scurried along the building, keeping close to the house, until she reached the corner where the drainpipe ran down the wall. Closing her fingers around the cold zinc, she shook it. Seemed solid enough.

For a moment she stood beside the drainpipe, trying to collect herself. Breathe in. Breathe out. Breathe in. Breathe out. It was no good; the residual dizziness persisted. A rope and a karabiner would have been very useful right now, but her equipment was at home in her wardrobe.

Quickly taking off her boots, she gripped the pipe, braced her feet against the wall and climbed.

Just above the cornice that separated the ground floor from the first, there was a crunch. The bracket holding the pipe had come away from the wall. Fragments of stone pinged into her face as the pipe bent outwards. Laura's fingers curled into the hole where the bracket had just broken off, her feet and lower legs clamping around the drainpipe.

There was a metallic crack, but the pipe held.

Gradually she pulled herself further up the pipe, until she reached the cornice on the second floor and placed her bare feet on the jutting stonework that ran around the house. To her right, about seven metres away, was the open bathroom window. Pressing herself against the wall, she shuffled her way to the nearest window and peered through the glass into the darkened room. Empty. Not a single piece of furniture. A soft rustling in the garden made her prick up her ears. Her gaze flitted downwards, past her feet. Suddenly the cornice seemed much too narrow and altogether too far above the lawn.

She gasped for air, clinging to the window frame and squeezing her eyes shut.

Fuck you, Mr Walker!

In normal circumstances she could stand on a bungee crane sixty metres in the air without a trace of vertigo, and now she was shitting her pants over nine piddling metres?

She opened her eyes, forcing herself not to look down. She shifted further, centimetre by centimetre, remembering all the people she'd harnessed into the ropes, how pale they often were, with their narrow lips and anxious faces. Despite that, nearly all of them had jumped.

If they could bring themselves to do it, then you can manage a few metres!

When she finally reached the bathroom window, she pulled out Gandalf's Swiss Army knife from her jacket pocket. Her slim wrist just about scraped through the gap, and she managed to loosen the screws on the brass strut holding the window in place. By the time she climbed into the bathroom, her legs were trembling.

In the air was a hint of perfume, men's aftershave, something woody and rather old-fashioned. She wondered whether her father had used that scent.

Gazing into the mirror above the sink, she tried to imagine him standing there. What did he look like now? Was his hair thinning? Grey? Were there bags underneath his eyes? All that came to mind was the fact that he was never there. Work, work, work. As if he'd been permanently on the run. Mostly he'd travelled to Vienna or other cities in Austria. At the age of five or six she'd started asking why. 'Property,' her mother answered.

'What's property?'

'Houses, Laura. He looks after houses and apartments.'

'Are there lots of houses, then?'

Her mother frowned. 'Why do you ask?'

'Because he's away so much,' answered Laura.

Her mother smiled. 'Yes. Lots. Some of them are really big, with lots of apartments.'

'And is it stressful?'

Her mother nodded.

Laura had quickly come to realise that someone with such a stressful job didn't have much tolerance for extra stress, and she'd heard often enough from her mother that she was a troublesome child. So she did her best not to get on his nerves when he was at home. He still didn't come back much, though.

Maybe it was because he didn't get on with her mother any more.

For a while she'd got the impression he didn't care whether she was there or not. Later she'd often thought it might be better if they'd never had her at all. On those days her mother seemed tormented by an invisible thorn, and her eyes met Laura's with icy coldness, sometimes even hatred. Yet they still had good times: birthdays, Christmas, card games and laughter, watching TV – and the first time she'd pushed her mother to the gate in her wheelchair. She'd been nine. And, suddenly, important.

She'd pushed her many times after that. Sometimes her reward was thanks. Sometimes hatred. More and more she'd felt like she was going crazy, because she never knew what to expect from them. Until her mother made a decision once and for all.

Nordholm.

A chill settled around her heart at the thought.

Enough with the memories! She shook herself out of it. Think of the revolver.

Rising from the edge of the bathtub, she softly turned the handle and emerged into the darkened corridor.

To her right were the stairs, with a grey runner, and directly opposite lay her father's study. Her feet sank into the soft pile of the carpeted floor. This house seemed to swallow every noise. The handle to her father's study turned as if freshly oiled, and the hinges made no sound as she slipped into the room. Through the barred window came a gloomy light, dimly illuminating the contours of the furniture. The black desk was in the same spot it had always been, with the same old steel lamp, the same heavy Montblanc fountain pen, the same books on the same shelves. It was like stepping into a museum.

She went straight to the bookcase, pulled out a book with a wide, dark-red spine and opened the cover. The book was hollow, and inside lay a box of ammunition, half full.

What was missing was the revolver.

Chapter Twenty

Berlin, 20 October, 1.21 a.m.

Laura swore noiselessly. She felt like chucking the book into the corner in disappointment. Instead she put it on the desk. The ammunition jingled faintly in the box.

Where else could he have hidden the gun?

Her gaze fell on the Etruscan vase that stood at eye level in the middle of the shelf. It was an heirloom from her grandfather, black at the top and bottom, with black figures on a faded yellow background.

Lifting the vase off the shelf with the tips of her fingers, she reached inside.

No revolver.

There was, however, a bundle of notes. He was still keeping money in there, then. She counted nearly three thousand euros, then stuffed the bundle into the pocket of her jeans and replaced the vase on the shelf.

At that moment she heard the handle move behind her, loudly, as if someone had pushed it down so clumsily it sprang back up.

Spinning around, she saw the door open and the light from the corridor stream past the shoulders of a figure in a wheelchair.

'You!' gasped Laura.

'Who were you expecting?' Ava Bjely's face was shrouded in darkness. Her hair, however, pulled severely back from her face, glinted pale grey. 'Your father, perhaps? He's not here.'

He never is, thought Laura.

'Did you think I wouldn't make it up here in my wheelchair?'

Laura said nothing.

'We had a lift put in. Your father didn't like it, but he agreed in the end.'

'He could never refuse you anything.'

'It almost sounds like you feel sorry for him.'

Laura didn't respond.

'I asked him. Why should he refuse me?'

'Asked? Demanded, surely?'

'Either way. Better than saying nothing. Like him. Or you.' Ava Bjely's eyes went to the dummy book on the desk. 'The revolver's the best example. Do you imagine I'd want a thing like that lying around in my house?' Her mother gave her a challenging stare. 'I took it. You don't need to keep searching.'

Laura gritted her teeth.

'Did you think you could just climb in and help yourself? Well, that's hardly surprising. You were like that even as a child. Never asking. Just taking.'

'When did you ever give me anything willingly?'

'Perhaps you should have shown more patience,' retorted her mother icily.

Laura snorted.

'Instead you'd rather break in here and steal. And he lets you.'

'What do you mean by that?'

'Think I don't know about the vase?'

Laura's breathing faltered. Involuntarily she took a step back and bumped into the bookcase.

'How many times did you come and take money from that vase? Twenty? Thirty? Did you never wonder why he always put more in there? Towards the end you found less and less in it, didn't you?'

A cold finger ran down Laura's neck. It was true. Once or twice the vase had been empty.

'*I* took the money out,' said her mother. 'I didn't tell him, but when I discovered what was going on I removed it. I thought you'd stop when you found nothing in there. Until I saw he kept refilling it.'

Laura stared at her mother in disbelief. Her father had deliberately been leaving money in the vase? He *wanted* her to find it?

'At some point,' continued her mother, 'I realised the old fool probably assumed it was you taking the money, so I simply left it in there. A few times after that I heard you up here, like today. So I put more money inside myself.'

'You? Why?'

Her mother was silent a moment. Although Laura couldn't quite make out her features she could have sworn she saw a cold, thin-lipped smile that robbed her face of any loveliness it might once have possessed. 'Can't you guess? I didn't want him to think you were coming to him. I wanted it to stop.'

'He was always more kind-hearted than you,' said Laura quietly.

'Kind-hearted? Don't make me laugh.' Her mother's lip curled. 'If he were kind-hearted, I wouldn't have had to do all this. Do you know how much effort it took to crawl up here? We didn't have a lift back then, so I always waited until he was away before getting out of that damn chair and hauling myself along . . .'

Laura got a vivid mental image of her mother inching grimly up the stairs, her legs dragging behind her. She'd probably had to hoist herself up on the bookshelves, maybe sitting on the desk chair and snatching at the vase with the tips of her fingers.

'Kind-hearted!' Her mother banged her left hand against the armrest of her wheelchair, making her bangles jingle. 'As if your father had a heart. A guilty conscience, that's all he had!'

'And you?' asked Laura. 'You didn't even have that.'

'I had responsibility. It weighs more heavily than guilt. No one with responsibility can afford a conscience.'

Laura's throat tightened. Responsibility? This was absurd. 'No,' she said softly. 'You don't feel guilty because' – she broke off, swallowing – 'because you hate me. You always have. I don't know what I did, but—'

'Shut your mouth,' said Ava Bjely, her voice uneven.

' . . . but no child deserves to be treated like that, no matter how horrible they are.'

'You have no idea,' said Ava Bjely. 'Almost everything I've done, I've done because I loved you – in spite of everything.'

'I've had enough,' replied Laura. 'I'm going.' Stepping away from the bookcase, she walked around the black desk and towards her mother. 'Let me pass.'

'On one condition.'

'Condition? Did you really just say condition?'

'I want you gone too. I mean *properly* gone.'

Laura stared at her mother. 'What do you mean, "properly gone"?'

'Exactly what I said. Gone from my life. Don't ever come back here. Gone from Berlin, gone from Germany.'

'Why would I do that?'

'I . . .' Ava Bjely hesitated, her eyes dropping to the floor. 'I'd give you money.'

'You'd do what?'

'A million. Into a bank account. For a new life somewhere. The condition is that your father and I would never see you again.'

Laura stared at her mother uncomprehendingly. 'This . . . this isn't really happening, is it? You didn't just say that.'

Ava Bjely stared mutely at the carpet.

'You know what?' said Laura angrily. Tears were welling up in her eyes, and she hated herself for them. 'You can shove it! Keep your fucking money. I'll go where I like. And there's no way I'm leaving Berlin.'

Ava Bjely gave a long and heavy sigh, as if she'd expected nothing less.

'Now get the hell out of my way,' demanded Laura. 'I want to get through.'

Ava Bjely didn't move. She sat bolt upright in her wheelchair as if it were a throne, blocking the door.

Furious, Laura grabbed the wheelchair by the armrests and pushed, but Ava Bjely slammed on the brakes and the wheels locked. Laura tried to peel her hands away from the brakes, but her mother was tenacious; decades in the wheelchair had given her arms an unnatural strength.

Laura tugged at her mother with all her might. Her forearms were trembling, as were her mother's; she smelled the ileostomy and the hot breath on her face. Both women were grunting with the effort, then suddenly her mother's left hand flew off the brake and the wheelchair jerked backwards. Laura overbalanced, banging her head against the doorframe and tumbling to the floor. The carpet cushioned her fall, but stars still danced before her eyes and pain radiated like fire above her ear.

She felt something hard at her shoulder, the wheelchair step, with which her mother was trying to shove her back into the room.

Her body gave way, and she rolled from her side onto her stomach. She could see the wheelchair in the light of the corridor; its tyres had dug furrows into the soft pile of the carpet. She threw out her arm to stop her mother closing the door, but it was too late. It slammed shut, and darkness descended. A key turned in the lock, a familiar sound. It wasn't the first time her mother had locked her in a room.

Tears came to her eyes.

Everything was upside down in her throbbing head: her mother, the eyes of the tattooed man, the gallery with its white, floating women's bodies. She thought of Jan and the voice of the tattooed man: *I can only protect you from him if you tell me his name.*

How could she warn Jan about that lunatic if she was locked up in here?

I've got to get out, she thought, dazed.

She tried to get up. First on all fours, then onto her haunches. But her muscles refused. In her father's pitch-black study, stars were dancing, tightly packed. Her eyelids fluttered. The carpet scratched at the side of her face, and a dull clatter reached her eardrum.

Door open. Wheelchair in. Door closed. Lift down.

She wished she had her father's revolver in her hand, itching to shoot through the wall at the lift or the cables holding it.

Then she slipped into unconsciousness.

Chapter Twenty-One

Berlin, 20 October, 11.13 a.m.

There was a crash. Jolted out of sleep, Jan needed a moment to remember where he was.

He was lying in Laura's bed, and the loud noise was echoing from the inner courtyard of Laura's building. An overturned wheelie bin, perhaps, or a front door slammed in irritation. Jan rubbed his forehead. Headache. Great. He sank back into the pillow, where a hint of citrus fruit still lingered. It smelled like the perfume next to Laura's washbasin. Fahrenheit by Dior, a classic – originally intended for men. Lying in her bed and breathing in her scent was an ambivalent pleasure: nothing brought home to him more clearly that she wasn't there.

Jan sat up and reached for his phone. The display showed 11.13 a.m. He'd slept miserably, spending hours gazing up into the darkness. Only in the early hours of the morning had tiredness finally caught up with him. He yawned, went into the kitchen and opened the fridge, just as he'd done last night. No bodies. Just brown bread, margarine, canned pineapple and water.

While he ate, the questions that had bothered him all night long came flooding back. Laura was in danger. So was he, most likely. The man with the red eyes would stop at nothing, even murder.

He forced himself to ignore his pounding skull and break his thoughts down logically.

Possibility Number One: the man with the red eyes had Laura. If that was so, then the chance of finding her was virtually nil – he hadn't the faintest idea who the guy was, let alone where he lived.

Possibility Number Two: Laura was being followed by the man – for whatever reason – and had gone to ground. Which she would only do somewhere she felt safe.

The photos popped into his head. Laura had lived for years on the street. Was there any better hiding place than an anonymous doss under a bridge, or some abandoned building, maybe, an industrial site or disused train tunnel?

He pulled out his smartphone and found the images he'd taken in Laura's hallway. Each one showed a section of wall with thirty or forty photos, mostly close-ups. He zoomed in on a few areas, trying to make out the details, but was foiled by the grainy resolution. The individual photographs were simply too small, too blurry, too pixelated. He kept having to break off because his eyes were burning.

Nothing. No clues, no places he knew or to which Laura seemed to have a particular connection. Around two, the phone began to ring again. Unnerved, Jan put it on silent.

Shortly before four, he was standing in the hallway in front of the empty walls.

Where the hell are you?

Suddenly he remembered the photo in his jacket. Crossing into the bedroom, where his Belstaff jacket lay beside the futon, he reached into the inner pocket and took out the picture. Laura was sitting by the bank of a river, under a bridge of some sort. In the background was a blurry building and three chimneys against a grey sky. As far as he could remember, another picture had been pinned to the wall beside this one, showing Laura sleeping at the same place. There had been the one with the star scribbled on it in marker, and her birth date, 7 August, in the lower right-hand corner.

Jan paused.

His heart beat more rapidly. Where would someone who lived on the street want to be on their birthday? Their favourite place.

He examined the three chimneys towering into the sky. Then he slipped into his jacket and pocketed the photo and two mobiles. The river Spree was only five hundred metres from Laura's apartment, and he was itching to scour its banks. She might be just around the corner.

It was misty outside. The sky had turned into grey soup, and the damp air crept down his neck. He shivered and pulled the zipper up all the way, walking down Bremerstraße towards the river. From behind him came the wail of a police siren, which approached then fell abruptly silent. He threw a glance over his shoulder and saw the flashing blue light drawing level with Laura's apartment.

It could only mean one thing. They had come for him. He picked up speed, went left into Turmstraße and broke into a run almost before he'd turned the corner. As he crossed the four-lane road somebody honked their horn, as a BMW swerved frantically and missed him by a whisker. Only a few metres later, outside a large church, he ran right into Krefelder Straße.

He slowed his pace at once. Don't make yourself too obvious! With a bit of luck the police hadn't seen him, but were going to Laura's apartment instead.

His heart was racing. How had they found him so quickly?

With brisk steps he kept walking, heading towards the riverbank. Only now did it occur to him that he'd left the new baseball cap in the apartment. Shit, shit, shit.

He cast another glance over his shoulder, but there was no sign of the police.

After two hundred metres he reached the Spree. The river wound like a snake, bridges to the left and right of him hiding the water from view.

Jan swore quietly. In the photo the river was dead straight, and the banks were thick with bushes and trees. The section he was looking for was probably much further out.

He took the photo from his jacket pocket, threw a last glance over his shoulder – and nearly tripped. Barely a hundred metres behind him, the nose of a police car was emerging out of Krefelder Straße at a walking pace and preparing to turn in his direction.

His eyes darted frantically around him. To his left was the Spree, in front of him the street. He plumped for the street, coming to a crossing ten metres later.

Hardly had he rounded the corner before he took to his heels. A taxi was parked on the pavement, a dirty beige Mercedes. An old lady was extricating herself laboriously from the back seat, putting one shopping bag on the kerb before reaching for a second one still in the car.

Jan went up to her. 'May I?' he asked breathlessly.

The woman looked at him in confusion. Jan put the bag on the pavement, leapt onto the back seat and pulled the door shut. The driver, his wallet still in his hands, turned and gave him a baffled look. He was bald, with small lethargic eyes behind dark, thick-rimmed glasses and an enormous belly.

'To the main station,' said Jan. 'I'm in a rush, my train leaves in fifteen minutes.' It was the best he could come up with to highlight the urgency.

'Jus' a stone's throw,' said the bald man. His sausage fingers snapped the wallet shut. 'Don't you worry. Be there in a jiffy.'

Jan looked out of the back window. The police car might appear at any moment. 'I'm sorry, but I'm *really* in a hurry. I've got to get up to the platform too.'

The driver mumbled something and tucked the wallet into the glove compartment. As he did so he dropped a packet of chewing gum into the footwell, bending down to retrieve it with a grunt. In the middle of the dashboard sat the taxi driver's mobile, and at that moment Jan's brain made a connection. His phone! They'd tracked him via the SIM card in his mobile. God, how could he have been so dim?

His eyes flew to the rear window. Nothing. *Still* nothing.

Without taking his eyes off the crossing, he took his phone out of his jacket and removed the plastic cover from the back. The taxi drove off with a lurch, precisely at the moment when the police car reached the crossing. Jan shook the battery out of his mobile and peeled out the SIM card with trembling fingers, then wound down the window a crack and tossed out the small chip card. The police car was driving down the street at a walking pace, before it came to a sudden halt and grew rapidly smaller in the rear window. A few hundred metres later the taxi driver merged onto a multi-lane road, and the police car disappeared entirely. Jan gave a sigh of relief and sank back into the black leather upholstery.

The driver eyed him in the rear-view mirror, but Jan avoided his gaze. Outside the houses flew by.

A ringing sound in his left jacket pocket made him jump.

Laura's mobile.

Frantically he fished it out. The number on the display was all too familiar, and he felt instantly uneasy. 'Hi, Katy,' he said, his voice strained.

'Shit. Jan?'

'Why are *you* calling Laura's number?'

'I just tried your phone but only got voicemail. And I knew you had Laura's mobile.'

'Fine. Anything specific to report?'

'Look, do you know what's going on here? They're searching for you. Like they're after a dangerous criminal.'

Jan felt the blood shoot to his head. He pressed the phone closer to his ear, throwing an anxious glance at the taxi driver and hoping Katy's voice didn't reach him.

'They've got four men outside the door and asked me a million questions. You're lucky Greg wasn't here or he'd definitely have told them about Laura—'

'Greg? I thought you were back home?'

'Are you still on about that? It doesn't matter now. I've got the police outside my door telling me my brother's wanted for murder. They said they found a body in your apartment. Is that true?'

'Katy – please! Calm down. I'll explain later, but I can't right now . . .'

'Shit,' groaned Katy. 'That's a yes. Is it Laura?'

'Laura?' asked Jan obtusely. 'Why would you think that?'

'How should I know? The police wouldn't give me any details. Ongoing investigation, blah blah blah. They only asked whether the name Laura meant anything to me.'

The taxi driver threw another glance into the rear-view mirror, and Jan got the distinct feeling that he heard every word.

'*No*. It wasn't Laura, it was my neighbour. Katy, it's insanely complicated, but I can't tell you anything else right now, honestly.'

'They've been to see Dad, too. He just called me.'

Jan froze. Not that, too. Despite how angry he was with his father, he immediately felt guilty. 'Leave Dad out of this,' he said hoarsely.

'*Me*? *You're* the one getting us into this mess. He's got heart trouble. Or did you forget?'

'Please, Katy. I can't explain everything right now . . .'

'Do you realise what you're doing?'

'I know,' whispered Jan. 'But I . . . I found out something.'

Silence. Only the quiet murmur of the Mercedes, a click from the driver's radio and the crackling signal.

'Do you trust me?'

More silence.

'Katy, please!'

'I . . . lately you've been so . . .' She broke off and sighed. 'Shit. Why didn't you tell me about this yesterday?'

'If I had, how would you have reacted when the . . .' – another glance at the taxi driver – 'when they showed up on your doorstep?'

'I . . .' she paused. Said nothing for a moment. 'OK. I understand.'

Jan exhaled.

'So – what did you find out? Do you know where Laura is?'

'Not exactly. But I have an idea. You know your way around Berlin, right?' asked Jan.

'Better than you, at least.'

'Exactly. I'm looking for somewhere on the Spree. A bridge where the river runs quite straight, overgrown with bushes, and with three chimneys nearby, all the same height, equidistant from each other. Does that ring a bell?'

'Hm. In the city itself? Or further out?'

'Don't know, but probably further out, I think. You can't see much of the city.'

'Directly on the Spree, you say? Can't think of anything off-hand, although . . . hang on . . .'

Jan stared straight ahead, through the windscreen. Directly in front of him towered an enormous glass building, and the taxi pulled up. The bald man half-turned towards him. 'Here we are, main station. Bang on schedule.'

'Er, yeah. Just a minute,' murmured Jan. 'Katy? Can we talk later?' He hung up without waiting for answer.

'That'll be eight fifty.'

Jan put the mobile away and rummaged around in the pocket of his jeans, pulling out a tenner, which he pressed into the driver's hand. Then he flung open the door and swung his legs out of the Mercedes.

'Hey, your chimneys . . .' said the driver.

Jan turned. 'Yeah?'

'Don't want to be indiscreet or anything, I just caught a bit of what you were saying . . .'

'Yes, and?' urged Jan. 'Do you know where they are?'

'Well. Not on the Spree, that's for sure. Sounds to me like Teltow canal, because the chimneys, they could be Lichterfelde power station.'

Jan's jaw dropped. The *canal*. Of course! Those straight banks looked much more like a canal than a river! 'Do you know how far away that is?'

The bald man shrugged. His eyes blinked behind the thick glasses. 'Quite a way. Ten miles or so, maybe.'

Jan was virtually buzzing with excitement. He yanked his legs back into the taxi and pulled the door shut. 'Take me there, please.'

'What about your train?'

'Not so important.'

The bald man raised his hairless eyebrows, reset the meter to zero and threaded the Mercedes back into the busy traffic by the train station.

Chapter Twenty-Two

Berlin, 20 October, 5.13 p.m.

Jan watched as the taxi idled in traffic on Königsberger Straße, crawling over the bridge across Teltow canal. Not more than a hundred metres from the bridge was a petrol station. A well-chosen spot, he thought. A place to sleep with a mini supermarket around the corner that's open round the clock.

The bridge was a soulless, functional piece of construction. Two lanes in each direction, curving street lamps left and right, a cycle lane and pavement, all wending gently to the right. *Emil Schulz Bridge* was wrought in iron letters on the greyish-blue railing. Teltow canal was visible only once you reached the bridge. The surface of the water looked like liquid lead, smooth as a bed with the covers pulled tight. Mist rose up between the banks, which were overgrown with bushes and trees. Not too far away emerged the outline of Lichterfelde power station's three chimneys, which stood directly on the edge of the canal.

Jan crossed the bridge, peering over the canal from the other side and comparing the view with the photo from Laura's apartment. The perspective was right, but the photo had been taken from the bank itself.

A tall chain-link fence at the end of the railing barred the way down to the water, and a sign forbade unauthorised entry.

Lifting part of the fence out of its concrete socket, he wriggled through and shuffled along the bridge, soon coming across a track that led to the canal through thick bushes. Gingerly he clambered down the steep slope, grabbing every handhold he could find along the way. At around the midpoint a branch broke, and he fell and skittered a few metres on his bottom.

Jan picked himself up and rubbed his tailbone. The head of the bridge ended here, the track leading through thick bushes beneath the bridge. Pushing the branches aside, he peered around the corner.

The area underneath the bridge was mostly concreted over, and somewhat sloping. On the other side, next to a dense bush, lay a mat, a sleeping bag – or were they blankets? – several plastic bags and various other bits and bobs.

His heart beat faster. Was this where Laura slept?

Jan hesitated. Above him, on the four-lane bridge, traffic was rumbling. The canal ran silently south-west, past the power station. The spot was windless, and the mist seemed denser here, immediately on the water.

He looked up to where he'd come from, then back at the abandoned sleeping mat.

Slowly he stepped forward and went underneath the bridge. Tiny stones crunched beneath his soles. Otherwise the ground was surprisingly clean: hardly any old leaves, no branches, no litter.

A loud ringing sound made him jump. Hastily he pulled Laura's mobile out of his jacket pocket.

'Hello?' he whispered.

'You were going to call me,' complained Katy, in her best big-sister voice.

'Katy!' Jan groaned and came to a halt. His gaze rested on the sleeping bag and the undergrowth behind. 'Dammit. Can't you just—' He broke off. Had he just seen something move?

'Jan? Hello?'

He lowered the phone.

'Ja—an!' squawked Katy's voice from the telephone.

He hung up and switched off the phone, without taking his eyes off the bushes.

'Laura?'

No answer. With slow steps he approached the sleeping bag.

'Hello? Are you there?'

No sound, no movement. Only the cars above him and the placidly flowing canal.

He bent down to pick up a plastic bag, removing the red rubber band that held it closed. The plastic rustled loudly. Inside was a ball of scrunched-up aluminium foil, a little packet of tobacco, a half-full bottle of Johnnie Walker Red Label, a wind-proof lighter – and a wallet that looked like Laura's.

Jan's heart was pounding. He peered inside to make sure. In the wallet was Laura's ATM card, her ID card and a surprisingly thick bundle of notes. Fresh green hundreds, perhaps twenty or more.

'Take your paws off my things!' a hoarse male voice suddenly rang out behind him. At the same moment a dull pain exploded between his shoulder blades, and a second blow to his side struck him in the kidneys. Jan toppled to the floor, and some-body threw himself on top of him. A hand roughly grabbed his hair and pressed his face into the dirt.

'Gotcha now, you shit.'

Jan moaned. Tiny stones were digging into his face like pins, and his forehead was burning.

'Don't move a muscle, or I'll wring your neck. Got it?'

'Yes,' gasped Jan. Fear crept into his limbs. Was this *him*? The man with the facial tattoos?

'What do you want here? What are you doing?'

'Where . . . where is Laura? What have you done with her?' panted Jan.

'Laura? You mean Lory. How do you know her?'

'Lory?'

'I asked you a question,' roared the voice. It sounded husky, and Jan smelled alcohol.

'I . . . I'm looking for Laura, she's—'

'Why? What do you want with her?' The hand yanked Jan's head back by the hair, so that he could hardly breathe.

'She's gone missing, I—'

'Are you the bastard that kidnapped her?'

'What?'

'Take me for an idiot, do you? She told me everything.'

'Shit, no!' groaned Jan. 'I didn't kidnap her. I'm her friend. I've been looking for her for days.'

The grip on his hair loosened a fraction. 'And I'm s'posed to believe that, am I?'

Jan gasped for air. 'For Christ's sake, if you'll just let me go . . . I can explain everything.'

'Why were you going through my stuff then, eh?'

'I thought they were Laura's things. I'm worried.'

The man wheezed, then he let go of Jan's hair and lumbered to his feet. Jan groaned with relief and sat up. Before him stood a tramp with a deeply lined face and bushy grey beard. He was around sixty, astonishingly strong, and wore a green parka, baggy brown trousers and a stained pullover. Jan recognised him immediately. He'd seen him in numerous photos in Laura's apartment.

'Sorry 'bout that,' growled the man, sitting down next to Jan. 'I'm Gandalf.'

'Gandalf? Like in *The Lord of the Rings*?' Jan's eyes wandered over the long grey hair and beard.

'Yeah. It stuck.'

'I'm Jan. Jan Floss.'

Gandalf squinted, as if seeing his interlocutor with fresh eyes, or as though the name meant something to him, but a moment later his gaze was turned inward again.

'Did I understand that right? Laura was here?' asked Jan. 'Is she OK?'

Gandalf shook his head from side to side. 'Lory is tough. But kidnapping . . .'

'What kidnapping? What did she tell you? When was she here?'

'Just yesterday. Found her the night before, took her here. First she just slept. Then she told me she'd been kidnapped by some psycho. One who kills women.'

So it was true. Jan swallowed, thinking of Nikki Reichert. 'And she escaped?'

Gandalf shrugged. 'She doesn't know how she got out.' He clicked his fingers. 'It just happened.'

'Just like that? What do you mean?'

'No idea. Better ask Lory.'

'Was she hurt?'

'Didn't see anything,' reflected Gandalf.

'And where is she now? The police station?'

'Would've been smart, 's what I told her. But she never wanted anything to do with the police. Can't blame 'er. Said there was something she had to do. Then she left, yesterday evening. Borrowed my pocket knife.'

'Great,' sighed Jan. 'And why did she leave her wallet?'

'How do I know?' said Gandalf gruffly. 'She jus' left it. I'm looking after it.'

Jan stared at him in silence, deciding to accept this answer for now. He had no intention of antagonising the man. 'And she didn't say *what* she had to do? Or where?'

Gandalf shook his head. 'Nah. She thought . . .' He broke off, hunting for words. 'She thought this bloke knew where she lived. Couldn't go back home. So she wanted to stay here with me for a while.'

'But why isn't she back yet?'

Gandalf shrugged his shoulders.

Jan sighed, rubbing his hand over his face in exhaustion. 'Maybe she went to the police after all.'

'Not Lory. Too scared they'll put her away.'

'Put her away?' Jan raised his eyebrows. The skin of his forehead was burning. 'How do you mean?'

Gandalf's eyes narrowed. 'Don't seem you know much about Lory. You're asking a lot of questions.'

Jan felt himself blush. 'I know her from before, from school. But then she went to boarding school and we lost touch for a while. We only reconnected recently.'

'Reconnected. I see.'

Jan nodded.

Gandalf hadn't failed to notice his change in colour, and grinned into his beard. 'Got you pretty bad, hasn't she?'

Jan grimaced. *Got you*. Yeah, that was about right.

Gandalf's smile broadened, the folds in his face becoming dark grooves. 'Get the feeling you don't know what you're letting yourself in for . . .'

'Feels that way to me too.'

'Got any cash?'

'Cash?'

'Yeah,' rumbled Gandalf. 'Up there,' he pointed over their heads, 'is a petrol station. Just started selling disposable grills, sausages and that.' He grinned slyly. 'If I'm going to talk about Lory, I need something in my belly. Something to warm my bones.'

Jan nodded. He looked past Gandalf, into the thickening mist, and shivered. 'Not a bad idea,' he said. As he got up, his kidney twinged where Gandalf's blow had landed.

'And Johnnie Walker Red Label, while you're at it,' called Gandalf after him.

Chapter Twenty-Three

Berlin, 20 October, 7.32 p.m.

Laura was listening attentively. Were those voices? Quite faint? Going over to the basement wall, she put her ear to the brick-work, which was chilly and rather damp. A thick drainage pipe ran vertically down the wall in front of her face.

A few hours ago she'd woken up on a thin mattress with a headache, nausea and a sweetish smell in her nose. She was lying in the middle of an empty room on the bare stone floor. The only source of light was a row of thick glass bricks just below the ceiling. The door opposite came from another age: old, solid wood, painted grey, the handle silver, worn. The shape seemed oddly familiar, as did everything in the room. Suddenly she knew where she was.

In the basement of her parents' house.

The same brick walls, the same doors, the peculiar glass bricks that seemed out of place in such an old house, the smell. This was the storeroom round the back. She hadn't realised it at first, because in the past it had always been full of boxes and crates. It was empty now except for a few plastic bottles of water, a fan heater, a bucket, several tins of food, boxes of biscuits and a ten-pack of toilet paper.

She tried to focus. Suddenly she needed a drink so badly that it nearly pushed everything else out of her head, but the only drink in the room seemed to be water. The events of the last few days were pinging around in her brain like beads on a snapped necklace: the gallery of women's corpses, her father's study, the tattooed man, Jan's father's house in Èze, Gandalf and the bridge . . .

She touched her skull and flinched as her fingers brushed the painful swelling.

It all came back to her in a flash. The break-in at her parents' house. The gun that wasn't where it should be. Her mother catching her, offering her money to vanish from her life. Then a scuffle, ending in a collision with the doorframe.

How, though, had she managed to get her down here? With Fanny's help? Or had her father come home and helped out?

Suddenly Jan popped into her head, and she knew she had to warn him. Please don't let anything happen to him! The voice of the tattooed man was still ringing in her ears. *Make things right.* On his lips it had sounded like a threat. She thought of the spectral figures in their glowing cages, and shuddered. What in God's name did that psycho want with her? To protect her, he'd said. Had he 'protected' all those other women?

Summoning all her strength, she got up and staggered over to the door. Locked. Of course, she thought. Remembering Gandalf's pocket knife, she fumbled for it her trouser pocket, but the knife was gone. So was the money from the vase.

Furiously she beat her fist against the door. Once. Twice. Until her hand ached.

She was trapped – in her parents' basement, of all places. Tears welled up uncontrollably, but she clamped her lips shut and forbade herself to cry.

To help herself think, she ate a few biscuits and drank some water. Mr Walker resurfaced in her mind. A few minutes later she felt a twinge in her bladder; there was no toilet, so she used the bucket.

She was still feeling sick as a dog, which she attributed to being drugged rather than the liquor, and the stench of urine wasn't helping. Sooner or later it would reek like a cesspool down here. Her gaze fell on the wide drainpipe on the wall. Close to the ground there was a fork in the pipe – a dead end, probably a connector for a washing machine or something.

Trying to twist the cap off the end of the pipe, she broke into a sweat. Her knuckles were white and sore from exertion. She was just about to give up when the cap yielded with a grating sound. She was met by an unpleasant smell. Swiftly she poured in the contents of the bucket and screwed the cap back on.

She knew it was silly, but it was a minor victory nonetheless. Even if all she'd done was trade the smell of urine for that of the drainage pipe.

She lay back down on the mattress and stared at the glass bricks, beyond which night was falling. She could have turned on the ceiling lamp – there was electricity, and even a socket for the heater – but somehow she wanted to see the daylight for as long as possible.

As it grew dark, all of a sudden she could hear voices.

Not individual words, only the muffled echo of a conversation somewhere in the house.

She put her ear to the wall, but it didn't make the voices much clearer. What was above the storage room? The kitchen? Laura's gaze fell on the drainage pipe. Dropping quickly to her knees, she took off the cap and put her ear to the opening.

Now the voices were easier to hear: one was unmistakably her mother's, the other that of a man. '. . . do you think you can just call me to heel like a dog, without so much as a please or thank you?' It sounded hoarse, guttural, a worn-out voice. She wasn't sure whether she knew him.

'What do you want?' asked her mother.

'What everybody wants. A little house, a few square metres of garden, something to eat, a beach chair by the ocean.'

Her mother laughed – her Ava-Bjely-lady-of-the-manor laugh. 'You? *You?* A nice little bourgeois idyll? I don't buy it. I give you three months before you whore it all away, like you always do. Look at yourself, you've already got another bottle in your hand.'

Laura heard footsteps, and then, quite close by, the sound of gurgling and trickling. Only a moment later, liquid ran down the pipe past her ear.

'Satisfied?' asked the man.

Her mother said nothing.

'Look here, I can always leave again. What'd you do then, eh? Ask Fanny?' He snorted contemptuously. 'You're a cripple, and you know it. Can't even go to the toilet by yourself. Down to the basement? How are you going to manage that?'

'Do you think you're any less crippled than me?'

'Always up on your high bloody horse,' complained the man. 'You don't seriously believe that I'm going to come here for peanuts and empty your basement, haul your little girl downstairs, turn the key and then just smile nicely and go?'

Laura's heart beat faster. So this was the man who'd brought her down. Her mother had rung someone she knew from the old days. But who could it be?

'What's supposed to happen now?' he asked.

Laura's mother cleared her throat. 'Don't give me the third degree. She can't stay here for ever. At some point he'll come back. He'll remember.'

'See what I'm saying? What will you do then?' The man snorted noisily and spat into the sink.

'Tell me what you want,' demanded her mother coldly.

'Give me the mansion.'

For a moment silence reigned.

Mansion? thought Laura. What mansion?

'You got your share, and more. Why should I let you loot the rest?'

'Come on,' said the man, coughing. It sounded rough, hard and unhealthy. 'That was over thirty years ago.'

'It was almost seventeen million. For most people that would last a lifetime,' retorted her mother.

'I learned my lesson. Losing everything you have brings you back down to earth with a bump. Makes you humble.'

'Humble, eh? The mansion!'

'Come on, that old box has been standing empty for ages. I don't want to move in. I want to sell it. Then I'll buy myself a little house. Not in Amsterdam, somewhere further up, on the coast, and I can live on the rest of the money till I'm in my grave. I mean, look at you, here in this bloody great eyesore. You've got your grand house and your fortune. Just give me the empty old box. Then I'll keep my mouth shut and help you.'

Help? With what? wondered Laura. She felt cold as ice. What were they planning to do with her?

Her mother was silent for a while, then coughed slightly. 'Fine. On one condition.'

'Which is?'

'You take Laura to the mansion.'

Laura froze. Was her mother just handing her over to this guy?

'What?' asked the man. 'To *my* house?'

'It's not your house.'

'It is now.'

'Only after you take Laura with you.'

'Take her how? For how long? What am I supposed to do with her, for God's sake?' asked the man irritably. 'What the hell are you thinking?'

'Buck, will you kindly calm down,' said her mother.

Laura was startled. Buck? Was *that* his name?

'Calm down, Buck,' the man imitated her. 'How am I supposed to be calm with all this madness going on, eh?'

An oppressive silence fell.

'Fine, then,' Laura heard her mother say. 'Go back to Amsterdam. Crawl back into your hole. I'll find another solution.'

Laura heard a faint shuffling sound and wondered what it could be, until she realised that it was probably her mother's wheelchair. That had always been her final card to play: rolling out of the room, head held high.

'Hey, wait,' said the man. 'Wait a minute.'

Laura heard her mother speak again, this time so quietly she couldn't understand what she said.

'Would you please just wait, goddammit . . . *hey* . . .' cried the man. Evidently he was following her mother, because his voice grew fainter. Laura only caught a few more scraps of conversation, then all was still. They must both have left the kitchen.

She kept listening for a while, then put the cap back without screwing it on.

Who was this Buck? How did he know her and her mother? And why in the world had he been given seventeen million? For what?

But the worst of it was that her mother was clearly happy for him to take her away, to this 'mansion', whatever that was. And what would happen to her there?

She sank down onto the mattress, pulled her knees up to her chest and hugged her arms around them. Tears ran down her cheeks. If only she'd never come to this godforsaken house. How could she have been so stupid?

That bloody revolver and the vase of money had seemed like a last piece of home. And now her mother had taken them too.

Chapter Twenty-Four

Berlin, 20 October, 8.23 p.m.

Jan watched Gandalf swill down the last bite of sausage with a tot of Johnnie Walker then screw the cap back on. His greasy fingers left prints on the glass.

Night had fallen; the world outside the bridge no longer existed. Only the cars' headlights, flitting through the fog like ghosts on the edge of their vision, reminded them that there was something else above them.

After cooking the sausages, Gandalf had shaken the embers from the grill onto the floor and tossed on a few pieces of dry wood. The fire was meagre, especially since the air was so damp, yet this spot beneath the bridge felt like the centre of the world.

Gandalf leant forward, bringing his gnarled hands closer to the meagre flames, and grunted. 'Really don't want any?' he asked, nodding at the bottle of Johnnie Walker.

'No.'

'How long since you stopped being able to get her out of your head?'

'Well, since . . . I guess since I was thirteen.'

Gandalf raised his eyebrows.

'But there was a long break in the middle.'

'A break, eh?' Gandalf slowly shook his head. 'I got divorced. 'S a kind of break too.' He gave a crooked grin. 'My father was a builder. Burger, maybe you know . . '

Jan shook his head.

'Probably before your time. Big deal, in his day. Lot of money sloshing around. I worked for him. He paid a few bribes – nothing special, the others were doing it too. But he got busted, and then it all went down the drain . . '

Jan nodded. 'And Laura, how long have you known her?'

'Ah, for ages now. Dunno which year any more, don't notice that sort of thing. First time I saw Lory on the street she was sixteen, I think. Realised straight off her family was stinking rich. Don't get many o' those.'

Jan frowned. 'I have a couple of photos of her from those days. Didn't she already have that punk hairstyle? And the piercings?'

'Yeah. And more of them, later. But that's all bullshit,' growled Gandalf. 'She could've had ten times as many piercings – it'd still've been plain as a pikestaff where she came from.'

Jan thought of his visit to Ava Bjely, and tried to imagine how Laura and her mother had got on. He couldn't. 'Did she tell you why she ran away?'

'Nah, not really *told*, no. Just bits and pieces. I thought sometimes it was the other way around, that it was the mother that chucked *her* out. Fourteen, Lory said she was, when out of the blue she's told she has to go to boarding school. Came as a bit of a shock.'

'And her father? What about him? Did he want that too?'

A spark flew into the air with a crackle. Gandalf glanced at it and shrugged. 'Didn't have much say in the matter, far as I know. He was never there – always withdrew into his work. That was all Lory told me about him.'

Jan stared into the flames. He could still see her in his mind's eye: pale, long dark hair, looking lost, somehow, yet with an energy like silent fire. Katy had said she had a tendency to cut and run, but he had never noticed that. He'd been far too self-absorbed back then, though: Theo's death, his mother leaving, his obsession with his own ugliness.

'Any idea why Laura was sent to boarding school?' asked Jan.

Gandalf sighed and scratched his beard with greasy fingers. 'Nope. Nor did she. It was in November, she told me.' He was silent a moment, also gazing into the fire. 'I remember because Lory always said how much she hated November. "That November was the end of everything," she used to say. "That's when my mother fucked up my life once and for all."'

November. Jan did some mental maths: Laura was thirty-four now, so if she'd been fourteen at the time then she was talking about November of 1992. Something must have happened. 'What about after that?'

Gandalf reached for the whisky and unscrewed the top thoughtfully. 'Just about everything, like all these boarding schools.'

'Everything? What do you mean?'

'Well. A bunch of problem children who've been sent away by their parents because they can't cope with their brats.'

'I'm not asking for a definition of "boarding school", I want to know what went on there.'

Instead of answering, Gandalf took a long swig. The whisky glowed reddish gold in the firelight, which was refracted through the bottle and played across his features. He waved the bottle in front of Jan's face. 'You know. Alcohol, drugs, parties, bullying . . .'

Jan turned away, gazing into the fog. In the distance he could hear an ambulance.

'Give me the bottle,' said Jan at last.

'Want some after all?' Gandalf grinned.

Jan merely nodded, took the whisky Gandalf passed him and sipped it. It burned in his throat, velvety and scratchy at the same time, and tasting of peat, smoke and juniper. Pretty drinkable, for twenty euros – except that they'd screwed forty out of him at the petrol station. He raised the bottle and tilted it with deliberate slowness until whisky started trickling onto the floor.

Gandalf goggled at him, slack-jawed.

'I didn't buy you this stuff so that you could feed me a load of half-baked rubbish. I might as well use it to water the weeds.'

Gandalf pulled an angry face. 'Give me the bottle, boy, or I'll take it off you. And you're not going to bloody like it . . .'

'Only this time you'll have to look me in the eye.'

Gandalf's eyes shifted from Jan to the bottle and back again. His face took on a deeply sulky aspect. 'All right, all right. Not sure if Lory would mind, that's why . . . don't have to do that.'

'Oh yeah?'

Silence. Above them a car honked its horn.

'So what now?' asked Jan.

'Well,' said Gandalf, 'at the boarding school, somebody – died.'

'A pupil?'

'Nah, a teacher.'

'So?'

'It's jus' a feeling,' said Gandalf hesitantly. 'Lory always said he was a bastard, he deserved it. And the way she said it . . . well . . .'

'What? What are you trying to say?'

Gandalf gave him a look that was hard to read. Then he scratched his neck. 'The bloke was beaten to death. In the woods behind the school.'

'Beaten to death?' Jan lowered the bottle.

Gandalf nodded.

'You . . . you think . . . Laura had something to do with it?' asked Jan, bewildered.

'Didn't say that.'

'But you thought it.'

Silence.

'How old was she then?' asked Jan.

''Bout fifteen, sixteen. Then she ran away from it, from the boarding school, I mean. That was when I met her on the street for the first time. Only told me later, though. Much later. Didn't like to tell you much about herself straight off . . .'

Jan puffed his cheeks and let the air escape out loud. Then he took another sip from the bottle. 'So what was this boarding school called?'

'Not sure now. Nordland . . . Nordschloss . . . something with Nord, anyway.'

'Nordland,' whispered Jan. The whisky was going to his head. The halogen lights of a car sliced through the fog, whizzing along the edge of the bridge. For a second he thought he glimpsed a figure in the darkness behind Gandalf, where the bushes grew.

You're letting your imagination run away with you, he told himself. 'What else do you know about Laura? How long was she—' Jan broke off. Was that a twig snapping in the undergrowth?

'You going to give me back the bottle?' asked Gandalf.

'Did you hear that too?'

'What?' asked Gandalf. 'The cars? It's always like this.' Leaning forward, he stretched his hand past the fire to take the bottle from Jan.

Behind Gandalf's back, a figure detached itself from the darkness: tall, black-clad, wearing a hood, the face beneath it patterned with radiant blotches between black decorative streaks. Jan's fingers clenched around the bottle.

'Give it here,' complained Gandalf, tugging at the whisky.

Jan was paralysed.

'Come on, man.' Gandalf shook the bottle, the golden liquid sloshing to and fro. The figure seized his grey, stringy hair and yanked his head back.

'Hey!' Gandalf's protest echoed underneath the bridge. The figure's other hand darted across his throat. Something glinted in the firelight. Gandalf's neck yawned darkly, blood pulsing out of the carotid as though out of a leaky garden hose. Gandalf's fingers slipped from the bottle. A dreadful sound emerged from his open throat as he tried frantically to gulp the air.

The man with the knife let go of Gandalf's hair. His eyes wide open, the tramp slumped over, landing on the ground with a dull thud.

The man now drew himself up to his full height, towering in front of Jan. The tattoos – or was it some kind of paint? – lent him an alien, almost diabolical appearance. His lips were pale, dry and cracked.

His eyes?

Jan had expected them to be red, but they were simply watery and grey, with a reddish shimmer in the fire.

'Hello, Jan Floss,' whispered the man. Jan could do nothing but stare at the dry, cracked lips, the only thing real about his face.

Chapter Twenty-Five

Berlin, 20 October, 8.51 p.m.

The knife sat warm in his right fist, the blade angled to the floor. Fjodor gazed down at Jan. Look at him crouching there, clinging to his bottle! Small, slender; like fucking innocence incarnate.

He smiled grimly, enjoying the fear in Jan's eyes. For a moment he was reminded of the doctor all those years ago, the way he'd stood there in the garage between his precious bloody Benz and Porsche. The pompous twat had had the same look on his face, his mind refusing to accept the obvious: that he was going to die. Right here and now.

How long ago was that? More than half a lifetime.

He cocked his head. Breathed. Stared at the birthmark on Jan's face. He'd already seen it in the photo online, of course, but he hadn't pictured it so large and dark. He found it ugly.

Surely Laura found it ugly too. Was she really chasing after this pussy?

'Who . . . who are you?' stammered Jan.

'I'm the one who's going to make things right.'

Jan opened his mouth – and closed it again.

'What do you want here?' hissed Fjodor.

'I'm . . . I'm looking for Laura.'

'Didn't I warn you?'

'Where is she? What have you done with her?'

'I should be asking *you* that!'

Silence.

The fire snapped and popped.

Leaning forward imperceptibly, Fjodor shot out his left arm at lightning speed, grabbing Jan's hair and pulling him close over the flames, pressing the knifepoint to his birthmark, directly underneath his eye.

Jan's gaze was fixed on the bloody knife. 'What do you want with Laura?' Suddenly he looked up straight at Fjodor, almost challengingly, with eyes that seemed virtually black in the darkness, a mirror of the restive fire.

The eyes of a liar, thought Fjodor. Laura belonged to him, how dare that bastard try to steal her. Laura had spat at him because of this man.

Feeling a surge of hatred, he gathered his saliva and spat in Jan's face.

The liar blinked. Fjodor pressed the blade harder against his red skin, wondering what kind of sound his blood would make as it spattered into the fire. What it would smell like. He stared at the mark, and suddenly his fingers itched to cut it out.

'Just you and me, Jan Floss. Here, under this bridge. There's nothing else. There never will be. Forget about Laura. She'll never belong to you.'

'Belong?' Jan's voice was a hoarse whisper. 'I don't want her to belong to me.'

'You're lying. You've already put your fingers on her. But that's over now. I'll cut them off and make you choke on them.'

Chapter Twenty-Six

Berlin, 20 October, 9.02 p.m.

The man's strange eyes bored deep down inside him. Jan's pulse was racing, his neurons firing like machine guns. The blade to his face. The point sticky with blood. The scorching heat of the fire beneath his chin. The acrid smoke, the fog.

And yet he was rooted to the spot. Nothing worked any more, as if those peculiar eyes had the power to transfix.

No eyelashes. Pale grey, or blue. A faint and sudden flutter of the iris. Or was it? No. It was gone.

Why had his eyes fluttered?

Jan's mind revved like a stuttering engine.

His fingers were cold, the bottle of Johnnie Walker a smooth foreign object in his right hand.

'Do you know where I'm going to begin?' asked the man, bending so close that his face was directly in front of Jan's.

His fingers tightened around the bottle.

The tattooed man traced the point of the knife over Jan's mark. A flash of light caught the blade, dappling his face, and his irises changed colour: instantly his eyes were red.

Jan stared at him.

The man stared back.

Don't look away, thought Jan, holding his gaze.

His left hand slid beneath the bottom of the bottle. The right one was still holding the neck so firmly that his knuckles ached.

Then he jerked the bottle upward with all his might, smashing it into his attacker's chin. Jan heard his teeth slam together, and the man's head flew back. He let go of Jan, tumbled backwards and tripped over Gandalf's body.

Jan took to his heels, racing out from underneath the bridge and around the corner.

In an instant all was shadow. A grey, dull gloom. No more firelight, only bushes and fog, and somewhere far above the diffuse glow of a street lamp. Jan scrambled up the steep path as quickly as he could among the clawing bushes, slipped and smacked face first into the hard earth on the slope.

From underneath the bridge came a howl of fury, then footsteps. Jan tried to find his footing, scrabbling on all fours up the track.

The street lamp.

Made it!

Behind him he heard his pursuer wheezing, soles slipping on the embankment.

Jan bolted down the pavement, the bridge at his back. The fog swallowed everything in his immediate environment: cars, people, houses. Street lamps floated above him like blunted suns, headlights becoming ghostly will-o'-the-wisps. The footsteps behind him were still there. Apparently effortless, quick and unerring.

Jan's legs were getting heavy, as though someone were sucking the energy out of him with a straw. His lungs began to burn. Too little oxygen, too many breaths. Why the fuck had he stopped working out?

He ran right. A hundred metres, then left. He ran around a man whose dog barked; tripped over it, got up again, ran on. His lungs were about to burst. The steps behind him wouldn't fade away.

Right, again.

A passageway opened into a courtyard just before the next street lamp.

He raced inside. The passageway was black as pitch. A few metres before the courtyard he paused, pressed his back against the clammy wall and kept his eyes on the open gate, which was just visible through the glowing fog. His lungs pumped strenuously, his pulse droned in his ears, and his legs trembled with the exertion.

He waited for the steps to come closer, for the man to run past. But nobody came.

Slowly Jan retreated towards the courtyard, his eyes fixed on the gate. A soundless figure stepped into the pool of light, a vague outline Jan recognised immediately by his hood.

He held his breath, praying that the man wouldn't see him in the dark passageway, and groped his way backwards along the wall. Reaching the end, he slipped around the corner. The courtyard was a dead end: four high walls loomed around him, the roofs disappearing in the fog. Lights were burning behind some of the windows. In one apartment flickered the familiar blue glow of a television.

He was a sitting duck. There was only one way out.

Jan's eyes darted from the bins to the parked cars to the basement windows. Bars everywhere. But directly above some steps leading down to the basement level, a window on the raised ground floor was open. The bottom third of the window was blocked, the bars cemented into the wall, but there was enough space above them to climb through. Assuming he could get that far up. The windowsill was only two metres above the paved courtyard, but the steps didn't make things any easier. He'd have to jump over them.

Jan bolted straight towards the wall. Leaping into the air and throwing his arms in front of him, he managed to grab the lowest bar, but slammed into the wall so hard that he nearly let go again. His own bodyweight tore at his arms. He tensed his stomach muscles, drew up his legs and tried to find purchase with his feet.

The rubber soles of his Converse trainers scuffled over the façade, breaking off some plaster, as the noise echoed through the courtyard. He pulled himself up the bars as if on a climbing frame, panting. Just as he heard footsteps near the entrance, he got his feet onto the sill, pushed the window all the way open, tugged a heavy curtain to one side and clambered over the bars into the room.

Immediately he bolted the window and drew the curtains shut.

His heart was pounding wildly.

It was pitch black in the room. The smell was musty, a human scent, and something else he couldn't identify.

At that moment there was a bang against the wall of the house. Jan heard the scrabbling of shoes on plaster. Instinctively he shrank back from the window, bumping into something hard with his elbow. It sounded like plastic, with a metallic echo, and something rustled frantically.

A muffled grunt echoed through the windowpane, then came a loud banging. A fist on glass. Jan could picture the tattooed man standing on the sill, hanging onto the bars with one hand and trying to shove the window open.

What next? Would he try to break—

A loud, dull blow shook the glass. Jan held his breath.

He stretched out his arm and felt for the wall. There! Where there was a wall, there had to be a door.

Another dull blow shook the windowpane.

Jan's fingers met an edge, and something clunked to the ground. Where the fuck was the door?

Suddenly there was silence.

Then there was a sharp thwack, followed by the splintering of glass.

The knife! The thought shot through Jan's head. He hit the window with the handle of the knife. The curtain billowed, opening a crack.

More glass clinked.

Jan lurched towards the curtain, smacked his thigh against a heavy obstacle and fell across a table top. Several objects clattered to the floor.

'Oi!' rang a voice through the courtyard. 'What's going on? What are you doing?'

It sounded like it was coming from one of the upper storeys. Jan got up slowly and moved past the table. Between the two halves of the curtain he saw a hand reach through a hole in the pane.

'Hey, you!' the voice echoed through the courtyard. 'Come down from there. I'm calling the police!'

The hand fumbled for the bolt. Jan tore back the curtain and made to grab the tattooed man's hand, intending to rake it across the sharp edges of the jagged glass, but at the last moment the man pulled it back from the window. For a few seconds they stood opposite each other in the darkness.

'Do you hear me? I'm calling the police. Bloody scum!'

A moment later the man had slid down from the sill, hanging from the bars for a second before letting himself fall.

A dark shadow hurried across the courtyard and disappeared into the passage.

Jan's hands were sweaty. He was quivering.

Again he heard the frantic rustling, and wondered whether anyone was in the apartment.

With the curtains open he could just see the outline of the door; immediately next to it was a light switch. He squinted as three halogen bulbs blinked on above him. The room was a bedroom and study, with an unmade bed against one wall and an old dining table covered with a chaotic jumble of papers, textbooks, a laptop and dirty cups. A few of them had fallen to the floor.

On top of a poorly preserved Biedermeier chest of drawers was a hamster cage with a yellow plastic tray. Three agitated mice were scurrying around among the wood shavings. One of them paused in the middle of the cage, looking at him. Its thin whiskers trembled as it contemplated his scent. Unlike the other two animals, its coat was snowy white and its eyes red. An albino, thought Jan.

That was the moment when it struck him.

Of course! The red eyes. The pale skin between the black streaks. An albino.

Chapter Twenty-Seven

Berlin, 20 October, 10.13 p.m.

Laura heard footsteps, jarring her awake. A key was slid into the lock and turned, then the handle moved. In the doorframe stood a man with a balaclava and a drill.

Buck, thought Laura.

He wore a tatty pair of ochre cargo pants, baggy at the pockets, and a green-and-blue checked flannel shirt that was marginally too short, and stretched tight across his stomach. Between his belt and shirt, a strip of hairy skin peeped out.

Laura was confused. The man's clothes were somehow ridiculous, but the balaclava and drill made his appearance terrifying.

In hindsight she couldn't say why she did what she did. It was pure instinct, driven by desperation and adrenalin.

She flung herself at him.

Buck, who was hardly any taller than her, gave an angry yell. The drill clattered to the floor as Laura grappled with him; his arms beneath the flannel shirt were surprisingly slender. Lashing out, she kneed him between the legs, but didn't quite hit her target. Buck groaned and crumpled, but grabbed her arms and held them tightly. As they struggled, Laura managed to seize the balaclava and tear it off his head. Deep-set black eyes glinted at her. His mouth was twisted with exertion. Laura was trying to wriggle out of his grip when suddenly his head shot forward, colliding with the very same spot she'd banged against the door-frame only a few hours earlier.

She screamed. Buck threw her back onto the mattress, pulled a roll of duct tape out of his pocket and wound it round her arms and legs.

Panting hard, he got to his feet. 'Fucking bitch.' He rummaged around in his pockets and took out a drill bit, plastic dowels and two reinforced eyelet screws, then fetched a stool from the corridor and drilled a hole in the ceiling directly above her, in the middle of the room. Dust fell into her face, making her cough.

Then he fixed one of the eyelet screws into the ceiling, made a second hole directly beside the door and put the other screw in. He said nothing, merely began to whistle quietly. Janis Joplin: 'Mercedes Benz'. Then he handcuffed her – in addition to the duct tape – threaded a synthetic rope through the middle, worked it through the eyelet screw on the ceiling and drew it from there to the eyelet by the door.

There he paused, his forehead and bald spot glittering with sweat. Mid-fifties, Laura estimated. He looked just as raddled as his voice had sounded during his conversation with her mother. 'All right, sweetheart,' he said. 'This is how it's going to go: whenever I come in, you're going to stand up. Got it?'

Laura clamped her lips together furiously. She was still aching from the headbutt, and taking orders from this arsehole was the last thing on her mind. And anyway – she couldn't. Not without help.

Buck nodded, as if he'd expected nothing less. He reached for the rope running through the eyelet by the door and tugged.

Laura felt her arms jerk into the air. Bound at the wrists and ankles, her body was being hoisted like a wet sack, stretching her upwards as the handcuffs cut painfully into her skin. Only once she was standing upright and her arms reached nearly to the ceiling did Buck stop pulling, tying the rope firmly to the eyelet.

'Your mother told me to look after you.'

'Did she also tell you to hang me up like this?'

He shrugged, but a smile played around his lips. 'It's your own fault. It didn't have to be like this.'

'I don't believe a word you say.'

Again, Buck shrugged his shoulders. His eyes looked her up and down. She wondered whether he'd take her away immediately, to the mansion – wherever that was – but decided not to ask. Better that he didn't know she'd overheard them. 'What do you want from me?' she asked instead.

'What do *I* want from you?' He seemed to be considering the question, as if he hadn't really thought about it. 'Well, like I said, your mother asked me to look after you.'

'But hanging me up like this? I doubt that's what she meant. So let me down.'

He raised his eyebrows. 'Well, will you look at that? Same tone as your mother. Probably runs in the family.' He gave a dry laugh.

Laura was silent.

'Y'know, now that I think about it, your mother didn't say very much about *how* to look after you. That bit's up to me. And you certainly won't get much help from your mother down here,' he added softly.

Until then Laura had simply been angry – at her mother and at being locked up – but now she was struck by another, thoroughly disquieting feeling. All at once, Buck seemed unpredictable. 'Why am I here?' she asked. 'What does my mother want?'

'I'm supposed to ask you a question,' said Buck.

Laura knew at once what it would be. She would never leave Berlin voluntarily, but given the current situation she had no choice. 'What if I said yes?'

Buck squinted, sizing her up. 'Not sure,' he said slowly, 'if I want to ask you yet. This is all moving too quickly for me.'

At first Laura thought she'd misheard. 'My mother wants an answer, and she wants it as soon as possible – trust me, I know her. So here's my answer: yes. I'll do it.'

Buck approached her, unhurried. 'You're saying yes to a question I haven't asked yet?'

'My mother already asked me herself. I'm saying yes. Now let me go.'

'There she is again – Ava's daughter,' said Buck, circling her. 'Every bit the lady of the manor. I could never stand that about her, did you know that?'

'Who *are* you? How do you know my mother?'

'Ha!' exclaimed Buck. 'Sounds like her. She never told you about me, did she? Well, you'll find out soon enough.'

Soon enough? She swallowed. How long was this imprisonment supposed to last? 'Whoever you are, please let me go. I told you: my answer is yes. Please tell her.'

Buck wiped his nose and prowled past her, his eyes sweeping across her breasts. 'You know, it's never good to let Ava get what she wants too quickly. I'll tell her you said no.'

Laura's blood ran cold. She was totally at the mercy of this arsehole, and of the simmering long-harboured rage he evidently felt for her mother. 'Sooner or later she'll find out you lied.'

Buck snorted. 'So? A deal's a deal. I'm not looking for brownie points.' He halted behind her. 'And the longer it takes, the surer I can be that *I'll* get what I want.'

Suddenly she felt his hands on her hips. She froze as his sweaty fingers fumbled at her waistband, then he yanked her trousers and underwear down to the tape at her ankles. Laura held her breath, pressing her legs and lips together. She wanted to scream, hoping her mother might hear her; yet at the same time she knew how absurd it was to expect help from her.

'Are you afraid?' Buck was standing directly behind her, breathing down her neck. She heard the clink of his belt buckle, its metal brushing her backside, and she flinched. Her muscles were so rigid that it hurt. Suddenly she felt something warm and fleshy sliding down between her buttocks.

'You've got a sweet arse. Behave yourself, or Uncle Buck'll be down every couple of hours. And I'll be putting in more than just my finger.'

Chapter Twenty-Eight

Berlin, 20 October, 10.34 p.m.

Jan had quickly switched off the light once he'd orientated himself in the room. It appeared he was alone in the flat – apart from the mice. The white one had now joined its grey companions in sheltering underneath a thick clump of wood shavings.

He'd stepped softly out into the tiny corridor and briefly switched on the light, glimpsing a bathroom and a narrow kitchen. In the kitchen window hung a colourful string of heart-shaped fairy lights. Far away, he could hear a siren.

Swiftly he rummaged through the wardrobe. The most suitable item seemed to be a woman's blue trench coat and a tweed flat cap, which he pulled down low over his face. His Belstaff jacket he stuffed hastily into a plastic bag.

His heart pounding, he stepped out onto the street. The fog enveloped him, and as the police cars whizzed past a minute later he silently thanked the man who had summoned them. Gandalf's killer would hardly have given up the hunt voluntarily.

Then he phoned Katy.

A few minutes later he was standing outside Greg's front door. *Gregor Wilke* was written in neat handwriting on a scrap of paper Sellotaped next to the bell. Jan looked around him one more time before pressing it.

Standing in the lobby, he inhaled that new-build smell. Smooth and fresh. It suited the all-American surfer boy, thought Jan, climbing the stairs to the second floor. Katy opened the door barefoot, wearing boxer shorts much too large for her and one of Greg's Hollister T-shirts.

With a jerk of her head she motioned him inside. As they stood in the hallway she hugged him. It felt good. The last time had been long ago. 'You're shaking,' she observed.

Jan grimaced.

'Did anybody see you?'

'Don't think so. You sure they're not allowed to keep tabs on you?'

'Quite sure,' said Katy, guiding him into the kitchen. The apartment felt bleak. Greg had only moved in six weeks earlier, and there were still piles of boxes in the hall. Only the kitchen was nearly finished, with a solid pinewood table in the middle of it.

'How do you know that?'

'Greg,' said Katy. 'He knows a bit about that stuff.'

Jan raised his eyebrows incredulously.

'Don't give me that look. Greg's OK.'

Jan did not reply. His legs were suddenly giving out. Supporting himself on the table, he sank down onto a chair.

Katy gazed at him in concern. 'Honestly. Don't let it worry you. I've got to be officially under suspicion before the police are allowed to monitor me or my phone. The fact that you're my brother isn't enough. Of course, your phone's another matter.'

'I chucked out the SIM card.'

Katy nodded, fetching a bottle of water from the fridge. With her left hand she adjusted Greg's boxer shorts. 'All right then. Tell me everything. Or would you rather wait until Greg's here?'

'Where is he, anyway?'

'Getting beer at the petrol station.'

Jan paused. 'Right. Are you sure?'

Katy gave him a long look. 'Listen, you're talking rubbish.' She put the water bottle down on the table in front of Jan. 'You don't seriously think he'd grass you up?'

Jan shrugged. His head ached, and so did his arms, shoulders and knees. Now that the adrenalin was dissipating came the pain. 'I don't know what to believe any more.'

'He's just on his way back from work. I called and asked him to bring beer. That's why he's not here yet.'

Jan nodded and glanced around. 'Fine. When I called I thought you were . . . at home.'

'Jan, please!'

'What do you mean, *please*?' asked Jan testily.

'You're acting like I owe you an explanation for just being here. If anything, you're the one who owes *me* an explanation. I lied to the police for you, remember?'

'I'm worried about the girls. This is pretty shitty for them,' he grumbled.

Katy took a deep breath, as if she had plenty to say that she nonetheless bit back. 'I can't be around them at the moment.'

'What do you mean? *You're* taking a break, and your kids just have to deal with it? I don't want to interfere, but—'

'You always do, though.' Katy's expression grew hostile.

'Have you forgotten what it was like? Or was it only *my* mother who took off?'

Katy bit her lip. All at once her hostility was gone. 'I can't be around them right now,' she said softly, 'because they remind me so much of *him*.'

It took Jan a few seconds to understand what she meant. 'That bad?'

Katy couldn't meet his eye. Her gaze was fixed on the floor, tears welling up. 'Sören's wrong for me. Just wrong, Jan. I can't explain it, but . . .' She broke off into silence.

Suddenly Jan felt mean. 'I'm sorry, I—'

'It's all right,' said Katy. 'It's all right.' She wiped away her tears with the back of her hand. 'But that's not why you're here, is it?'

'No.'

The front door opened, and a moment later Greg came into the kitchen, wearing a corduroy jacket, jeans and dark-brown Converse shoes. He had bags beneath his eyes, and his face looked haggard. Wearily he dumped a six-pack on the kitchen table. The noise echoed strangely in the quiet room. Suddenly it occurred to Jan that he didn't even know what Greg's job was.

'So there's the fugitive,' remarked Greg, without a shred of irony. He handed Jan and Katy a can of beer each, opening one for himself too. 'Let's have it, then.'

Clearing his throat, Jan told his story. Katy's eyes grew wider and wider. When he was finished he realised that he hadn't drunk a single drop of beer. He opened the can, and the air escaped with a loud hiss. The cold beer did him good.

'But what's the point of kidnapping someone then letting them go again?' asked Katy.

'Frankly, I have no idea. Him letting her go is just speculation, anyway. Maybe somebody helped her get out.'

'Sounds pretty unlikely,' murmured Greg.

Katy nodded. 'Do you think he's looking for her?'

'Guys like him don't look,' said Jan. 'They hunt.'

'And now he's hunting you too,' observed Katy.

For a moment there was silence.

'For him it's about Laura, not me,' said Jan eventually. 'He wants me to keep away from her.'

'Which you're not doing.'

'What are you trying to say?'

'Have you considered turning yourself in?'

'What about Laura?'

'I'm not thinking about Laura,' said Katy.

'Well I am.'

'If your brother turns himself in,' interjected Greg, 'then sooner or later he'll be pegged for two murders. First the neighbour, then this Gandalf bloke. His fingerprints will probably be on the grill and the bottle. It won't take long for the police to match them.'

'And that's proof enough?' asked Katy. 'I mean, this story has got to make the police reconsider. Laura has actually disappeared, after all, and her name was written on – what was her name again?'

'Nikki.'

'On Nikki's forehead. *NOT LAURA*. Then there's the video on the phone, and us as witnesses. There are some clever people in the police, they'll listen.'

Greg shrugged. 'It's all pretty thin. And so far none of the relevant facts are in Jan's favour. All in all, I don't think I'd risk it at the moment.'

Katy fell awkwardly silent.

'The most important thing is to find Laura,' said Jan. 'And I can't do that if the police arrest me. The way things stand, they'd definitely put me in custody. I'd be stuck in jail, and that psychopath could do whatever he wants to Laura.'

'Who is he? What do you think he wants with her?' asked Katy.

'I don't know.' Jan said nothing for a minute, thinking it over. 'But it seems to me that it's personal. Something to do with Laura's past. I just don't know what.'

'I still don't understand,' remarked Katy, 'why Laura didn't go to the police.'

'Apparently she doesn't trust them. That's what Gandalf told me, at least. She lived on the street for years, and who knows what happened to her out there. Then there's that business with the boarding school.' Jan shook his head. 'Somehow I can't shake the feeling that it's all connected.' He put the can to his lips and emptied it. Exhaustion crept into his eyes, and he blinked.

'This guy, this albino,' said Katy, 'he must be a total nutcase. Otherwise he wouldn't go running around the neighbourhood like that, would he?'

Jan nodded quietly. Something kept nagging at him. 'Do you know what he said to me under the bridge? *Forget about Laura. She'll never belong to you.*'

'So?'

'Well, for a start I think it's weird the way he talked about "belonging". He wasn't just saying it – he meant it seriously. In his head it's completely normal for someone to "own" another person. He thinks Laura belongs to him. That's why he's so angry with me – because he thinks I want to own her too.'

Katy said nothing, looking pensive.

'What's the other thing?' asked Greg.

'The other thing is that Laura is practically allergic to the whole concept of ownership. She's much too stubborn for anyone to imagine for more than five minutes that she "belonged" to them.'

Greg's mouth twisted. 'All I'll say is this: a thirty-minute ego trip in the supermarket loos without letting anybody know.'

'The main point,' continued Jan, 'is that if he's known her for a long time – and I'm fairly sure he has – then he must already realise that. But he doesn't care. He's steamrollering ahead regardless. He wants Laura for himself: she belongs to him, even though he knows it's not what *she* wants.'

'OK. But I still don't see how that gets us any further,' said Katy.

'It doesn't. Not directly,' admitted Jan. 'But it tells us how he's wired. He's probably extremely dominant. For him, owning and controlling someone seems to be normal. That speaks to a powerful urge to control and dominate, maybe even to a compulsion. His appearance backs that up. And as soon as that control threatens to slip away from him, he's ready to kill. That's pathological.'

'Pathological?' Greg frowned.

'It means he's ill,' translated Katy. 'One of Jan's favourite words. He learned it at uni.'

For a moment all three were silent. 'The albino thing,' she asked eventually, 'are you sure about that?'

'Well, only albinos have red eyes.'

'Didn't you say his eyes were only red for a split second?'

'People don't usually have red eyes – not even albinos, as far as I know. They lack pigmentation in the iris, which means that when light falls directly into their eyes it passes through largely unfiltered and bounces back as red. It's like the red-eye effect, only more intense. And for a second I got the impression that his pupils were trembling.'

'*Trembling?*'

'Do you have a laptop?' Jan turned to Greg.

Greg nodded and went into the next room. When he came back, he passed Jan an iPad. 'I assume this'll do the job.'

Jan nodded and opened the browser, typing in 'albinism' and clicking through the results. 'Here,' he said eventually. '*Dancing eyes*. The medical term is nystagmus. Most people with pronounced albinism suffer from it to a greater or lesser degree. Without proper pigmentation, too much light gets into their eyes, and they can't focus properly. That's why their pupils dance around like that, because they're constantly trying to focus.'

'But that would mean he's got bad eyesight, wouldn't it?'

'It says here that they generally only have a visual acuity of 0.1 to 0.5. Just enough to ride a bike – if that. It'd be easy to overlook pillars or bollards. And driving a car is out of the question.'

'But he did drive a car in France,' objected Greg. 'Think of the video on Laura's phone.'

Jan paused and considered. 'Yeah, his eyesight seemed pretty good to me too.' He scrolled further down the article on the iPad. 'It also says that albinism can manifest in very different ways, including in terms of vision and nystagmus. But, either way, he must have some sort of visual impairment.'

'Hm.' Katy looked from Greg to Jan. 'If he's really got albinism, then it might help us find him quicker. Plus he's got those distinctive tattoos, or whatever they are.'

'And how are you planning to do that?' Greg opened a second can of beer. 'There's no database of albinos.'

'Maybe at some university? Somebody doing a study?'

Jan yawned and shook his head. 'Way too complicated. Firstly we'd run into problems with data protection, secondly we'd have to find out which university might have done one, and thirdly, well, who knows whether our guy has ever participated in a study like that?' He reached for a second can, opened it and drank. 'If he genuinely is compulsive about control, as I suspect he is, then he'd never put himself in such an uncertain and open-ended situation. If I were in his shoes I'd rather live in hiding, somewhere secure that I could shape exactly as I liked.'

'Phew!' sighed Katy, gazing at him.

'What do you mean, *phew*?'

'Sometimes you're creepy.'

'Why?'

'Well, this Sherlock Holmes routine.'

Jan shrugged. 'I liked clinical psychology, at least at university. I just couldn't stand working at a clinic.'

'Might that be an idea?' suggested Greg. 'Asking around at psychiatric clinics?'

'We'd never get access to patient records. And who knows what part of Germany he's from.'

'So what now?' asked Greg.

Yawning again, Jan shifted back and forth on his chair. No matter how he sat, some part of his body ached.

'Now Jan's going to lie down,' said Katy. 'You look done in.'

There she is again, thought Jan, my big sister. This time, however, it felt nice. 'First I want to know what that boarding school was called, the one where Laura was.' Picking up the iPad, he went back to Google and typed in 'Nord' and 'boarding school'. 'I can't get that story about a death at the school out of my head,' he muttered. 'I think I'll have to see her again tomorrow.'

'Her? Who do you mean?' asked Katy.

'Ava Bjely,' replied Jan. Hardly had he said her name before he yawned again. He suddenly felt abruptly cold, and knew it wasn't just fatigue.

Chapter Twenty-Nine

Berlin, 21 October, 2.05 a.m.

Fucking *chaos*! Fjodor took one of the black make-up sticks from the jar. *Never* had his face felt or looked like this. Swellings, painful teeth, messy lines! Tonight he could have made everything right. He could have washed and celebrated his victory. And now this! It made him incandescent with rage.

The soap burned on his chafed skin. He washed off the smears on his chin, drawing new lines over the clean patch. What was the point of washing when things weren't right, before every line was in its place?

Ritual was ritual.

He *hated* that pussy.

Worse still, Laura hadn't reappeared. He'd been so sure that she'd go back to her flat. Yet, for some reason, she hadn't. Twice he'd been there in person and checked, phoning her landline at regular intervals and each time waiting, waiting, waiting for her to pick up. Just to pick up. That was all he wanted.

But she wasn't there.

Surely she knew he wasn't a threat to her any more. He'd made that more than clear with the wallet.

So he'd driven to the bridge by Teltow canal. And there, suddenly – *him*.

Just dropped into his lap.

First he'd got rid of the rubbish. As expected, the pussy had just crouched there like a moron and stared at the blood.

Exactly. A pussy. Incapable of action.

And then?

He could count himself lucky that the bottle hadn't broken – it might have slit his throat. As it was he'd nearly bitten off his own tongue, and his jaw was still aching from his teeth slamming together.

In hindsight he wondered whether the problem had been with his vision. Yet he saw almost perfectly. Better than all the others those doctors had tried to lump him in with.

He could still remember the visit to the ophthalmologist, although he couldn't have been older than eight or nine. Going to the doctor had always been a special event. Doctors wore white coats. Going to the doctor meant he didn't have to wear make-up, though he'd often get odd looks because of his dyed-black hair. His mother would simply shrug. 'It's what the boy wants.'

The doctor was a lanky man with thinning hair and horn-rimmed glasses. He'd wondered at the time whether someone with glasses like that should even be allowed to practice ophthalmology. How could you examine other people's eyes if your own were so terrible? He came to dislike doctors more and more, despite their nice white coats.

During the examination the doctor had kept muttering to himself. 'I don't believe it. It's just not possible.' Or: 'How very unusual.'

At the end of it he'd taken off his glasses and rubbed his tired eyes with his spidery fingers. 'Well, your son's a very lucky lad. He does have albinism, but I can't see any of the ocular defects you'd usually get. Hardly any, at least. It's . . . well . . . such a mild case is more than unusual. As I said, he's very lucky.'

Very lucky? How so, he'd wondered. The truth was the opposite. He was unlucky. Unlucky to have been born wrong. The fact that he could see quite well, especially when things were further away, didn't change that.

Fine. Later he'd understood what the doctor had meant. His eyes trembled only rarely, and when they did it was minimal. And issues with spatial vision? Also rare. His visual acuity was above seventy-five per cent.

The other twenty-five per cent he could make up for. Compensation. Anticipation.

But how the hell had he not noticed the bottle? Was it just the missing twenty-five per cent?

He felt his hatred growing minute by minute. That wretched parasite!

In the mirror he examined the lump underneath his chin.

It was all crying out to be put right.

For too long other people had made decisions for him, until he'd finally started calling the shots. He could still remember creeping back into the house after what had happened with Jenny.

He'd locked himself in the bathroom and stood in front of the mirror, wearing his father's white trousers, with the white shirt and black pattern on his face. He'd been high on his own virility, pumping himself dry. Then he washed that powerful person off his body, and Froggy re-emerged, bringing doubt, fear, shame, dismay.

In the morning his mother discovered black streaks in the sink and asked where her eyeliner was. He had no answer, not even when she found his father's white trousers in the laundry, and the white shirt.

The black streaks in the sink weren't so bad. Hair dye left black streaks too, and dying your hair was good.

Altogether worse were the white clothes. His mother hated white clothes. Once, as a child, he'd put on a doctor's coat from a costume set. He'd been happy, cheered by the thought that someone as important as a doctor wore such a very white garment. For a while he'd played doctor every afternoon – the coat was like a second skin. When his mother found out, however, she cut the coat into pieces, and he went two days without any food.

Eating had been difficult anyway, because eating and make-up didn't mix. Not for kids, at least. When he joined kindergarten at the age of four, his mother began to paint his face, making it darker. He had to look normal. Had to be allowed to feel like the other children, she said.

But when he bounced around at kindergarten, when he ate or drank and wiped his face with his sleeve or fingers, it would always spoil his make-up. He never noticed, but his mother had a sharper eye.

So he wasn't allowed to eat or drink anything at kindergarten any more. Playing and messing around in the sandpit were also too much of a risk. If he came home with his make-up smudged, there'd be no food until next lunchtime.

Only when evening came could he shower and wash himself white. After that he wasn't allowed to leave the house, and he quickly learned it was better not to leave his room either. His mother didn't want him in her sight. For a while he'd lain secretly on the stairs and watched TV. Until 26 December 1969, when his father had caught him there.

After that they'd locked his bedroom door at night, and there was nothing to do but stare at the blank wall. It wasn't until three years later that he'd found the magazines in the basement, hidden in a big box. Most of the girls inside were naked. He liked the pale blondes best of all. Gradually he started snipping out a few of them and tacking them up on his bedroom wall at night, turning his desk lamp towards them so that they glowed in the darkness.

Glowed, like him.

That way he'd been less alone.

It was high time to get Jan out of the way once and for all. He'd have to think it over carefully and make a plan, and that was best accomplished in solitude, surrounded by his closest family.

He hurried off. By the time he opened the door his heart was full of peace and calm. Mostly, anyway. Entering the gallery, he felt as though a whisper rippled down the rows. Reverent. Fearful. He switched on the light, and they all stepped almost literally out of the darkness. White and pale blonde. Humble and obedient.

Everything surrounding him was his.

Chapter Thirty

Berlin, 21 October, 9.47 a.m.

The morning was friendly, with a blue sky and low sun, as if the fog had wiped away all evil overnight. Even the icy house was radiant as a palace. The light fell through the iron gate, casting sharply contoured shadows on the road.

Jan opened the passenger door, got out of the Cherokee and nodded to Katy, who was at the wheel. Greg had let her borrow the car.

'Turned your phone to silent?' asked Katy.

Jan nodded. 'It's Laura's, remember.'

'And you're still sure you want to risk this?'

'Katy, we've been through this. Until they put me on the news, nobody's going to know they're looking for me. Why would she call the police?'

Katy shrugged. 'I'm just being careful.'

'All right then, big sister.' Jan smiled, although he didn't really feel like it. 'Call me if you see anything that looks wrong.'

'Isn't it usually the little one who's left as a lookout for the big one?'

'I *am* big,' replied Jan. He swung the passenger door shut with rather more energy than necessary, and looked at the house. Ava Bjely and her coldness repulsed him. But it was worth a try.

He stepped up to the gate and rang the bell.

After a while there was a crackle. 'Yes?' It wasn't Ava Bjely's voice. The home help, perhaps, thought Jan.

'Good morning. Jan Floss. I'd like to see Ava Bjely. I was here just recently. It's about her daughter Laura.'

'One moment.'

Crackle. Silence. A soft gust of wind blew through the gate, carrying a few withered leaves.

'Frau Bjely is not available,' announced the voice.

'Tell her there have been more deaths.'

'Excuse me?'

'The death at the boarding school – tell her I know about that. And now there have been more.'

Silence.

Then another crackle.

Laura was glad the night was over. She was lying on the mattress in the middle of the basement. A diffuse early light fell through the glass bricks. She would have liked to get up and walk around, but Buck had given the rope only just enough slack for her to lie down. It was too short to go to the wall or the door, so her range of movement was limited to a circle in the middle of the room.

She hadn't slept a wink all night. Her thoughts revolved endlessly around how to free herself and warn Jan. She was still desperate for a drink, too.

Shortly after dawn, she'd been racked with hunger. She'd tried to reach the water and biscuits, but the rope was too short for that, and only by stretching out her feet had she managed to shuffle them over. The bucket, however, remained out of reach. She'd put it by the pipe herself, and Buck had simply left it there.

For that reason she drank as little as possible, although she was parched. She was gazing longingly at the bucket when suddenly, very quietly, she heard voices.

'No. Tell him to clear off. I won't see him.' Her mother. Unmistakably. She must have been shouting, or else her voice wouldn't have reached Laura. She wished she could have unscrewed the top from the drainage pipe to hear better, but the rope made it impossible. So she held her breath and listened.

There was silence for a while.

Then she heard a second voice, further away, an incomprehensible murmur.

'What did he say?' cried her mother.

Again the other voice. Laura wondered where it was coming from. Maybe the front door?

'All right,' replied her mother. 'Open up and tell this Floss to . . .' The rest of the sentence was inaudible, but the name struck Laura like a bolt of lightning. *Floss*. Jan was here! She edged closer to the pipe, as close as the rope allowed.

The gate buzzed, and Jan stepped onto the property. At the open front door, Ava Bjely was waiting in her wheelchair, as straight as the pillars to her left and right. She wore black, the same as on his last visit, with the same bangles around her wrist and the same severe bun. This house was like a preserving jar. Behind her stood the home help. Fanny, if Jan remembered right.

'I've got to hand it to you, young man. You know what buttons to push,' remarked Ava Bjely.

'You leave me no choice,' replied Jan.

'There are people who claim I'm especially good at that. Follow me.'

Fanny made to roll Ava Bjely into the living room, but she waved her off and did it herself. 'You can go. See to my husband's rooms. I won't need you down here.'

Fanny nodded, and vanished without a word.

'We'll go over here,' said Ava Bjely to Jan, who had followed her. She pointed to the other end of the room, where a grey corner sofa stood. Jan sat down.

Ava Bjely rolled up to the low coffee table. 'What deaths?' she asked, without further ado.

'Did I frighten you?'

Ava Bjely snorted contemptuously. 'Do I look like I'm easily frightened? I'll ask again: what deaths?'

'I'm wondering why you care.'

'Young man, if you're planning to answer every question with a question, you'd better get out of my house right now.'

Laura hardly dared to breathe. Why couldn't she hear anything? Where was Jan? And where was her mother? Maybe they were speaking quietly. Or still standing at the door. She was on tenterhooks. The rope was taut as a bowstring; she'd come as close to the pipe as she could. She thought about screaming, in the hope that Jan would hear her sooner or later, but realised just in time that Buck would hear the screams too if he was around. And if Buck heard them *before* Jan, he'd come and shut her up.

She clamped her lips together. No. She had to wait until she could hear Jan's voice. Only then was it likely her screams would reach him – until then she mustn't make a sound.

She held her breath and listened. Nothing but the dull thud of her pulse.

'What if,' suggested Jan, 'we both answer a few questions. First you, then me.'

Ava Bjely gazed at him scornfully. She didn't like the situation one bit, but Jan could sense how curious – perhaps even worried – she was.

'So ask.'

'Why did you send Laura to boarding school?'

Ava Bjely ran her tongue over her incisors, as if cleaning out some unpleasant scrap of leftover food. 'What do you think? Why do parents generally send their children to boarding school? Because they're difficult. Laura *was* difficult. She always had been. But when she hit puberty, I couldn't control her any more. She cut class to roam around the town, and I was sure she was experimenting with drugs. She was going off the rails, as they say.'

'And that's why you sent her to Nordholm? Because of a few missed classes and experiments with drugs?'

'You're acting as if Nordholm were a prison. Have you ever been there?'

'I've seen pictures of the building online. But that's irrelevant. It could be the prettiest boarding school in the world – Laura didn't want to go.'

'Sometimes you have to force children to be happy.'

'Happy? Do you know what Laura said about it? "My mother fucked my life up."'

'Who told you that? Laura?'

'A friend.'

'Don't believe everything you hear. Most people fuck their own lives up. "We are each our own devil, and we make this world our hell." Oscar Wilde. But it's always nice and simple to pretend other people are responsible.'

'But why so suddenly?' asked Jan.

'How do you mean?'

'Well, normally people switch schools at the end of the year, or maybe the term. But Laura left in November 1992, towards the middle of the school year. Why?'

Ava Bjely gazed past Jan into space, as if searching for the answer there.

The silence hummed in Laura's ears. Jan, where are you! she begged. The handcuffs were cutting into her skin, and screams were already building up in her throat. She cursed the moment when she'd put the cap back on the pipe. Maybe Jan was already in the house, and she just couldn't hear him? Her gaze fell on the water bottle. Might that work? She picked it up, turned towards the drainage pipe, aimed at the cap – and threw.

The bottle missed the cap by a whisker, knocking instead against the pipe. A dull, hollow clang echoed through the room.

Jan's eyes flew to the kitchen, where he'd heard a sound. Ava Bjely, who was sitting with her back to the kitchen, didn't react. Only her eyes indicated that she'd heard it too.

Finally she shrugged and muttered: 'Fanny isn't getting any younger. Now and again she breaks things.'

Jan raised his eyebrows, wondering how Ava Bjely treated her employee. Would she deduct something from her pay? 'November 1992,' he remembered, picking up the conversation. 'Why did you change Laura's school?'

'It just seemed to be the right moment. There was no particular impetus, so far as I recall.'

Jan said nothing. It was clear she was lying. Something must have happened. 'And why not a school in Berlin? Nordholm is more than three hundred kilometres away.'

'I wanted her to have a fresh start, I think. Meet new people. In any case, there was nothing adequate closer to Berlin. This was 1992, relatively soon after the Wall fell.'

Jan nodded. It sounded plausible, yet he was certain she was leaving something out. 'Last time you said Laura was a sickness, and if she disappeared you wouldn't care.'

Ava Bjely gazed at him, her face expressionless. 'I didn't say I wouldn't care. I said if she never came back it would be better.'

Jan took a moment to digest her answer. What was going on inside this woman's head? 'I just can't figure out why you hate Laura so much.'

'Hate? No. I don't hate my daughter.'

'What, then?'

'You wouldn't understand.' Ava Bjely stared at the table. Her features had hardened.

'If you don't hate her, then why do you treat her like this?'

'Do you hate your birthmark?'

Jan hesitated for a moment. 'No.'

'But you'd rather be rid of it.'

He didn't reply.

'Because it's like a mark the devil has spat onto your face, and everything that's gone really wrong in your life is connected to it. Am I right?'

Jan swallowed. Suddenly he understood. Maybe Laura wasn't the cause of Ava Bjely's bitterness at all. He thought of Katy, and the two young daughters she couldn't bear to look at because they reminded her so much of Sören.

He surveyed Ava Bjely sitting there with narrowed lips. 'What is this really about? Your husband?'

It was suddenly silent in the room.

Above them there was a faint clatter, then Jan heard the heavily muffled sound of a vacuum cleaner.

'Leave my marriage out of this,' said Ava Bjely coldly.

'Why are you punishing Laura for a grudge against your husband?'

'God, you're self-righteous,' she hissed. 'What about your parents? Why do you think your mother left?'

Jan sat there, thunderstruck.

'Because your father's a pig? Do you think it's that simple?'

'Don't talk about my family,' blurted Jan.

'You're the one who started reopening that wound. So why do you think she left? Because your little brother died?'

'Stop.'

'Because you didn't buckle him up? Or is it more complicated than that?'

'Enough!' yelled Jan.

Wasn't that Jan's voice just then? Laura held her breath.

'I'm trying to save your daughter's life, for Christ's sake! Why can't you get that through your skull?'

Yes, it was Jan! Very clearly.

'Jan,' she screamed. 'Jaaaaaan! I'm here! Help!'

'I can look after my own daughter,' she heard her mother say, loudly and shrilly. 'I don't need some bloody moraliser coming here and telling me what . . .'

'Jaaaaaan!' she screamed with all her might.

'Your daughter's been kidnapped, and you couldn't give a shit?'

'JAAAAN! HELP! I'M IN HERE!'

'She hasn't been kidnapped. You don't know the first thing about my daughter.'

'I do know one thing. Someone like you should never have been allowed to have a child. What happened? Was it too late for an abortion?'

'Out!'

'JAAAN! Help!'

'Get out. Right now!'

No! thought Laura. Please, no. Don't go!

'JAAAN!' She tore at the rope. Grabbing the water bottle again, she flung it as hard as she could against the pipe. 'JAAAAAAN!' Her heart was racing, her vocal cords burning. But she had no choice – this was her only chance. 'JAAAAN!' Her voice tumbled over itself. Echoed.

She listened into the silence.

Hoped for an answer.

But none came. No sound. Nothing but her own pulse.

'JAAAAAN.'

Then came the panic: he might simply leave without hearing her. She screamed until her vocal cords were aching. Then she sank to the floor and began to cry uncontrollably.

'Jan,' she sobbed, drawing up her knees and burying her face in her hands.

Suddenly she heard the key turn in the lock. Full of hope, she raised her eyes.

The door swung open.

In the frame stood Buck.

He jerked the rope, and she didn't have the strength to resist. Her arms stretched painfully above her, she stood there defenceless and forlorn.

'What's all this? Why are you screaming?' asked Buck.

She tried to hold back her sobs, but couldn't quite manage it. She would have liked to shout and rail at him, but didn't have the energy.

'Didn't I warn you?'

She didn't reply, overcome by fathomless despair.

Chapter Thirty-One

Berlin, 21 October, 10.19 a.m.

Jan leapt into the Cherokee and slammed the passenger door. 'Drive, please. Quickly!'

Katy threw him a worried look and stepped on the accelerator. The diesel engine roared, and the car jerked forward. 'What's wrong? Did she call the police?'

'No. She didn't.'

'Why the hurry?'

'I just want to get out of here, OK?'

Katy exhaled noisily, but said nothing. Jan stared at the walls, fences and houses whizzing by. Now and again came the monotonous clicking of the indicator. Jan registered that Katy wasn't driving back to Greg's, but didn't bring it up. His mind was still full of Ava Bjely, and he wondered what could have happened to make somebody like that.

'Do me a favour, all right?' he said finally. 'Go and see Anna and Nele. Visit them.'

'Jan, I told you yesterday—'

'Spare me. Just do it, OK?'

Out of the corner of his eye, he saw her jaw tense. Her hands clenched the steering wheel, and tears came to her eyes. He couldn't care less.

He still couldn't imagine how Laura had survived such a mother. Psychiatrists had patients queuing up to talk about their parents. Some had suffered less than Laura, others even worse.

Somehow she'd come out the other side with a halfway healthy psyche, where someone else might have been crushed. Only the other week he'd been reading an article about it in *Psychology Today*. *Immune to Fate?* it was called. It was about resilience, a kind of inner strength that many people had, allowing them to survive even the most terrible situations. Clearly Laura belonged to that group. He decided to read the article again. First of all, though, he had to uncover more about Laura's past and the time she'd spent at boarding school.

The Cherokee jolted and Jan came out of his reverie. Katy had parked on the kerb. She opened the door and got out.

'What are you doing?' asked Jan.

'Buying make-up. And anyway, I need some fresh air.'

Make-up? Now? Before he could protest, Katy slammed the door. Jan watched her go, irritated. When she still wasn't back after a quarter of an hour, he decided to use the time and make a phone call. It took a moment for him to find the number and get put through; the conversation itself lasted barely five minutes.

Afterwards he tried to reach Katy. Unsuccessfully.

Only after another fifteen minutes did she reappear, carrying a shiny white bag with light-blue lettering. Jan closed his eyes and counted to three, trying to keep his annoyance in check.

'So?' asked Katy spikily. She was sitting back in the driver's seat. 'Perhaps *now* you'd like to tell me why you're so upset? Has something happened?'

Jan grimaced. 'I'll tell you on the way.'

'On the way where?'

'We're going to Schleswig-Holstein.'

'Where?'

'To Schleswig-Holstein, on the Baltic Sea. Not far from Flensburg.'

'That's at least five hundred kilometres!'

'Three hundred,' corrected Jan. 'If you don't want to come, you can get out.'

'And do without the pleasure of your company? Not likely. Anyway, this is Greg's car. He lent it to me, not you. We're going together or not at all.'

Jan smiled, although he didn't really mean it.

'I assume you want to go to the school?' asked Katy.

'That's brother-sister love, isn't it?'

'What is?'

'Not having to say very much.'

Katy looked at him with an expression he couldn't quite read.

'Why did you buy make-up?' asked Jan.

'For you.'

'For me?' asked Jan, taken aback.

Katy sighed. 'That brother-sister love thing only seems to work one way.'

'I don't get it.'

'Look in the mirror, Jan. What do you think is the first thing they'll see if we hit a police checkpoint?'

They stopped at the next large café and went into the men's bathroom. As they disappeared into the WC together, a man in his mid-fifties shot them a disapproving yet rather envious glance. Jan sat down on the toilet seat and tilted back his head. Katy tied his hair back from his forehead and busied herself with powder and foundation. It irritated his skin, and Jan found it hard to sit still, especially with the stench of ammonia and urinal cakes in his nose.

When Jan stood before the mirror above the sink, he saw a stranger gazing back at him. The birthmark had disappeared, bringing his eyes and the symmetry of his facial features to the fore. His port-wine stain had sometimes felt like a tedious magnet: when he was talking to people, he often saw their pupils dart down to it. But now there was nothing for them to dart to. His even complexion gave him a strangely smooth appearance.

His skin, however, felt stiff and tacky. He got the urge to scratch. Touching his face was out of the question. He thought of the albino's black stripes and wondered whether he felt the same – assuming they weren't tattoos.

'What happens if I sweat?' he asked.

'The woman at the beauty counter thought the foundation plus fixing powder combination would be practically waterproof. But I wouldn't take a shower in it.'

Jan nodded. 'Thanks.'

A few minutes later they were travelling north, before taking the A10 west. Jan told her about his encounter with Ava Bjely.

After three hours, shortly after Kiel, they turned off onto a smaller road. The landscape was flat, and the sun made the autumn leaves glow. In Eckernförder Bay, the Baltic lay smooth and calm beneath the cloudy sky. Picture-perfect weather. Having passed Eckernförder, they kept left. After a small patch of forest, they saw a green sign with a gold crest and the word *Nordholm*. It pointed left.

The narrow private road led towards the Baltic Sea. Trees fringed the road on either side, offering glimpses between them of a sports ground, outbuildings, tennis courts. The Cherokee stirred up golden leaves.

As the grand building with its early classical façade came into view on their right, Katy puffed out her cheeks. 'Pretty posh round here.'

'One of the best-known boarding schools in Germany,' said Jan. 'And one of the most expensive. I did a bit of research online.'

'How much does it cost to send your little nippers here?'

'Between forty and forty-five thousand per child per year,' answered Jan.

Katy raised her eyebrows. 'Laura's parents dug deep into their pockets, then.'

'Money was never the problem,' said Jan bitterly. 'They had more than enough of that.'

The pale gravel crunched beneath the tyres as Katy steered the Cherokee into the car park and pulled up. 'What now?'

Jan glanced at his watch. 'Just before three. In about half an hour we've got a meeting with Dr Breitner, the headmaster.'

Katy stared at him, baffled. 'You've got a meeting? When did you arrange that?'

'Earlier, while you were buying make-up.'

'And you got one the same day?'

Jan smiled. 'I said we were considering sending our children here, but first we wanted to see the place in person. Since I'm travelling abroad tomorrow and won't be back for a while, now is the only time that works.'

'I didn't realise you had any kids.'

'I don't, but you do. I used your name when I rang – hope that's OK.'

Katy's jaw dropped. 'My baby brother,' she murmured, giving him a look in which vexation and respect struggled to gain the upper hand.

Dr Peer Breitner was a rangy man with manicured fingers, an elegant complexion and a vigorously strong chin. Jan judged him to be in his late forties. His bearing was that of a person unlikely to go without a suit and tie even on the hottest days of summer.

'Welcome to Nordholm.' His pale-blue eyes scrutinised them alertly as he shook hands. Jan wondered why he didn't use their names. Not proper etiquette, perhaps. 'Please, sit down.'

Jan and Katy seated themselves before a white oak desk, the headmaster into a large leather armchair. Behind him, stacks of books were sorted by size and colour on a room-height bookshelf nearly five metres wide, while on the desk in front of him were a few well-organised files, a designer lamp from the Seventies, and a bronze sculpture of a man bowed beneath the weight of the globe on his back.

'I suggest,' he began, 'that you spare me your cock-and-bull story and come straight to the point. Why are you here?'

Jan, who'd just been about to say something, stopped short in astonishment. He made a quick calculation: clearly his only chance was to go full steam ahead. 'I have a few questions about a former student here.'

'You mean the student you mentioned as a reference during our telephone conversation?'

'Yes. Laura Bjely,' replied Jan. As he spoke he got the feeling it had been a mistake to mention Laura. Perhaps that was precisely what had blown their cover.

'To be frank,' said the headmaster, pursing his lips, 'I scarcely remember her. Surely your best course of action would be to speak with Ms Bjely herself. As a former pupil, she knows the school well.'

'I'd like to do exactly that,' replied Jan. He paused. 'But she's disappeared.'

Dr Breitner would not be drawn. His face betrayed neither surprise nor curiosity, merely reserve. 'In that case I would advise you to inform the police.'

'I would have.' Jan leant forward demonstratively. 'But then I heard about an incident that took place here at Nordholm.'

The headmaster almost imperceptibly wrinkled his brow. 'What incident?'

'It happened about twenty years ago.'

'Ah. I don't recall anything of particular note.'

'Do you really not remember Laura Bjely? Long brown hair, slim, almost thin, pretty face. She was fourteen years old when she arrived. Not the usual enrolment procedure: she left school in Berlin in November and came here.'

'Twenty years ago, you say? Listen, young man, that's a long time. Many pupils have come and gone through our gates since then. In those days I wasn't yet headmaster. Do you seriously imagine I remember everything and everybody?'

Jan smiled icily. 'Do you see the bookshelf behind you?'

'Excuse me?'

'The books. They're not organised alphabetically, but by size and colour.'

'I don't quite understand what you're getting at.'

'It's very simple,' said Jan. 'People with bad memories tend to arrange their books alphabetically. That way they're quickly and reliably to hand. Someone who organises their books by size and colour has to have much better recall. They have to know not just the author or title but the approximate size, shape and colour of the book. For novels, that's perhaps not so remarkable.

But the shelves behind you are full of academic books. Lots of very similar shapes and colours and titles.'

Dr Breitner surveyed Jan in silence.

'I'm sure you remember. After all, we're talking about a death on school grounds.'

'You may be right,' conceded the headmaster. 'But I have no intention of discussing it with you.'

'Clearly you didn't buy my story about wanting to enrol twins at the school. Correct? So why did you agree to see us?'

'It's not my practice to reject things out of hand. I prefer to form my own opinion first.'

Jan nodded. 'And it's about your reputation, isn't it? Better to hear someone out before taking a risk. And that's exactly the point.'

Dr Breitner raised an eyebrow and contemplated him sceptically.

'Twenty years ago a teacher here was beaten to death, and not long afterwards a student went missing. Kind of thing that might give rise to speculation. Imagine me going back home without getting any answers, and being so annoyed that I spread rumours online about the incident. Unpleasant rumours. Rumours that might come back to bite you.'

Dr Breitner's eyes had narrowed. 'Are you trying to black-mail me?'

'I don't care what you call it. I simply need a few answers. A woman has gone missing, and we're trying to find out what happened.'

'You won't get very far. Our reputation is spotless.'

'I'm afraid, Dr Breitner, that you underestimate the internet. Take United Airlines, for instance. In 2008 a false newspaper report about the company surfaced online, and within minutes their stock price had plummeted by seventy-five per cent.'

'We're not an airline,' replied the headmaster drily. His face, however, had blanched.

'Of course. It's a poor comparison. Especially since the newspaper saw the false report and recalled it, so the stock price recovered. But the rumours I'm going to spread about your school will multiply in places where you'll never control them or get them retracted. And I'm sure you'd rather not risk that.'

Dr Breitner looked at him stony-faced. Suddenly Jan wasn't sure he'd judged the situation right. What if the headmaster called the police?

'Fine. Ask.'

Jan exhaled. He felt Katy relax somewhat in the seat next to him. 'What exactly happened back then?'

'If I tell you, can you assure me it will go no further?'

'Absolutely.'

The headmaster sighed. 'Laura Bjely was a bit of a wild child. At first all you saw was a shy, reserved young lady from a good family. But she simply wouldn't do as she was told. She'd hear you out, yes, but if something didn't suit her she'd silently ignore it. As if she simply couldn't stand keeping to the rules. I liked her, but she was . . . well, frankly she was a nightmare. She would listen, and you'd think, fine, she understood, and then she'd go and do exactly the opposite. She should never have been accepted here, really. Even then we had a substantial waiting list. But the headmaster gave in to the parents' pleading, and made an allowance. It happens from time to time.'

'Presumably if the parents put a bit more money in the pot, I suppose?'

Dr Breitner said nothing.

'Did you meet her parents?'

'At the headmaster's request, I gave Frau Bjely a tour of the school so that she could get a sense of the place.'

'And? What was your impression of her?'

'She seemed deeply anxious.'

'Anxious?' asked Jan. That was the last thing that came to mind when he thought of Ava Bjely.

'Frau Bjely asked an extraordinary number of questions. About the security of the grounds, when the gates were open, whether the pupils' accommodation blocks were locked at night, whether the caretaker kept an eye on the pupils after dark . . . all sorts of things. She seemed to know her daughter very well.'

'What do you mean?'

'Well, as I said, Laura didn't pay much attention to the rules. She was frequently . . . absent.'

Absent. A nice euphemism for skiving or running away, thought Jan. 'And what about the death of your colleague?'

'Death.' Dr Breitner sighed and scratched his neck. 'Yes, well. I'm not sure I'd call it that.'

'Why not?' asked Jan, surprised.

'Well.' Headmaster Breitner placed his arms on his chair and shifted in his seat. 'Strictly speaking he disappeared.'

'How do you mean, "strictly speaking"?'

'The matter was rather complicated.' He cleared his throat. 'On the night our colleague disappeared, a student had absented himself from the grounds.'

'You mean he ran off.'

Dr Breitner winced visibly. 'You see, a runaway, as you call it, is someone who has absented themselves from the grounds and doesn't return. It presupposes a lengthy period of time. Benno Fröhlich – that was the pupil's name – was only away for one night. That's bad enough, of course, but . . .'

'OK, I understand,' interrupted Jan. 'Before we get stuck splitting hairs, perhaps you can tell me what actually happened.'

'Well, this Benno Fröhlich came back in the middle of the night, completely hysterical. It must have been about two in the morning. He reeked of cigarettes and beer, and the words just came tumbling out. He'd found Herr Nolte, he said, in the woods, dead, bleeding from a serious head wound. Someone had caved in his skull, he kept telling us. He was clearly in shock. I set off at once with some colleagues. Benno led us to the spot, but there was nothing there.'

'Why didn't you call the police?'

'Benno was drunk. I wasn't quite sure, and I didn't want . . . but then we discovered that Herr Nolte wasn't in his bed, nor in the building or anywhere else. And his clothes hung untouched in his wardrobe. Even his wallet was still there. And Benno had sworn blind that he was telling the truth. When Herr Nolte still hadn't appeared the following day, we went to the police. Herr Nolte has been considered missing ever since.'

'And there were no clues?'

'None whatsoever.'

Jan was silent for a moment, glancing at Katy.

'So what's the connection with Laura?' asked Katy.

'With Laura Bjely, you mean?' The headmaster gazed at her, puzzled. 'There is no connection.'

Jan thought of what Gandalf had told him, and Ava Bjely's reaction when he'd mentioned the death. 'There must be.'

'I don't know what it would be.'

'Did Laura and Herr Nolte know each other?'

'What a question. Of course. Every pupil knows every teacher here – and vice versa.'

'What kind of teacher was Herr Nolte?'

'He was . . . he taught art and PE, and sailing.' Dr Breitner looked out of the window, where a few sailboats were moored at the school's jetty in the distance.

'Unusual mixture,' said Jan. 'But I meant what he was like. Any foibles? Was he liked or feared by the students?'

'Liked . . .' Dr Breitner seemed to be considering the question. A fraction too long, Jan thought. 'Yes, as far as I recall.'

Jan gave the headmaster a sceptical look. 'But?'

'What do you mean, "but"?'

'Listen, Dr Breitner. Something's not right here. You say Herr Nolte vanished. But Laura, like Benno Fröhlich, said he was beaten to death. Do you know what else she said?'

'No.'

'She said he deserved it.'

Dr Breitner paled. He opened his mouth, then shut it again.

'Why would she say something like that if Herr Nolte was genuinely liked?'

The headmaster gazed out over the Baltic again, towards the white bellies of the boats. Then he sighed. 'You'll find out sooner or later. Herr Nolte . . . he pestered one or two of the female students.'

'He *what*?'

Dr Breitner avoided his gaze. 'As I said: he pestered some female students.'

'I'm not sure whether I fully understand you,' pressed Jan. 'What does *pestered* mean to you? Are we talking about verbally overstepping a few boundaries, groping, abuse or what?'

At the word *abuse*, Dr Breitner's expression froze into a mask. Yet he didn't deny it.

A chill ran down Jan's spine. What was the connection to Laura? Had Nolte harassed her? Suddenly he was filled with rage at the headmaster's stonewalling. 'So you're saying you had a teacher under your roof who was abusing schoolgirls. And you did nothing about it?'

'That's not entirely accurate,' said Dr Breitner. 'For one thing, I was still only deputy headmaster in those days. For another, we didn't know about it. I only found out four years later, from a former classmate, a psychologist. She treated Herr Nolte before he came here.'

'He was in treatment? For his sexual attraction to minors? And she broke doctor–patient confidentiality to tell you that?'

Red blotches appeared on Peer Breitner's cheeks. 'Herr Nolte had already been missing for several years. Basically . . .'

' . . . you both thought he was dead.' Jan finished the sentence. 'So it didn't seem that bad. Right?'

Breitner nodded reluctantly.

'Do you have a photograph of Herr Nolte?'

The headmaster stared at him for a moment, then got wordlessly to his feet and went over to the bookcase, where he picked up a book from a row of identical tomes on a hip-height shelf. It was a yearbook, with the number 95 embossed in gold beneath the Nordholm crest.

Flicking through a page or two, he laid the open book on the table in front of Jan and Katy. There were about a dozen photos on a double-page spread: students sailing, an evening party of some sort. 'We celebrate the beginning of sailing season every March,' said Dr Breitner. 'And this is Peter Nolte.' He tapped one of the photos with his index finger.

Jan leant forward and froze; he felt Katy do exactly the same beside him. Nolte was in his early thirties with an athletic build, not good-looking, exactly, but somehow attractive, with a pale skin tone that might simply be down to the flash. His right cheek was marked with two curving parallel scars.

The most striking thing about him, however, was his eyes. They were fixed directly on the camera – and they were red.

For a moment Jan was transfixed. Then he came to his senses. Of course his eyes were red: the picture had been taken with flash, after all, and Nolte was looking straight at the camera. So it didn't mean anything. Or did it?

Jan's gaze shifted to the girl standing immediately in front of Nolte. Her face was narrow and sensitive yet full of defiance, a face that had haunted his dreams for years.

Laura.

Jan raised his eyes and looked at Dr Breitner. 'Do you know whether Peter Nolte suffered from albinism?'

'Albinism?' Dr Breitner's eyes narrowed. 'What makes you say that?'

'Just a thought.'

'Albinism . . .' Breitner shook his head. 'Not that I know of.' He hesitated, and for a split second Jan got the feeling that something had struck him. But a moment later his face was blank again. 'I don't think so, actually. I'd have noticed, wouldn't I?'

Chapter Thirty-Two

Berlin, 21 October, 4.11 p.m.

Laura's stomach was still aching. On his last visit, Buck had thumped her in the belly as hard as he could.

She'd been crumpled on the mattress ever since, exhausted, shaken and deeply dejected. She couldn't understand how Jan had been so close without hearing her screams. At least there was one comfort, however: he was still alive.

Whatever the tattooed man had planned for him, he hadn't been able to carry it out, and a tremendous weight was lifted from her shoulders. She would never have been able to forgive herself if Jan had been harmed because of her.

Again and again over the last few hours she'd closed her eyes, unable to sleep, conjuring up those moments with Jan in Èze instead. His brown eyes. His birthmark. His lips. Her own heat, against the cold rain on her neck. And then that peculiar sensation of intimacy, of safety, of being welcomed home, which she felt whenever she thought of him.

Breaking in on her thoughts was the sound of the key turning in the lock.

The door opened.

Reality was back.

Preparing herself for what was coming, Laura sat up.

Buck entered the room and yanked the rope, making her stand up and stretch her arms above her head. Tying the rope firmly to the eyelet screw by the door, he surveyed the room.

Having discovered the drainage pipe last time, he'd stuffed it with insulating material so that Laura caught nothing of the conversations in the kitchen – and made absolutely sure that nobody would hear her if she cried for help.

Buck was evidently someone who learned quickly. And he still seemed to have enough respect for her mother not to dare lay a hand on her – apart from the blow to the stomach.

For the first time, Laura felt something like gratitude for her mother's presence.

'Have you spoken to her?' asked Laura. Her voice was grated raw from the screaming.

'Of course I have.'

'And?'

'She regrets very much that you haven't come round to her point of view,' said Buck mockingly.

'Fucking arsehole,' growled Laura, between clenched teeth.

Buck gave a pinched smile, grabbed the rope and tugged vigorously. The handcuffs cut into Laura's skin, and her shoulders felt about to burst from their sockets. She cried out in pain.

'Got the upper hand again, eh?' remarked Buck.

Laura panted as the pain ebbed away.

Then she noticed Buck unscrewing a red cap from a small, dark-brown bottle. 'It's time to move.'

Oh no, thought Laura, not the mansion.

'I'm looking forward to the pleasure of interacting with you a little more freely. I do feel a little . . . restricted . . . in this house, I must admit.'

'No matter what you have in mind, my mother will find out. Even if you take me to the mansion.'

Buck raised his eyebrows. 'Well, well, well. You know about the mansion?' His eyes wandered to the drainage pipe. 'Eavesdropping, were you? It won't help you. Do you seriously believe that your mother's just going to drop by after so many years of avoiding it like the plague?'

Laura bit her lip. How did he know so much about her mother? Things she didn't even know herself. 'Let me go,' she said. 'If you do, I'll give you the money my mother promised me.'

'That's a very gracious offer.' Buck nodded appreciatively, curling his lip. 'Money's great. Truly, it is. I'm very fond of it. But, sadly, it isn't everything. And I've always been the type to hanker after *everything*.' His eyes caressed her body. 'Why should I settle for the money? Day in and day out she ordered me around. Do this, stop that. God, I was so pleased when she had that accident. Paraplegic. I thought – now there's an end to her ladyship's high-handedness. Shit, was I naïve. Seventeen million they fobbed me off with. And the rest of it to her. The property alone was worth three times that. When I suggested I might get involved in managing the money, she laughed in my face. Whores were what I knew, she said. I should invest my savings there.'

Laura felt dizzy. She didn't understand what he meant, but clearly this was about more than just money. 'I . . . I can't help it if you have a problem with my mother. I've got a problem with her myself. I . . .'

'Who gives a shit whether you can help it? Is that going to be on some gravestone?' He cocked his head. 'I'm taking you with me. I'll do what I like with you for a while, then bury you in the forest or wall you up somewhere, and tell my stupid sister that you finally came to your senses so that I can get the money.'

Laura stared at Buck open-mouthed. *Sister?* The floor threatened to swallow her up. Buck was her mother's brother? She'd had no idea that her mother even had one. So *that's* what the money was about, the property. An inheritance.

As if he had all the time in the world, Buck moistened a cloth with the contents of the brown bottle. It smelled sweet.

Laura shrank back, but it was no use. With a grin Buck pressed the chloroform-soaked rag over her mouth and nose. Just before she lost consciousness, a wave of panic surged through her chest, taking her breath away. Her future wavered like a guttering flame before her eyes.

Waking up in an unfamiliar place.

Defenceless.

Dying.

Chapter Thirty-Three

Berlin, 21 October, 5.18 p.m.

Jan blinked. The sun was low in the sky, shining straight into the car. Katy squinted and flipped down the sun visor. She was hunched over the wheel, her eyes fixed stubbornly on the A24. There were still a hundred kilometres to go before they reached Berlin, and the Cherokee's V8 diesel engine hummed along at an even 140 kilometres per hour.

'Think Nolte's our psychopath?' asked Katy.

Jan examined Nolte's face on the photocopy. He'd got a picture of Benno Fröhlich, too, and his former address. His parents had lived near Munich. Finally he'd taken the name and telephone number of Dr Breitner's former classmate, the one who'd treated Nolte. 'I don't know,' said Jan. 'Going by the bone structure, and if I imagine him without hair, then maybe.'

'It would explain a few things, anyway,' said Katy, throwing a glance at the rear-view mirror.

'True. Maybe he was lying in wait for Laura in the woods. She fought back, and later Benno Fröhlich found Nolte and assumed he was dead. He ran up to the school, told Breitner, and everybody went to look for the body together. But Nolte wasn't dead after all. He couldn't go back, though, because he was afraid

Laura would talk, so he took to his heels and vanished, never to be seen again.'

'Then, years later,' continued Katy, 'he finds Laura and kidnaps her. But why wait such a long time?'

'Because she went to ground. Laura ran off shortly after that night, ending up back in Berlin and on the streets, according to Gandalf. Even if he did try to find her, it doesn't necessarily mean he succeeded.'

'Do you think it was coincidence that he bumped into her again?' Katy glanced again into the rear-view mirror.

'Bit too much of a coincidence, wouldn't you say?'

'Hm,' murmured Katy. 'Mostly I'm just wondering why he kidnapped her then let her go.'

'We don't know that he did. Maybe that wasn't how it happened. Gandalf said Laura couldn't remember.'

'OK,' said Katy. 'And what about your albino theory?'

'Albinism,' said Jan.

'Sorry?'

'It's called albinism.'

Katy groaned. 'My brother's being hunted by a homicidal psychopath, but we certainly can't forget technical accuracy, can we? You psychologists are nuts.' Her eyes kept darting to the rear-view mirror, then back ahead.

Jan acknowledged her remark with a shrug. 'If Nolte suffered from albinism, then Breitner must surely have noticed.'

'But Nolte probably wore make-up all the time, practically day and night.'

Jan gazed at the black-and-white photograph contemplatively. Nolte was gazing earnestly at the camera. His skin was shaved smooth, his complexion even. But Jan couldn't tell whether he wore make-up or not. 'It would fit the pattern of our psycho-path,' he muttered, then, more loudly: 'The man we're looking for makes categorical claims of ownership over people, and certainly over Laura. He's compelled to dominate and control, so the sexual molestation makes sense. He thinks he's entitled to use what belongs to him.'

'It fits with what must have happened to Laura in the woods,' added Katy.

Jan nodded.

'But what makes you say wearing make-up would fit the pattern?'

'Well, it's the same strict pattern of control he applies to other people – just turned on himself. He's probably got a very concrete idea of how things should be, for others and for him. And he enforces it. Obsessively. Down to the last detail. He can't do otherwise. A person like that would be expert at putting make-up on perfectly every single day, avoiding difficult situations, taking care not to smear it – if he did, it would be unbearable for him.'

'Is that what you call obsessive-compulsive disorder?' asked Katy, overtaking a lorry.

'I think it's anancastic personality disorder. That's a bit different. If you're OCD, you suffer terribly from your compulsions. You're a slave to them; they torment you. With anancastic personality disorder, on the other hand, you're convinced they're right. You're proud of them. And you can't understand why other people don't see it the same way. You're not a slave but a missionary.'

'A missionary,' murmured Katy absent-mindedly. Another glance in the rear-view mirror.

'Is there something back there?' asked Jan.

'Hm?'

'You keep staring at the mirror the whole time.'

'I'm not sure,' said Katy, 'but I think that black SUV has been tailing us since Nordholm.'

'What?' Jan looked right, into the wing mirror. 'I don't see anything. Can you move the mirror out a bit?'

Without having to think about it, Katy pushed a small switch on the door. Jan realised it wasn't the first time she'd driven Greg's car, and he wondered how long the two of them had been involved. The wing mirror jerked, then swung out with a whir to reveal the road behind them.

Jan saw the car immediately. A large black SUV, about a hundred metres behind them. The car in Laura's video had looked very similar. 'Since Nordholm? That's nearly two hours. Why didn't you say anything?'

'I didn't really notice until we started talking.'

'OK,' said Jan. 'Maybe we're seeing ghosts. Let's take the next exit and see what he does. But don't indicate, whatever you do, and leave the motorway at the last moment.'

Katy nodded apprehensively, taking her foot off the accelerator and lowering their speed to a hundred kilometres per hour.

The SUV kept its distance.

Silently they drove on. After two minutes a sign announced the Herzsprung exit in one thousand metres.

Katy continued to drive without slowing down, indicating or switching lanes. Only at the very final opportunity did she step on the brakes and turn abruptly right, directly into the bend at the bottom of the exit.

Its tyres squealing, the Cherokee obeyed. Jan was flung left by the centrifugal force. Out of the corner of his eye he saw the black SUV follow them. Without indicating. 'Shit,' he whispered.

At the end of the exit, the black vehicle came so close to them that they could see it clearly. A Range Rover with Berlin plates.

Katy's hands clenched around the wheel. 'What now?'

'Left, over the bridge.'

She nodded and turned off on the L18 towards Fretzdorf. The Range Rover followed them.

'What does he want from us?'

'No idea,' said Jan.

'Think it's him?'

'I hope not. Do you recognise him?'

'You mean, is it the same man as in France? I'm not sure. It was dark and raining like crazy.'

They drove around Fretzdorf in a wide arc. Ahead of them lay a long, straight stretch of road, forest to the left and right of them. The speedometer climbed to a hundred and thirty. Jan checked the wing mirror. The black vehicle was gone. Incredulous, he turned and looked over his left shoulder. What he saw made his heart stop.

The Range Rover had begun to overtake, driving onto the left lane diagonally behind them, and was rapidly approaching. The low sun flashed between the trees, blinding light whipping across the vehicle. The driver's face was shadowed by the light grey hood of a sweatshirt, but Jan didn't think he could see any black marks on his face. For a split second he hoped it would all dissolve into thin air, an absurd mistake, their agitation merely the distorted image of their fear.

Then he saw the window roll down on the passenger side of the Range Rover. The car was nearly level beside them, and the man reached for something that lay on the passenger seat.

'DRIVE!' yelled Jan. 'Step on the accelerator! Quickly!'

Katy jumped and the car swerved slightly – then jolted forward. The needle on the speedometer shot to one eighty, and the Range Rover fell back a few metres. 'He had something lying on the seat,' said Jan. 'Just don't let him come level with us!'

'What do you mean? *What* was lying there?'

'I have no idea. He's planning something!'

Katy was deathly pale, her knuckles white, and she was gritting her teeth. She swung into a soft bend to the left, and a signpost flew towards her. Rossow.

'Shit,' she said under her breath, moving into the middle of the road and stepping on the brakes. Going nearly a hundred kilometres per hour, she hurtled into the village. Katy braked again. Ninety, then eighty. The SUV kept tailing them, but stayed a few metres behind.

'He wants to get us outside the village,' said Jan.

'To get us? What do you mean, "get us"?'

'For fuck's sake, I don't know. All I know is that he's planning something.'

The houses flew by, then the signpost on the outskirts of the village. Ahead of them was the next long stretch of road, and Katy stepped determinedly on the accelerator. One sixty, one eighty, two hundred . . . at that speed the road shrank to a narrow bottleneck. Jan's stomach turned. Memories tumbled over him: the accident, the empty child seat, Theo's small body.

Ahead of them was the back of a red Mazda. They shot past it and moved back into their original lane as if it were a stationary obstacle. Two oncoming cars whizzed past them. Jan couldn't help but think of the collision speed: we're going two hundred, they're going one hundred, so three hundred kilometres per hour.

The Range Rover was practically glued to their rear bumper, but Katy gave it no opportunity to overtake or draw level with them.

'What do you think he's got? What's he planning?' asked Katy again.

'I don't know, maybe a gun?'

She raced towards the next village. Rägelin. Katy stepped so sharply on the brakes that Jan was afraid the Range Rover would drive into them. But nothing happened. As it had done in the previous village, the car kept its distance. They were doing eighty through the sleepy village when Jan suddenly noticed the camera. It was on a tripod to the right of the roadside, half hidden behind a car door.

'Brake, there's a—'

A garish red light flashed. The black car behind them slowed abruptly. Two hundred metres further down was a police car. A uniformed officer stepped out into the road, brandishing a red signalling disc.

Katy puffed out her cheeks, snorted, braked and moved right. The Range Rover came closer and closer, then passed them without being stopped. The black bumper disappeared around the next bend in the road like an evil spirit. Jan imagined him pulling into a side road and lying in wait, some sort of weapon on the passenger seat.

Through the windscreen, Jan saw the policeman approach. 'Is the make-up still OK?'

Katy surveyed him briefly and nodded. As she shifted the gearstick into neutral, Jan saw that her hand was trembling. She rolled down the window; the officer came up to them and looked inside. He was blond, with flawless skin and a crew cut, his cap positioned perfectly on top of it. Young, attractive, dynamic. Keen grey eyes. A man with ambition, thought Jan. The policeman's eyes rested on him for a long moment, as if he'd detected the make-up and was considering what it might imply. Then his gaze flitted across the interior of the car.

'Good afternoon. Name's Sänger. Traffic division.' He gave Katy a reproachful glare. 'You were driving too fast. Are you aware of that?'

Katy pulled a contrite face. 'Sorry. It's not my car. In a big box like this it's so easy to lose track of your speed.'

The policeman looked at her suspiciously, as if to say he'd seen that helpless-woman act plenty of times before. 'Whose car is it, then?'

'My boyfriend's.'

'Ah. Then I'd like to see your driving licence and vehicle registration, please.'

Katy drew her licence out of her wallet. Jan was profoundly relieved that he hadn't been driving. He almost never carried his licence – although today that didn't matter. With or without a licence, as soon as his name was checked he'd be arrested for sure.

'And the vehicle registration documents?'

'I'm sorry, I don't have them. They're with my boyfriend in Berlin.'

'Ah. And who is the gentleman beside you?'

Jan froze.

'Er – I don't quite understand,' said Katy. 'Does that matter?'

Wrong answer, thought Jan, shrinking into his seat. The seatbelt felt much too tight.

The officer gave Katy a searching look. 'If you put it like that, then yes. You wouldn't be the first person to take a stolen luxury vehicle over the border into Poland.'

Jan saw the next question coming.

'What's his name?' he asked, looking at Jan.

'Who do you mean?' asked Katy.

He stared first at her then back at Jan, who felt as if the man had seen the make-up and taken exception to it.

The officer coughed. 'I mean the owner of the vehicle.'

'Greg,' said Katy. 'I mean *Gregor*. Gregor Wilke. He lives in Berlin.' She gave him the exact address, complete with phone number.

The officer jotted it all down carefully and gave a military nod. 'Excellent. We'll check.'

'Can you do me a favour?'

The officer raised his eyebrows.

'If you call him, please don't say that I . . .' She jerked her head at Jan.

The policeman's expression gave no indication of whether he agreed to the request or not. His eyes rested on Jan once more, then he took his notebook and Katy's licence back to his patrol car.

Jan groaned and leant back in his seat. He was unbearably hot, and the make-up on his skin felt like glue.

'That was close,' remarked Katy.

'It still is. If he checks your name, he might find me.'

'Doubt it. Bengtson? There's no connection. Or does your licence give your birth name too?' Suddenly she felt unsure. 'Do you know?'

Jan shook his head apprehensively. 'I never looked. Doesn't apply to me, anyway.' He glanced across at the patrol car, where the officer and his colleague had put their heads together.

'Think he's waiting for us?' asked Katy.

'The guy in the Range Rover? It's possible.'

'Does he want to kill us?'

'I don't know. Maybe.'

Katy said nothing for a moment. 'Did you recognise him?'

Jan shook his head. 'He doesn't have any black marks on his face.'

'But it's him, isn't it?'

'Must be.'

'That means it's not tattoos but black make-up or ink?'

'Careful.' Jan gestured towards the patrol car. The policeman had got out and was coming towards them, this time with his colleague.

He gave Katy back her licence. 'So, Frau Bengtson, your details check out. There's still the speeding violation, however. Allowing for a margin of error, we measured a speed of seventy-nine kilometres per hour, twenty-nine more than you're allowed.'

Katy nodded respectfully and paid with her debit card, while the other officer stepped back out onto the road and flagged down a bright-yellow Golf.

Katy started the engine and closed the window. 'What now?'

At a single stroke, the fear was back.

Jan peered ahead, to the spot where the Range Rover had disappeared. 'Turn and go back a bit,' he suggested.

'To the motorway?'

'No, not that far. There was a fork in the road before then.'

Katy nodded, spun the wheel and did a U-turn. Jan kept his eyes firmly on the wing mirror. The policeman was standing on the side of the road, gazing after them and growing rapidly smaller. Nobody followed them. Katy turned right twice, then left, following the K6811 out of Rägelin towards Frankendorf. Jan turned and watched Rägelin disappear. The road was virtually straight; best of all, it was empty. No Range Rover. Nobody at all.

Yet he felt no relief. The whole situation had turned into an all-consuming nightmare. He looked over at Katy, who was sitting ashen-faced behind the wheel. 'Everything all right?'

'I'll be OK.'

She turned right without indicating, her gaze fixed on the road.

'Thank you,' said Jan softly.

'It's fine. I only have one baby brother.'

He swallowed.

A couple of trees flew past on the edge of the road.

'Think he'll try again?' asked Katy.

He was silent, not daring to speak.

'Jan?'

'Hm?'

'Is she really so important to you?'

'I can't stop now.'

'That's a yes, then,' she said flatly.

'Yes. She is.'

'You barely know each other.'

'It doesn't feel like that, though.'

Katy sighed. 'You do know it's not your fault she's missing, right?'

Jan nodded.

'Same goes for the accident, too. And Mum's vanishing act.'

Jan nodded again.

They were driving past a leaden lake, which appeared blue on the GPS.

'What do you want to do now?' asked Katy.

'I have a sort of idea,' he murmured, reaching into his jacket pocket and taking out Laura's phone. 'But first I'm calling that psychologist.'

'What psychologist?'

'The one who treated Nolte.'

Chapter Thirty-Four

Berlin, 21 October, 5.49 p.m.

'Shit. Answering machine,' growled Jan in an undertone. He left Laura's telephone number and urgently requested her to call him back. 'Would've been too convenient.' He stared through the windscreen. By now they were back on the motorway, heading for Berlin, and it had begun to drizzle.

'What about your idea?' asked Katy.

'Hm?'

'You just said you had an idea.'

Jan nodded absent-mindedly. 'More of a thought, really,' he said slowly. 'Assuming this psychopath does have albinism—'

'I thought you were sure?'

'Yes, yes. I basically am,' he said testily. 'So, let's say he *does* have albinism . . . and let's say, too, that he *doesn't* have tattoos on his face but puts those black marks on with make-up instead . . . what does that say about him?'

'He doesn't want to be recognised.'

'Hm. Perhaps. But then wouldn't it be more sensible to make yourself look normal? Blend in with the crowd? I think it's more that he doesn't want to be himself. He wants to be somebody else. He's painting *over* himself. Reinventing himself.'

'You mean he doesn't want to hide?'

'No, he does. He's hiding by becoming someone else.'

'Sounds a bit far-fetched,' murmured Katy.

'And this won't have been a recent development. These disorders tend to manifest in childhood or during puberty,' continued Jan. 'Do you know what that means?'

'Frankly, no.'

'Imagine someone like that at school! A kid with albinism is always going to stick out, and a weird one even more so. He would've been an oddball, for sure. Most likely he was bullied. No matter what school he went to, he would have been conspicuous.'

'You think we'll find him through the school?' asked Katy sceptically.

'He must have gone somewhere. Germany doesn't allow home schooling.'

'But where? We can hardly comb through every school in the country.'

'I think focusing on Berlin will be enough,' said Jan. 'One of my university friends works at the Educational Psychology Service in the city. It's the first port of call for cases like that.'

For a moment Katy didn't speak.

Jan gave her a sidelong glance. 'What are you thinking?'

'Do you have his phone number?'

'I don't, unfortunately. We should drop by. Now, ideally.'

Katy gave him an amused look. 'Do you know what time it is? It's a public sector office. They've got set hours.'

Jan glanced at his watch and swore. Just before six. He always forgot about set hours: in market research and in advertising, working late into the evening was the norm.

He picked up Laura's mobile, rang directory enquiries and was put through. A deep, husky woman's voice picked up: 'Berlin Educational Psychology Services. This is Frau Küttner. Good evening.'

'Good evening. My name's Floss. I'd like to speak with Eckhard Bär, please.'

'I'm sorry, but he's already left. Can I help?'

'Erm. I . . . I'm not sure. Yes, maybe. I'm doing a survey of people with albinism as part of my doctoral thesis,' he lied. Katy threw him a look and raised her eyebrows. 'I'm sure you can imagine how difficult it is to find participants.'

'Goodness, however did you hit on *that* idea?'

'Ha, don't ask!' laughed Jan. 'I'd change topic if I could, but I've already missed the boat on that. My advisor is absolutely obsessed with the idea.'

'Herr Floss, even if I wanted to help you, I obviously can't go giving out addresses – especially since I don't have any to hand at the moment. Perhaps you could put a flyer in the lobby?'

'But what about older cases?'

'Older? How old?'

Jan's mind raced feverishly. He'd only caught a brief glimpse of the man beneath the bridge, and the marks on his face had done a good job of disguising his age. 'The Seventies or Eighties.'

She laughed. It was a sound that had seen a lot of bars and ten thousand cigarettes, and he pictured a woman in her mid-fifties. 'You're asking the wrong person, then. I've only been here six years. And our records from those days were destroyed ages ago.'

'Would there be anyone on your team who might recall?'

'Someone with the memory of an elephant, you mean? That stretches back thirty or forty years?'

Jan sighed. The irony in her voice was unmistakable. 'I understand. It's more than a little unlikely,' he admitted.

'If you'd called three years ago, I would have put you through to our head of department, Dr Maria Hülscher. But she's retired now.'

Suddenly Jan was fully alert. 'Your former head of department? Could you give me her telephone number?'

Again, the hoarse laugh. 'Won't help you much.' Her voice suddenly turned grave. 'Dr Hülscher is in a care home now. Suffering from dementia.'

'What's the name of the home?'

There was silence on the other end of the line, and instantly Jan was kicking himself for blurting it out like that. Why hadn't he been more subtle?

When the woman gave him the name anyway, contrary to expectation, it felt like a punch to the gut. He thanked her mechanically, then hung up and closed his eyes.

Please, no, he thought. *Please, no.*

'It's crazy how well you can lie,' he heard Katy say. She sounded several miles away. The asphalt whispered beneath the Cherokee's tyres, and the headwind whooshed as if blowing straight through his brain. He kept his eyes closed and the phone in his motionless hand.

'Everything all right?' asked Katy, worried. 'Do you have an address?'

'Yes,' answered Jan tonelessly.

'Well? Don't make me drag it out of you word by word.'

'Dr Maria Hülscher is in the same home as Dad. The Blankenburg Residence.'

Chapter Thirty-Five

Berlin, 21 October, 7.18 p.m.

Laura was still woozy from the chloroform. Her head ached. Her surroundings were unbearably cramped: she lay hunched on her side, bound at the hands and feet. Darkness shrouded her like a bad dream. Everything was vibrating, and with each bump her head struck thinly upholstered metal. Suddenly gravel crunched beneath the tyres. It sounded as though the tiny stones were rubbing against her skull.

A faint scrunch, then the vehicle pulled up. It jolted, as if Buck were unloading something. Doors slammed. Then the boot opened.

Instinctively she closed her eyes. She was awake, but didn't want him to know. Buck – her uncle. The thought made her nauseous.

She hadn't known who he was, but she'd known from the beginning *what* he was. She'd met his type before, on the street. Blotchy skin, brittle yellow fingernails, bad teeth, burst blood vessels in the eyes. Alcohol, bruised pride and a cynicism force field three miles deep. She'd woken up in a pool of her own vomit too often not to recognise a part of herself in him – a part of the person she used to be.

At least, she hoped so.

She was grabbed by two hands. His armpits smelled of sweat. He yanked her rather than lifted her out of the boot.

She fell to the ground, her head smacking against the gravel. Or were they pebbles? Small, sharp stones poked at her skin. Pain and irrepressible rage welled up inside her. More than anything she wanted to punch and kick him.

For a moment everything was still.

She knew he was standing there looking down at her, gloating, as she lay crumpled and vulnerable at his feet. Then he hoisted her face-up onto a kind of frame.

A second later, the top end of the frame was raised a little. Her bare feet touched a chilly metal surface. She felt him tie ropes around her ribcage, belly and thighs, panting, and at one point he adjusted the position of her feet with cold, sweaty hands.

Once he'd fastened her properly, he grabbed the top of the frame, lifted it and pushed her jerkily forward. A handcart, she thought. He's tied me to a handcart. Cautiously she opened her eyes.

In front of her was a generously proportioned period building, two storeys, with an orangey-red tiled roof, dormer windows and a dirty grey façade. The entrance was a heavy wooden door, a monstrosity in oak or walnut, dark brown and imposing, with a few steps leading up to it.

Behind her, a crow cawed as it came flapping out of a tree. Buck turned the handcart around, pulled Laura backwards up the steps. He unlocked the door and rolled her into the hall. There was a dull bang as the door swung shut, and her chest tightened.

Buck left her facing the doorway and went into the house. Behind her back she could hear a bunch of keys jangle, then Buck rattled a doorknob. Not the right one, evidently. He growled in irritation, trying other keys. But none of them seemed to fit.

'Fucking hell.' He came closer, and she rapidly shut her eyelids. Grabbing the handcart roughly by the handles, he made a quarter turn, then hauled her up a step. Then another, and another. More stairs. She opened her eyes to see an entrance hall clad in dappled marble. Crescent-shaped staircases soared upwards on either side, leading to a gallery. Beneath the gallery was a closed door; on the upper level, however, a corridor led further into the building.

With every step, the frame dug painfully into her back. Buck's huffing and puffing mingled with the squeaking of wheels on marble. Reaching the top of the staircase, he paused briefly to catch his breath before continuing down the corridor.

There was no marble here, only bare concrete covered with dust and fragments of concrete, as if the first floor were suspended in a near-final phase of construction. To her right was a service lift in polished grey. Then, on either side, a series of numbered doors.

At the end of the corridor, outside the last door on the right, Buck stopped. This time the key fitted.

He pushed her into the middle of a stark room, cut her off the handcart and let her fall, still bound. As he left the room without a word, out of the corner of her eye she thought she saw him flick back the blade of a Swiss Army knife. Gandalf's knife.

Laura scanned the room. A bricked-up window, a light bulb on the ceiling. Nothing else. Not even a mattress.

Five minutes later he was back, bringing a heater, toilet paper, water, the drill and other tools.

She no longer made an effort to hide the fact that she'd regained consciousness. His eyes flashed when he noticed.

'Look at that. Back with us, eh?'

She already knew what was coming next. The screeching drill, eyelet screws in the ceiling and the wall, handcuffs, ropes.

'Up you go!'

Her hands were wrenched upwards. The rope twitched through the eyelets and jerked her mercilessly to her feet, until she was standing on her tiptoes. She groaned and swayed.

'How long have you been awake?' asked Buck.

She made no answer. What would be the point?

The blow struck her right cheekbone with such force that her head flew sideways. Then he hit her from the left, and she cried out in pain.

'Finally,' he snarled. 'There's no one to keep me in check. Nobody to hear you scream.' He looked at her, waiting for a reaction.

She didn't want to give him the satisfaction.

He rubbed his fist with his left hand, then slammed it into her stomach so that she doubled over and the handcuffs tore at her wrists.

'Do you know how crazy this is?' Suddenly he was giggling. 'You've got *her* to thank for this. The very woman you've inherited your nasty temper from.' He surveyed her from head to toe. 'All you got from your father was dark hair. Apart from that you're a carbon copy of her. A copy of a piece of shit.'

Buck tore at her top with both hands, but couldn't rip it off, which only seemed to make him angrier. He picked up the drill, switched it on and pointed it at Laura. First between her breasts, then, lowering the tool, between her legs. The polished steel drill was spinning barely a centimetre from her groin.

Laura tensed, frantically trying to find purchase with her toes and keep her balance, so she didn't sway to and fro.

'Shall I drill down there?' asked Buck. 'I've drilled my fair share of cunts. For a while I did nothing else. Three or four in a night sometimes. One time, in Amsterdam, I hired the whole damn whorehouse. Cost a fortune. Worth it, though. All of them just for me.' He laughed bitterly. 'Yeah, well. These days I eat dirt. And your mother's sitting on her fucking money. She could give me some of it, you know, but she won't. Acts like I don't exist, all high and mighty with her shitty morals. Practically the only thing she didn't do was dig out our mother's old cross and hang it on the wall.'

He held the drill very close to her face. 'And since those golden days are gone, I've got you. Least that way it feels a bit like *she's* paying for it.'

He tugged her top over her head, so that she could see no more than vague outlines through the cotton. He held the body of the drill right next to her ear, running it on the lowest setting. It crunched as if the gears were grinding bone.

Then the sound ebbed away.

The motor stopped.

A moment later she felt the cold steel of the drill bit against her left nipple. Although she couldn't see, the image was clear in her mind's eye: a spiralling, sharp-edged drill pressing into her breast, creating a hollow down to the ribs above her heart.

'My finger's on the trigger,' he whispered. 'And I wish *she* could see me now. Feel what you feel.' It didn't sound like he was talking to her at all. He was talking to himself.

Laura shivered. Inside her raged a hopeless chaos of fear, rage, bottomless exhaustion and wildly firing neurons. Tears welled up in her eyes.

Suddenly he took the drill away.

Instead he hit her. Holding back, as first, then with more and more abandon. On her bare stomach. On her breasts. On her fabric-covered face. In the gut. Tears ran down her cheeks in streams and into her shirt.

'Where is it now?' he roared. 'That Bjely arrogance? Eh?'

She clamped her quivering lips together, bracing herself for the next blow. He seemed to be waiting, as if tormenting her with her uncertainty.

All of a sudden the rope from which she was hanging relaxed. She staggered and fell.

'I'll be back,' he purred. 'And each time I'll take away more of your arrogance.'

She heard the wooden door slam into the frame, the key turn in the lock. Then she was alone.

With trembling hands she pulled her top back down and wiped her wet face. The salty tears burned on her skin. Her eyelids sore, she blinked in the stark light of the bulb.

Chapter Thirty-Six

Berlin, 21 October, 9.23 p.m.

Jan and Katy had parked the Cherokee outside Greg's front door. Katy had insisted, because she knew Greg needed to use it that evening. Then they took the underground to Blankenburg station.

The sky had clouded over, the temperature plummeting so abruptly that Jan shivered as they walked down Bahnhofstrasse.

It's *him*, he thought, not the cold.

The prospect of seeing his father made his innards twist. He knew he'd have to keep his emotions under wraps if he wanted to get through the meeting. If he'd had a neuroleptic in his pocket, he would have considered taking it to dull his nerves.

'We're here,' said Katy. A large sign marked the entrance to the grounds of the Blankenburg Residence. Four garish halogen lights bathed the sign in light.

'Do you really think we need him?' asked Jan.

Katy nodded. She knew how Jan was feeling – she could see it in his suddenly stiff and awkward movements. 'It's half nine. No one's going to let us in to see a senile patient, especially since we're not relatives. It'll be different with Dad.'

'Maybe we simply say we want to visit him, saunter in, and with a bit of luck we'll find Maria Hülscher by ourselves.'

'You really think this is a good plan? She's senile, remember.'

'It's worth a shot. With senile patients their long-term memory often works best. She may not remember where the toilet door is in her room or whether she's switched off the water, but the things from the distant past – those she can probably still recall.'

They turned down the path that led to the main block. Out of the night sky, the first few raindrops fell.

The care home was a rambling, four-storey building with large glass windows, which had been built six years earlier beside the Berlin-Pankow Golf Resort by a property fund. The left-hand wing housed small apartments for the active retirees like Karl Floss, Jan's father. In the right-hand wing were those who needed constant care, Maria Hülscher presumably among them. The two halves were separate from each other, although they were run by the same agency. On previous visits, however, Katy had seen connecting doors between the two wings.

They entered the foyer and walked past reception, a rounded wooden counter staffed by an equally rounded woman with a buzz cut.

'Good evening.' Katy nodded to her.

'Good evening, Frau Bengtson. You're visiting late.'

'Don't worry,' smiled Katy. 'I know the rules. And my father's never considered half nine to be late.'

The woman returned Katy's smile like a mirror.

Jan wondered how often Katy came here, and was immediately pricked by his conscience – a feeling he'd sworn to himself his father would never prompt in him again. His pace automatically quickened.

As he climbed the stairs, he pondered again how best to find Maria Hülscher's room. They could hardly ask a nurse. Maybe another resident?

'Turn right,' said Katy behind him, as they reached the second floor. From the corridor to their left came a muffled jumble of different TV programmes. The laminate looked like beechwood parquet. Wall lamps threw tasteful pools of light onto the wallpaper.

To their right were the lifts, and beyond them the door to the other wing. Jan had just put his hand on the wide, round plastic handle and was about to open the door when there was a gentle *ping*. The matte steel door of the lift in the middle slid aside like an electronic curtain. Behind the curtain stood his father.

Jan stared at him.

His father stared back with tired, anxious eyes, like Jan's apart from their advanced age and the dark rings beneath them. Unlike in earlier days he was badly shaven, his thinning hair rather too long, his cheeks sunken and lined. It felt bizarre to see him suddenly appear like that – on the other hand, it was typical of his father to show up precisely when he was wanted least.

'What the hell are you doing here?' asked Karl Floss. His voice was brittle and nasal, as if he had a cold. His eyes shifted, and he noticed Katy.

'Hi, Dad,' she said. Her attempt to sound insouciant failed miserably. 'We're looking for someone.'

'I was asking Jan.'

'We're looking for someone,' repeated Jan.

His father scanned his face, his eyes narrowed, as if seeking something. 'Did you remove that thing because of the police?'

It took Jan a moment to realise what his father meant. Then he nodded. 'So they called you too?'

'Didn't Katy tell you?'

'Yeah. She did.' He'd just forgotten.

'Could you please explain to me what this is about?'

'Dad, please,' interjected Katy. 'Let's not fight. Not here.'

'I'm not fighting.'

There was another *ping*, and the lift door closed again. Jan saw his father raise his cane and stick it in the crack. The movement was sure and accurate, although the long stick was visibly trembling in his hands. The door met the wooden stick, hesitated briefly, then opened again.

Karl Floss muttered softly and stepped out of the lift. 'If you're not here for me, then who're you looking for?'

'We'll manage, thanks,' said Jan, reaching for the doorknob.

'I wasn't offering to help, I was asking you a question.'

Jan drew back his hand and looked at his father. 'Is that a statement of fact? Or are you trying to provoke me?'

'You're ungrateful,' declared Jan's father.

Jan snorted. That's enough, he thought, and tugged the doorknob. The door, however, was locked.

For a moment he thought he glimpsed a satisfied twitch of his father's lips.

'Dad,' said Katy.

'What is it, my child?'

'We're looking for Dr Maria Hülscher. We know she's here in the care home, but not where. And we've got to speak to her. Can you help us?'

Karl Floss looked at Jan challengingly, his free hand gesturing towards Katy. 'See, that's how you do it. When you want help from someone, you ask them politely.'

'*Dad!*' hissed Katy. 'Do you know her?'

'Of course I know her. Maria's a psychologist – and senile. Odd mixture. Always babbling about her old cases. She's not supposed to, but who's going to stop her? After all, she's a bit confused. Can't just tape over her mouth.'

'We need to talk to her, Dad. It's really urgent.'

Karl Floss's gazed darted back and forth between Katy and Jan, then he nodded as if he'd made a decision. 'Wait here.'

He called the lift and disappeared behind the quietly rattling door.

A few minutes later he re-emerged from the lift, accompanied by another *ping*, grinning mischievously and holding up a key. 'Let's go, then.'

'Thanks,' said Jan, nonplussed. He reached for the key.

His father hastily drew back his hand. 'I'm coming with you, of course.'

'Out of the question,' protested Jan.

Karl Floss sighed. 'Now you listen here, my boy. I've been forced onto the bench and now I'm stuck here—'

'May I remind you that you're here voluntarily?' interrupted Jan exasperatedly.

'—boring myself to death. I may not have much strength left, true. My heart's pretty damaged, and who knows how long it'll last. But what would you do if your son never came to see you, not so much as one measly visit? If suddenly the police came asking for him, saying: *Herr Floss, we're looking for your son on a charge of murder. Not tax dodging or fraud or some other kind of scam. No. Murder!* And then he just shows up, your son. In the middle of the night, wanting to talk to a senile psychologist he doesn't know from Adam. No explanation, no nothing. What would you do, eh?'

'It's not the middle of the night,' said Jan.

'Ah! And this isn't a key.'

'Please just give me the key, all right? I don't want you getting dragged into this.'

'Rubbish,' snorted his father. 'I've already been dragged in. I'm your father, whether you like it or not. And if you don't want me coming with you now – that's fine. But then explain to me here and now what all this secrecy is about.'

'There's honestly no time for that.'

Karl Floss smiled like a grey wolf and held the keys up high with shaky fingers.

Jan took a deep breath. 'Fine,' he replied.

Karl Floss led them up the stairs to the third floor. There he opened the door on the right, threw a cautious glance down the corridor and motioned Jan and Katy to follow. A few spartan neon tubes bathed the PVC floor in greenish-grey light. The background noise was the same as on the other side, except that the TVs were louder here. Through one of the doors came a dull, tormented moan that was not of this world, over and over, at regular intervals. In small letters, the sign on the door read *Room 316: Borken, Walter.* A shiver ran down Jan's spine. It sounded so much like pain and suffering, like Walter Borken wanted nothing more than death. And yet there he lay, groaning like a soulless robot, with no one to release him.

His father pointed at the opposite door. *Room 315, Hülscher, Maria.* Evidently her title meant nothing here.

Karl Floss put his index finger to his lips. The tremor made his finger shake.

'Is she already asleep?' asked Katy softly.

Jan's father shook his head energetically. 'We shouldn't give her too much of a surprise. It overwhelms her sometimes.' He knocked. Waited. Then knocked again. Finally he opened the door.

A gust of wind blew into Jan's face. Maria Hülscher must have opened the window. Yet he could see nothing; the room was pitch black, bar a flickering lantern on the table by the balcony. Beside it, seated in an armchair, was a dark finger swaddled in a blanket. The candle gave her a diffuse, quivering halo of light.

'Maria? It's me. Karl Floss, from next door.'

'Karl? Is that you?' The voice was astonishingly high and clear, only the distinctive scratchiness betraying her age. 'Now come on in and close the door, or Sebastian will run out.'

Sebastian? Jan threw his father a questioning look.

'Her son,' he whispered. 'Wandered out of their apartment when he was four years old and got hit by a car.'

'Who are you whispering with?'

'I've got visitors, Maria.'

'Not more children,' groaned the old woman. 'Nothing but children, my whole life long.'

'No children, Maria. Adults,' said Karl Floss, entering the room and waving Jan and Katy inside before swiftly shutting the door. It smelled strongly of cleaning products, despite the open window.

'You shouldn't be lighting candles, Maria,' said Karl Floss gently.

Maria Hülscher frowned. The lantern made her face waver in the darkness. 'They can't order me around,' she declared sulkily. 'You're not allowed to do anything here. They take everything away from you, even my scent. Don't you smell it, that nasty stuff? Yuck! You can scarcely breathe. Who have you brought then, Karl?'

Jan stepped into the light of the candle flame. 'Good evening, Frau Hülscher. I'm Jan Floss, and this is my sister Kathrin Bengtson.'

'Floss?' The old woman looked first at Jan, then at his father. 'I've heard that name before. Karl, did you bring these people?'

Karl Floss nodded. 'Yes, Maria. Katy is my daughter, and Jan is my son.'

'What nonsense, Karl! We don't have a daughter. And our son is dead.'

'Maria, it's me, Karl Floss, from next door. We're at the care home,' he explained patiently. Moving closer to the chair, he placed his trembling hand on hers, with a naturalness that deeply unsettled Jan. Was that *really* his father? The former agency boss? The man who had always buried himself in his work?

'Maria's husband was also called Karl,' said Jan's father, as if that explained everything.

Maria Hülscher leant forward a fraction, stroking his father's cheek affectionately yet somehow absently with her free hand. He let her, smiling uncertainty. But something in his eyes told Jan that he was drinking up the human contact, as if Maria Hülscher's touch could heal wounds. The moment was so intimate and struck Jan with such force that it took his breath away.

Where on earth was this man when I was little? he wondered.

'I think they have a question for you, Maria.' Karl Floss turned to Jan and Katy. 'Why don't you sit down?'

Jan cleared his throat. Unable to reply, he took one of the three chairs around the table, as did Katy and Karl. The latter also picked up a blanket from the bed and wrapped it round himself. Through the open window came the patter of rain. The candle flame guttered in the damp, chilly air.

Jan coughed again. 'May I call you Maria, Frau Hülscher?'

'*Dr* Hülscher, please. Of course you may. All my husband's friends are allowed to call me Maria.' She flashed a winning smile.

'Um, great. So, Maria, you used to be head of department at the Educational Psychology Services in Berlin, didn't you?

Maria Hülscher wrinkled her brow. 'What a question. Certainly I was. Is your child having trouble? Can I do something for you? As soon as I'm back at my desk tomorrow morning I'll take care of it.'

Jan smiled. He was glad Maria Hülscher believed she was still doing her old job. 'I'm looking for someone. Someone specific. Perhaps he was one of the pupils you met.'

'Oh, I met lots. Lots and lots. So many hopeless cases. Difficult cases.'

'The case I'm thinking of is rather unusual. Does the name Peter Nolte mean anything to you?'

Maria Hülscher stared into the flame for a while, then shook her head.

Fine. That didn't necessarily mean anything, thought Jan. 'Can you remember, perhaps, whether you ever worked on a case with an albino? A pupil with very light skin?'

The elderly psychologist looked at him earnestly, then back into the flame. Her gaze was abstracted, and she was adamantly silent. Then she shook her head again. 'Not that I remember.'

'You're quite sure?'

'Jan, that's a stupid question,' interjected his father. 'You know Maria's condition.'

'Rubbish, Karl!' growled Maria Hülscher irritably. 'My memory's better than yours. I just have to . . . search a bit.'

'Perhaps you couldn't tell he had albinism. He might have been wearing make-up,' persisted Jan. 'A boy who was always made-up, always hiding. Hyper-controlled, compulsive . . . he might even have dyed his hair . . .'

Suddenly a light went on in Maria Hülscher's eyes. 'Oh. Yes. There was someone. I remember. Wait a minute . . .'

Bullseye! Jan felt the hair rise on the back of his neck. Hypnotised, he leant forward, hanging on the psychologist's every word.

'It wasn't an official case, you see. Sometimes you get that. You know something's going on, or somebody needs help, but there's nothing you can do. Because nothing bad happens. And because neither the parents nor the school officially calls us in. That's what it was like with this case.'

She broke off for a moment, and Jan was afraid she'd got lost in her memories, or was confusing them with the present.

'A younger colleague rang me up, her name was . . . hold on . . . no, it's not coming to me. Well, she rang me up because of an incident that occurred at a hostel during a trip. She woke up in the middle of the night. All the beds were empty, and there was noise and laughter coming from the shower room. She went to check at once, of course. The whole class was down there, standing in a circle around a boy. He was lying under the showers. He'd fallen over, broken his leg or sprained it or something. The class had probably surprised him in the shower. They said he was masturbating . . . well. But the funny thing was that the boy was pale as death. That's what she said, more or less. She'd noticed before that he was wearing make-up, but didn't know why. Now, though, seeing him in the shower room all miserable, naked, skin white as a hospital sheet . . .'

White skin. Make-up. Jan's heart beat faster. And then the shower – maybe a compulsion to wash. Sexual frustration. Everything seemed to fit. He was about to ask whether she could remember when this had been, but bit his tongue. The question would confuse her. He'd have to stick to the topic at hand. 'What happened then? Did you investigate?'

Maria Hülscher nodded absent-mindedly. 'The boy didn't want to talk, so I rang his parents. They said everything was fine, so I went to see for myself.' She gave a roguish smile. 'I'm not that easily shaken off.'

Jan refrained from asking the parents' names. He knew that the least interruption, like fishing around for a name, might stem the flow of memories. Nothing was so easily knocked off track as a senile mind.

'The boy's father had a shop. Hardware, I think. And he was an alcoholic, you could see that at once. The mother was different. Well turned-out, somehow. Very careful with her appearance.' She giggled, then instantly grew serious again. 'The daughter of a man who owned a perfumery, I found out later. It looked almost funny, seeing her standing there. So pretty and scented among all that flaking plaster. The house was very run-down – rather straitened circumstances, that family. Well . . . they wouldn't even let me see the boy. I didn't catch so much as a glimpse.'

'If you didn't even see him,' asked Katy, 'how come you remember so well?'

Maria Hülscher jumped when she heard Katy's voice. Gazing over at her, she squinted so she could see her better. Jan swore internally at the interruption, but bit back a rebuke. Any remark might make the situation worse.

'Because' – Maria Hülscher lowered her voice to a hoarse whisper – 'of the red eyes.'

Jan froze. An icy chill ran down his spine, although what the old lady had just said couldn't be true. 'Red eyes?' he asked. 'How do you know?'

The psychologist giggled. 'Aren't you a clever clogs! I don't know where my Karl dug you up, but you really are a clever clogs! You know, the whole thing never really left me. Do you know that feeling? When something haunts you, like a ghost? I dropped by once more, at the house. It was . . . hang on . . .' Maria Hülscher frowned, then waved her hand. 'Oh, I don't know any more when it was. Anyway, I saw the house and remembered. I rang the bell, and a young man opened the door. He looked quite normal. Brown hair, slim . . . only his eyes – they were light, very light. And his skin looked powdered. I asked him about his parents. He said they were dead. At the time I thought, well, perhaps it's for the best. Only, the *way* he said it, so . . . strange—'

He'd killed his parents? Was that what she meant?

Jan felt the damp, frigid air almost literally crawl beneath his clothes. He shivered, his hands ice cold. The pelting rain had risen in volume, reminding him of the night in southern France when Laura had disappeared.

'And there was something else,' added Maria Hülscher. 'There was someone in the house, a woman. Young, I think. She called to him, asking who was at the door. She said if it was her mother he should tell her to go to hell, that she'd wreaked more than enough havoc. That was the gist of it, anyway.'

Maria Hülscher nodded, as if wanting to confirm to herself that she remembered correctly. 'I remember it exactly because his answer was so cold. He shouted that she didn't have to worry. Her mother would never cause any trouble again. He was looking at me the whole time, with those eyes.' Maria Hülscher paused, as if she could still sense his gaze. 'And then they turned red, his eyes. Very suddenly, just for half a second. I swear they did. Red! I'll never forget the sight of it. You might think I'm crazy, but . . . that's what happened . . .'

Maria Hülscher fell silent. For an instant no one in the room drew breath. The only sound was the rain.

'I believe you,' said Jan softly. 'Tell me more.'

'More . . . yes.' She sighed. 'He said I should go. I wasn't needed. I . . . I got the impression that if I didn't leave immediately he might get dangerous. So I made tracks.'

Again she sighed. A shiver ran through her skinny body under the blanket. Her grey hair formed a tangled aura around her head, catching the yellow candlelight. For a while she stared wordlessly into the guttering flame.

'Karl?' she asked unexpectedly. 'Who gave permission to put a candle there?'

And just like that, the thread was broken. Karl Floss was about to say something, but Jan shooshed him with a vigorous wave of his hand. 'Maria? Can you remember the name of the family? Or the name of the boy?'

No response.

'Maybe the name of the street where they lived? Or roughly when this took place?'

Still nothing.

As if the well had run dry.

Then, very suddenly, her face lit up. She raised a triumphant forefinger. 'It was something with an "O", I remember that much.'

'Maybe Nolte,' nudged Jan. 'Peter Nolte.'

'No, no. It wasn't so ordinary. Or was it?' Maria Hülscher scratched her head. 'Wait! Annie Hall!'

'What?'

'*Annie Hall*. By Woody Allen. It had just won an Oscar. So did Diane Keaton. I love Diane Keaton. I saw that film three times.

'Wasn't that at the end of the Seventies?' asked Katy.

'I don't know. Karl? What do you think? Didn't we go together?' Suddenly she flinched. 'Karl, it's raining, do you hear it? Sebastian's still outside. Can you go and fetch him?'

Chapter Thirty-Seven

Berlin, 21 October, 10.29 p.m.

Fjodor breathed calmly and intently, although it was a struggle. Inside he was seething. He knew, however, how important it was to keep it together. Especially now. Especially after the last few hours.

Applying the streaks was the best way to achieve a higher internal order. The pressure of the stick on his skin, the removal of the lines, which he'd drawn thousands of times over more than thirty years.

At no other moment did he feel himself more intensely. His whole will, concentrated in the tiny black eyeliner stick as it moved across his skin with a gentle, unyielding pressure. He felt every stroke, every movement. First his face, then his throat. He kept swapping the sticks as they grew blunt. For the back of his head, he mostly closed his eyes. The outer lines he could draw blind; he was guided by the skin of his scalp. Only when filling them in did he need the side mirror.

Afterwards he sharpened the blunt sticks, each with fourteen half-turns of the sharpener. He didn't have to check to see if they were the same length. He knew they were. He used to line them up next to each other, but these days he placed them upright in a glass. Thirty-seven sticks in all – no more would fit. He liked the way they looked. Black, vertical stakes.

He felt better once he'd finished. The turmoil had left him, the lines were sharp again.

Reaching for the telephone, he dialled Laura's landline for the seventeenth time that day.

Nobody picked up.

Why wasn't she back at her apartment? Why was she hiding from him? He'd even taken down the photos from her front hall so she didn't have to endure them any more.

At least he now knew she wasn't with Jan; he was still looking for her too. Was that why she was hiding? Was she afraid of Jan?

No. He knew that was what he *wanted* to believe. But it wasn't true. She'd been pining for him even in the south of France. He'd recognised it at once. Refusing to disclose his name, fighting for that pussy!

Thus far his main goal had been to get Jan out of the picture. But now that Laura had dropped off the face of the earth, he felt the loss more keenly than ever before. He regretted letting her go. It was against the nature of things. A planet had to revolve around its sun, but for some reason Laura could never stick to her orbit. As if she were a will-o'-the-wisp, and not a planet at all. It was all Jan's fault. That pussy was like a fucking asteroid on a collision course! One bearing down implacably on Laura, just as she was bearing down on him.

Gravitation. It was all a question of attraction.

Laura had to be brought back into orbit. Permanently. And to do that, he needed Jan. Attraction would take care of the rest.

He knew now what he had to do. First of all, however, he had keep the chaos to a minimum.

Too many planets around a single sun was bad news.

You couldn't stay on top of things. You lost track of who was turning where.

Standing outside the gallery, he turned left and went to the nearest door. The lock clicked as the key went in.

A breath of warm air and the faint scent of faeces struck him as he entered. Repulsive, but today he'd have to shrug it off.

From the back wall came a soft rasp. Bare skin on concrete.

'Hello, princess,' he whispered.

Nothing. No answer.

Since the mishap four days ago she'd been barely responsive. As if her wits had drained away with that little bit of blood. Perhaps it would have been better to let her die then and there, instead of turning off the small white tap on the hose. Somehow, however, it hadn't seemed right.

Look at her crouching there in front of her bunk! Always the same expression, always covered by the blanket, even though it was much too hot in here, always drawing up her legs in the same manner so that he couldn't see her crotch or breasts. His mind flew automatically to Laura. Suddenly the word princess sounded utterly hollow, the way it had just slipped out. This was no princess. Not while Laura was alive.

Laura was a princess.

This woman wasn't. This woman was one planet too many.

'Do you know why gravitation is so important?' he asked.

Silence. No answer.

'Without gravitation, chaos takes over. People like my father. People like Jan Floss. Or doctors. All sorts of forces are exerted over you. There's no longer any right and wrong. No clear paths of orbit. The wrong ones live, and the right ones perish.'

Still no reaction.

'You could at least nod.'

She nodded.

'But you don't understand, do you?'

After a moment's hesitation, she shook her head.

'Imagine a doctor. A senior one. This senior doctor is an arrogant, presumptuous shit. He's an asteroid. And you're orbiting. You're orbiting where you've been put. That's all as it should be. Predetermined. You travel your path. Now, along comes the doctor. You know he's been paid to kill you during your next operation. The money's changed hands, and he's on a collision course. If he hits you, he'll destroy you. Wouldn't you want me to pay that bastard asteroid a visit?

'I'd go to his house and hide in his garage. About two in the morning the garage door moves as if by magic. Remote control. Two round headlights. He rolls in with his expensive bloody Porsche, fucking loud thing. I'm hiding behind his other car, a Benz.

'The garage door closes, the fluorescent bulb comes on, and the doctor gets out. He's the asteroid that's going to kill you, remember. He's aiming at you. Like in *Armageddon*. The thing's hurtling towards you like in a Hollywood film.

'I stand up so he sees me, and put my finger to my lips. He just gasps, doesn't even manage a scream.

'I'm by his side in two paces, holding a knife to his throat.

'"Who . . . who are you?" he stammers.

'I just smile.

'"What do you want? Money? I . . . my wallet's—"

'"I don't want your money," I interrupt him. "I want you to cancel the operation. I want you not to kill her."

'He stares at me aghast, horrified that I know everything, and tells me: "I'm not going to kill anyone."'

'And at that moment I know the conversation is pointless. He's going to fly and fly and he won't stop. I've got to make a decision. I'm Bruce Willis. I've landed on the fucking asteroid. What am I going to do? What would you expect?'

She didn't reply. She just crouched there, looking at him with her fixed, dull eyes. Her long stretch in captivity had worn her down, like all the others before her. But there was no better way to achieve the skin tone she needed.

'I'll tell you what you'd want. Do it, you'd be thinking. Blow the damn thing into the air. Maybe you wouldn't say it, but you'd think it. And I'd do it. For you! Would you be grateful?'

He saw her hesitate – how *could* she?

Finally she nodded.

'So you should be,' he whispered. 'Sometimes you have to do the wrong thing because it's right. Because that's what makes the right thing possible. Sometimes there's not enough room in the universe for the right thing.'

Again she nodded dumbly.

'Then you understand that I need room. For the two girls.'

He could tell she still didn't get it.

Only when she saw the sharp, glinting blade did she scream.

His heart light as a feather, he went over to her. He knew that this was right.

Eliminate the planets. Keep track.

But *was* it right?

Or was he about to lose control because of one bloody asteroid?

Didn't control also mean being able to put up with things?

Being able to sit tight?

Maybe there was another possibility. Maybe it would be worth keeping her. Halloween was in ten days. Maybe by then things would be different.

Too many maybes, he thought.

Maybe is Froggy.

I'm Fjodor.

He stared at her, a pale, miserable wreck. She could still be made a princess.

Without a word he turned on his heel and hurried out of the room. One of the girls would be enough, he thought. That in itself would reduce the number of planets.

Chapter Thirty-Eight

Berlin, 21 October, 10.38 p.m.

Jan left the care home by the front entrance with his father and Katy. Rain was hammering down wildly onto the porch roof. A heavy stream ran down from the left-hand edge, splattering onto the road.

Karl Floss passed his son a dark-grey umbrella.

'Thanks,' murmured Jan.

'You still owe me an explanation or two,' said his father. His eyes were small, and he looked like he'd been in urgent need of rest for hours.

'You also owe me an explanation or two, but I'm never going to get them.'

'What explanations would those be?'

Jan gawped at him in disbelief. 'Are you serious?' The conversation with Maria Hülscher was suddenly at the back of his mind. 'You throw me out on my ear then sell the company without discussing it with me? And you're asking what explanation you owe me?'

Karl Floss shook his head reluctantly. 'I did you a favour. I don't understand a word of this ungrateful gibberish.'

'A *favour*?'

'What else would it be? I know you don't want to work in the industry. You never have. Advertising! You've always considered it the lowest of the low. I couldn't do that to you. So I turned down Eisner's offer with a heavy heart.'

'Turned him down?' repeated Jan.

'He would have paid me more if you'd stayed at the agency. But I insisted you had to leave.'

Jan felt as if someone had knocked him clean off his feet. 'Why didn't you ask me before deciding something like that, for Christ's sake?'

'Ask? Ask?' grumbled his father. 'I know what you're like.'

'Oh yeah? You think so? I'm not sure I've got anything against advertising.'

'Yes you do.'

'I had something against working at your company. With you as a boss. With the demands you make. I—' Jan broke off, feeling Katy's hand on his back.

His father stared at him open-mouthed, deeply hurt. 'I did that for you.'

'Great,' blurted Jan, raising his hands in a gesture of helplessness and bewilderment then letting them fall.

No one said anything.

Jan felt lonelier than he had in a very long time, yet he knew his father had been serious. He'd genuinely believed he was doing the right thing. We're like a puzzle missing some connecting pieces, he thought. What if Theo were still here? What if his mother had stayed?

His father sighed. It sounded almost like a growl. 'If I was wrong, I'm sorry.'

Jan nodded. He knew it was an apology, but it didn't feel like one.

'I think we should go home,' said Katy softly.

Home. Where was that, wondered Jan. Greg's? The idea struck him as grotesque, but it was accurate. 'Yeah. We probably should,' he said. Squaring his shoulders, he watched Katy say goodbye to their father. He couldn't bring himself to hug him, so instead he opened the umbrella, nodded curtly and left.

'Good luck,' his father called after him.

Jan turned around and saw him standing on the porch, an old man with a cane and a forlorn expression behind a curtain of rain.

'Thank you,' called Jan. 'For before, with Maria Hülscher.'

His father raised his hand and gave a short, stiff wave. Katy tucked her arm in his and slipped beneath the umbrella.

On the train a few minutes later, they were still silent. Water dripped from the umbrella onto the floor, creating a puddle.

Her smartphone in her hands, Katy began to type. '*Annie Hall*, by Woody Allen,' she said at last. 'It was 1977.' She lowered the phone. It was typical of Katy not to bring up Jan's argument with their father. And he was more than grateful for it.

Nineteen seventy-seven. Jan did some mental maths. As quickly as the conversation with Maria Hülscher had faded into insignificance, it now seemed all-consuming. 'In the Nordholm yearbook for 1993 Peter Nolte was in his early thirties. That means he'd be in his early fifties today, and in 1977 roughly twenty. Both would fit.'

'And you really think he managed to hide his albinism from the school?'

'If you think of the story Maria Hülscher just told us, then yeah. He's clearly been doing it since childhood, and at school. Being caught like that in the shower must have had catastrophic consequences for him. He'd have been more careful after that. I bet he controlled things down to the last detail.'

'Surely a control freak like that would stick out.'

'Perhaps I should call Breitner again tomorrow morning.'

'You think he'll talk to you after today's performance?'

'Depends on my choice of words,' said Jan. He attempted a smile, but it turned into more of a grimace. 'There's something else bothering me. I keep wondering how this guy found us. First he was in my apartment. Fine, my address isn't a secret. If he knew my name he could find out where I lived. Then he suddenly shows up under the bridge. Maybe because it's one of Laura's favourite places, and because there's some connection between them he knows about it too. Perhaps he was even the one who took the photos.

'But how in the hell did he track us to Nordholm? Did he follow us all the way from Berlin?'

'That struck me too,' remarked Katy. 'I glanced into the rear-view mirror plenty of times on the way there, and I'm certain he wasn't tailing us then.'

'Then someone at Nordholm must have tipped him off.'

'Hang on,' said Katy. 'This guy had Berlin plates. And from Berlin to Nordholm is three hours. That doesn't add up. We'd have been long gone again by the time he made it to Nordholm.'

'Unless,' Jan said thoughtfully, 'the headmaster called him. He was the only one who knew in advance that we were coming.'

'But you didn't give him your real name. That means . . .'

'That he knew who I was anyway.' Jan finished her thought. 'And he did, didn't he? Breitner seemed to know right from the start that something wasn't right about my name . . .'

Katy fell into uneasy silence. 'Are you saying,' she asked after a while, 'that Breitner is involved somehow?'

Jan nodded grimly. 'Something's fishy there. I just don't understand what the hell it is. But the way he tried to fob us off when we first asked about Nolte, I got the sense there was more at stake for Breitner than the good name of his school.'

'Do you think he lied, and the two of them are still in touch?'

'That would explain a few things, at least.'

'Shit,' muttered Katy. She'd gone pale. Jan knew only too well what was going on inside her head. She was afraid, and rightly so. If Breitner was mixed up in this business, then Katy might be in danger too. Why on earth had he dragged her into it?

When Jan and Katy got off the train, it was still raining. Street lamps and headlights threw glittering islands onto the asphalt. They kept turning around, with the vague sense that they were being followed. Jan kept thinking of Laura. Where the hell had she got to?

At Greg's front door, Katy fumbled a key out of her jeans and opened up. As they entered the apartment, some of his tension dissipated. Here, at least, they were safe. A leaden tiredness overwhelmed him, although he'd also eaten nothing for ages. 'Think Greg might have some food and a can of beer in the fridge?'

Katy grinned faintly. 'If you're looking for a frozen pizza, then Greg's not your guy. But beer – very possibly. Hey, what's that smell?'

'No idea.' Jan trudged towards the kitchen, already imagining the beer pouring down his throat. He opened the kitchen door and stopped as cold as if he'd run into a wall. An acrid smell came to meet him out of the darkness. Instinctively he pressed his hand to his nose and mouth, groping for the light switch. Finding it, he flicked it on.

The ceiling light flared.

Jan shrank back in horror.

Behind his back, Katy screamed.

In the middle of the kitchen sat Greg, his body fastened to a chair with plastic wrap. Only his head was left uncovered. His face was dotted with tiny burn marks. The place where his right ear should have been was charred; around the blackened, reddish wound the skin had blistered. In his wide-open mouth was a ball of cling film, and his eyes had lost all brightness and expression.

Chapter Thirty-Nine

Berlin, 21 October, 10.46 p.m.

Laura could hear faraway steps. Unlike her previous prison, this house carried noises easily. The wooden door looked solid, but it didn't appear to be soundproof. The marble staircase and the corridor formed a kind of funnel, which captured every sound and magnified it. Like Buck's footsteps, which were now coming up the stairs.

Laura stood up. She didn't want to stumble around in front of him when he tugged the rope. She wanted to meet him on her own two feet, at least. Her jaw tensed, her teeth already gritted in anticipation of further pain and humiliation. Her skin was still burning from the earlier blows. What if he had something worse in mind this time?

She had feverishly considered how to escape from Buck.

Was she strong enough to grab the rope, swing herself up and throw her legs around his neck? Her legs were free, and if she could get his throat between her thighs she could try to throttle him.

But what then?

Even if she overpowered him, what would be her next move? She'd still be hanging from the rope, her arms stretched way above her head. How would she get hold of the key to the handcuffs?

The footsteps echoed down the hall, coming inexorably nearer.

How many metres to go?

Six, maybe? Or eight?

'Stop!' A voice sliced through the corridor.

The footsteps ceased instantly.

What was that?

'Turn around,' ordered the voice. Laura's heart jumped. That wasn't Buck.

For an endless moment, all was silent. Laura pictured Buck standing in the middle of the corridor as if rooted to the spot, slowing turning around.

'You?' He sounded disbelieving, as if the man the piercing voice belonged to knew Buck. Laura was about to make a noise and call for help when she heard the voice again. This time it wasn't piercing; it was cold, soft and emphatic. 'What the hell are you doing here, Buck Stelzer?'

The cry got stuck in Laura's throat. Her stomach twisted. She knew that voice. It was the psycho with the red eyes, the tattooed man.

She began to tremble.

More footsteps in the corridor.

'This is my house,' said Buck. He sounded aggressive and anxious at the same time, and was audibly retreating down the hall. 'I'd like you to leave.'

'Tell me what you're doing here,' said the tattooed man.

'Whoever you are – why would you give a shit what I'm doing? It's none of your damn business,' said Buck.

'You know a thing or two about shit, don't you, Buck? You've always wallowed in it. Your whole life. First with money, then without.'

Laura held her breath. The tattooed man seemed to have known Buck for ever. What on earth was going on?

'Who are you, for God's sake?' Buck was standing directly outside Laura's door.

'Put that thing away,' said the tattooed man. 'You're making a fool of yourself.'

'Keep away from me. Get out of my house.'

'And you think if you wave that pocket knife around a bit then I'll let you go? Think you're as untouchable as you used to be?'

'Who the fuck are you?'

'I'm your recurring nightmare, Buck Stelzer. You've got to look through the stripes on my face. Part of me is still there, between the lines. But perhaps it'll help if I unbutton my shirt. Maybe that'll jog your memory.'

For a moment all was quiet. Laura thought she could make out the rustle of clothing.

'You?' gasped Buck in disbelief. 'It's *you*?'

Suddenly Buck laughed, a loud bleat. He sounded almost relieved, as if all the fear had lifted from his shoulders. 'You're right, I do remember. I can still see you standing under that shower, dick in hand, my sister's name on your lips. Man, you were whiter than the tiles on the wall. And now you've got the balls to come here and act all scary?' Buck laughed again. 'Once a freak, always a freak, eh?'

'Do you feel strong?' asked the tattooed man. 'Invincible? Like the old days?'

'Invincible. Like the old days,' Buck mimicked. 'I was never invincible. But for someone like you, Froggy, I was more than a match.'

Laura froze. What had Buck said?

Froggy?

'Froggy isn't here any more,' whispered the tattooed man.

No, thought Laura. That can't be right. Not that name. Her heart skipped a beat.

It's impossible.

But there was only one person she knew who'd once gone by the name of Froggy. She wondered how she'd failed to notice, why she hadn't recognised him herself – from his voice, his posture, as he stood there before her while she was on that bloody chair, bound and kidnapped, by him.

She thought back to that strange feeling she'd had, beyond all the fear. The feeling that something had stirred inside her, that something seemed familiar.

Yet she hadn't recognised him.

'How can Froggy not be here any more when he's standing right in front of me,' scoffed Buck. 'You'll always be Froggy. To your final fucking day, you got that? Once Froggy, always Fro—'

A dull bang made Laura jump. The door shuddered. For a moment the air was more than silent. Then she heard a moan.

Another bang.

And another.

With every one the door vibrated, and with every one there came a groan.

A body slid down the door.

She heard the voice of the tattooed man very close to the door, whispering, full of hatred. 'Froggy isn't here any more. There's only me left. And I can do anything I want.'

A last dull blow, then a noise like someone sticking a knife into a sack of meal.

'*Anything!*'

Footsteps receded, moving down the marble steps, at last cut off by the reverberations of the front door closing.

Laura stared at the red puddle seeping in through the crack beneath the door, dark as a shadow, seizing her and dragging her into the abyss. Tears welled up in her eyes. Her whole body shook in rebellion. Her mind refused to believe what she'd just heard.

Buck was dead.

But that meant nothing any more. She felt neither relief nor dismay.

There was only one thing she could think about:

Froggy.

Chapter Forty

Berlin, 21 October, 11.07 p.m.

It felt like an eternity before Jan could move again. In reality it was no more than thirty seconds.

Spinning on his heel, he took Katy's arm and pushed her out of the kitchen into the bedroom, where he sat her down on the bed.

Her face was ashen, her chin wobbling. Carefully he placed the duvet around her shoulders. Greg's duvet.

Jan's mind raced. Why Greg? What had he wanted from him?

Suddenly he felt guilty. All this time he'd been judging Greg, without considering for a second that for Katy he might be much more than a cheap distraction from the frustrations of marriage.

'Is . . . is he dead?' asked Katy.

Jan nodded. 'Yes,' he said softly, pressing her to him.

'Are you sure? You didn't check . . .'

'I don't have to check, Katy. He's dead.'

Silence.

He waited for her to cry. But she didn't. 'Why did he do that?' she stammered. 'Why Greg?'

'He's after me,' said Jan.

'But how did he know about Greg?'

'Greg was with us in France.'

'No, I mean, how did he know where Greg lives?'

'He must have followed us somehow. Maybe he knew even before then.'

Katy said nothing, ceaselessly kneading her hands. The sound of skin rubbing against skin, and the scent of burned flesh hung in the air.

'If you're the one he wants and he followed us here, then why did he wait until we left before killing Greg?'

'I don't know,' said Jan.

More silence.

Rubbing hands.

Racing mind.

'What did he do to Greg?' Katy's voice trembled.

'I think he . . . it looks like he . . .'

'Tortured?' whispered Katy. The word echoed in the stillness.

'Yes.' Jan swallowed. The idea was truly monstrous.

'What could Greg have told him? Where we were? He had no idea.'

Jan stared into space. That was precisely the question. What did Greg know that this monster could use? Plenty about Katy, he thought. But about me?

Suddenly he felt Katy go rigid beside him. Her left hand clutched his forearm. 'Oh my God,' she breathed.

'What?'

Katy pointed at the small beside table. 'The photo.'

'What photo?' asked Jan. There was nothing but a chunky digital alarm clock on the table.

'A little picture from a photo booth. I tucked it into a slot in the alarm clock.'

'Katy, what was the photo *of*?'

'Nele and Anna.'

Jan felt like he'd been hit by a freight train. His heart began to race. In a flash, all the pieces started coming together.

Everything this psychopath has done is about me, thought Jan.

He was in my apartment. He wanted to kill me. He tracked me to the bridge and found me in Greg's apartment. Each time I got away, and each time someone else has paid for it.

Anna and Nele.

His chest tightened. How could he have been so naïve? It had only been a question of time before the tattooed man started using his family to draw him out.

'Please tell me this isn't happening,' whispered Katy.

Jan leapt up, pulled Laura's mobile out of his jacket pocket and dialled 110 for the police. Pressing the phone to his ear, he felt a vein throb in his temple.

Booop.

Katy sat there as if paralysed, staring in bewilderment at the slot in the alarm clock where the photo should have been.

Booop.

'I'm not allowing this,' Jan choked out. 'I'm – not – allowing – this!'

Chapter Forty-One

Berlin, 21 October, 11.24 p.m.

When Jan hung up, Katy was standing in front of him. She'd got to her feet without him noticing. Her fingers were clutched convulsively around her phone. 'Nobody's picking up at home,' she said hoarsely.

'Have you tried Sören's mobile?'

'Both numbers.'

They looked at each other.

Katy had tears in her eyes. 'He always puts things on silent in the evenings. "Got to have some peace and quiet sometime," he keeps saying.'

Jan simply nodded.

'I've got to go back,' said Katy, her voice cracking.

Greg's car keys lay in the hall. As they dashed out of the house onto the pavement, Jan pressed the button to unlock the car, and there was a flash of orange roughly thirty metres to their left.

'Let me drive.' Katy held out her hand for the keys.

Jan looked at her trembling fingers. 'No way.'

'They're my kids,' protested Katy.

'And my nieces.' Jan started the car. 'Anyway, you're in shock.'

Sitting for the first time behind the wheel of the Cherokee, he was surprised how quick yet cumbersome the vehicle was. He rarely drove, and was glad to see the automatic gear box.

'Take a right up ahead,' said Katy.

Jan spun the wheel, following his sister's directions. He could probably have found the way on his own, but she would know the shortest route.

Katy sat beside him, endlessly redialling Sören's number. Jan threw her a worried glance. 'We'll be there in five minutes,' he said, trying to calm her. His voice held a hollow note of uncertainty. Guilt bored into his gut.

'I can't bear it,' moaned Katy, balling her fists and digging her nails into her palms.

Houses flew past. Jan ran two red lights where no one else was waiting, but at the next one he had to stop. Several vehicles were crossing the street, including a bus. The road was barely clear before he stepped on the accelerator.

'Do you think the police are already there?'

Jan considered the question. Eight minutes had passed since he'd called them. 'I hope so.' It was all he could manage to say. Instead he tried to focus on the traffic.

Three minutes later they turned onto Fontanestraße. Street lamps bordered both sides of the road, yellow points of light in the dark. Detached houses with gardens under the black sky. No flashing blue lights for miles. The house belonging to Katy and Sören Bengtson was at the end of the street. Built in the Fifties and in reasonably good condition, it had yellow plaster and a steep peaked roof above the first floor. Underneath the grey tiles of the roof were the children's bedrooms.

The house was dark.

Jan switched off the headlights and let the car roll the last few metres in the dark. Then they got out.

Jan threw Katy a warning glance, putting his finger to his lips. They closed the doors of the Cherokee softly. At the garden gate, fear caught up with Jan. Suddenly he saw Gandalf in his mind's eye, recalling the ease with which the albino had killed him – to say nothing of his brutality towards Greg. He felt exposed without a weapon, or anything else that might help him keep this psychopath at bay.

The narrow path to the front door stretched and grew. The lawn hadn't been mown in a while, the bushes and roses not cut back. Sören didn't seem bothered about the garden.

Katy grabbed his hand and held him back. 'What do we do now?' she whispered.

'Ring the bell.'

Her eyes widened. 'What if he . . .'

Jan's gaze fell upon the sandpit Sören and Katy had built for the twins. A rusty children's trowel with a wooden handle lay inside it, and he picked it up with grim determination. The wood felt brittle and sodden.

'Where the hell are the police, goddammit?' muttered Katy in an undertone. Her breath was condensing in the air, her eyes flitting from one dark window to the next.

'We'll ring the bell,' whispered Jan. He motioned Katy towards the right of the front door, positioning himself to the left. Gripping the trowel with both hands, he raised it above his head, the sharp edge pointing downwards, and nodded to her.

Katy pressed the bell.

Jan held his breath. The electronic chime wrenched at his nerves.

Nothing.

Breathe, thought Jan. Despite the damp, chilly air, he felt hot. He prayed the wooden handle wouldn't break when he had to strike. 'Again,' he whispered.

Katy rang once more.

Lights switched on in the hall. Through the frosted glass door a figure appeared, a blurry smudge growing ever larger.

Katy shrank back from the door as Jan readied himself; he only wished he was holding an axe instead of a trowel.

There was a crunch. A chain was removed. The door swung open, and a man emerged into the bright rectangle of light. 'What on earth—'

Seeing Jan with the raised trowel, Sören Bengtson froze.

Relieved, Jan let his arms drop.

Behind Sören, standing in the doorway, was a blonde woman who looked to be in her mid-twenties, wearing a dressing gown Jan had previously seen on his sister.

'Where are the girls?' asked Jan hoarsely.

Sören's gaze shifted back and forth between Jan, Katy and the trowel. 'Have you gone totally mad?' he asked, pale as a corpse. 'What are you doing here?'

'Where are Nele and Anna?' repeated Katy.

'Listen,' said Sören, retreating into the house, 'if you want to take them, fine. But not like this, OK? Please. Not like this!'

'I don't give a flying fuck who you're screwing. That's just business as usual. But I want to know right now where our children are.'

'Mum?'

Peering over Sören's shoulder, Jan saw Nele coming down the stairs in her pyjamas. Behind her, a drowsy-looking Anna appeared.

'Anna, Nele!' Katy pushed past Sören and the blonde woman, ran to the staircase, pressed her children close and sobbed.

A weight was lifted from Jan's heart.

Behind him echoed the sound of a single siren.

At that moment he realised he had to get out of there. Immediately.

Giving the visibly upset Sören a dismissive glance, he turned on his heel and ran to the car, the trowel still in his hand.

As he reached the corner, the blue light bathed the street in a garish light. A police car rushed at high speed down the little street, whizzing past him.

Turning the corner, Jan breathed a sigh of relief.

Unexpectedly, Laura's telephone rang in his jacket pocket. He took it out with one hand, trying not to take his eyes off the road, and pressed the green button with his thumb. 'Hello?'

'Herr Floss? Ava Bjely here. We've got to talk, right now.'

'Me? With you? Why?'

'Does my daughter still mean something to you?'

Jan swallowed. 'Yes.'

'Then don't ask stupid questions. Just get over here.'

Jan hung up with sense of deep unease. How did Ava Bjely know she could reach him on Laura's mobile? Then it occurred to him that he'd told her himself about finding it. Still, he was surprised she even knew the number.

Chapter Forty-Two

Berlin, 21 October, 11.49 p.m.

Jan turned the wheel, and the Cherokee leapt over the threshold of the open gate. The headlights bounced upwards, skimming the house. All was pitch black in the garden. He braked and the car jolted a little, sending a few pebbles spraying to one side. Not far from the door, he came to a halt.

Jan switched off the engine and sat there motionless in the silence. His heart was hammering in his chest, his hands trembling. After sixty seconds, the interior lights went off. In the darkness he could still see Greg. The dead eyes. The black wound in place of an ear. The stench of burnt flesh.

Jan threw open the door and climbed out.

He glanced down at the trowel, which was in the footwell on the passenger side. As ridiculous as the rusty thing was, it was better than nothing. He was unlikely to need it with Ava Bjely, however.

The house was scarcely visible in the darkness, except for the light through the open door, where the silhouette of a woman in a wheelchair appeared. Ava Bjely's shadow fell between the columns, reaching the edge of the lawn.

As he approached, he could see the agitation in her face.

'I may have made a mistake,' she said instead of greeting him.

Jan stopped in front of her. Ava Bjely made no move to get out of the way: evidently she preferred to discuss the matter on the front porch.

'What kind of mistake?'

'What have you done to your face?'

'I had to put make-up on,' said Jan curtly.

Ava Bjely pulled a face.

'What kind of mistake?' repeated Jan.

'Do you have siblings?'

'A sister. Why?'

'Then perhaps you'll understand.' She took a deep breath, as if she had to take a run-up. 'You can't choose your siblings. You're stuck with them all your life. Like children.'

Jan lost his temper. 'For Christ's sake, can you just tell me what's going on here? What do you want? Why did you call?'

She was silent a moment, as if agonising over something. 'Laura was here.'

'What?' Jan's jaw dropped. 'When?'

'Last night. But that doesn't matter any more. What's more important is—'

'Why didn't you say anything?' interrupted Jan furiously.

'It doesn't matter now,' she repeated. 'What's more important is I'm worried.'

'*You're* worried? *You?*' Jan stared at Ava Bjely.

'Laura broke in here for the umpteenth time, and I caught her red-handed. I offered her money – lots of money – if she'd leave Berlin. Leave Germany, ideally.'

Jan's mouth remained open.

'She refused,' continued Ava Bjely. 'She was stubborn as a mule, and—'

'Where is she?' asked Jan sharply.

Ava Bjely dropped her gaze, examining her scrawny hands, which were folded together in her lap. 'I asked my brother to take her away.'

'Take her away?'

'I wanted her to come to her senses. He was supposed to take her away and put her in the mansion.'

'So?'

Ava Bjely groaned. Her breath was cloudy in the light from the door. 'My brother isn't the nicest of people.'

An icy hand brushed across Jan's neck. 'Do you think he's going to do something to her?'

'I don't know. But he should have checked in hours ago. I can't reach him.'

The chill spread from Jan's neck to the rest of his body. 'Where is this mansion?'

'Quite nearby, Drosselweg 37. My father was having it converted into a clinic, but it was never used as such. He died a few months before it could be completed.' She handed him a key. 'Be careful inside. It's derelict now, and it might not be safe.'

Jan stared at the key – and Ava Bjely.

'Well, what's it to be? Do you like my daughter or not?'

Jan took the key, spun wordlessly around and went back to the car. The orange lights of the Cherokee glowed like warning lamps as he unlocked it. He could scarcely think straight. His brain had knotted together. Mechanically he started the car and entered Berlin, Drosselweg 37 into the GPS. Mistyping, he smacked the dashboard angrily with his palm and had to re-enter the address.

The tyres dug a bald spot into the gravel, then he whooshed out of the gate.

It took seven minutes before the GPS told him he had reached his destination. There was no house number to be seen, not on the broad outer wall or the driveway.

He parked and picked up the trowel from the passenger-side footwell. For the first time in his life, he wished he had a proper weapon.

The gate was a copy of the wrought-iron one at Ava Bjely's house, though the building beyond it was somewhat larger. To the left was a small annexe with an open garage, in which he could make out the contours of a white delivery van. Above the roof, a sharp crescent moon cut through the sky.

The gate refused to open. Jan found a spot on the wall overgrown with ivy, threw the trowel over and climbed across to the other side. Damp, unkempt grass, weeds and withered flowers brushed his trousers. His pulse raced. The trowel felt oddly light in his hand. Outside the front door he was dwarfed: almost three metres high, it was double-leafed and made of solid dark wood.

It took him more than one attempt to get the key into the lock. Bloody nerves! He had to get a grip.

He'd expected a creak as he opened the door. It was well oiled, however, and made no sound. In the darkness of the hall he couldn't see very much, only that the floor and walls were of light-coloured marble. Staircases soared into the air on either side, leading up to a gallery. Directly in front of him was another door. Ignoring the stairs, he went up to it and tried the key.

But the door wasn't locked. Slowly, with bated breath, he swung it open.

More darkness.

He fumbled around the door for a light switch, but found none.

Gripping the trowel with both hands and holding it in front of him like a shield, he placed one foot in front of the over. After six or seven metres the metal trowel knocked into yet another door. His fingers groped for the lock. The key fit. The room beyond was a black hole.

His fingertips scrabbled across the bare wall. Dry plaster and small fissures. Then a cable mounted on the wall, leading to a small switch.

He flicked on the light and squinted. Scanning the room, his heart began to pound.

He was surrounded by the living dead.

Never in his life had he seen anything so terrifying yet so ethereal and gruesomely beautiful. He felt sick.

He closed his eyes. Opened them again.

Not a dream.

Reality.

The room before him looked like a gallery. In the middle was a solid wooden chair with a high back, evidently bolted to the floor. Jan walked down the row of large transparent blocks with women hovering inside them. Naked, young, deathly pale, similar as sisters, with long blond hair fanned out around their heads as if petrified mid-movement. They stared at him with their wide dull eyes, and he couldn't help thinking of Nikki Reichert, of the way she'd been huddled in his freezer.

Hesitantly he approached one of the blocks. Somewhere behind the bodies was a source of light that gave them a radiant aura. His hand slid across the transparent surface. Artificial resin. Smooth as glass. As if someone had taken great pains to polish away every inconsistency.

His gaze fell on the woman's wrists. At both veins were neat dark dots, like puncture marks. Somebody had bled them dry before immersing them in resin.

The fascination these women held for him despite the way they'd died disturbed him deeply.

He stood there spellbound. And didn't hear the footsteps behind his back.

Chapter Forty-Three

Berlin, 22 October, 12.53 a.m.

Laura was still stunned.

Froggy.

The idea that Froggy was the tattooed man tipped her world on its head. She kept picturing his face, the pale skin marked with black stripes, the eyes, the voice – she wondered whether she should have known from the start.

But she had no memory, no image of Froggy to compare with the tattooed man. It was simply too long ago. Where the memory of him should have been, there was nothing but empty space.

With each passing minute her anger increased. And anger was good. Better than fear. Better than the horror that had overwhelmed her, threatening to drag her down into the abyss with such irresistible force that nothing would remain.

After the echo of his footsteps had died away she'd kept listening, thinking every second that he'd come back, to her.

She wondered what he'd say. Most of all, she wondered what she'd say to him.

But as time passed, she began to doubt he even realised she was in the house. And if he didn't, she thought, then what would become of her?

Would her mother look for Buck if she didn't hear from him? Would she send someone?

She glanced around the room.

She had nothing more than a plastic bottle with a litre of water. It wouldn't last long. To her right stood the bucket with the open packet of toilet paper, and beyond that the heater, still humming on Setting 3 and keeping the room relatively warm.

The rope connecting the handcuffs around her wrists to the eyelet screw on the ceiling and the second one by the door gave her just enough room to lie down or come within a metre of the walls.

Her mind turned to Jan, and how only yesterday he'd been scarcely a few paces away from her. Only now did she understand why he was in danger, and why the tattooed man hated him so much. Tears came to her eyes. How long had she been waiting for a sign? Now it had come – and brought her deep unhappiness.

He'll kill Jan, she thought. Like he killed Buck. And all those women. Jan would die – because of her.

Her eyes wandered feverishly across the room, searching for something she might have overlooked. Some way of getting round that bloody rope and the door.

The warm stream of air from the heater caressed her legs. She shifted closer, letting it blow into her face. Just don't start crying again. The salt was still burning on her skin. She stared into the spinning fan and glowing filament inside.

Chapter Forty-Four

Berlin, 22 October, 1.44 a.m.

Jan woke up as something cold touched his scalp. From there the cold radiated down over his face, his closed eyelids, his lips and chin, dripping off him in long streams. The liquid tasted of nothing. Water, he thought.

He blinked woozily, and immediately the water ran into his eyes. Instinctively he made to rub them, but it was as though his hands were turned to stone.

He tried to blink away the water. Droplets clung to his eyelashes, making everything a little blurry. He squinted down at himself, and was gripped by icy horror. His arms were bound to the chair all the way to the cuffs of his shirt, his chest and legs equally tightly wrapped. His neck ached horribly, as if he'd been struck by something hard.

In a flash his memory returned. The mansion. The women's bodies. The chair bolted to the floor.

He looked up.

Barely a metre away stood the tattooed man.

He was clad all in white. The black, stripe-like pattern on his skin had razor-sharp edges. Between them was the pale skin of an albino. His wan lips weren't twisted with hatred, as at their last meeting; the smile they wore was almost relaxed, assured of victory.

In his right hand he was continuously twirling an open water bottle, sloshing the remaining water around at the bottom. Behind him, in the dim light, glowed the spectral corpses of the dead women.

'You used waterproof make-up,' remarked the albino. His voice was as soft as it was emotionless.

Jan did not reply.

'Did you want to get rid of it?'

'Get rid of . . . what?' asked Jan hoarsely.

'Your mark. What else?'

Jan tried to shake his head, but the pain in his neck held him back. Gingerly he attempted to move his legs, trying to move anything at all. Unsuccessfully.

'My mother used to use waterproof make-up too. Only, when I ate or played it wouldn't stay put. Did your mother want you to use make-up?'

'No.' God, how feeble his voice sounded! So weak-spirited.

'Do you want to know my name?'

Jan breathed, trying to stay calm. *Just don't panic!*

'You're a psychologist. Psychologists always try to call people by their names. Creates a personal connection.' He cocked his head. 'Do you think that might help?'

Jan swallowed. His throat hurt. His head was in a whirl.

'I'm F-j-o-d-o-r.' His lips almost painted the name.

Fjodor. A Russian name, thought Jan. Could Fjodor be Ava Bjely's brother? Had she even mentioned her brother's name?

'I'm going to kill you now . . .'

Jan gasped for air. The offhandedness of the announcement took his breath away. Panic surged inside him. Concentrate! Do something, goddammit! Talk to him!

'. . . and it doesn't matter what you say. You were already dead under the bridge. Actually, you were dead in France, when you got into her head.'

'How do you know Laura?' asked Jan, his voice husky. 'Who are you?'

Instead of answering, Fjodor picked up a thin, round object from the floor. Only when he pulled apart the wooden handles did Jan recognise the distinctive wire. It was a garrotte.

He felt paralysed, his mind whirling chaotically.

'She spat at me, you know that? Me! Because of a pathetic nobody like you!' The streaks moved like black vipers as he gathered spittle in his mouth. Then Fjodor spat emphatically.

Jan squeezed his eyes shut as the saliva flew into his face. In a flash he came to his senses, as if someone had emptied a bucket of cold water over his head. 'Where is she?' he asked. 'Where is Laura?'

'She's gone, dammit!' screamed Fjodor. His calm, emotionless whisper had vanished. 'Do you know how much that hurts? Do you know what I've done for her? How I've suffered? How much restraint I've shown? I've earned her. Year by year. Every centimetre of her skin. Every hair on her head is mine. And then you come along and just *take* her?' His forehead glinted, patches of sweat appearing on his shirt. 'I won't let that happen.'

Fjodor tensed the garrotte with a jerk, and the metal wire quivered. Jan's mind raced. Fjodor didn't know where Laura was? But hadn't Ava Bjely said her brother had brought her here? Laura must have escaped by herself, then. But what if Fjodor wasn't the brother? What if this were all just a horrible coincidence? If that were so, then Laura had to be here somewhere . . .

No! Coincidences like that simply didn't happen.

Or did they?

But then who was Fjodor? Peter Nolte?

Jan stared at Fjodor, trying to make out his features behind the pattern and mentally comparing it with the photo of Peter Nolte. 'What happened in the Nordholm Woods all those years ago?' he asked.

Fjodor lowered the wire. 'What do you think? You were there. Asking questions. Using your nieces as an excuse. Getting your sister mixed up in all this. And that pretty boy . . . Gregor. Doesn't look quite as nice without his ear, does he? How many people have died on your account, Jan Floss?'

With a quick movement Fjodor flung the wire around his neck and pulled the ends so that the metal dug into his throat.

Jan gasped for air; this could be his last breath. The garrotte would cut through his flesh like a knife through butter.

'Now I've got you, she'll come back. Sooner or later she'll look for you.' He increased the pressure.

Jan gagged, his vision growing dark. 'Why . . . would she come?' he choked out.

'Gravitation,' whispered Fjodor. His eyes sparked.

Jan struggled for air, rearing up, but the cling film kept him glued to the chair. He saw stars before a midnight-blue sky, the corpses of the women hovering like ghosts.

It was his last moment.

And the silence in that final instant was indescribable. Nothing could be heard: no breath, no wind, no cars, no insects, nothing at all – besides his own heartbeat.

And a key being turned in a lock.

Fjodor's head turned. His grip relaxed, and Jan drew a rattling breath.

The door swung open.

Jan's heart skipped a beat.

In the doorway stood Laura, breathing heavily, her face covered in soot, with matted hair and singed clothes. Around her wrists were handcuffs, and in her right hand was a Swiss Army knife with a bloody blade. An acrid, burnt smell wafted into the room.

Laura's gaze brushed past him, then jerked back in confusion, apparently searching for his birthmark. Then she turned to Fjodor. She stared at him as if he were the devil incarnate. But there was something else in her eyes that Jan didn't understand. It was neither anger nor fear, but pain.

Her ribcage rose and fell.

She opened her mouth and said: 'Hello, Dad.'

Chapter Forty-Five

Berlin, 22 October, 1.58 a.m.

'Or should I call you Froggy?' Laura's breathing was ragged. Speaking was difficult, her tongue dry with soot. 'Ava told me once that she used to call you that.'

Her father stared at her open-mouthed.

Laura could do nothing but stare back. Standing there all in white, his head covered in those demonic black marks, the tattooed man had seemed so huge. But her father looked much smaller.

'Hello, Laura,' he whispered rawly.

The hairs on the back of her neck prickled, and her instincts were bellowing *run*! But running was not an option. Without Jan she wasn't going anywhere.

Her father still wasn't moving.

'Let him go,' she said, her fingers closing around the knife. It was sticky with Buck's blood.

Her father went behind Jan and pulled the garrotte warningly around his neck. 'Stay where you are.'

Laura swayed; she had to support herself against the doorframe.

'How did you get here?'

'Buck brought me here. Ava wanted me gone.'

It took her father a few seconds to make the connection. 'Good thing I killed him. Buck was always a nasty piece of work,' he said. 'How do you know?'

'Know what?'

'Who I am.'

'You can't even say it, can you? You're my father, and I don't even know you. For me you were always invisible.'

He gazed at her steadfastly, but his hands were trembling. 'Didn't you find the money I put in your wallet?'

'What money? I thought you kept my wa—' She broke off, realising what that meant. 'Gandalf,' she murmured, taken aback. He must have taken her wallet as he changed her out of her wet clothes.

'Ah. So the tramp pinched it.' Her father curled his lip in disgust. 'I should have known. Should have tied up that loose end long before now.'

Laura froze. 'You mean . . . Gandalf's dead?'

He didn't respond.

'That's a yes, then,' she groaned. Tears welled up in her eyes. Gandalf's betrayal was bad enough, but his death tore a hole in her heart. 'Do you know how often he took care of me? How often he rescued me?'

'He stole from you.'

'So what? You don't know what it's like out there. Without him I wouldn't have made it.'

Rage flared up in her father's eyes. Involuntarily he relaxed the garrotte a fraction. Jan didn't dare move. Around his neck was a sharp red line.

'Where do you think you'd be without me?' hissed her father. 'Without me you wouldn't exist at all. Your mother didn't want you. Your grandfather didn't. They wanted to get rid of you before you were even born.'

Laura felt the strength drain from her legs. 'You're lying,' she whispered.

'The only one who wanted you alive was your grandmother Charlotte. But not for your sake – only because she was so fucking Catholic. Crosses all over the house, falling to her knees at church on Sunday . . . and then suddenly she finds her daughter's pregnant and wants an abortion. Do you know what happened?'

Laura shook her head mechanically.

'She got carried away with the milk of human kindness and turned violent. Ava took a tumble down the stairs, with you in her belly. But somehow you survived. Can't say quite the same for your mother. Ava lay in hospital for months.

'You surviving was a sign, you understand? You wanted to come into the world. It simply had to happen. Once Ava was fully conscious again, it was too late for an abortion. But she wouldn't accept it! Even lying in her hospital bed unable to move, she was making plans with me to get rid of you. By which I mean *she* made plans. I just held her hand, listened and thought about what I could do for *you*. I was your advocate. I wanted you to live.' He took a breath.

'You had powerful opponents. In the end Ava managed to convince Wolfgang. Your grandfather. You never met him. He spoke to the senior doctor at the clinic, a sort of doctor-to-doctor thing. Money changed hands. A little mishap in the operating theatre. It happens. Nobody would have thought twice about it afterwards. Even your grandmother would have swallowed it. You would have been thrown away with the medical waste. So do you know what I did?'

Laura didn't answer. She merely listened. As if through cotton wool, she watched Jan and the wire. He was struggling to breathe.

'The only right thing to do. The doctor had to go.'

'Go?' asked Laura in a choked voice. Tears ran down over her soot-smeared face.

'Go,' repeated her father. 'And to make your grandfather finally shut up, I told Charlotte what I'd done. He did make a second attempt. Ava was desperate, of course. It wasn't over yet.'

Laura wanted to run screaming out of the room. But she was transfixed, the words roaring in her ears.

'Ava begged me. Offered me money. Me! To bribe the surgeon who was about to operate on her.'

'Why? Why didn't she want me?' whispered Laura.

'I took her money and calmed her down,' continued her father undeterred, his gaze fixed as if he were somewhere far away. 'But I didn't do anything. I watched over you until you were born.'

'For Christ's sake, tell me why they didn't want me!'

Her father's lips narrowed into a hard, pale line.

'It had nothing to do with you,' Jan choked out. He flicked his eyes towards her father. 'Must be because of him. She didn't want a child with him, maybe—'

Her father silenced Jan with a tug of the garrotte. 'She loved me,' hissed Fjodor. 'She was a cripple. And I did everything for her. Everything!'

Laura stared first at Jan and then at her father.

'But if you did everything for her, and if you wanted me to stay alive that much, then why were you never there?'

For a moment silence reigned.

'I *was* there. You just never saw me. But I was always near you. Your whole life.'

'You mean the money you left for me in the vase? The photos you took of me when I lived on the street?'

'I was your guardian angel.'

'*Guardian angel?*'

'Think of Nordholm. I was there.'

Laura wiped her wet cheeks with her sleeve. The chain between the handcuffs clinked softly. 'I didn't need you in Nordholm,' she said. 'I'd have managed with Nolte. He wouldn't have tried it again. OK, maybe I hit him too hard, but what else could I do? I didn't have anything except the stone. But I could have explained everything, even if he'd been dead. Maybe he *was* dead. But then you had to show up and interfere, didn't you? Did God-knows-what with him. For years I was terrified he was just lying low, waiting to come after me. I don't know what you did with him, but whatever it was you did it for yourself. Not for me! For me it just made everything worse.'

'I was your guardian angel,' insisted her father, as if she hadn't said anything.

'I don't need a guardian bloody angel!' shrieked Laura. 'And definitely not one that kidnaps me. I needed a father. One who was there. One I could see, and touch.' She sobbed, her eyes turning to the pale women hovering around them. 'What are you doing?' she whispered. 'What kind of hideous monster are you?'

'Me? A monster?' he asked angrily. 'What does that make your mother, then? She wanted to kill her own child! And your grandparents? And *my* mother? My father? The doctor? And Buck? And that teacher, Nolte?'

Laura stared at him slack-jawed.

'Don't look at me like that. I could go on for ever.'

'You kill these women and . . . why do you do it?'

'Because I can.'

'Because you . . . what?'

'Because I can. I can do what I want. Nobody's going to make me answer for it.'

Laura could barely breathe. 'You kill women because you can? Just like that?'

Her father was quiet, and looked down at Jan.

Jan twisted his neck in the garrotte as if he wanted to say something, but her father pulled the wire so tight that nothing but a gasp emerged from his throat.

When her father looked up again, his eyes bored into hers. 'Now you're finally back, I want to know where I stand.'

'Where you stand?'

'I'm giving you the chance to take back control of your life.'

'I *had* control over my life,' whispered Laura. 'Until you showed up.'

'No. *He* had control. Look at yourself. Standing there gaping at him. Wondering what you can do to help him. You sat here yourself once, and made your decision then – you chose him! You'd rather have bitten off your tongue than betray him. Your life was on the line! His name for your life. And what did you do? Throw it all away for this pathetic loser's sake.'

'What do you want?'

'You.' His eyes virtually glowed as he looked at her.

'What do you mean?'

'Come over here. Take my place. It's very easy! Just a few seconds. One tug and you're free. Cut his throat!'

Laura froze.

Jan's eyes widened. Fear was etched into his face, and he tried to meet her gaze.

'Decide.' Her father clutched the handles of the garrotte in his fists, his arms tensed, and didn't take his eyes off her.

'And if I don't?'

'If I told you that, it wouldn't be a *real* decision.'

The pocket knife shook in her hand. Did she have any hope at all? She was handcuffed, and so weak she could barely stay on her feet, let alone help Jan escape.

'Come here and do it,' he whispered. 'It's quick, and then you'll be free.'

Jan tried to shake his head, chafing the skin of his neck as he did so.

She took an uncertain step forward, although what she really wanted to do was run. She wanted to get out of there. To be under the bridge. Or by the sea. Foam-crested waves. Warm winds. Rushing water. The knife felt slick between her fingers.

'Let go of it,' he whispered. 'You don't need it.'

Jan's eyes said the opposite.

She didn't want to let the knife go. But what use was it? What could she do to stop him? She took another step forward, stumbled, and caught herself.

'I know you can do it. You could do it even at Nordholm,' he whispered. His voice seemed to be inside her head, as if it were her own. 'Don't think about him. Think about yourself. Free yourself. It's the only way to survive.'

Survive. She'd learned that on the street. And at Nordholm. I'm me. Everyone else is everyone else. Take what you need . . .

'Let go of it.'

She obeyed. Opened her hand. The knife dropped to the floor with a clatter. He was so close now! Pale corpses shimmered to his left and right. In her father's eyes she saw individual capillaries, and in his irises the women were reflected like small white flakes.

'You or him!' he breathed.

A plume of smoke drifted over Laura's shoulder, followed by a puff of hot air.

She avoided Jan's gaze, looking past him at the wall. 'I'm sorry,' she whispered.

Chapter Forty-Six

Berlin, 22 October, 2.13 a.m.

Fear had constricted Jan's throat so tightly that he barely noticed the pressure of the wire. His heart raced. Memories shot wildly through his brain. He thought of Theo, how intent he'd always looked when he knitted his small brow and fiddled with the orange button on the seatbelt. How indignantly he'd reacted when Jan told him not to play with it. He felt the force of the accident, saw his mother's back, her hand gripping her suitcase, disappearing through the snow-covered front garden. Then his father's back, not turning around even once, not in all his life, and himself, bound to a chair. He wished he had an orange button he could press, an ejector seat to get him out of this madness.

But there was no button.

She swayed past the chair and went behind him. Only the burnt smell of her clothing still hung in the air like a poisonous cloud.

He felt Laura's hands take the garrotte from her father's. The heat grew more intense. Was it fear, or was it really this hot?

He closed his eyes, refusing to believe she'd do it. He was still hoping, although he knew how naïve that was. He would have reared up, but the cling film wouldn't let him.

He would have said something, if there had been anything to say.

But there was nothing equal to the situation.

Nothing that might make it better.

It was what it was.

Over.

Chapter Forty-Seven

Berlin, 22 October, 2.16 a.m.

The wire went taut with a jerk, cutting into his neck. His mouth flew open, struggling vainly for air – and a second later the garrotte sprang lightly onto his lap before dropping with a clatter to the floor.

Behind him he heard a dull thud, then a moan. The back of the chair shuddered.

He tore his eyes open.

Through the open door thin plumes of smoke came reaching for him, and beneath the closed door beyond he could see a flickering strip of orange.

Oh God! Was that fire?

Behind him he heard heavy breathing. 'Laura?' he croaked.

His only answer was a blow to the back of the head, and darkness fell.

Darkness and silence.

Only after a few minutes did a sound like the crackling of an open fire reach his ears.

He forced open his heavy eyelids. He was still sitting in the chair, still bound with plastic wrap. Raising his eyes, he turned towards the corridor. The door to the front hall was half open.

Orangey-red flames were mirrored in the marble. The air billowed with heat, and acrid smoke was filling the gallery.

The house was burning down!

Instinctively he made to jump up, but the cling film held him in the chair.

His eyes darted across the room.

'Hello?' he shouted.

No answer.

Where were Laura and her father?

By his feet, almost within reach, lay the garrotte and Swiss Army knife. He strained at the plastic wrap with his arms and legs, adrenalin giving him new strength, but still it wouldn't tear.

'Help,' he bellowed. 'HELP!'

He was immediately overcome by a fit of coughing. His eyes streamed and he gasped for air. How long did it take to die of smoke inhalation? Increasingly dense plumes were pouring through the door, taking on bizarre forms. In their midst was a shape almost like a human being. Jan squinted.

A figure drifted through the smoke, naked and chalky white, as though one of the women had stepped out of the wall and was coming straight towards him. His heart stopped. It had to be a hallucination.

The ghostly apparition came even closer, walking bent over, lurching, and suddenly shaken by a fit of coughing.

The woman was real!

He tried to call for help but could only wheeze. 'Quick! Please . . .'

The woman dropped to her knees in front of him. With trembling hands she picked up the Swiss Army knife, jabbed it into the plastic underneath his arm and tore it towards herself.

Reluctantly it gave way, and his right arm was free. 'Thank you,' gasped Jan with a painful effort.

The woman nodded and coughed, the knife slipping out of her hand. It clattered to the floor. Panicking, Jan scrabbled with his fingers at the tightly wrapped plastic around his left arm. The woman picked up the knife again – much too slowly, as if it were immensely heavy. Jan was running out of time. 'Give it to me,' he wheezed. She was seized by a fresh attack of coughing, her fingers cramping around the handle. Jan couldn't wait any longer. He grabbed the blade and tried to yank the knife out of her hand. It cut into his flesh, and white-hot pain shot through his hand. Finally she let go.

Gritting his teeth, he stuck the knife into the cling film and freed his left arm. The woman had sunk to the ground, and was dragging herself towards the door.

Jan cut the rest of the plastic wrap, lurched to his feet and glanced quickly behind him. The gallery was empty. No Laura. No Fjodor. As he tried to run away, he fell sprawling onto his face.

Picking himself up, he crawled on all fours towards the exit. His right hand left bloody prints, and his lungs felt about to burst. Catching up with the woman, who was barely inching forward, he half lifted her and dragged her along with him.

It was blisteringly hot in the corridor.

When he pushed the second door open all the way he was struck by a blast of scorching heat. The flames were mirrored garishly in the marble. A crash came from somewhere up above. Out of the corner of his eye he saw a burning beam come tumbling down and flung himself aside, pulling the woman with him. A split second later the beam slammed down next to him onto the marble floor. The heat struck him in the face like a fist, the sparks pricking like hot needles.

He heaved the woman over to the front door. Tearing the shirt from his body, he prayed it wasn't locked. With his hand wrapped in the fabric he pulled down the scorching handle and the door swung open. Fresh air whipped past him, making the fire surge.

Oxygen gave him new energy. He grabbed the woman under her arms and pulled her down into the garden, coughed, sucked the clean air greedily into his lungs, then floundered on, sinking onto the damp grass about twenty paces from the house.

Behind him he heard the sound of shattering glass.

As he turned around he saw the first flames come bursting through the windows. The garage around the side of the house was open, the white delivery van gone. In the glow of the fire he could see wide tyre tracks: they led straight across the lawn towards the open gate.

Jan unwrapped the shirt from his hand and made to put it around the shoulders of the woman, who was coughing and wheezing as she huddled on the grass next to him. She shrank back, but then let him do it. 'Thank you,' he said hoarsely.

She said nothing, just rocked back and forth.

'Were you locked up in the house?'

She nodded.

Her pale skin, blond hair, the resemblance to the women encased in resin – it spoke for itself. 'How long?'

'March.' Her voice was thin and fragile. 'He already had a . . . a place for me, with the others. He showed me on the first day.'

Jan swallowed. Since March. Almost nine months. 'How did you get out?'

'There was a woman, before. Dark hair . . . her face all sooty . . .'

'Laura,' said Jan. 'She's called Laura.' He felt a twinge in his chest as he said her name.

'She opened my door and took off the chains, asked me what I . . .' She swallowed. 'She gave me the key. Told me to be quiet . . . then she went into the room where you were. I wanted to go, but the door was open and I was afraid he'd see me. So I hid, then when he was gone . . .' She broke off and inhaled gulps of air.

'Thank you,' Jan repeated gently. He wanted to touch her, to give her a hug, but from the way she'd flinched before he judged it was better not to.

He turned back to the burning house, the open garage and the tyre tracks. The fire couldn't have gone unnoticed. In a few minutes the fire brigade would be here, probably the police too. For a brief moment he was overwhelmed by the urge to simply flop back onto the grass, wait for the police, explain everything and hand the matter over.

At least now he had a witness. Somebody to confirm that this maniac really existed.

The woman beside him sobbed, breaking his chain of thought. Her shoulders shook. She had put her arms through the sleeves of his shirt and was trying unsuccessfully to do up the buttons with trembling fingers. Kneeling in front of her, Jan carefully took the bottom half of the shirt and helped her.

She let him.

At the sight of her pale skin he couldn't help thinking of the gallery, and he was gripped by a powerful sense of rage. Kidnapping all those women, taking their lives and encasing them in resin spoke of a cruelty that took his breath away. Fjodor hadn't just killed them; he'd taken possession of them, even in death. The thought suddenly made his heart clench – his fingers, which had kept buttoning mechanically – froze.

He was ice cold. Suddenly he knew he couldn't wait for the police, not if he was right about what Fjodor wanted to do with Laura. They wouldn't just take his word for it. They'd ask questions, wasting precious time. Time Laura didn't have.

Reaching into his trouser pocket for Greg's car keys, he sighed with relief as his fingers found them.

'I've got to go,' he said, his voice raw.

The woman shot him a distraught look, but nodded.

In the distance came the howl of sirens. 'They'll look after you.' He got up painfully. 'One more thing. The man who did this to you, his name is Fjodor Bjely. He lives in Finkenstrasse. Can you remember that?'

'Bjely. Finkenstrasse,' she repeated dully.

'Tell the police, please. It's urgent.'

She nodded again.

Jan wasn't sure she'd really understood him, but he had no choice. Time was running out. He turned on his heel and walked towards the road. Cold air streamed over his bare chest, and he began to freeze. By the gate he felt briefly dizzy and had to grab the black bars. On the other side of the street a group of alarmed neighbours was gathering, clad in pyjamas and hastily thrown-on coats, watching the fire in consternation.

Jan kept close to the wall, hurrying along to the Cherokee.

He hoisted himself trembling into the driver's seat.

The engine started with a gurgle.

He switched on the heated seats and adjusted the climate control until it was blasting out hot air. The cut in his right hand twinged sharply as he shifted gear into drive. He accelerated much too quickly, making the car lurch forward and shoot across the street. He spun the wheel just in time. Then he heard the polyphonic sirens of an approaching fire engine.

After barely three hundred metres he turned abruptly right. There was only one place he could imagine Fjodor feeling safe enough to do to Laura what Jan feared he might. And he prayed he was right about that.

Chapter Forty-Eight

Berlin, 22 October, 2.32 a.m.

Finkenstrasse was silent beneath the sharp crescent moon. The Bjely house's black gate was closed.

Jan pulled up near to the wall. As he got out, a cold wind shivered across his bare chest. He closed the door softly. Taking the first-aid kit out of the boot, he hurriedly taped a bandage around the cut on his right hand. His gaze fell on a grey fleece blanket that lay crumpled next to the wheel case. Using the scissors from the kit he made an incision in the middle, stuck his head through and taped it around his upper body.

Climbing onto the bonnet then the roof, he scrambled over the wall. The grass rustled faintly beneath his Converse shoes as he approached the house, which loomed before him like a fortress. He wondered whether Ava Bjely had installed an alarm system, and how Laura had repeatedly managed to break in.

He had no tools, let alone a weapon.

He remained standing irresolutely on the lawn outside the house. Did Ava Bjely know what her husband was up to? Probably she was just as much in the dark as Laura. And since she was stuck in a wheelchair there must be rooms and corners in that house she'd never entered – maybe the basement, maybe the attic.

He stared at the gloomy front of the house. At that same moment, a shot tore through the silence.

Then another.

Jan flung himself onto his stomach in the grass. His heart thudded dully yet with crazed speed. The scent of wet earth was in his nose. He peered up at the house. The porch was just as dark as before. Where the hell had those shots come from? Was that Fjodor?

'Whoever's there' – Ava Bjely's voice rang out through the garden – 'get lost, or I'll put a bullet in your brain!'

Jan breathed a sigh of relief, but at the same moment he realised the sound must have warned Fjodor. 'Frau Bjely!' he called in a low voice. 'It's me. Jan Floss.'

Silence.

'I'm going to stand up and come over to you. Don't shoot!' He got to his feet and walked over to the house. The light went on in the front hall. Ava Bjely was waiting by the open door. In her lap glinted a silver revolver. She eyed Jan from head to toe. 'Why not use your damn phone?'

'Where's your husband?'

She knitted her brow. 'How the hell should I know? I'm more interested in what's happened to my daughter and my brother.'

'Your brother is dead. His body's probably still at the mansion, which is burning to the ground as we speak.'

The corners of Ava Bjely's mouth twisted, but otherwise she showed no sign of emotion. 'And Laura?'

'Your husband has her.'

'My husband?' In a heartbeat Ava Bjely went chalk-white. Instinctively she reached for the revolver. 'Oh God, no,' she whispered.

'Are you sure you don't know where he is?' asked Jan.

She stared at her hands as if paralysed.

'Frau Bjely!'

'What happened?' she asked tonelessly.

'There's no time for that. I've got to find your husband. He's going to kill Laura.'

Ava Bjely nodded, as if she'd been expecting nothing else for years.

'Are you sure he's not here?' repeated Jan. 'What about the basement? Or the top floor?'

She shook her head. 'Since you left I've been sitting in the dark and staring at the wall. Trust me – I would have heard him,' she said resignedly. 'He's gone. I don't know where.'

'But you must have some idea where I might find him, surely?'

Ava Bjely gazed emptily into the night. Her usually straight back was hunched; she seemed literally to have collapsed in on herself. An oppressive hush fell.

'Is that really all you have to say?' Jan was getting angry. 'You're just giving up?'

'You have absolutely no idea,' she replied wearily.

'No idea that you did everything you could think of to have Laura aborted? Or that you're paralysed because your mother physically attacked you?'

Ava Bjely's eyes narrowed. 'Who have you been talking to?' she asked hoarsely. 'My husband?'

'Help me!' urged Jan. 'If your daughter means anything at all to you, then for God's sake *talk*. You might remember something that could help me find him.'

Ava Bjely sighed and sat up in her chair. 'Push me inside. You may be right.'

'But I warn you,' added Jan, 'I'm sick of you fobbing me off with bits and pieces.'

'Just push me in. It's not the kind of thing you discuss on the doorstep.'

A few minutes later they were sitting opposite each other at the dining table. Ava Bjely put the revolver down in front of her. 'Perhaps I should begin with my real name. I was born Jenny Ava Stelzer, and this is my parents' house.'

Chapter Forty-Nine

Berlin, 22 October, 2.38 a.m.

Laura felt a gust of air on her neck as the front door closed behind her.

'Welcome.' He took the blanket off her shoulders, revealing her duct-taped wrists. The smell of her soot-covered clothes reminded her of the burning mansion and of Jan, who was bound to the chair at the mercy of the flames.

'Just walk,' he murmured, jabbing two fingers into the small of her back. 'Straight on, past the stairs. I want to introduce you to someone.'

Laura stumbled down the long hallway. The duct tape around her legs gave her just enough room to shuffle slowly forward. To her left a floating wooden staircase led up to the first floor. The corridor ran parallel to it, leading to a large door inlaid with panes of glass.

'Do you see that?' he whispered from behind into her ear. She hated the sound of his voice. She wanted to punch him.

All she saw was a dark room beyond the door.

Another prod from behind, between her ribs.

'Go on in.'

Laura went up to the door and pushed it with her bound hands. To the left at the back she thought she saw the outline of a bulbous old TV.

'On the right, in the corner,' he said.

Laura took a few steps into the room. To the right there was a niche, but she could make out nothing definite.

'Wait, I'll put the light on.'

A bulb flashed for a split second, then the filament burnt out with an electric hiss and all was dark again. He snarled. Then he went over to the television and switched it on. Grey fuzz appeared in the depths of the dull screen. Black-and-white snow flickering in the gloom.

In the light of the television she realised she was standing in front of two massive blocks of resin.

In the right-hand block was an elderly woman: naked, sunken and drained of blood. There were numerous cuts at her wrists and ankles. In the left-hand block floated an obese man. Laura's breath caught in her throat at the sight.

He was as naked as the woman. Where his genitals should have been gaped a black wound. His head seemed tinged blue, and from his mouth protruded a bloody hunk of flesh.

'I'd like to introduce you to my parents, princess. Don't worry. They can't hurt you. I've been making their decisions for them for a long time.'

Laura opened her mouth to scream, but her throat produced a choking gasp instead.

'It's time,' he whispered, 'for me to make a decision for you too.'

Chapter Fifty

Berlin, 22 October, 2.48 a.m.

'Jenny Ava Stelzer?' asked Jan.

'My mother Claudia was the scion of a Viennese family of private bankers.' Ava Bjely coughed. 'Derenberg. Perhaps you've heard the name?'

Jan shook his head.

She responded with a regretful, almost scornful smile. 'My father, Dr Wolfgang Stelzer, came from a medical family. When I was little, he went to the United States for three years. In those days plastic surgery was a growing industry. When he came back, he wanted to open a private clinic. It was small change to my mother, so she bought an old mansion house nearby and my father began to renovate it. Those were golden days for my family. Money, reputation, big plans. I was blonde, good-looking, young and healthy, with plenty of opportunities to while away my time with boys. Until 31 October 1977.'

'My parents were away, and my brother Buck wanted to take advantage of that. He organised a Halloween party at the house. Nobody did that sort of thing back then. Say what you like about my brother, but when he threw a party he didn't do it by halves.'

Nineteen seventy-seven, thought Jan, doing a quick mental calculation. 'And Laura was conceived at that party?'

Ava Bjely gave a bitter smile. 'I admire your perspicacity.'

'Did you meet your husband at the party, or had you already got to know him?'

'Both, in a sense.'

Jan wrinkled his brow.

'Laura was the product of a rape.'

Jan swallowed.

A rape? It took him a moment to digest the information, but suddenly the pieces fell into place in his head as if of their own accord . . . and a thought occurred to him. 'But if your husband really is Laura's father,' he said, thinking out loud, 'then you married the man who—' He fell silent. The thought struck him as monstrous.

Ava Bjely's mouth twisted. 'It was Halloween. He was dressed all in white, his face and head all covered in a strange pattern. He looked like a voodoo priest or something. I never would have dreamt it was Froggy under there.'

'Froggy?'

'That was his nickname at school. My brother gave it to him. Froggy was always an outsider. He came to school in make-up with his hair dyed black, even in the first grade. I think his mother made him.'

Another piece of the puzzle, thought Jan. 'He had albinism, didn't he?'

Ava Bjely nodded. 'But nobody knew. He was always good at hiding.'

'You just said his mother made him – did you ever meet his parents?'

Ava Bjely shook her head. 'The first time I went to his house, his parents were already dead.'

'His house?' Jan's ears pricked up. 'You mean the house he grew up in?'

'His parents' house, yes.'

Jan felt a tremor run through his whole body. He thought of Dr Maria Hülscher, who had probably stood on that very doorstep decades before. 'Is the house still there?'

Ava Bjely looked at him. Clearly the same idea had just come to her. 'You think he'll take Laura there?'

'Where else?' asked Jan.

'You don't know how many properties my family owns.'

'Here? In Berlin?'

'No,' admitted Ava Bjely. 'Most of them are in Vienna. But he runs them.'

'He's got to feel safe,' said Jan. 'He needs to feel everything's under his control.'

Ava Bjely gazed at him, her eyes wandering over Jan's bandaged hand and fleece blanket and coming to rest on the swollen red line around his throat. Finally she nodded, as if making a decision. 'I'll show you the way. Help me into the car.'

Jan shook his head. 'We're calling the police. They'll get there faster.'

Ava Bjely gave a crooked smile. 'No police.'

'Excuse me?' Jan stared at her in disbelief.

Ava Bjely laid one hand on the revolver. 'No police.'

'If you don't want to call the police, that's fine by me. I'll do it myself!'

'That won't help you. You need the address. And you won't get it without me.'

Jan stared at her, agog. 'This is your daughter we're talking about, for Christ's sake. Don't you get that? Only a few hours ago you were packing me off to help her.'

'I still want to help her,' said Ava Bjely with icy coolness. 'Just not with the police.'

'Why? What do you have to hide?'

Ava Bjely said nothing, and turned her face away.

Jan clenched his fists. He knew there was no more time to waste. 'Fine,' he said grimly.

Chapter Fifty-One

Berlin, 22 October, 2.56 a.m.

Jan flung the passenger door of the Cherokee wide open, grabbed Ava Bjely under the arms and lifted her out of the wheelchair.

Her fingers were clamped around the revolver. Jan felt the weapon graze his stomach as he hoisted her onto the seat, and devoutly hoped the safety catch was on.

'Where to?' he asked, once he was behind the wheel.

'Straight on, then the second right, down Clayallee,' said Ava Bjely.

Jan stepped on the accelerator. The Cherokee roared and shot forward. The burnt smell that still clung to his body filled the interior of the car. Just before Clayallee he braked sharply, spun the wheel and turned down the narrow road with a squeal of the tyres. Ava Bjely was still gripping the revolver tightly, staring out through the windscreen.

'What happened afterwards?' asked Jan.

'After the rape, you mean?'

Jan nodded.

'My brother found me. I was unconscious. And he had a problem.'

'How do you mean?'

'He'd thrown a party without our parents' permission, the house looked like a pigsty, and now his stupid sister was lying half dead in their bedroom, stark naked, with strangulation marks all over her neck. Meanwhile the last few stragglers were stubbing out their cigarettes on the parquet downstairs. Not exactly the kind of situation where you call an ambulance or the police.'

'You mean he didn't fetch *any* help?'

Ava Bjely's eyes were fixed on the road ahead. 'He put me on the bed and tried to wake me up. At some point he succeeded. I was in so much pain I could barely move, and I felt like my back was broken – it turned out later that when I fell onto the bedframe I cracked a vertebrae. I screamed at Buck to call our parents. Then I begged, and finally threatened. Eventually he gave in. Our parents came back from London immediately. You can imagine what a performance there was.'

'Because of the rape?'

'Oh good God, no. I kept that quiet. I didn't want to talk about it, least of all with my parents. I told them he'd *tried* to, but that was it.'

'Did you go to the police?'

'Certainly not! In a family of doctors and private bankers? You learn to keep a lid on everything. No hospital, no police, nothing. The staff tidied up the house, my father treated my cuts and bruises, and my mother went to church and prayed for me.'

'Prayed?' A red light flew towards Jan. He was forced to brake, pulling up at the crossing then accelerating again.

'Every single day. Dyed-in-the-wool Catholic, you see. My father had affairs and my mother went to church. She thought I'd been drunk. Drunk, meaning it was my fault.' She pointed straight ahead with her left hand. 'Just keep driving, onto Hohenzollerndamm.'

'And when you realised you were pregnant, you wanted an abortion.'

'Yes. I did. I made an appointment in secret, but my mother found out and went crazy. The pregnancy came as a shock, yes, but abortion was a mortal sin.'

'But you'd been raped,' objected Jan. At least 150 metres ahead of him a traffic light switched to amber, and he accelerated above a hundred kilometres per hour. The speed brought a cold sweat to his brow.

'She didn't want to hear it. It was my fault, and that was that. In the end it all spiralled out of control. As you said before, she turned violent during one of our arguments, and ever since then I've been in this bloody chair.'

Jan tried to concentrate on the road. The wheel was dripping with sweat beneath his hands, the wound making it more than a little awkward to drive. Ahead of them appeared a large intersection.

'Go left. Take the A100 to Charlottenburg.'

Jan took the corner at high speed. Thank God for the motorway, he thought. No traffic lights, no junctions. 'And your husband?'

'What did he tell you?'

'That he foiled all your attempts to get an abortion.'

'That he *what*?'

Jan hesitated a moment. 'He called himself Laura's guardian angel. From before she was even born. He thought there was some big conspiracy going on. Apparently he even killed a doctor who'd been bribed by your father.'

Ava Bjely made a strange noise and rubbed her face with her hand. 'Oh my God, if I'd only known! Froggy simply turned up that first day at the hospital. I was lying there with a baby in my belly and the knowledge I'd be crippled for life. At first I used to send him away. I didn't like him. Didn't like his presumption, just showing up at my bedside. It was as if he was trying to tell me I was just like him now: an outsider. A tragic figure. Someone who deserved to be pitied. Pity was the last thing I wanted.

'Yet he kept coming, every day. In the end he was the only one interested in me. The only one I could trust. Or so I thought. He seemed to accept me as I was, long before I could: a paraplegic condemned to a wheelchair for the rest of her life, carrying a rapist's baby.'

'When did you realise you'd married the man who raped you?'

'October 1992. At Halloween, if you can believe it. Laura was fourteen by then. He and I – we'd always had separate beds, and separate floors of the house. I'd got used to him spending most of his time in Vienna and other places, taking care of our property interests.

'He came home late, between three and four, but I was awake. I heard the front door. The door to the living room was ajar. He was so agitated he didn't even notice me, like something had gone wrong. His face and his whole body were covered with those black stripes. It was the face of my rapist.

'At first I thought, Oh God, he's back. It's happening again. I didn't make any connection whatsoever between that man and my husband. Until he went upstairs with my husband's tread. And took a long, long shower in his bathroom, the way only my husband used to do. Then I knew.'

'Is that why you sent Laura to boarding school?'

Ava Bjely nodded. 'She was just entering puberty, and apart from my blond hair she looked uncannily like me. After seeing him in that ... that make-up ... I mean, I knew what he was capable of. I was afraid for Laura.'

'Do you know what he was doing that night?'

'I can imagine.'

'And you did nothing to stop him?'

'I made sure my daughter was safe.'

'Safe? By sticking her in some boarding school? For God's sake! You should have called the police. Your husband's a psychopath, a killer. He's murdered more than a dozen women. All of whom look near identical to you and Laura. You could have prevented it.'

Ava Bjely sat ramrod straight in her seat. 'How do you know that?'

'I saw it with my own eyes. He encased their bodies in resin and bricked them into the mansion's walls.'

Ava Bjely was audibly fighting for air.

Jan moved into the right-hand lane and whizzed past a slower car. Ava Bjely's horror didn't seem remotely feigned.

'Encased in resin, you said? Bricked into the walls? Oh my God. Why ... why does he do it?'

'Because he's possessive. A narcissist and a control freak, with his own particular view of the world,' said Jan, switching back into the left lane. 'Anyone who gets in his way is as good as dead. And anyone he's attracted to he wants to possess, or at least control. Like you. Like Laura. You two seem to be the only people he couldn't – or wouldn't – kill. So he made sure other women were in his power instead. Encasing them in resin is like' – he struggled to find the words and read the street signs flying by at the same time – 'like the ultimate form of control. He's controlling them even in death. As if he were God.'

'But if you think he can't kill me or Laura, why—'

'He couldn't *so far*. But things have got completely out of hand. I'm afraid there's only one way for him to wrest back control . . .' He paused, barely able to say the words. 'He'll want to put Laura in resin.'

Ava Bjely sat there as if turned to stone. She didn't speak. Her jaw was grinding mutely, her fingers clenched around the gun.

A few droplets of rain pattered against the windscreen, and a gust of air tugged at the car. Ava Bjely pointed mechanically to the right. 'Up there . . .' Her voice gave out, and she cleared her throat. 'You've got to go down Siemensdamm.'

'The house is in Siemensstadt?'

Ava Bjely merely nodded. Her teeth were grinding so violently that Jan thought he could hear them over the noise of the road.

Chapter Fifty-Two

Berlin, 22 October, 3.13 a.m.

Jan turned down the narrow street. At this time of night the residential area was deserted. 'Here?'

'Here,' nodded Ava Bjely.

Street lamps hung over parked cars, which created a narrow path down the middle of the road. Ava Bjely didn't have to say anything else. Jan identified the house immediately; on the pavement outside was a white delivery van.

He steered the Cherokee into a parking space, then switched off the light and the engine. A handful of raindrops beat loudly against the roof of the car.

Either side of the street were three- and four-storey blocks of flats, with identical balconies jutting out like open drawers. Fjodor Bjely's parents' house looked like something from another era: a detached house with a half-hipped roof overgrown with wild vines. Autumn had swept off the leaves. What remained were knotted branches, like a wickerwork of dry veins. Beneath it was the house, dismal and stained. The once bright red roof tiles were covered in dark blotches, as if the house had metastasised, the shutters were closed, and the garden fence had disappeared beneath thick ivy.

'Do you really think she's here?' asked Ava Bjely.

Jan nodded forcefully and pointed to the delivery van. 'That was parked in the garage outside the mansion.' Then he gestured at the revolver. 'If you want to see Laura again you should give me that thing.'

'I don't want you calling the police.'

'Oh, for Christ's sake! He's in there right now doing god-knows-what to Laura.'

Ava Bjely bit her lip. 'Ten million.' She stared at him through narrowed eyes. 'Ten million if you shoot him.'

Jan gazed at her speechlessly. 'You're sick.'

'Not as sick as he is. Ten million.'

'I couldn't give a fuck about your money,' blurted Jan indignantly. 'Now *give me the goddam gun.*'

Ava Bjely surveyed him. 'There he is,' she said softly. 'The wolf beneath the sheep's clothing.' She handed him the revolver. Jan's fingers closed around the rough, skin-warm grip. The weapon felt heavy; he'd never held anything like it before. On the barrel, the words Smith & Wesson were etched into the metal. Beside the cylinder was a kind of lever. 'Is that the safety catch?'

'The only safety catch is your finger.'

Jan nodded, took a deep breath, then swung himself out of the Cherokee and walked around the car. In the boot the first-aid kit was still open. He put the scissors in his back pocket, found an old torch next to the breakdown triangle, sent a silent word of thanks to Greg and tucked the Smith & Wesson into his waistband.

It was raining harder now.

As he walked past, his gaze brushed over Ava Bjely. She looked small on the passenger seat.

A mossy path ran from the garden gate to the front door. Jan padded quietly around the house. The shutters were closed and boarded over. A shed leant up against the side wall. There was no back door or basement entrance, nor any glint of light.

At the front door, he briefly switched on the torch. The metal doorknob looked as if it had been recently touched. A sharp gust of wind buffeted his back. Wet leaves had been trodden flat around the doorstep. Cautiously he rattled the doorknob. Locked, of course.

He took a step back. In the wall above the shed was a window. Unlike the others, it wasn't boarded up.

Round the back of the shed was a waist-height plastic rain butt, full to the brim with scummy water. Supporting his weight on the edge of the drum, he pulled himself up onto it. White-hot pain shot through his hand, and he clenched his jaw and flattened himself against the wall of the shed. The thin plastic drum wasn't particularly stable. Water sloshed around inside, soaking his shoes. Panting, he clambered onto the roof of the shed, then crawled over the corrugated roofing felt towards the house.

The weather-beaten shutters were bolted from the inside. Pulling the scissors from his trouser pocket, he jammed them into the crack and jemmied back the bolt. The hinges squeaked as he opened the shutters.

Behind the window it was so dark he could see the outline of his own face reflected in the glass. Cutting off a piece from the blanket, he wrapped it around the torch and smashed in the pane. Instantly he ducked down, whipped out the gun and held his breath.

For a long, agonising moment he listened. Nothing but the wind and rain.

Then he reached through the hole in the glass, unlocked the window and climbed into the house.

Inside he covered the torch with his hand to block the light and switched it on. His fingers glowed red, a faint light emanating between them. Jan saw a single bed, two chests of drawers, a tiny desk, books and a desk lamp, all of them blanketed in a thick layer of dust. Pictures hung on the walls either side of him, about a dozen photographs in plain black frames. He took his hand away from the torch in order to see them better. At first he thought they were of Laura. Until he saw the blond hair. The young woman had the proud and upright bearing of a ballerina. It was Ava Bjely – or rather, Ava when she was still Jenny Stelzer.

The torchlight hit upon a murky block of resin on one of the chests of drawers, solid and somewhat larger than a shoebox. Jan leant forward and found himself looking into the dead eyes of a striped kitten, which was floating in the resin as if caught mid-bound.

He inhaled sharply, and couldn't help thinking of Laura. He felt sick to his stomach. He switched off the torch and the cat vanished like a ghost. Wan moonlight fell through the window, allowing him to see no more than the outlines of the furniture.

Gingerly he opened the door and slunk into the corridor. The house was deathly still. Diffuse light fell through a window in the roof, and a staircase led straight down to the ground floor. His wet shoes squeaked on the wooden floor. Stopping immediately, he slipped out of his Converse and crept down step by step.

At the bottom of the stairs he paused. Opposite him was the front door, so he reached out and carefully tried the handle. The door swung inwards, a gust of wind carrying a few leaves over the threshold and scattering them across half a dozen milky plastic canisters. Jan picked one of them up. It was heavier than a bucket of water, with a viscous fluid slopping around inside. Resin, he thought. The glinting barrel of the Smith & Wesson trembled in his hand.

At the end of the corridor was an open door, offering a glimpse of a clunky old TV beyond. On the left were the steps leading down to the basement, and on the right another door, presumably the toilet. Slowly, gun raised, he went over to the basement stairs.

His heart was hammering.

He didn't dare switch the torch back on. The dark-tiled steps down to the basement were narrow, walled on either side. They ended at a grey door.

Warily he turned the handle and pushed, the hinges grinding like sand between teeth. He slid into the basement on his tiptoes.

A short corridor. Three doors. Whitewashed brick either side. The far door wasn't quite shut, and a ray of light fell almost to his feet. A caustic chemical smell reached his nose. The resin! A final step, and he was standing directly in front of the door. He could hear someone grunting with effort, as if lifting something heavy.

Jan kicked the door and it flew open with a crash.

He was blinded by a dazzling light.

In a room tiled floor to ceiling in white stood Fjodor Bjely, scarcely three metres from Jan, staring down the barrel of the gun. His white clothes were flecked with soot. He held Laura in his arms like a bridegroom carrying his new wife across the threshold, and was in the act of placing her into a large tiled basin that stood in the middle of the room. But this bride was bound with duct tape at the hands and feet, and wore only a slip and bra. Her face was still smeared with soot and tears, yet her eyes flickered with a sudden hope.

Jan aimed the gun at Fjodor's head. 'Put her down.'

On Fjodor's face was a twisted smile. The pattern on his right cheek was smudged. His eyes shone with a blend of puzzlement and sheer hate.

'Put her down. NOW!' repeated Jan.

Fjodor didn't move a muscle. His irises were pale as ice, his gaze focused on the quivering barrel of the gun.

Jan let go of the torch and used his left hand to hold the revolver steady.

'If you shoot,' said Fjodor slowly, 'I'll drop her and she'll bang her head on the tiles.'

'If you put her down I won't shoot.'

Silence.

Stalemate.

I'm not putting her down, said Fjodor's eyes.

Jan watched him, sensing Laura's gaze. He thought of Greg, Nikki Reichert, Gandalf, the woman at the mansion – would he ever feel safe if he didn't pull the trigger? The wound on his neck burned, the tiles beneath his feet cold as ice. He saw Laura's mouth form a word, noiselessly and in slow motion.

S – h – o – o – t!

His finger curled around the trigger, the sinews tensed to snapping point.

He wondered how far he'd have to pull before the gun fired.

A third of the way . . . nothing.

He raised the weapon a fraction, now gazing straight down the barrel between Fjodor's eyes.

Halfway . . . still no shot.

The hammer wasn't budging. Did the revolver even work? Ava Bjely had fired it . . .

Two thirds . . .

When the hell was the hammer going to lift?

'Fine,' growled Fjodor. 'I'll put her down.'

Jan's index finger froze.

Fjodor sank to his knees, laying Laura down next to the tub. Jan tracked his head with the barrel of the gun. The tub was a quarter full of a clear, viscous fluid. Beside it were dozens of canisters.

Laura's eyes were pleading. *Shoot!*

Fjodor placed Laura gently on the ground. Jan was still aiming at the bald, painted head, almost wishing Fjodor would try something so he could put a bullet through his skull and watch his sick brain splatter across the floor.

And yet he was afraid of that moment.

His finger loosened imperceptibly.

As if sensing Jan's hesitation, Fjodor jumped aside.

Instinctively Jan fired.

There was an ear-splitting bang. The recoil jerked the weapon upwards, and for a split second Jan's arms and shoulders vibrated to the marrow. White ceramic splinters pinged through the air like needles.

Chapter Fifty-Three

Berlin, 22 October, 3.36 a.m.

Laura screamed.

The next moment Fjodor hurled himself at Jan, grabbing the hand with the gun and tearing it upwards. The force of the attack toppled Jan backwards against the edge of the door-frame. Fjodor ducked underneath his arm and wrenched it violently.

His shoulder felt like it was twisting out of the joint, and his hand burned as if he'd stuck an electric cable in it. He lost control, relaxed his grip, and Fjodor wrestled the revolver off him. Frantically Jan scrabbled for the gun with his left hand. Fjodor's fingers had nearly closed around it, his index finger curling around the trigger and the barrel lurching threateningly towards Jan's chest. Jan pushed back, forcing the revolver away. His muscles were trembling, almost tearing. Fjodor's face was right next to his. Sweating. Panting. Distorted with rage. Instinctively Jan lashed out with his forehead, slamming it into Fjodor's temple. Fjodor staggered and Jan worked his other hand free, grabbed the barrel of the gun and tugged.

In the middle of the tussle a shot exploded. Laura screamed again. Jan let go of the gun like a red-hot poker.

The moment seemed impossibly drawn-out.

He waited for the pain, wondering where the bullet had struck him.

He perceived everything as if through smoke: the echo of the shot, his empty hands, Fjodor reeling backwards into the wall by the sink, where, slowly, his back against the tiles, he sank to the floor. Fjodor's moans. Fjodor's hand clutching the revolver, and the short silver barrel he was pointing at Jan.

'Stay where you are,' he hissed through gritted teeth.

Jan didn't move, his eyes flitting between the Smith & Wesson and the red stain on Fjodor's white shirt. The stain was at the level of his stomach, and blossoming rapidly. Fjodor's index finger on the trigger was white as snow.

This was it. This time he wouldn't be able to push the gun aside. Fjodor was too far away. Now nothing stood between Jan and a bullet. Fjodor raised the revolver so that Jan was staring straight down its black maw. 'I should have finished you off in France,' he snarled.

'No!' shrieked Laura.

Fjodor's eyes darted towards her. He lowered the weapon a few inches and grimaced. The black marks on his face were grotesquely smudged. Fjodor looked to be coming undone. 'No?' Pain and fury mingled in his expression. 'When *he's* got the gun you whisper *shoot*, and when I've got it you say *no*?'

Laura was about to answer, but thought better of it.

'I should spread his fucking brains across the walls.' Fjodor tried to straighten up, but sank back moaning. 'It looks' – he glanced at the wound in his stomach – 'as if he'll have to do something for me first.' Fjodor's eyes bored into Jan's. 'Finish it.' He nodded towards the canisters.

Laura froze.

Jan stared at him open-mouthed, shaking his head.

'I don't want to hear any more fucking nos!' bellowed Fjodor. 'Nobody gets in my way. Nobody!' He aimed the gun at Laura, his eyes feverishly bright.

Jan's breath caught in his throat.

'Do you think you can refuse? You think I'll let you?'

Jan stared at Fjodor, his gaze full of loathing. Pouring resin over Laura was the last thing he had in mind.

'You won't survive either way, in the end ... that's what you're thinking, isn't it? Have you really made your peace with that? If so, then congratulations. You're free. You can afford to be all high and mighty with your morals.' Fjodor lowered his voice. 'But where were her morals when it came to your shitty little life? Or have you already forgotten? Didn't you see it in her eyes? Didn't you hear her phoney apologies?'

Jan clamped his lips shut.

'Jan, please!' begged Laura. 'Don't believe a word, I—'

'Shut your mouth,' hissed Fjodor. 'She betrayed you, you pathetic moron. In the end she just betrayed you, she pissed all over your morals. Like she did to me.'

'I betrayed *you*?' Tears ran down Laura's sooty face. 'I grew up without you all my bloody life. You might as well have been dead. But you weren't!' she yelled. 'I always heard you. Your steps, sometimes your voice through the wall ... only I never saw you. You were a fucking ghost. And I always wondered what I did that was so wrong that my own father didn't want to see me. Why didn't you want to see me? What's so wrong with me that you didn't want me?'

Fjodor was breathing heavily, the gun still pointed at Laura.

'*Why?*' she shrieked.

'You had the wrong skin colour.'

Fjodor's words rang through Jan's skull like a shot. Was that the reason? Was it that horrifyingly simple? Suddenly he felt he could see the whole situation clearly.

'The wrong skin colour?' Laura gazed at her father uncomprehendingly.

'He's got albinism,' said Jan in a husky voice.

'I don't understand what that . . .'

'He didn't just hide from you. He hid from everybody. Dyed hair, make-up, creams. And all the while he was obsessed with finding someone like him, with white skin,' said Jan. 'When Ava got pregnant he thought you might also be . . .'

' . . . an albino,' whispered Laura.

Fjodor's eyes seemed to look straight through her. His head was leaning against the bottom of the sink, his right hand – holding the gun – resting on his thigh.

'So because I didn't have the right skin colour I was worth nothing to you?' asked Laura. 'All because I wasn't what you wanted?'

Fjodor's mouth was a narrow line. His eyelids fluttered, and he pressed his left hand against his bleeding abdomen.

'All those women,' asked Laura, 'were they supposed to be like you too?'

Deafening silence.

'And your parents?'

'You could never understand.'

'And me? Why me? First you do everything you can to make sure I'm born. Then you never let me see you. You follow me in secret like some peeping fucking Tom because you supposedly want to protect me – and now you want to kill me? Because I betrayed you?'

'You're out of control.'

'*You're* out of control!' screamed Laura. 'You're a fucking narcissist. A nutjob living in your own crazy world and dragging everybody else down because you can't cope in your miserable, stinking hole by yourself.'

The corners of Fjodor's mouth twitched. His fingers trembling, he cocked the Smith & Wesson.

A soft, tiny click.

Laura fell silent.

'The layer of resin in the tub is hard enough.' Fjodor turned to Jan. 'Clean her face before you put her in the tub.'

Jan didn't move.

'It's very simple,' hissed Fjodor. 'If you refuse, I'll shoot you both right now. First her, then you.'

A surge of hatred welled up inside Jan. Fjodor smiled derisively. 'All you had to do was pull the trigger. Once, twice, three times. Instantly, without all that put-her-down crap. But you're a bloody coward. When push comes to shove and you've actually got to *do* something, you choke and curl up shivering in the corner. Oh, but I mustn't do anything *wrong*. I mustn't get my hands dirty. I mustn't take responsibility. What happened in your tiny little life to make you constantly shit your pants like that?'

Jan clenched his fists.

'Hurry up, or she's dead. Five ... four ...'

Jan's mind raced. Time. He needed time. Ten, maybe fifteen minutes. Fjodor's strength was waning rapidly.

'Three ...'

The thought of drowning Laura in resin with his own hands was unbearable. But it was his only chance to buy time.

'Two . . .'

'All right, all right,' said Jan hastily.

'Clean that muck off her face.' Fjodor gestured to a stack of white face towels next to the tub. Jan's throat was dry as dust as he picked one off the top. The material was stiff and old, but clean. With leaden limbs he went over to the sink. Fjodor was only inches away now. One kick and he'd drop the gun. But Fjodor seemed to read his mind. Groaning, he dragged himself away from the sink, leaving smears of blood on the white floor.

Jan turned the water on. It shot gurgling from the tap, clear and icy cold. The dry material absorbed it greedily. In the mirror above the basin he searched for something that could help him, but there was nothing besides the tub, to which Laura was tied, a toilet and a heater. That was it. Not even a window. The only opening in the wall was a large ventilation shaft.

'Hurry up,' snarled Fjodor, 'or I'll start counting down from two.'

Jan turned off the tap. His heart was pumping dully yet at frantic speed as he knelt beside Laura.

'Don't touch her. You're only supposed to clean her face.'

Jan took the face towel and wiped the soot from her skin. Tears flowed from the corners of her eyes, yet she didn't blink or take her eyes off his, as if breaking eye contact might snap the thread between them.

'Shhh,' he said.

She swallowed.

Twenty years. A few heated kisses at his father's house. And now this. It couldn't be the end. Their eyes folded around each other as though in an embrace, and he never wanted to let go. He wanted only to sink into those eyes, in which Ava's green and her father's pale blue were mingled.

Christ! He still didn't know who she really was. He only knew that he couldn't give her up, and a boundless rage overwhelmed him.

Chapter Fifty-Four

Berlin, 22 October, 3.47 a.m.

Fjodor stared at Laura, the child who wasn't his child at all.

The midwife had pressed her into his arms after the delivery, a breathing, pulsing little bundle wrapped in a towel. Seeing her skin and the down on her head, he'd been stung with disappointment. His hands had stiffened, cramping, like his belly, his heart, his whole body.

This was what he'd fought for?

His first impulse was simply to drop her, but for some reason he couldn't.

And so it had remained, until today.

Drop her! – I can't.

Hadn't he freed himself from everything? Fulfilled his childhood dream? More than anything else he'd wished for invisibility. And he'd got it. He *was* invisible.

Froggy was gone, obliterated, once and for all. Gone, too, were all inhibitions and restraints. He could do whatever he wanted. No limits, no rules, no nos.

Until Laura had come into the world.

Drop her! – I can't.

As if he'd rejected her at first and then, against his will, accepted her.

He'd kept away from her. And yet he'd filled the vase, watched over her, protected her at Nordholm, photographed her thousands of times from a safe distance, with a telephoto lens as long as his forearm. He'd watched her flee Nordholm, cut her hair and dye it grotesque colours, booze, put on weight, stick holes in her ears, anything so long as she looked nothing like her mother in appearance – as if that were her single greatest goal. And every time someone had got too close, he'd done what fathers were supposed to do.

He'd never taken his eyes off her. Even when he'd gone away for a few days, he always knew where to find her. He had everything in hand. Until the moment she disappeared. Without any warning. Without any trace.

For months he'd searched, looking under every single bridge, every park bench. It was like she'd vanished into thin air. For eighteen years. Until a few days ago, when he'd glimpsed her on the edge of the street, quite by chance, an unearthly creature.

It had been instant déjà vu. Almost like that time at Buck Stelzer's party. *Jenny!* Jenny, only with dark hair. He'd sat in the car and got hard. Fucking hell! He'd followed her to Èze, imagining what it would be like to sit her in his chair, the way she'd look with pale skin and white blond hair, naked and shaved, the way she'd bleed out as he . . . no! Stop.

He swallowed.

He should have recognised Laura. But eighteen years was eighteen years. And all he knew about Laura's whereabouts during that time was what he'd learned from that blond surfer boy Greg with the stupid tan, while he burned his ear.

'She left because of that guy she met,' he screamed.

'What guy?'

'I . . . I don't know.'

'What guy? What did he do to her?' Fjodor let the flame lick Greg's ear until he howled. 'Nothing! He didn't do anything to her!'

'How do you know?'

'I . . . from her . . . she . . .'

'Don't lie.' He held the flame very close to Greg's eye.

'I'm not lying,' sobbed Greg. 'She told Katy.'

'Katy. Aha. And? Where is she?'

'Katy said she went into rehab. In some clinic. She wanted to turn her life around . . .'

'Why?'

'I don't know . . . because of that guy, I think.'

'Who is he?'

'I don't know! . . . Please! That's all I know!'

And eventually Fjodor had believed him. That ear hadn't looked very good. And Greg wasn't as hard as his build led you to believe.

Run off. Rehab. Turn her life around.

As if it were that easy!

Well, fine – he'd thought later – she was Jenny's daughter, after all. And Jenny was like steel when she had to be.

He felt indescribably angry when he thought of what Laura had done to him. And yet he was powerless.

Even now.

That left only one solution: the resin.

Fjodor stared along the barrel of the revolver. That bastard was wiping the soot from Laura's face like it was part of some sort of foreplay. More unbearable still, however, was the thought of Laura lying forever in the resin with her face covered in dirt. 'Enough,' he said hoarsely. He could feel his strength failing. 'Put her in the tub!'

The bastard didn't move. He just kept staring at Laura.

Fjodor gritted his teeth, swallowed and tasted blood. He was itching to blow the guy's brains out, but that would have to wait until Laura was ready. 'DO IT!' he roared.

Finally! He was picking her up, one arm under her knees and the other beneath her shoulder blades.

'Other side of the tub. I want to see you put her in there.'

Look at him walking around the tub! Tentative and weak. No backbone. What a pussy. Fjodor's eyes wandered over Laura's body, and he hated himself for the muddle he felt.

He blinked. His vision was fading. Not a good sign.

Jan was standing behind the tub.

'What are you waiting for? Put her in.'

Without a word Jan lifted her over the edge; then Laura vanished from Fjodor's line of sight. She was lying in the tub. How he wished he could look at her now. But standing up would cost him precious minutes. And there was still so much to do. He blinked again. His eyes flickered. 'The canister with the letters ER. Pour it into the tub. All of it.'

The pussy's arms were shaking as he poured the first canister into the tub. It glugged, and the distinctive scent of resin wafted through the air. Fjodor could see Laura in his mind's eye, lying on the bottom layer of resin, which would already be hard by now, the fresh stuff forming a pool around her. 'Keep going.'

The pussy hesitated.

'If you don't keep going I'll shoot you in the stomach, then I'll crawl up to the tub and kill her right in front of you.'

That was all he had to say. The pussy wiped his face with his sleeve. Beneath the make-up his birthmark re-emerged: red, violet, ugly.

The second canister, then the third, then the fourth.

Where was the resin now? Already up to her ears?

He was working much too quickly. He knew that. It had taken years to perfect the technique. The preparation, the immersion bath beforehand, the hardened bottom layer, the careful prevention of air bubbles. But he was running out of time.

The seventh canister, the eighth.

Laura didn't seem to be fighting it. She made no sound. Had she understood that it was better this way? Or was she already having to hold her breath? He thought of Jenny. Jenny would have kept silent out of pride. Maybe that was it.

The pussy was sweating. The bandage around his right hand was drenched in blood, the red line around his neck swollen.

The fifteenth. Sixteenth. Laura coughed and choked. The resin was trickling into her mouth, forcing its way into her lungs.

'Push her under!' he ordered. It seemed to him as if the words were said by someone else.

The pussy's eyes were wet. He leant down, put all his weight on his left hand and pushed. Fjodor involuntarily gritted his teeth; suddenly he wanted to close his eyes. Froggy had come knocking! But he wouldn't let him in.

Laura choked and spat again.

The pansy pressed, shaking. His face was covered in soot, sweat and tears.

Then there was silence.

Fjodor blinked. He could hear his own breath. Rattling, feeble. 'Now the canister with the big H on it,' he said dully.

The pansy's mouth was a straight line. Fjodor tried to read his expression, but his eyes kept going out of focus like a broken camera. He heard the hardener pour into the tub. The sharp chemical smell was overpowering.

Peaceful.

Suddenly he heard a noise – a kind of shuffling. A noise that didn't belong. Fjodor's gaze shifted to the doorway, and what he saw there stopped him dead.

Chapter Fifty-Five

Berlin, 22 October, 4.01 a.m.

Jan ceased to breathe. Ava Bjely was crawling through the doorway, panting, dragging herself onwards with the strength of her arms alone. She stopped abruptly when she saw Fjodor, the black make-up on his face, the gunshot wound and the revolver in his hand. 'Where's Laura?'

Fjodor was gazing at her as if she were some spirit come to life.

Jan prayed Ava Bjely wouldn't be capable of looking over the edge of the tub.

'Where – is – Laura?' repeated Ava Bjely.

Fjodor's lips were whitish blue and quivering. 'Ask him,' he said, pointing at Jan.

'Well?'

Jan's knees gave way. For a moment he had to support himself on the edge of the tub. His head was feverish and hot, his thoughts tangled and erratic. What should he say? The truth? A lie?

'Where the hell is she?' spat Ava Bjely.

'She's . . . in there.' Jan nodded at the tub.

'In there? You mean she's . . .'

Jan nodded and looked away.

Ava Bjely seemed to crumple. Utter silence. 'I want to see her.'

Anything, just not that! Jan shut his eyes. 'Please don't do that.'

'You useless piece of shit,' hissed Ava Bjely. 'I want to see her, so help me.'

Jan shook his head.

'Help her,' said Fjodor.

Ava Bjely's head twisted towards him. 'I can manage without you, you sick bastard.'

Fjodor ignored her and raised the gun. 'HELP HER!'

Jan looked into the tub, his heart pounding. As if in a trance he went over to Ava Bjely and picked her up. Nothing scared him more than what was coming next. Just one wrong word would do it.

'There's nothing there.'

Three wrong words.

Dead silence.

'Nothing but a tub full of some smelly stuff.'

Jan's heart hammered in his chest.

It took Fjodor a moment to process the words. 'What?'

'There's nothing there. Tell me right now where Laura—' Ava Bjely broke off abruptly. The realisation had hit her.

Fjodor gave an animal roar, his fingers curling around the trigger.

'No!' Ava Bjely threw up her arms and flung herself to the side, dragging Jan half-turning after her. The black muzzle flashed, the shot rang out with a crack, and a shiver ran through Ava Bjely. At the same instant Jan felt as if a metal pipe had been rammed through his side. He gasped for air and dropped Ava

Bjely, tripped over her body and launched himself at Fjodor. A second shot, and Jan felt a dull blow to his leg. Fjodor bellowed in pain as Jan landed on top of him. Grabbing Fjodor's left arm he pushed the weapon aside, then seized his throat with his other hand and squeezed.

Fjodor rasped. His larynx pumped up and down, his eyes popping. There was no hint of red in his irises, only a strangely translucent watery hue. Jan's shadow fell across his face. Beneath the black marks, the skin was turning blue. Fjodor twisted his neck, the sinews so taut they were virtually snapping. Black make-up had rubbed off onto Jan's hand, and his muscles were on fire. Fjodor reared up one last time, freeing the arm holding the gun with a powerful jerk and pointing the barrel at Jan's head.

Jan's fingers loosened around Fjodor's throat. With a deep wheeze, Fjodor inhaled. The Smith & Wesson shook. Jan saw the white index finger on the trigger. Saw the firing pin draw back. Fjodor's eyes glowed cold, supernaturally huge. Time compressed. Thoughts and sensations poured in their thousands down a single split second.

Everything inside Jan was screaming. He couldn't believe what he was seeing: a round black opening wobbling in front of his eye socket. He smacked Fjodor's arm away as hard as he could, but it was too late. He'd pulled the trigger all the way back. The firing pin shot forward.

There was a metallic click.

No blast. No shot.

Jan slammed Fjodor's arm to the ground, but he managed to wrest it free and struck Jan in the back of the head with the gun. Jan saw stars, wondering why he was still conscious. No doubt because Fjodor had precious little strength left. Fjodor struck a second time. Then a third.

If only he'd had a knife, or even a stone! Suddenly he remembered the scissors from the first-aid kit. Reaching one hand behind him he shoved it into his pocket. They were still there.

Then the next blow fell.

All the lights seemed to flicker.

He pulled out the scissors, the oval handles pressing hard into his hand, and stabbed the blunt, rounded blades into Fjodor's chest, forcing them between the ribs and into flesh.

The revolver fell clattering to the floor. Between one second and the next Fjodor's body lost all tension; he twitched and collapsed.

Jan let go of the scissors.

Panting, he rolled off Fjodor. Stared at him.

Shivered.

Waited.

Breathed.

'Jan?'

'Yeah,' he answered hoarsely.

From behind the tub came a sob.

'I'm coming.' Jan tried to get up, but the pain in his calf and side held him back. Blood was oozing from both gunshot wounds.

He gritted his teeth and looked at Fjodor. Beside him lay a Swiss Army knife, which had evidently fallen out of his pocket.

Jan picked it up, then crept away on all fours, past Ava Bjely, who was staring at the ceiling with dead eyes, and around the basin to the other side, where Fjodor couldn't see – to where Laura lay.

When he reached her he took her face in his hands. 'You all right?'

Her chest rose and fell unevenly. 'Is he . . .'

'Yes.'

She said nothing, merely shook her head.

Jan opened the knife and cut through the duct tape. 'Are you hurt?'

She shook her head. Jan felt her breath on his face, gazed into her eyes. Her lips quivered.

Again he took her head in his hands, stroking her cheeks. He tried to smile, but the pain was too intense.

'What about my mother?'

He shook his head.

She closed her eyes a moment. Swallowed. 'Don't let me go again, OK?'

Suddenly a hoarse whisper came from the other side of the tub. 'Hey . . . scum.'

Jan froze. He reached for the knife, and his fingers closed firmly around the red plastic. 'Wait here,' he murmured to Laura.

Sitting up, he dragged himself back to the sink. Fjodor Bjely's eyelids fluttered with exertion. 'Come closer,' he whispered in a thin voice.

Jan hesitated.

'Look at me. Are you still afraid?'

Fjodor's voice was so soft that Jan leant forward in spite of himself.

'Jan?' Laura, from behind the tub.

'I'm here. Everything's fine.'

Fjodor's gaze was directed inward, but for a brief moment his eyes shone. 'She's my daughter. Despite everything. Do you understand what I mean?'

'No she isn't. You didn't want her.'

A mocking laugh crossed Fjodor's black-smeared lips. 'My blood, my daughter. You'll never be safe. Think of the mansion. Think of Nordholm.'

The mansion. Nordholm. The hair prickled on the back of Jan's neck.

'You don't know her . . .'

'I know her. I know who she is.'

'But you still want to know what happened, don't you? Then . . . come closer . . . I don't have much strength left . . .'

Jan raised the knife threateningly, putting it to Fjodor's throat and bringing his ear close to his lips. The words rattled faintly out of Fjodor's mouth, etching themselves letter by letter into Jan's memory. Mid-sentence he heard someone move behind him. Slim, strong fingers closed around the fist that held the knife, jabbing the blade into Fjodor's throat and dragging it back. A weak stream of blood spurted out of the carotid, a few drops spraying into his face.

With a gurgle and a long-drawn sigh, Fjodor fell silent.

Laura, still holding Jan's hand firmly, sank to her knees behind him.

'I'm sorry,' she said. 'He's already poisoned my whole life. I don't want him to do it any more.'

Chapter Fifty-Six

Berlin, 5 November, 9.33 a.m.

Jan pushed the door leading out of Moabit prison and stepped into the open air. He was still limping a little.

The sky lay heavy and grey above the city. Powdery snow-flakes fell onto cold, dry ground. In the slipstream created by the traffic on Alt-Moabit, the snow was carried across the lanes and danced among the headlights of the cars.

Jan's breath materialised in the frosty air. He wasn't prepared for the sudden onset of winter, and the fierce cold crept beneath his thin windbreaker. Walking rapidly past the round, brick-red guard tower, he headed straight for the massive open gate. Behind him loomed the prison, a star-shaped building with beds for thirteen thousand inmates.

Two weeks in custody during the investigation had been hard on him, although he'd spent most of the time in the prison hospital. He'd been extraordinarily lucky with those gunshot wounds, the doctors had assured him. No injured organs, no smashed knees. The Smith & Wesson had been loaded with full metal jacket bullets, meaning the shot to his side had been a clean through-and-through that left only a small exit wound behind. Even the one to his leg wasn't as bad as they'd first thought.

After a brief grace period the interviews had begun. Endless interrogations, probing, constantly repeated questions – he kept feeling like nobody believed him. The whole story seemed so outrageous that he could scarcely believe it himself.

Then, at last, his lawyer Paul Stegner had said it was over. He was free to go tomorrow morning.

And he was.

At the gate Jan saw a thickly swaddled figure. His heart beat faster as he stepped across the threshold. He'd been longing for this moment, yet it frightened him too. During his imprisonment Laura hadn't been allowed to visit, since both she and Katy were witnesses. *Danger of collusion*, they'd called it. That Laura had pushed the knife into Fjodor's neck he didn't mention.

He knew Laura would have questions. And then there was what Fjodor had told him. Like poison, his last words had insinuated themselves into Jan's mind, and he still wasn't sure whether they were final proof of Fjodor's madness, of his desperate compulsion to pull the strings even after death, or if there was some truth to them.

Laura looked ready for a Siberian winter, wearing a dark, oversized man's coat over sturdy dark-brown jeans, heavy boots and a thick woollen scarf. She'd piled her hair beneath a woolly hat that caught the snow.

'Hi,' she said.

Jan hugged her.

Her cheek was cold against his; she must have been waiting for some time. She smelled of Fahrenheit, and he couldn't help but be reminded of their last embrace, in her father's white-tiled basement. No Fahrenheit, only soot, cold sweat, the stench of death and artificial resin.

He kissed her, and despite the chill he grew warm. How does she bloody do it? He was in his mid-thirties, yet he felt – just like in France – as though he was back in the playground at school, longing for exactly this moment. Twenty years, and his feelings hadn't changed.

Yet everything was different.

Laura took her lips from his. Hot breath steamed in the air. She cast a quick glance upwards at the sky. 'Whenever we kiss it's raining or snowing.'

'Better snow in Berlin than rain on the Côte d'Azur.'

Laura unbuttoned her coat. Beneath it was revealed a light brown tweed coat with a belted waist. 'I thought you might be cold.' She handed it to Jan.

He took it gratefully and slipped it on. 'Pre-warmed,' he remarked with a smile. 'Shall we take a walk?'

Laura nodded. She was pale, dark shadows under her eyes.

They turned left and walked down Alt-Moabit.

'How are you?' asked Laura, looking at his leg, which still couldn't take his full weight.

'My leg and side are fine. I was lucky,' he said. 'And I'm glad to be out. What about you?'

She shrugged. 'The days are fine.'

He grimaced. The nights weren't. How could they be?

They turned left down Rathenower Straße and headed to Fritz Schloss Park.

'How exactly did she die?' asked Laura.

No beating around the bush. He'd have preferred a little small talk first. 'Your mother?'

Laura nodded.

He cleared his throat and stuffed his cold hands into his coat pockets. 'She literally threw herself in front of me. If she hadn't, the bullet would have hit me.'

Laura was quiet.

'You were the one she cared about, though. She wanted to save you.'

'But she hated me so much,' murmured Laura.

Yes and no, thought Jan.

'He said she wanted to kill me. Do you know why?'

The question he had feared.

A truck boomed past them, swirling the falling snow and giving Jan a moment to think. Haltingly he began to tell her what he knew. Laura only nodded. Her expression was impenetrable, a wall of self-protection.

'If she really wanted to protect me,' she said at last, 'I mean, if she knew what kind of person he was, then why didn't she say anything?'

Jan shrugged. 'Maybe he had a hold over her. Somehow the two of them were chained together. Perhaps he made her complicit in something.'

'Do you think she knew about the women?'

Jan shook his head. 'I'm sure she didn't. He managed all their properties, and your mother hardly ever left the house. The clinic at the mansion was his kingdom. The perfect hiding place. Did the police find anything there that they could use after the fire?'

'Mostly bone fragments. They're still working on their analysis. There were lots of tubs in the basement, plus an old operating table and an electronic fork lift. That's probably how he moved around the finished blocks of resin.'

The thought sent a chill down Jan's spine.

'I still don't understand why my mother didn't call the police. He nearly killed her. How could she live under the same roof as him for so long?'

Jan was silent a moment. 'I'm sure there's a reason. She certainly wasn't the kind of person to do something without good reason – or to let something happen.'

Laura nodded mutely and let the matter rest.

To their right was Fritz Schloss Park, and they stepped onto one of its snow-covered paths.

'How is Katy?' asked Jan.

'Hm?'

'How's Katy? Is she coping all right with what happened to Greg?'

'More or less. She's living back at home.'

'Really?' Jan's feelings were more than ambivalent on the subject of Katy's husband.

'But she's chucked Sören out.'

'Oh. I see.'

'She asked if we'd drop by later.'

Jan came to a halt, gazing at the snow-covered track that led further into the park. 'I'm too cold for a long walk. I just needed to feel like I was properly outdoors.'

'Want to take the train?'

Jan nodded. Suddenly he thought of his father, of their last meeting and the way he'd stood under the porch roof at the care home. He felt the old knot back in his belly and promised himself he'd call.

Standing next to him, Laura was trying to read his expression. 'What shall we do now?'

'Go to Katy's, I thought.'

'No, I mean, you and me . . . about us . . .'

'Is that a serious question?'

She said nothing. Her eyes looked grey, reflecting the sky. All at once she seemed forlorn.

'I'm sorry.' He gave her a hug. 'I'm here.'

Thanks . . .

. . . are due first of all to Meike, Janosch and Rasmus. Two feet in the job and a head full of books meant you often got a raw deal, so I'm deeply grateful for the fact that you nonetheless showed so much understanding and curiosity about my writing. The same goes for your psychologist's couch, Meike, where my protagonists and my story have so often lain.

Heartfelt thanks to you too, Katrin. Your editorial eye made me think, grumble and sometimes laugh at myself. And it always made this book better. Julia, thank you for your enthusiasm right from the word go. An agent is one thing; a good agent is something else entirely. Dear 'Ullsteiners' – and by that I mean all of you – without your work I'd have had a good story but not a book reaching so many people. Thank you for that.

Dear Annette and Norik, when you gobble down the first pages I know I'm heading in the right direction. All the more so when you keep going.

And to Verena, Peter, Wilfried, Henrik and all the friends and acquaintances who gave me criticism and feedback, a huge thanks! I may have been the one to write the book, but all of you contributed.

About the Author

Marc Raabe owns and runs a television production company. He lives with his family in Cologne. *The Shock* is his second thriller.

The page-turning thriller that took Europe – and then the UK – by storm – available now as a Manilla paperback and e-book.

Read on for a sneak peek . . .

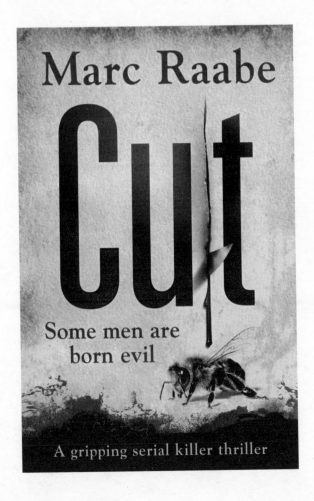

Prologue

West Berlin – 13 October, 11.09 p.m.

Gabriel stood in the doorway and stared. The light from the hall fell down the cellar stairs and was swallowed by the brick walls.

He hated the cellar, particularly at night. Not that it would've made any difference whether it was light or dark outside. It was always night in the cellar. Then again, during the day, you could always run out into the garden, out into the light. At night, on the other hand, it was dark *everywhere*, even outside, and ghosts lurked in every corner. Ghosts that no grown-up could see. Ghosts that were just waiting to sink their claws into the neck of an eleven-year-old boy.

Still, he just couldn't help but stare, entranced, down into the far end of the cellar where the light faded away.

The door!

It was open!

There was a gaping black opening between the dark green wall and the door. And behind it was the lab, dark like Darth Vader's Death Star.

His heart beat in his throat. Gabriel wiped his clammy, trembling hands on his pyjamas – his favourite pyjamas with Luke Skywalker on the front.

The long, dark crack of the door drew him in as if by magic. He slowly placed his bare foot on the first step. The wood of the cellar stairs felt rough and creaked as if it were trying to give him away. But he knew that they wouldn't hear him. Not as long as they were fighting behind the closed kitchen door. It was a bad one. Worse than normal. And it frightened him. Good that David wasn't there, he thought. Good that he'd taken him out of harm's way. His little brother would've cried.

Then again, it would've been nice not to be alone right now in this cellar with the ghosts. Gabriel swallowed. The opening stared back at him like the gates of hell.

Go look! That's what Luke would do.

Dad would be furious if he could see him now. The lab was Dad's secret and it was secured like a fortress with a metal door and a shiny black peephole. No one else had ever seen the lab. Not even Mum.

Gabriel's feet touched the bare concrete floor of the cellar and he shuddered. First the warm wooden steps and now the cold stone.

Now or never!

Suddenly, a rumbling came through the cellar ceiling. Gabriel flinched. The noise came from the kitchen above him. It sounded like the table had been scraped across the tiles. For a moment, he considered whether he should go upstairs. Mum was up there all alone with *him* and Gabriel knew how angry he could get.

His eyes darted back to the door, glimmering in the dark. Such an opportunity might never come again.

He had stood there once before, about two years ago. That time, Dad had forgotten to lock the upper cellar door. Gabriel was nine. He had stood in the hall for a while and peered down.

In the end, curiosity triumphed. That time, he had also crept down into the cellar, entirely afraid of the ghosts, but still in complete darkness because he didn't dare turn on the light.

The peephole had glowed red like the eye of a monster.

In a mad rush, he had fled back up the stairs, back to David in their room, and crawled into his bed.

Now he was eleven. Now he stood there downstairs again and the monster eye wasn't glowing. Still, the peephole stared at him, cold and black like a dead eye. The only things reflecting in it were the dim light on the cellar stairs and him. The closer he got, the larger his face grew.

And why did it smell so disgusting?

He groped out in front of him with his bare feet and stepped in something wet and mushy. *Puke. It was puke!* That's why it smelled so disgusting. But why was there puke *here* in the first place?

He choked down his disgust and rubbed his foot clean on a dry area of the concrete floor. Some was still stuck between his toes. He would've liked a towel or a wet cloth right about now, but the lab was more important. He reached out his hand, placed it on the knob, pulled the heavy metal door open a bit more, and pressed on into the darkness. An unnatural silence enveloped him.

A deathly silence.

A sharp chemical smell crept into his nose like at the film lab where his father had once taken him after one of his days of shooting.

His heart was pounding. Much too fast, much too loud. He wished he were somewhere else, maybe with David, under the covers.

Luke Skywalker would never hide under the covers.

The trembling fingers on his left hand searched for the light switch, always expecting to find something else entirely. What if the ghosts were here? If they grabbed his arm? If he accidently reached into one's mouth and it snapped its teeth shut?

There! Cool plastic.

He flipped the switch. Three red lights lit up and bathed the room in front of him in a strange red glow. Red, like in the belly of a monster.

A chill ran up his spine all the way to the roots of his hair. He stopped at the threshold to the lab; somehow, there was a sort of invisible border that he didn't want to cross. He squinted and tried to make out the details.

The lab was larger than he had thought, a narrow space about three metres wide and seven metres deep. A heavy black curtain hung directly beside him. Someone had hastily pushed it aside.

Clothes lines were strung under the concrete ceiling with photos hanging from them. Some had been torn down and lay on the floor.

On the left stood a photo enlarger. On the right, a shelf spanned the entire wall, crammed with pieces of equipment. Gabriel's eyes widened. He recognised most of them immediately: Arri, Beaulieu, Leicina, with other, smaller cameras in between. The trade magazines that were piled up in Dad's study on the first floor were full of them. Whenever one of those magazines wound up in the bin, Gabriel fished it out, stuck it under his pillow, and read it under the covers by torchlight until his eyelids were too heavy to keep open.

Beside the cameras lay a dozen lenses, some as long as gun barrels; next to them, small cameras, cases to absorb camera operating sounds, 8- and 16-mm film cartridges, a stack of three VCRs with four monitors, and finally, two brand-new camcorders. Dad always scoffed at the things. In one of the magazines, he had read that you could film for almost two hours with the new video technology without having to change the cassette – absolutely unbelievable! On top of that, the plastic bombers didn't rattle like film cameras, but ran silently.

Gabriel's shining eyes wandered over the treasures. He wished he could show all of this to David. He immediately felt guilty. After all, this was dangerous, so it was best that he didn't get David involved. Besides, his brother had already fallen asleep. He was right to have locked the door to their room.

Suddenly, there was a loud crash. He spun around. There was no one there. No parents, no ghost. His parents were probably still quarrelling up in the kitchen.

He looked back into the lab at all of the treasures. *Come closer*, they seemed to whisper. But he was still standing on the threshold next to the curtain. Fear rose in him. He could still turn back. He had now seen the lab; he didn't have to go all the way in.

Eleven! You're eleven! Come on, don't be a chicken!

How old was Luke?

Gabriel reluctantly took two steps into the room.

What were those photos? He bent down, picked one up from the floor, and stared at the faded grainy image. A sudden feeling of disgust and a strange excitement spread through his stomach. He looked up at the photos on the clothes line. The photo directly above him attracted his eyes like a magnet. His face was hot and red, like everything else around him. He also felt a bit sick. It looked so real, so . . . or were they actors? It looked like in the movie! The columns, the walls, like in the Middle Ages, and the black clothes . . .

He tore himself away and his eyes jumped over the jumbled storage and the shelf, and finally rested on the modern VCRs with their glittering little JVC logos. The lowest one was switched on. Numbers and characters were illuminated in its shining display. Like in *Star Wars* in the cockpit of a spaceship, he thought.

As if of its own accord, Gabriel's index finger approached the buttons and pushed one. A loud click inside the device made him jump. Twice, three times, then the hum of a motor. *A cassette!* There was a cassette in the VCR! His cheeks burned. He feverishly pushed another button. The JVC responded with a rattle. Interference lines flashed across the monitor beside the VCRs. The image wobbled for a moment, and then it was there. Diffuse with flickering colour, unreal, like a window to another world.

Gabriel had been leaning forward without knowing it – and now he jerked back. His mouth went totally dry. It was the same image as in the photo! The same place, the same columns, the same people, only now they were moving. He wanted to look away, but it was impossible. He sucked the stifling air in through his gaping mouth, and then held his breath without realising it.

The images pummelled him like the popping of flashbulbs; he couldn't help but watch, mesmerised.

The cut through the black fabric of the dress.

The pale triangle on the still paler skin.

The long, tangled blond hair.

The chaos.

And then another cut – a sharp, angry motion that spread into Gabriel's guts. He suddenly felt sick and everything was spinning. The television stared at him viciously. Trembling, he found the button and switched it off.

The image collapsed with a dull thud, as if there were a black hole inside the monitor, just like in outer space. The noise was awful, but reassuring at the same time. He stared at the dark screen and the reflection of his own bright red face. A ghost stared back, eyes wide with fear.

Don't think about it! Just don't think about it . . . He stared at the photos, at the whole mess, anything but the monitor.

What you can't see isn't there!

But it was there. Somewhere in the monitor, deep inside the black hole. The VCR made a soft grinding noise. He wanted to squeeze his eyes shut and wake up somewhere else. Anywhere. Anywhere but here. He was still crouched in front of his ghostly reflection in the monitors.

Suddenly, Gabriel was overcome by the desperate desire to see something pleasant, or even just something different. As if it had a will of its own, his finger drifted towards the other monitors.

Thud. Thud. The two upper monitors flashed on. Two washed-out images crystallised, casting their steel-blue glimmer into the red light of the lab. One image showed the hall and the open cellar door; the stairs were swallowed up by darkness. The second image showed the kitchen. The kitchen – and his parents. His father's voice rasped from the speaker.

Gabriel's eyes widened.

No! Please, no!

His father shoved the kitchen table. The table legs scraped loudly across the floor. The noise carried through the ceiling, and Gabriel winced. His father threw open a drawer, reached inside and his hand re-emerged.

Gabriel stared at the monitor in horror. Blinking, he wished he were blind. Blind and deaf.

But he wasn't.

His eyes flooded with tears. The chemical smell of the lab combined with the vomit outside the door made him gag. He wished someone would come and hug him and talk it all away.

But no one would come. He was alone.

The realisation hit him with a crushing blow. *Someone had to do something.* And now *he* was the only one who could do anything.

What would Luke do?

Quietly, he crept up the cellar stairs, his bare feet no longer able to feel the cold floor. The red room behind him glowed like hell.

If only he had a lightsabre! And then, very suddenly, he thought of something much, much better than a sabre.

Marc Raabe

Cut

Some men are
born evil

A gripping serial killer thriller

THE INTERNATIONAL BESTSELLER

THE CLEANER

ELISABETH
HERRMANN

Gisa Klönne

SILENT IS THE
FOREST

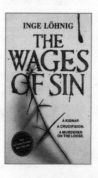

INGE LÖHNIG

THE WAGES OF SIN

A KIDNAP.
A CRUCIFIXION.
A MURDERER ON THE LOOSE.

MARTIN
KRIST

FIELD OF GIRLS

KARL OLSBERG
DELETE

A dangerous game - or
a murderous reality?

HEIDELBERG
REQUIEM

Wolfgang
Burger

HANNA WINTER

He must hunt her down.
Kill her.
Destroy her ...

SACRIFICE

Want to read
NEW BOOKS
before anyone else?

Like getting
FREE BOOKS?

Enjoy sharing your
OPINIONS?

Discover
READERS FIRST

Read. Love. Share.

Get your first free book just by signing up at
readersfirst.co.uk